THE WATSONS

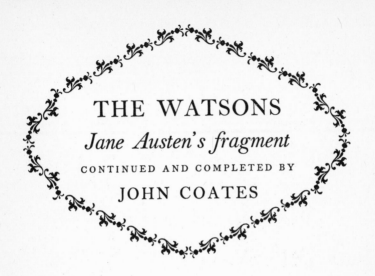

THE WATSONS
Jane Austen's fragment
CONTINUED AND COMPLETED BY
JOHN COATES

Thomas Y. Crowell Company
NEW YORK · ESTABLISHED 1834

To

AILEEN,

HENRIETTA

and

GEORGINA HOTHAM

1

The first winter assembly in the town of Dunford in Surrey was to be held on Tuesday, October the thirteenth; and it was generally expected to be a very good one. A long list of county families was confidently run over as sure of attending, and sanguine hopes were entertained that the Osbornes themselves would be there. The Edwards's invitation to the Watsons followed as a matter of course. The Edwardses were people of fortune, who lived in the town and kept their coach; the Watsons inhabited a village about three miles distant, were poor, and had no close carriage. Ever since there had been balls in Dunford the former were accustomed to invite the latter to dress, dine, and sleep at their house on every monthly return throughout the winter. On the present occasion, as only two of Mr Watson's children were at home, and one was necessary as a companion to himself (for the loss of his wife, which had occurred many years ago, still preyed on his spirits) only one could profit by the kindness of their friends. Miss Emily Watson, who was recently returned to her family from the care of an aunt who had brought her up, was to make her first public appearance in the neighbourhood; and her eldest sister, whose delight in a ball was not lessened by ten years' enjoyment, deserved some praise in cheerfully undertaking to drive her and her finery in the gig to Dunford on the important morning.

As they splashed along the dirty road Miss Watson thus instructed and cautioned her inexperienced sister:

"I dare say it will be a very good ball, and among so many officers you will hardly want partners. You will find Mrs Edwards's maid very willing to help you, and I would advise you to ask Mary Edwards's opinion if you are at all at a loss, for she has very good taste. If Mr Edwards's prognostics are favourable and he wins money at cards you will stay fairly late; if they are unfavourable he may hurry you home. Though if they are *extremely* unfavourable perhaps he will not play at all, but merely watch the others. That may be best as he is bound to find someone who loses, and his delight at his cleverness in reading the signs aright will put him in a good humour."

"His *prognostics*?" said Emily. "I thought Mr Edwards was a sensible man and a friend of my father's."

"My father seldom sees his friends these days," replied Miss Watson. "I do not think Mr Edwards particularly sensible myself, but he does no harm with his signs and omens. I believe he often provokes his poor wife, but Mary has learnt to arrange something propitious when it suits her. A matter of two pictures crooked on the wall or a piece of blue wool on the hearth-rug, I believe. You must be careful not to upset the salt at dinner as he takes that very amiss. I hope you will be in good looks at the ball. I should not be surprised if you were thought one of the prettiest girls in the room; there is a great deal in novelty. Perhaps Tom Musgrave will notice you; but I should advise against giving him any encouragement. He generally pays attention to every new girl, but he is a great flirt and never means anything serious."

"I have heard you speak of Mr Musgrave before," said Emily, "but you have not yet given me any account of him."

"He is a young man of good fortune, quite independent, and re-markably agreeable. Most of the girls hereabout are in love with him, or have been. I believe I am the only one that has escaped with a whole heart, and yet I was the first he paid attention to when he came into the country six years ago. And very great attention he did pay me. Some people say he has never seemed to like any girl so well since, although he is always behaving in a particular way to one or another."

"And how came *your* heart to be the only cold one?" asked Emily, smiling.

"There was a reason for that," replied Miss Watson, changing colour. "I have not been very well used among them, Emily. I hope you have better luck."

"Dear sister, I beg your pardon if I have unthinkingly given you pain."

"When we first knew Tom Musgrave," continued Miss Watson, without seeming to hear her, "I was very much attached to a young man by the name of Purvis, a particular friend of Robert's, who used to be with us a great deal. Everybody thought it would have been a match."

A sigh accompanied these words, which Emily respected in silence; but her sister, after a short pause, went on.

"You will naturally ask why it did not take place, and why he is married to another woman while I am still single. But you must ask him, not me. And you must ask Penelope. Yes, Emily, it was my own sister who set him against me with a view to gaining him herself. But it ended in his discontinuing his visits, and soon after marrying someone else. It has been the ruin of my happiness. I shall never love any man as I loved Purvis. I do not think Tom Musgrave can be compared to him."

"You quite shock me by what you say of Penelope," said Emily. "Could a sister do such a thing? But I hope it was not so. Appearances were against her and you have been misled."

"You do not know Penelope. I will say no more for she has her good qualities. When there is something to do in the house and Margaret has one of her headaches, which come on so convenient at busy times, Penelope does not shirk. I will grant her that. But she has no scruples if she can promote her own advantage. I have suffered from the lack. I wish most sincerely she was well married. I declare I would rather have her well married than myself."

"Than yourself! Yes, I can suppose so. A heart wounded like yours can have little inclination for matrimony."

"Not much indeed. But you know, Emily, we must all marry."

"I could do very well single for my part."

"A little company, and a pleasant ball now and then, would be enough for me, if one could remain young for ever," said Miss Watson. "But my father cannot provide for us, and it is very bad to grow old, and be poor and laughed at. I am beginning to feel the evil of it, and I am not as nice as I was once. I have lost Purvis, it is true; but few people marry their first love. I would not refuse a man because he was not Purvis. We must do the best we can for ourselves."

Emily said nothing, for it was not a sentiment she could approve of.

"Penelope, however, has had her own troubles," continued Miss Watson. "She was disappointed over Tom Musgrave, who paid her considerable attention some three years ago. But he never means anything serious, and when he had trifled with her long enough, he began to slight her for others, of whom Margaret is the latest. Poor Penelope was very wretched for a time. Lately I think she has been trying to make some match in Chichester. Margaret says she is after a rich old Dr Harding, uncle to the friend she is staying with now. The visit was arranged before we knew of your return. When we got your letter she said she did not wish to displease Mrs Shaw by a sudden change but I suspect she was more worried about the doctor."

"I am sorry for her anxieties," said Emily, "but I do not like her plans or her opinions. To be so bent on marriage, to pursue a man merely for the sake of situation, is a thing that shocks me deeply. Poverty is a great evil; but to a woman of education and feeling it ought not, it *cannot* be the greatest. I would rather be a teacher at a school, and I can think of nothing worse, than marry a man I did not like."

"I would rather do anything than be a teacher at a school," said her sister. "*I* have been at school, Emily, and know what a life they lead; *you* never have. I should not like marrying a disagreeable man any more than you, but I do not think there *are* many disagreeable men. I think I could like any good-humoured man with a comfortable income."

Being but newly arrived in her home and the youngest member of her family, Emily shrank from appearing to criticize her sister. She was, however, unable to refrain from saying gently:

"Marriage, Elizabeth, on which our future felicity must depend, is not to be lightly undertaken."

"You certainly speak truth when you say that our future felicity depends on marriage," replied Miss Watson. "For should anything happen to my father before we are settled we have nothing to look forward to but teaching in a school or a life of dependence on Robert and Jane at Croydon. I do not think your upbringing at my aunt's, with a governess and handsome young curate for instructors, will have prepared you for either."

"Indeed," said Emily, smiling, "Mr Jones is neither handsome nor young, and it would embarrass him considerably to know that he had been so described."

"Well we need not quarrel about his looks, as I have not seen him yet and doubtless never will. But it is true that my aunt has brought you up to be rather refined."

"I do not know, Elizabeth. My conduct must tell you how I have been brought up; I am no judge of it myself."

"Nevertheless I can see in a great many things that you are very refined. I have observed it ever since you came home, and I am afraid it will not be for your happiness. Penelope will laugh at you very much."

"*That* will not be for my happiness I am sure. If my opinions are wrong I must correct them; if they are above my situation I must endeavour to conceal them. But I would prefer to have my eyes opened by argument rather than ridicule."

"Penelope is a great tease," said Miss Watson. "I should warn you she makes Margaret very wild at times. But I do not heed her any more."

"There, certainly, I must try to imitate you."

Having said this, Emily was for a few moments silent. The course the conversation had taken could not but remind her of the recent change in her situation resulting from her uncle's death and her aunt's second marriage. She had been the single child in a genteel home, with affluence to support it; she had lately become the fourth daughter in a small parsonage, with no resources beyond a meagre stipend and the produce of a few sparsely-cultivated meadows. The welcome she had received from her father and eldest sister had been kind – kinder than she had allowed herself to hope – but the degree of difference in her immediate society and material surroundings produced an occasional dejection that even the excitement of the coming ball could not entirely disperse.

"Has Penelope much wit?" she asked.

"I do not know about wit; but she has great spirits, and never minds what she says."

"Margaret is more gentle, I think?"

"Yes; especially in company. She is all gentleness and mildness when anybody is by. But she is a little fretful and perverse among ourselves. Poor creature! She is possessed by the notion of Tom

Musgrave's being more seriously in love with her than he ever was with anyone else, and is always expecting him to come to the point. This is the second time within this twelvemonth that she has gone to spend a month with Robert and Jane on purpose to egg him on by her absence; but I am sure she is mistaken and that he will no more follow her to Croydon now than he did last March. He will never marry unless he can marry somebody very great: Miss Osborne, perhaps, or someone in that style."

"Your account of this Mr Musgrave gives me very little inclination for his acquaintance."

"You are afraid of him," said Elizabeth. "I am not surprised."

"No indeed; I dislike and despise him."

"Dislike and despise Tom Musgrave! No; *that* you never can. I defy you not to be delighted with him if he takes notice of you. I hope he will dance with you; and I dare say he will, unless the Osbornes come with a large party, and then he will not speak to anyone else."

"He seems to have most engaging manners," said Emily. "Well, we shall see how irresistible Mr Musgrave and I find each other. I suppose I shall know him as soon as I enter the ball-room; a man so elegantly endowed by nature and education must carry some of his charms on his face."

"You will not find him in the ball-room I can tell you. You will go early, so that Mrs Edwards may get a good place by the fire, and he never arrives till late. If the Osbornes are coming he will wait in the passage and come in with them. I should like to look in on you, Emily. If my father seems cheerful, I could wrap myself up, and James could drive me over as soon as I had made tea. I could be with you by the time the dancing began."

"What! Would you come late at night in this gig?"

"To be sure I would. There, I said you were very refined, and *that's* an instance of it."

"I was thinking of the danger to your health as much as of the impropriety, Elizabeth," said Emily. To forestall a further charge of over-refinement – for in her home at Stanton a young lady's health seemed more taken for granted than it had been at Eversleigh – she added: "Who will be in the Osbornes' party besides Mr Musgrave?"

"It depends whether they have guests. I shall know before you as

I shall hear the carriages pass. The road is bad, as you can see for yourself, but it saves them a mile from the castle. One carriage will mean Lady Osborne and her son and daughter. Two carriages will mean that Mr Howard and his sister have been dining with them. Mr Howard is the rector at Wickstead. His normal way in is by the main road so we see little of him as a rule. Indeed we see little enough of the others, if by seeing you would infer more than a mere glimpse as they pass. Lady Osborne stops twice a year to inquire after my father. Lord Osborne sometimes remembers to raise his hat; but I think Miss Osborne is unaware of my existence. Three carriages or more will mean that there are guests at the castle. However, they are very great folk and even if the report of their meaning to attend the ball is true, some whim may make them change their minds at the last moment."

"I trust that Lord Osborne, as the principal landowner in the district, is actuated more by a sense of what is due to his neighbours, than by sudden caprice," said Emily.

"Lord Osborne is a rich and independent young man of five-and-twenty," replied Miss Watson. "And like other young men of the same situation and age is doubtless more concerned with pleasing himself than others."

"We all have a duty to others, Elizabeth. And the greater the situation, the greater the duty."

"You must tell him so," said Elizabeth, drily. "I shall be interested to hear how he replies."

"Now you are not serious."

"Indeed I am not. And if I thought there was any likelihood of your exchanging two words with Lord Osborne tonight, I would not even have jested on the subject, for your embarrassment would be great enough without the recollection of any words of mine to add to it."

Emily for a moment made no answer. At last she said:

"I wish, Elizabeth, you had not made a point of my going to this ball. I wish you were going instead of me. I am a stranger here and know nobody but Mrs Edwards and her daughter. My enjoyment, therefore, must be very doubtful. Yours, among all your acquaintances would be certain. It is not too late to change. Very little apology would be requisite to the Edwardses, who must be more

[13]

glad of your company than of mine; and I should most readily return to my father. Your clothes I would undertake to find some means of sending to you."

"My dearest Emily," cried Elizabeth warmly, "do you think I would do such a thing? Not for the universe! I shall never forget your good nature in proposing it; but I am not so selfish as to take advantage of you. No; although I am nine years older, I would not be the means of keeping you from being seen. You are a pretty girl and it would be very hard if you should not have as fair a chance as we have all had to make your fortune. Whoever stays at home this winter, it shall not be you. That is what I did with Penelope and Margaret their first year, and it has become our custom."

Emily expressed her gratitude. Though there were phrases in it she would not have used herself, she could not but be moved by the kindness of Elizabeth's speech. Elizabeth on her side had been touched by Emily's offer; and for a little they jogged on in silence, sensible of an increased feeling of intimacy.

Elizabeth spoke first.

"You will take notice whom Mary Edwards dances with?"

"I will remember her partners if I can; but they will all be strangers to me."

"Only observe whether she dances with Captain Hunter more than once. I have my fears in that quarter. Not that her father or mother like officers — red is such an unlucky colour, he considers — but if she does it is all up with poor Sam. And I have promised to write him whom she dances with."

"Is Sam attached to Miss Edwards?"

"Did you not know *that*?"

"How should I know it, Elizabeth? How should I know in Shropshire what is passing of that nature in Surrey? It is not likely that circumstances of such delicacy should have made any part of the scanty communication that has passed between you and me in the last fourteen years."

"I wonder I never mentioned it when I wrote. Since you have been at home I have been so busy with the house, my poor father, and our great wash, that I have had little leisure to tell you anything important. But indeed I think I concluded you knew it all. He has been very much in love with her these two years, and it is a great disappointment to him that he cannot get away to our balls. But Mr Curtis does not often spare him, and just now it is a sickly time at Guildford."

"Do you suppose Miss Edwards inclined to like him?"

"I am afraid not; she is an only child and will have at least ten thousand pounds."

"But she may still like our brother."

"The Edwardses look much higher, Emily. Her father might perhaps be brought round, but her mother would never consent to it. Sam is only a surgeon you know. Sometimes I think she *does* like him; but Mary Edwards is grown rather reserved lately and does not talk to us as she used to."

"Unless Sam feels on sure ground with the lady herself, it seems a pity that he should be encouraged to think of her at all."

"A young man must think of somebody," said Elizabeth. "And why should he not hope to be as lucky as Robert, who got a wife with six thousand pounds?" Miss Watson gave another sigh to the remembrance of Purvis. "I have been unlucky enough myself so far; and I cannot say much for you, as my aunt married again so foolishly. Well, you will have a good ball, I dare say. The next bend will bring us to the turnpike; you can see the church-tower over the hedge, and the White Hart is close by. If you have to cough when Mr Edwards is by, cough three times – otherwise it means he will lose money. I shall long to know what you think of Tom Musgrave."

Such were the last audible sounds of Miss Watson's voice before they passed through the turnpike gate, and entered on the pitching of the town, the noise of which made further conversation undesirable. The old mare trotted heavily on, wanting no direction from the reins to take the right turning, and making only one blunder, in proposing to stop at the milliner's, before she drew up at Mr Edwards's door.

2

Mr Edwards lived in the best house in the street, and the best in the place if Mr Tomlinson, the banker, might be indulged in calling his newly-erected house at the end of the town, with a shrubbery and carriage sweep, in the country. The house was higher than its neighbours, with four windows on each side of the door. The windows were guarded by posts and chains, and the door was approached by a flight of steps.

"Here we are," said Elizabeth, as the gig ceased moving, "safely arrived; and by the market clock we have only been five-and-thirty minutes coming, which I think is doing pretty well, though it would be nothing to Penelope who claims to have done it in quarter of an hour less. The Edwardses have a noble house, you see, and live quite in style. The door will be opened by a man in livery with a powdered head, but I suppose that is nothing out of the ordinary to you."

Emily had seen Mrs Edwards and her daughter only one morning at Stanton. They were therefore all but strangers to her; and though her spirits were by no means insensible to the expected joys of the evening, she felt a little uncomfortable at the thought of all that was to precede them. Her talk with Elizabeth, by giving her some not very pleasant feelings with respect to her own family, had made her more open to disagreeable impressions from any other cause, and increased her sense of the awkwardness of rushing into intimacy on so slight an acquaintance.

There was nothing in the greeting of Mrs or Miss Edwards to make Emily change these ideas. The mother, an educated, respectable woman, strove to hide an anxious and nervous manner under a great show of formal civility. The daughter, a genteel-looking girl of twenty-two with her hair in papers, seemed to have caught something of the formal style of the mother. Elizabeth was obliged to hurry away; and some polite remarks on the probable brilliance of the ball, interspersed by some fretful speculations from Mrs Edwards about the whereabouts and employment of her husband, were all that broke a silence of half an hour before they were joined by the master of the house.

Mr Edwards had lived long enough in the idleness of a town to become something of a gossip. His peculiarities had made him neither furtive nor reserved. Though he treated his superstitions with more solemnity than they deserved, he was quite open about them, and indeed found his chief pleasure in discussing his beliefs with a sympathetic listener. In this he differed from Mrs Edwards whose anxious manner was due to the strain of pretending to herself, and in so far as it was possible to others, that his peculiarities did not exist.

Mr Edwards greeted Emily and inquired after her father and family.

"For your father, Miss Emily, is one of my oldest friends," he said. "It is a great concern to me that he should be such an invalid, and that I should see so little of him these days. I know nobody who likes a game of cards, in a social way, better than he does, and very few who play a fairer rubber. We have lately started a little Whist Club that meets three times a week at the White Hart. If he was in health, how much he would enjoy it!"

"I dare say he would, sir; and I wish with all my heart he was equal to it."

"Your club would be better fitted for an invalid," said Mrs Edwards, "if it did not keep you up so late."

This was an old grievance. As soon as he had been an hour or two out of her sight Mrs Edwards would begin to wonder who, by trading on his weakness, might be taking advantage of her husband. In this she gave herself an unnecessary worry, for Mr Edwards's money was in the safe keeping of Mr Tomlinson, his friend and banker. It was seldom, even when the omens were most favourable – when the moon was full, when he had burnt his tongue on a hot potato, when there were three pieces of cork in his glass of wine, and he had severely bruised his elbow – that Mr Edwards risked more than an additional half-crown on his game of whist.

"So late, my dear! What are you talking of?" he cried. "We are always at home before midnight. At the castle they are but just getting up from dinner at midnight. Which reminds me, I have some news for you: the Osbornes will certainly be at the ball this evening. I heard it stated definitely at the White Hart."

"I am glad of it," observed Mrs Edwards, "because their coming gives a credit to the assembly. Indeed we shall feel the benefit of it throughout the whole series."

"I cannot entirely agree," said Mr Edwards, gravely. "It gives me no pleasure to make an unfavourable forecast, but facts must be faced, and I can see no reason to suppose that the winter balls will be a success. Those responsible have chosen the most inauspicious day on which to begin."

It was some moments before Emily realized that the cause of his displeasure was the day's date – the thirteenth of the month. Mr Edwards's remark brought a silence to the room. Mrs Edwards, apart from a deep sigh – which indeed might have been occasioned by some other cause – paid so little attention that she appeared not to have heard him; and Mary was looking thoughtfully at the carpet. Even Emily felt unable to make the rational reply required of her by politeness.

Mr Edwards seemed a little put out by the effect of his warning. He was a friendly, cheerful man, and it was far from his intention to depress the spirits of his young companions.

"Come, come," he said. "I was speaking in a general way. I have no doubt that Mary and Miss Emily will enjoy themselves; and to tell the truth I stumbled over an old shoe in the passage this morning. I have no idea how it came there as I saw it yesterday safe in the cupboard; if it had not been for that I might have been tempted to stay at home. I think we may take it that no harm will come to anyone of *this* household through the balls; but that when we look back from a few years hence and see the season in perspective we shall realize that it was less noteworthy than those that preceded and followed it."

It was then that Mary raised her eyes from the carpet, met Emily's glance for a moment, and quickly looked away. Emily was left in doubt about who was responsible for the shoe having been so conveniently in Mr Edwards's path. The matter of the propitiousness or unpropitiousness of the date, however, had now been arranged to the satisfaction of all parties, and they chatted with great briskness till Mrs Edwards's time for dressing arrived.

The young ladies ascended with her. Emily was shown to a very comfortable apartment; and as soon as Mrs Edwards's civilities could leave her, the happy occupation, the first bliss of a ball, began.

The girls, dressing in some measure together, grew unavoidably better acquainted. Emily found in Miss Edwards a sufficiency of politeness, an artless, unpretending mind, and a great wish of obliging. When they returned to the parlour where Mrs Edwards was sitting, respectably attired in one of the two satin gowns which would go through the winter, and a new cap from the milliner's, they entered it with easier feelings and more natural smiles than they had taken away.

Mrs Edwards, with no cause for anxiety now that her husband was by her side, complacently viewed her daughter's good looks. Mr Edwards, not less satisfied with Mary, paid some compliments of good-humoured gallantry to Emily at her expense. The discussion led to more intimate remarks, and Miss Edwards gently asked Emily if she was not often reckoned very like her younger brother. Emily thought she could perceive a faint blush accompany the question, and there seemed something still more suspicious in the manner in which Mr Edwards took up the subject.

"You are paying Miss Emily no great compliment, Mary," he said hastily. "Mr Sam Watson is a very good sort of young man, and I dare say a very clever surgeon. The profession is considered by many to be a lucky one. But his complexion has been rather too much exposed to all weathers to make a likeness to him very flattering."

Mary apologized in some confusion. She had not thought a strong likeness at all incompatible with very different degrees of beauty. There might be a resemblance in countenance, while the complexion and even the features were very unlike.

"I know nothing of my brother's beauty," said Emily, "for I have not seen him these fourteen years."

"You will certainly not recognize him from your own looks," said Mr Edwards. "My dear, do you perceive the least resemblance?"

"Not the least," replied his wife, with great firmness. "Miss Emily Watson puts me very much in mind of her eldest sister; and sometimes I see a look of Miss Margaret. But I cannot perceive any likeness to Mr Samuel."

"No more can I."

Mr and Mrs Edwards, it seemed, were in full agreement on one point. Miss Edwards was not for Sam.

"I am sorry my brother is not coming to the ball tonight," said Emily, who felt she owed something to her family. "I would like to make his acquaintance. However, it is a fair journey; and there may be reasons against it of which we know nothing."

"True enough," said Mr Edwards, somewhat restored to good humour. "A ride of thirteen miles is not to be lightly undertaken at such a season. Mr Sam has more sense than others of his age. Dr Richards says he is spoken of as a steady young man in Guildford.'

But neither his steadiness, nor his sense of the dangers inherent in a journey of thirteen miles, recommended him to the ladies. Mary, now as prim and reserved as before she had dressed, looked dissatisfied at this explanation of his absence; Mrs Edwards sighed again and murmured that he still had his way to make in the world; and the subject was allowed to drop.

Mr Edwards, wanting to know more of the circumstances of his young guest than had reached him, then said:

"I think, Miss Emily, I remember your aunt about thirty years ago. She was a very fine woman then, but like other people I suppose she is grown somewhat older since that time. I hope she is likely to be happy in her second choice."

"I hope so; I believe so, sir," said Emily, in some agitation.

"Mr Turner had not been dead a great while, I believe?"

"About two years, sir."

"I forget what her name is now."

"O'Brien."

"Irish! Ah, I remember; she is gone to settle in Ireland. I do not wonder that you should not wish to go with her into *that* country, Miss Emily."

"I was not so ungrateful, sir," said Emily, warmly, "as to wish to be anywhere but with her. It did not suit Captain O'Brien that I should be of the party."

"Captain!" repeated Mrs Edwards. "The gentleman is in the army then?"

"Yes, madam."

"Aye; there is nothing like your officers for captivating the ladies, young or old. There is no resisting a cockade, my dear."

"I hope there is," said Mrs Edwards gravely, with a quick glance at her daughter. And Emily just recovered from her own perturbation in time to see a second blush on Miss Edwards's cheek, and to remember what Elizabeth had said of Captain Hunter.

"Elderly ladies should be careful how they make a second choice," observed Mr Edwards.

"Carefulness and discretion should not be confined to elderly ladies or to a second choice," added his wife. "They are quite as necessary to young ladies in their first."

"Rather more so," he replied. "Because young ladies are likely to feel the effect of it longer. When an old lady makes a mistake it is not in the course of nature that she should suffer from it many years."

Emily drew her hand across her eyes, and Mrs Edwards, in perceiving it, immediately changed the subject to one of less anxiety to them all.

3

A very good dinner, elegantly served, occupied them for barely an hour; and with nothing to do but expect the time of setting off, the afternoon was long to the young ladies. The entrance of the tea-tray at seven o'clock was some relief. Mr and Mrs Edwards always drank an extra cup and ate an additional muffin when they were going to sit up late, which lengthened the ceremony almost to the wished for moment.

At a little before eight o'clock the Tomlinsons' carriage was heard to go by, which was the constant signal for Mrs Edwards to order hers to the door. In a few minutes the party was transported from the quiet and warmth of a snug parlour to the bustle, noise and draughts of the broad entrance to an inn. Mrs Edwards, carefully guarding her own dress, and attending with yet greater solicitude to the proper security of her young charges' shoulders and throats, led the way up the wide staircase, while no sound of a ball but the first scrape of one violin blessed the ears of her followers. Mr Edwards had left them on business of his own; and Mary, on hazarding the anxious inquiry of whether there were many people yet come, was told by the waiter, as she knew she would be, that Mrs Tomlinson's family was in the room.

In passing along a short gallery to the assembly room, brilliant in lights before them, they were accosted by a young man in morning-dress and boots, who was standing in the doorway of a bed-chamber apparently on purpose to see them go by.

"Ah, Mrs Edwards, how do you do? How do you do, Miss Edwards?" he cried, with an easy air. "You are determined to be in good time, I see, as usual. The candles are but this moment lit."

"I like to get a good seat by the fire, Mr Musgrave," replied Mrs Edwards, coolly.

"I am just about to dress," he continued, undismayed by her cool-
ness. "I am waiting for my stupid fellow. We shall have a famous
ball. The Osbornes are certainly coming; you may depend on *that*,
for I was with Lord Osborne this morning."

The party passed on. Mrs Edwards's satin gown swept along the
clean floor of the ball-room to the fireplace at the upper end, where
one party only were formally seated, while three or four officers,
clustered together like companionable cattle, walked in and out of
the card-room. A very stiff meeting between the near neighbours
ensued; and as soon as they were duly seated, Emily, in a low whisper, which became the solemn scene and the empty room, said to
Miss Edwards:

"The gentleman we passed in the passage was Mr Musgrave,
then. He is reckoned remarkably agreeable, I understand."

Miss Edwards answered hesitatingly:

"Yes; he is very much liked by many people. But *we* are not very
intimate."

"He is rich, is he not?"

"He has about eight or nine hundred a year, I believe. He came
into possession of it when he was very young, and my father and
mother think it has given him rather an unsettled turn. He is no
favourite with them."

There were, it now appeared, a number of points on which Mr
and Mrs Edwards were in agreement. Neither Sam, Captain Hunter
nor Mr Musgrave were entirely desirable connections.

The cold and empty appearance of the room, and the demure air
of the small group of females at one end of it, quickly gave way to a
brighter scene. The cheerful sound of other carriages was heard;
and a succession of portly chaperones, each with a string of smartly
dressed girls, took up their stations at an ever-increasing distance
from the fire. The young gentlemen, of whom there were soon a considerable number, seemed as fearful as the officers of quitting the
safety of each other's company; but after sufficient encouragement
in the way of a smile, or a quick glance followed by downcast eyes,
one would occasionally walk across the floor, bow, engage a fair
creature for a pair of dances, and retreat swiftly to the crowd by the
entrance. The older gentlemen were more forthright in their search
for pleasure, and as a rule made straight for the card-room. Mr Ed-

wards was something of an exception, for on his entry he approached the ladies and asked whether they were comfortably settled. Then, his hand on a lucky charm in the shape of a rusty nail that had once penetrated through his slipper and into his heel (where it set up an inflammation that caused his wife a week's broken rest) passed on to seat himself at the third table set for cards on the right-hand side of the door looking east.

Among the increasing number of military men one now made his way to Miss Edwards with an air of obvious gallantry that informed her companion he was Captain Hunter. Emily, who could not but watch her at such a moment, saw her looking rather embarrassed, but by no means displeased, and heard an engagement formed for the first two dances, which made her think her brother's case a hopeless one.

Emily in the meantime was not unobserved or unadmired herself. A new face, and a very pretty one, could not but attract attention, and her name was whispered from one party to another. No sooner had the signal been given by the orchestra's striking up a favourite air than she found herself engaged to dance with an officer introduced by Captain Hunter.

Emily Watson was not more than of middle height, well made and plump, and with an air of healthy vigour. Her skin was very brown, but clear, smooth and glowing; which, with a lively eye, a sweet smile, and an open countenance, gave beauty to attract and expression to make that beauty improve on acquaintance. Beneath this pleasing exterior were hidden a seriousness of mind and firmness of principle that few would have suspected and fewer still came to know. Her manners and address were those usually met with in a young lady of nineteen summers, and not many people had yet troubled to look for more in one who already showed to such advantage. Having no reason to be dissatisfied with the lady under whose protection she had appeared, or with the partner to whom she had been introduced, the evening began very pleasantly for her. Her feelings perfectly coincided with the reiterated observation of others that it was an excellent ball.

The first two dances were not yet over when the returning sound of carriages attracted general notice. "The Osbornes are coming! The Osbornes are coming!" was repeated round the room. After some minutes the important party, preceded by the attentive master of the inn to open a door that was never closed, made its appearance. It consisted of Lady Osborne; her son, Lord Osborne; her daughter, Miss Osborne; Miss Carr, her daughter's friend; Mr Howard, formerly tutor to Lord Osborne and now clergyman of the parish in which the castle stood; Mrs Blake, a widowed sister who lived with him; her son, a fine boy of just eleven years old; and Mr Tom Musgrave.

In their progress up the room they paused almost immediately behind Emily to receive the compliments of some acquaintance, and she heard Lady Osborne observe that they had made a point of coming early for the gratification of Mrs Blake's little boy, whose birthday it was. Emily looked at them all as they passed. Her chief interest was in Tom Musgrave, who was certainly a genteel, good-looking young man; then she was struck by the thought that the former Lord Osborne must have been extremely handsome, for his children were tall and well-featured, while Lady Osborne herself was small, had a very red face, and was almost entirely without the customary elegance of rank.

A closer inspection only heightened Emily's first impression. Lady Osborne's gown was less fine than Mrs Edwards's; her voice was loud and masculine; and the words in which she entreated Mr Howard, an agreeable-looking man of little more than thirty, to get her out of the crush and into the card-room, were not well chosen. Miss Osborne seemed concerned at being as unlike her mother as possible. She was dressed in the height of fashion, her complexion was fair, and there was a suggestion of haughtiness in her expression and carriage. Lord Osborne himself was a fine young man. His countenance was good and his bearing distinguished. But there was a lack of ease about him, an air of shyness and even of awkwardness, which seemed to speak him out of his element in a ball-room. As it appeared he was not fond of women's company and seldom danced, it looked as though Emily's assessment of the reasons for his presence was a correct one. He came, in fact, only because it was judged expedient for him to please the borough. Miss Carr was a vapid, pretty creature, with a neat figure, a ready laugh, and a total want of distinction.

At the conclusion of the two dances Emily found herself seated next to the Osbornes' party. She immediately noticed the fine countenance and animated gestures of the little boy, as he was standing before his mother, inquiring when they were going to begin.

"You will not be surprised at Charles's impatience," said Mrs Blake, a lively pleasant-looking woman of five- or six-and-thirty, to a lady near her, "when you know what a partner he is to have. Miss Osborne has been so kind as to promise to dance the first two dances with him."

"Oh yes! We have been engaged this week," cried the boy.

Beyond him, Miss Osborne, Miss Carr and a group of gentlemen were engaged in a very lively conversation; and soon afterwards Emily saw the smartest officer in the room walk off to the orchestra to order the dance, while Miss Osborne turned to her expectant little partner and said:

"Charles, I beg your pardon for not keeping my engagement, but I am going to dance these two dances with Colonel Beresford. I know you will excuse me, and I will certainly dance with you after tea."

Without staying for an answer she turned again to Miss Carr, and in another minute was led away by Colonel Beresford to begin the set. If the boy's face had in its happiness been interesting to Emily, it was infinitely more so under this sudden reverse. His mother, stifling her own mortification, tried to soothe him with the prospect of Miss Osborne's second promise. But though he continued to utter, with an effort of boyish bravery, "Oh, I do not mind it!" it was evident from the increasing agitation of his features that he minded it as much as ever.

On a sudden impulse, and without pausing to reflect on the possible consequences of her action, Emily offered herself as his partner.

"I shall be very happy to dance with you, sir, if you like," she said, holding out her hand.

The boy, in one moment restored to all his first delight, looked joyfully at his mother. Then, stepping forward with an honest "Thank you, ma'am," was instantly ready to attend his new acquaintance. The gratification of Mrs Blake was more diffuse; she turned to the young lady with repeated and fervent acknowledgements of so great and condescending a kindness. Emily, with perfect truth, assured her that she could not be giving greater pleasure than she felt herself; and Charles having been called back, provided with his gloves and told to keep them on, they joined the set which was now rapidly forming. It was a partnership which could not be noticed without surprise; and it gained her broad stares from Miss Osborne and Miss Carr as they passed her in the dance.

"Upon my word, Charles, you are in luck," said the former, as she turned him. "You have got a better partner than me."

To which the happy boy, with the frankness of youth, replied simply:

"Yes."

Tom Musgrave, who was dancing with Miss Carr, gave Emily many inquisitive glances; and after a time Lord Osborne himself, under pretence of talking to Charles, came to look at his partner. Though rather distressed by such observation, Emily could not repent of what she had done, so happy had it made the boy and his mother. Her little partner, she found, though chiefly bent on dancing, was not unwilling to speak when her questions or remarks gave him anything to say. She heard that he had two brothers and a sister, that they and their mamma lived with his uncle at Wickstead, that his uncle taught him Latin, that he was very fond of riding and had a horse of his own given him by Lord Osborne, and that he had been out once already with Lord Osborne's hounds.

At the end of these dances Emily learnt that they were to drink tea. The tea-room was within the card-room; and Mrs Edwards, who had been placidly watching the dancers and gossiping with her neighbours since she arrived, entered the latter in some anxiety. Seeing neither piles of gold in front of her husband's opponents, nor the deeds of his house in his hand – seeing in fact that he was merely engaged in a quiet game of whist – she sighed, this time with relief, and passed on. In the centre of the room, however, the passage was straitened by tables, and the party was brought to a halt again. It happened close by Lady Osborne's casino table. Mr Howard, who belonged to it, spoke to his nephew; and Emily, on perceiving herself the subject of attention to both Lady Osborne and him, just turned away her eyes in time to avoid seeming to hear her young companion exclaim delightedly:

"Oh uncle! Do look at my partner; she is so pretty."

As they were immediately in motion again, Charles was hurried off before Emily could hear his uncle's reply.

On entering the tea-room, in which two long tables were prepared, Lord Osborne was to be seen quite alone at the end of one, as if retreating as far as he could from the ball to enjoy his own thoughts. Charles instantly pointed him out to Emily.

"There is Lord Osborne. Let you and I go and sit by him."

"No," said Emily, laughing. "You must sit with my friends."

"Very well. Do you think Miss Osborne will keep her word and dance with me when tea is over?"

"Oh yes; I suppose so," replied Emily, though she had no better reason to give than that Miss Osborne had *not* kept it before.

"When will you come to Osborne Castle?"

"Never probably. I am not acquainted with the family."

"But you can come to Wickstead and see mamma, and she can take you to the castle. There is a monstrous curious stuffed fox there, and a badger. Anybody would think they are alive. It is a pity you should not see them."

On rising from tea there was a scramble for the pleasure of being first into the ball-room, which happened to be increased by one or two of the card-parties having just broken up, and the players being disposed to move in exactly the opposite direction. Among these was Mr Howard, his sister leaning upon his arm. No sooner were they within reach of Emily than Mrs Blake called her notice by a friendly touch, and said:

"Your goodness to Charles, my dear Miss Watson, brings all his family upon you. Give me leave to introduce my brother."

Emily curtsied, the gentleman bowed, and made a hasty request for the honour of her hand in the next two dances, to which as hasty an affirmative was given, and they were immediately impelled in opposite directions. Emily was well pleased with the encounter; there was a quietly cheerful, gentleman-like air about Mr Howard which suited her. A few minutes afterwards the value of her engagement increased. She was waiting somewhat screened by the door for Mrs Edwards, when she heard Lord Osborne, now at an empty card-table, call Tom Musgrave towards him and say:

"Why do you not dance with the beautiful Emily Watson? Dance with her, Tom, and I will come and stand by."

"I was determined on it this very moment, my lord. I will be introduced and dance with her immediately."

"Aye, do."

"I will go this minute, my lord. I shall find her in the tea-room. Mrs Edwards has never done with tea."

Away he went, Lord Osborne after him; and Emily lost no time in hurrying the other way towards Mrs Edwards's seat by the fire.

"We had quite lost you," said Mrs Edwards, who followed her with Mary in less than five minutes. "I had not seen you go on ahead."

Emily was saved the trouble of apologizing by their being joined at that moment by Mr Musgrave, who, requesting Mrs Edwards aloud to do him the honour of presenting him to Miss Emily Watson, left the lady without any choice in the business but that of testifying by the coldness of her manner that she did it unwillingly. The honour of dancing with her was solicited without loss of time, and Emily, however she might like to be thought a beautiful girl by lord or commoner, was so little disposed to favour Tom Musgrave himself that she had considerable satisfaction in avowing her previous engagement. He was evidently surprised. The style of her last partner had led him to believe her not overburdened with applications.

"My little friend, Charles Blake," he cried, "must not expect to engross you the whole evening. We can never suffer this. It is against the rules of the assembly, and I am sure it would never be permitted by Mrs Edwards. She is too nice a judge of decorum to give her licence to such a dangerous particularity."

"I am not going to dance with Master Blake, sir."

The gentleman, a little disconcerted, could only hope he might be more fortunate another time; and being unwilling to leave her, though Lord Osborne was waiting in the doorway for the result, he began to make civil inquiries after her family.

"How comes it that we have not the pleasure of seeing your sisters here this evening? Our assemblies are accustomed to be so well treated by them that we do not know how to take this neglect."

"My eldest sister is the only one at home, and she could not leave my father."

"Miss Watson the only one at home! You astonish me; it seems but the day before yesterday that I saw them all three in the town. But I am afraid I have been a very sad neighbour of late, and I confess it is a shameful length of time since I was at Stanton. But I shall *now* endeavour to make amends for the past."

Emily's calm curtsy in reply must have struck him as very unlike the encouraging warmth he had been used to receive from her sisters. The dancing now recommenced. Miss Osborne deputed her engagement with Charles to Miss Carr; and Tom Musgrave's curiosity was appeased on seeing Mr Howard come forward and claim Emily's hand.

"That will do as well for me," was Lord Osborne's comment, when his friend carried him the news; and he was continually at Mr Howard's elbow during the two dances.

The frequency of his appearance there was the only unpleasant part of the engagement, the only objection Emily could make to Mr Howard. In himself she thought him as agreeable as he looked. Though chatting on the commonest of topics, he had a sensible, unaffected way of expressing himself which made all his opinions worth hearing; and she only regretted that he had not been able to make his pupil's manners as unexceptional as his own. The two dances seemed very short, and she had her partner's authority for considering them so. At their conclusion, the Osbornes and their train were on the move.

"We are off now," said his lordship to Tom. "How much longer do you stay in this place – till sunrise?"

"Not I, my lord. I have had quite enough of it, I assure you. I shall not show myself here again when I have had the honour of attending Lady Osborne to her carriage. I shall retreat in as much secrecy as possible to the most remote corner of the house, where I shall order a barrel of oysters and be famously snug."

"Let me see you soon at the castle; and bring me word how she looks by daylight."

Emily, who had overheard this, could not but disapprove of the way the command was given, and indeed of the command itself. If Lord Osborne was in truth interested in her day-time appearance she considered that he should have made an opportunity for examining it himself: which, Stanton being situated between the castle and Dunford, and she herself in the habit of taking a daily walk, he could have done without over-exercising his ingenuity. He was certainly a fine young man; but this incident, and his behaviour during the dances, had lessened him in her eyes.

She parted from Mrs Blake as from an old acquaintance; and Charles shook her by the hand and wished her good-bye at least a dozen times. From Miss Osborne and Miss Carr she received something like a jerking curtsy as they passed. Lady Osborne stared at her with curiosity, then gave her a brief nod and a loud good-night. This was not the last of the party, however, for Lord Osborne came back after the others were out of the room to beg her pardon and look in the window-seat behind her for the gloves that were visibly compressed in his hand. But Tom Musgrave was seen no more, so we may suppose his plan to have succeeded and imagine him mortifying himself with his barrel of oysters in dreary solitude, or perhaps assisting the landlady in the bar to make fresh negus for the happy dancers above. Emily could not help missing the party by whom she had been, though in some respects unpleasantly, distinguished; and the two dances which followed and concluded the ball were rather flat in comparison with the others. Mr Edwards had had good luck, his fortunate stumble over the shoe having outweighed the unauspicious date, and they were among the last out of the room.

"Here we are back again," said Emily, sorrowfully, as she walked into the dining-room where the candles were being lighted. "My dear Miss Edwards, how soon it is at an end. I wish it could come all over again."

Mrs Edwards, with a look of complacency which showed that she took appreciation of the assembly in some measure as appreciation of herself, admitted that it had been an elegant ball; and even Mr Edwards spoke in praise of the meeting, and trusted they would not have to atone for its fullness, brilliancy and spirit by gloom and dullness for the rest of the season. Having been fixed the whole time at the same table in the same room, with only one change of chairs, he was hardly in a position to pass judgement on the scene in the ballroom. He meant that he had won four rubbers out of five and was in hopes that his luck would not change.

His daughter felt the advantage of his good fortune in the course of the remarks and retrospections which ensued over the welcome soup.

"How came you not to dance with either of the Mr Tomlinsons, Mary?" said her mother.

"I was always engaged when they asked me."

"I thought you were to have stood up with Mr James for the last two dances. Mrs Tomlinson told me he was gone to ask you, and I heard you say two minutes before that you were *not* engaged."

"Yes; but it was a mistake. I had misunderstood. I thought it was for the two dances after, if it went on so long. But Captain Hunter assured me it was for those very two."

"So you ended with Captain Hunter, did you Mary?" said her father. "And with whom did you begin?"

"Captain Hunter," admitted Mary, in a very humble tone.

"Hum! That is being constant at least. Whom else did you dance with?"

"Mr Norton and Captain Styles."

"And who are they?"

"Mr Norton is a cousin of Captain Hunter's."

"And Captain Styles?"

"One of his particular friends."

"All in the same regiment," added Mrs Edwards. "Mary was surrounded by red-coats all the evening. I should have been better pleased to see her dancing with some of our old neighbours. I had particularly hoped she would dance with Mr James." For though Mrs Edwards disapproved of a number of Mary's suitors she did not intend that her daughter should remain for ever unmarried.

"Yes, yes. We must not neglect our neighbours," said her husband. "But if these soldiers are quicker than other people in a ballroom, what are young ladies to do?"

"I think there is no occasion for their engaging themselves so many dances before-hand, Mr Edwards."

"No, perhaps not. But I remember, my dear, when you and I did the same."

Mrs Edwards sighed, but said no more. She was mistress of the finest house in Dunford; she had a powdered footman and neat maids. Her carriage was smart, her horses good and her drawing-room elegant. She was the leader of the society in the town and visited many of the county families. But three fears troubled her. She was afraid lest her husband, misreading the signs, might one day lose his money. She was afraid lest other people, in the privacy of their homes, might sometimes laugh at her on account of his silliness. And she was afraid lest Mary, after the unpredictable manner of daughters, might one day form an imprudent attachment. On balance her life was satisfactory; when she forgot to be an anxious woman, she was a contented one. But as Emily went to sleep that night, her head full of Osbornes, Blakes and Howards, Mrs Edwards lay awake and sighed.

4

The next morning brought a great many visitors. It was the way of the place to call on Mrs Edwards the morning after a ball, and this neighbourly inclination was increased in the present instance by a general spirit of curiosity on Emily's account. Everyone wanted to look again at the girl who had been admired the night before by Lord Osborne. Many were the eyes and various the degrees of approbation with which she was examined. Some saw no fault, and some no beauty. With some her brown skin was the annihilation of every grace, and others could never be persuaded that she was half so handsome as Elizabeth Watson had been ten years ago. The morning passed quickly away in discussing the merits of the ball with this succession of company, and Emily was astonished at finding it two o'clock, and remembering that she had heard nothing of her father's gig. After this discovery she walked twice to the window to examine the street, and was on the point of asking leave to ring the bell and make inquiries, when the sound of a carriage driving up to the door set her heart at ease. She stepped again to the window, but instead of the convenient, though very unsmart family equipage, perceived a neat curricle. Mr Musgrave was shortly afterwards announced, and Mrs Edwards put on her stiffest look at his entry. Not at all dismayed, however, by her chilling air, he paid his compliments to each of the ladies with no unbecoming ease; and, continuing to address Emily, presented her with a note, which, he said, he had the honour of bringing from her sister, but to which he must observe a verbal postscript from himself would be requisite.

The note contained a few lines from Elizabeth saying that their father, in consequence of feeling unusually well, had taken the sudden resolution of attending the Visitation of the Sick that day. As his road lay wide of Dunford it was impossible for her to come home till the following morning, unless the Edwardses would send her, which was hardly to be expected, or she could meet with any chance conveyance, or did not mind walking so far.

She had scarcely run her eyes through the whole before she was obliged to listen to Tom Musgrave's postscript.

"I received that note from the fair hands of Miss Watson only ten minutes ago," he said. "I met her by chance in the village of Stanton. She was in quest of a person to employ on her errand, and I was fortunate enough to convince her that she could not find a more willing or more speedy messenger than myself. Remember I say nothing of my disinterestedness. My reward is to be the indulgence of conveying you to Stanton in my curricle. Though they are not written down I bring you your sister's orders on the point."

Emily felt distressed. She did not like the proposal, nor did she wish to be on terms of intimacy with the proposer; and yet, fearful of encroaching on the Edwardses, as well as wishing to go home herself, she was at a loss how to decline what he offered. She thanked the gentleman but professed herself very unwilling to give him so much trouble. The trouble did not exist, he replied. It was honour, pleasure, delight. What else had he or his horses to do? Still she hesitated. She believed she must beg leave to decline his assistance; she was rather afraid of that sort of carriage. The distance was not beyond a walk.

Mrs Edwards then inquired into the particulars, and said:

"We shall be extremely happy, Miss Emily, if you can give us the pleasure of your company until tomorrow; but if you cannot conveniently do so, our carriage is quite at your service, and Mary will be pleased with the opportunity of seeing your sister."

This was precisely what Emily had longed for; and she accepted the offer most thankfully. The plan was warmly opposed by their visitor.

"I cannot suffer it, indeed. I must not be deprived of the happiness of escorting you. I assure you there is not the possibility of an accident with my horses. Your sisters all know how quiet they are. They have none of them the least scruple in trusting themselves with me. In truth," he added, lowering his voice, "*you* are quite safe; the danger is only *mine*."

Emily was now even less disposed to oblige him than before.

"As to Mrs Edwards's carriage being used the day after a ball," he continued, "it is a thing quite out of the question, I assure you, never heard of before. The old coachman will look as black as his horses, will he not, Miss Edwards?"

No notice was taken. The ladies were silently firm, and the gentleman found himself obliged to submit. His air of earnest entreaty faded, and for a moment he looked quite glum. It was not, however, in his character to remain low for very long.

"What a famous ball we had last night," he cried, after a short pause. "How long did you keep it up after the Osbornes and I went away?"

"We had two dances more."

"It is making it too much of a fatigue, I think, to stay so late. I suppose your set was not a very full one?"

"Yes; quite as full as ever, except for the Osbornes," said Emily, somewhat against her conscience. "There seemed no vacancy anywhere, and everyone danced with uncommon spirit to the very last."

"Indeed! Perhaps I might have looked in on you again, if I had been aware of as much, for I am rather fond of dancing than not. Miss Osborne is a charming girl, do you not think?"

"She is certainly handsome," replied Emily, to whom all this was chiefly addressed.

"Her manners too are delightful. And Fanny Carr is a most interesting little creature. What do you think of Lord Osborne, Miss Watson?"

"He would be handsome, even though he were *not* a lord, and perhaps better mannered. Perhaps more desirous of pleasing, and showing himself pleased, in the right place."

"Upon my word, you are very severe on my friend! I assure you Lord Osborne is a very good fellow."

"I do not dispute his virtues, sir, but I do not like his awkward air."

"If it were not a breach of confidence," replied Tom, with an important look, "I might be able to win a more favourable opinion for poor Osborne."

Emily gave him no encouragement, and he was obliged to keep his friend's secret. He was also obliged to put an end to his visit, for

Mrs Edwards had ordered her carriage. Mrs Edwards parted from her guest with many expressions of kindness, and hoped to have the pleasure of welcoming her again on November the tenth. Miss Edwards accompanied her home; but as it was dinner hour at Stanton stayed only long enough for Elizabeth to walk round her twice, admire her new bonnet and pelisse, thank her three times for conducting her sister home, send her respects to Mrs Edwards and inquire after half a dozen Dunford acquaintances; all of which was accomplished without a pause in a very few minutes.

"Now, my dear Emily," said Miss Watson, as soon as they were alone, "you must talk to me for the rest of the day without stopping or I shall not be satisfied. But first of all Nanny shall bring in the dinner. How nice Mary Edwards looks in her new pelisse. And fancy them sending you home in the coach! Now tell me how you like them and what I am to say to Sam. I have begun my letter. Jack Stokes is to call for it tomorrow as his father is going within a mile of Guildford the next day." Here she was interrupted by the arrival of the dinner. "We will wait upon ourselves," she continued, "and then we shall lose no time. And so you would not come home with Tom Musgrave?"

"No; you had said so much against him that I did not wish either for the obligation or the intimacy which the use of his carriage must have created."

"You did very right; though I wonder at your forbearance, and I do not think I could have done the same myself. He seemed so eager to fetch you that I could not say no, though it rather went against me to be throwing you together, so well did I know his tricks. But I longed to see you and it seemed a clever way of getting you home. It was my baking day, you know, and I had been too busy to think out a proper plan. Besides, it will not do to be too nice. Nobody could have imagined the Edwardses letting you have their coach after the horses had been out so late. But what am I to say to Sam?"

"If you are guided by me you will not encourage him to think much of Miss Edwards as things stand at present. The mother is decidedly against him, and the father shows him no favour, though as you said yesterday, he might be brought round. His weakness for predictions in general makes his own conduct somewhat unpredictable. As to Sam's interest with Mary, I feel he is the only person to judge that. But I cannot pretend I am very optimistic. She danced twice with Captain Hunter, and I think shows him as much encouragement as is consistent with her disposition and the situation she is placed in. She once mentioned Sam, and certainly with a little confusion; but that was perhaps merely owing to the consciousness of his liking her, which may very probably have come to her knowledge."

"Oh dear, yes!" said Elizabeth. "She has heard enough of that from us all. Poor Sam! He is out of luck as well as other people. For the life of me, Emily, I cannot help feeling for those who are crossed in love. Do you not find it so with yourself?"

Her opinion having been thus requested by her eldest sister, Emily found herself more capable of saying what she thought on the subject than had been possible the day before.

"I am unable to help feeling for friends who are misused," she replied. "But we must draw a distinction in these matters. Society has laid down certain conventions to be followed by those of refinement, and indeed by all of natural respectability. There are many ways by which a gentleman can show his regard before he reaches the stage of a formal proposal. And there are as many ways whereby a young lady can inform him whether his regard is returned or not. If the gentleman persists in spite of the lady's opposition, or if the young lady allows herself to become attached before being assured of the gentleman's intentions, censure rather than sympathy is called for."

"Upon my word, you lay down very strict rules!"

"It is not I who lay them down, dearest Elizabeth, it is society. I think Sam, indeed I think *everybody*, would be well advised to follow them. We should then hear less talk of people being crossed in love."

"That is all very well," said Miss Watson, the memory of Purvis recurring to her mind, "but you have left out of your calculations parents and family and situation. It is not seldom that one or another play a considerable part in match-making and match-breaking."

"Situation certainly must be taken into account by the principals. If it is given due weight by them it is unlikely that opposition will be encountered from parents, whose duty it is to oppose only an imprudent marriage. For the rest the matter should be left to the mutual regard of the parties concerned. If Sam is really unable to leave Guildford we must give him what information he asks. As he is our brother, we can also add our advice; but more we should not do. The fact that Miss Edwards has heard of his attachment from his sisters may already have lowered him in her eyes. It cannot be pleasing to anyone of refinement to know that such things are a matter of public discussion."

Emily had spoken with considerable earnestness. She held her opinions with all the sincerity of which she was capable. They had been implanted in her by her governess, her uncle, the good Mr Jones, and even by her indulgent aunt, during the years she had lived at Eversleigh, an only child whose work and play, reading and entertainment, had been the concern of a number of adults. The occasion of her aunt's second marriage, and the break-up of the household, following so soon on the death of her uncle, had severely distressed her; but her opinions were by then too firmly rooted to be changed.

Elizabeth's opinions were as different as her education. Brought up partly at Miss Stokes's school in Dunford, and partly in a household that had lost the guiding hand of its mistress, forced at an early age to undertake that place of mistress herself, she had had no time to meditate on the niceties of behaviour. Her duties were the care of her father and the respectable settlement of his family. If those ends could be attained she would not be too particular of the means employed. She listened attentively to her sister, and then answered with her usual good humour.

"It is very fine talk, Emily, and would read very well in an essay too, I dare say. But young ladies are vain as well as refined; and I doubt if one has ever yet broke her heart through being told she was admired. It may be that Penelope and Margaret talk too much, and I am not much good myself when it comes to holding my tongue; but we are all fond of Sam which must be our excuse. However, we can discuss this another time; at the moment I would rather hear an account of everything that happened last night."

Emily was too sensible to expect any sudden revolution as a result of a few words from one who was, after all, but a younger sister. She readily did as she was bid and described the ball. When Elizabeth heard that she had danced with Mr Howard, she exclaimed:

"Dance with Mr Howard! My! He is quite one of the great and grand ones. Did you not find him very high?"

"His manners are of a kind to give me more ease and confidence than Mr Musgrave's."

"Well, go on. I should have been frightened out of my wits to have anything to do with the Osborne's party."

Emily concluded her narrative, omitting those parts that touched Lord Osborne's admiration for her.

"And so you really did not dance with Tom at all. But you must have liked him. You must have been struck with his appearance."

"I do *not* like him, Elizabeth. I allow his person and his air to be good; and his manners to a certain point – his address rather – to be pleasing. But I see nothing else to admire in him. On the contrary, he seems very vain, very conceited, absurdly anxious for distinction, and absolutely contemptible in some of the measures he takes to achieve it. A friendship that has a careless *Tom* on one side, and an obsequious *My lord* on the other, is amusing to an observer. Indeed there is a ridiculousness about him that entertains; but his company gives me no other agreeable emotion."

"My dearest Emily, I am fast coming to the conclusion that you are like nobody else in the world. It is as well Margaret is not by. You do not offend *me*, though I hardly know how to believe you. But Margaret would never forgive such words."

"I wish Margaret could have heard him profess his ignorance of her being out of the country. He declared it seemed only two days since he had seen her."

"Aye; that is just like him. Yet this is the man she *will* fancy so desperately in love with her. He is no favourite of mine, as you well know, but if Margaret could fix him I would have to rejoice. It would be as good a match as she could hope for."

To this Emily made no reply; and after a short pause Miss Watson continued:

"I must own that it is a relief to me to find you can speak as you do of Tom Musgrave. I only hope it will last and that he will not come to pay you too much attention. It is a hard thing for a woman to stand against the flattering ways of a man when he is bent on pleasing her."

"How is it that you do not know Mrs Blake?" asked Emily, turning to a subject of more interest to her than Mr Musgrave.

"Mr Howard is very intimate with the Osbornes."

"I am surprised a woman of Mrs Blake's understanding should find that an overwhelming obstacle to an acquaintance between the families of neighbouring clergymen."

"You must blame me rather than Mrs Blake, for she is only recently come into the neighbourhood, and I did not presume to wait on her. We are not rich enough for new acquaintance, Emily: that is the truth of the matter. The people we know are those who remember my mother when she was alive, or my father when he used to go about. It is good for us they were well loved; otherwise they would have had a dull time of it."

"I believe Mr Howard was once tutor to Lord Osborne?"

"For many years. The living was promised him as a reward, but he has had to wait for it. It is only within the last few months that old Mr Stapleton died, and he is come back to the district."

"Is the living a good one?"

"Better than my father's," said Miss Watson, with a sigh. "Some six hundred and fifty a year, and he is known to have a little in the funds as well."

"He is not then so *very* rich as to put him quite out of our sphere?"

"Not by himself; but Mrs Blake has been left very well off, and there is his connection with the castle. Lord Osborne is said to have a great respect for him."

"That is to Lord Osborne's credit. And to Mr Howard's too," said Emily, and was somewhat surprised at the satisfaction the second sentiment gave her. She had not learnt Mr Howard's name, but she knew she would have thought less of him than she did if she had heard Lord Osborne address him with a careless Dick or Bob. Then, considering that she had spoken enough of Mr Howard she added: "Did you not say that Lady Osborne called here sometimes?"

"No, indeed," replied Miss Watson. "Nothing of the kind. She has never set foot inside the parsonage. But every now and then when she sees me in the road she stops her carriage and inquires after my father."

"She honoured me with a good night when she left the ball-room yesterday. There is an openness in her manner which goes some way to redeem the inelegance of her person; but I was very surprised at the dress she wore. It was ten years out of fashion at the least."

"She has no wish to be smart herself," Elizabeth explained. "It is enough for her that her horses and carriages are the best in the district. I have seen her in summer in Dunford rub some dust off the door of her barouche with her own glove. Great folk have their foibles, and that is hers."

As their quietly sociable little meal drew to an end Miss Watson could not help observing how comfortably it had passed.

"It is delightful to me," she said, "to have things go on in peace and good humour. Though we have had nothing but fried beef, how good it has all seemed. I wish everybody were as easily satisfied as you; but poor Margaret is very snappish and Penelope says she would rather have quarrelling going on than nothing at all. She teases Margaret so much that I sometimes believe her."

Mr Watson returned in the evening, none the worse for the exertion of the day, and consented to sit by the parlour fireside instead of retiring upstairs to his book-room. His illness was not imaginary, and at times even gave him pain; but Emily had already observed that if he chose to exert himself – as having no curate he was frequently forced to do – his duties were within his capabilities. The intelligence of his sudden excursion had been an excuse to question Elizabeth more closely than hitherto on his state of health. Emily had learnt of his occasional painful bouts, and of his general want of spirits since his wife's death. The latter was of more importance than the former, her sister informed her, for he was a temperate man and his gout was not severe. Had he been able to accustom himself to a little regular exercise, had he, at the right time, been able to master the loss of his wife with a proper degree of fortitude and re-enter the society of his friends, he would have been less of an invalid. But he had allowed his misfortune to overcome him. Though grateful for the attentions shown to his children he seldom visited or received people himself. He was now settled in his ways and soon became fretful and gloomy if he had more than a single companion to attend to his needs and look after his candles. Indeed, concluded Miss Watson, with Penelope and Margaret perpetually squabbling, there was little enough to tempt him down.

That evening, however, was an exception. Emily saw her father as the man of sense and education he was; and she could not but picture the parsonage as it might have been if her mother were still alive – the meadows cultivated, the household well-managed, Elizabeth's many good qualities enhanced, and expectation instead of uneasiness in her own heart at the thought of the meetings still in front of her. Poor, they would still be; neither the economy of her mother nor the exertions of her father could have made them rich; but it would be a poverty easily borne, mitigated by useful tasks and intelligent occupations, by serious reading and rational discourse, a poverty without the stigma of low-minded ignorance attached to it.

Not foreseeing any particular interest to herself in the occurrences of a visitation, she had been busy with her own thoughts during the chief part of her father's description; but when she heard Mr Howard spoken of as the preacher, and as having given an excellent sermon, she could not help listening with a quicker ear.

"I do not know when I have heard a discourse more to my mind," Mr Watson was saying, "or one better delivered. He reads extremely well, with great propriety and in a very impressive manner, yet at the same time without any theatrical grimace or exaggeration. I do not like much action in the pulpit. Nor do I like the studied air and artificial inflexions of the voice which your very popular preachers generally have. I try and avoid them myself. A simple delivery is better calculated to inspire devotion and shows a more educated taste. Mr Howard reads like a scholar and a gentleman."

"And what had you for dinner, sir?" asked his eldest daughter.

He related the dishes, and told what he had eaten himself.

"Upon the whole," he said, "I have had a very comfortable day. My old friends were quite surprised to see me and treated me very kindly. But what pleased me as much as anything was Mr Howard's attention. There was a steep flight of steps up to the room we dined in, which did not agree with my gouty foot. Mr Howard walked with me from the bottom to the top, and made me take his arm. It struck me as very becoming in so young a man. I had no reason to expect it, for I have hardly spoken to him before in my life. He inquired after one of my daughters, but I do not know which. I suppose you know among yourselves."

"It would be Emily," explained Elizabeth. "He stood up with her last night after Mrs Blake had introduced them."

"Did he indeed?" said her father. "And how did you find him?"

"As you have described him, sir. Sensible, well-mannered and properly educated."

"And how are my old friends the Edwardses?" he inquired.

"Mrs Edwards was very kind and paid me every possible attention. It was not only that she sent me back in her coach; there were other and smaller courtesies whose omission would not have been noticed and of whose performance only I could be aware."

"I am told Mr Edwards has turned into a great fortune-teller lately," said Mr Watson. "He always had an interest in those matters, but of old it was a harmless one. He collected superstitions as others might collect quaint proverbs or old receipts. In his new idleness I believe he is grown to believe them."

"Some of his talk was very foolish, sir," replied Emily.

"It is a pity he should waste his own and other people's time. But we must not be too harsh. I believe him to be a good man; and goodness is not so common that we can afford to despise it, even when it is allied to qualities we cannot admire."

"Indeed, sir," cried Emily, "I did not mean to criticize one who was once your friend. I have no doubt at all of Mr Edwards's true worth; and I have seen at Eversleigh – in fact I have known as well as a pupil can know a loved teacher – a person in whom great goodness is combined with no little eccentricity."

Mr Watson asked who this was, and she spoke at some length in praise of Mr Jones, telling of the affection he inspired in all who knew him well. A little later, on Elizabeth's being summoned out of the room, her father returned to the subject.

"Through the kindness of your aunt," he said, "you have enjoyed a better education than I would have been able to provide for you. It has pleased me to find that this education has not been confined to a few accomplishments and elegancies of behaviour, but has included the development of your understanding. You have lately been dismissed from your aunt's home and have come to one which must appear sadly different to you. But Mr Edwards is by no means unique in this world. Goodness and foolishness are often combined in one person. You must never let the knowledge of your aunt's recent error displace the memory of her past kindness. Nor must you ever let the noise and bustle in this house, or the lack of refinement to which you have been accustomed, blind you to the real qualities of some of your brothers and sisters."

Emily immediately set at rest any doubts that may have existed in her father's mind about the affection in which she held, and would always hold, her aunt. She was going on to express her gratitude for the warm welcome she had received from Elizabeth when her father cut her short.

"I was not thinking solely of your eldest sister. I am too sensible of what I owe her for the manner in which she has attempted a task that would have daunted all but the bravest hearts ever to exclude her from my reckoning. But I hope you may also find friends among the others. I do not pretend they are without imperfections. But I leave it to your good understanding to discount superficial faults, which in truth very few of us lack, and to appreciate what is worthy of esteem."

At this point Elizabeth returned to the room. Mr Watson ceased speaking and never afterwards reopened the subject with Emily. His remarks had given her great satisfaction, and the meetings she had looked forward to with apprehension assumed a different aspect. Elizabeth, whose judgement was not always hers, had perhaps exaggerated her sisters' faults. The smallness of the house and closeness of their society would serve to emphasize minor blemishes of character. Perhaps she remembered a youthful fretfulness or a youthful petulance that had long been outgrown. So Emily reasoned, while the evening passed very comfortably.

5

At five minutes past three, on the third day after the ball, as Nanny bustled into the parlour with the tray and knife-case, she was called to the front door by the sound of as smart a rap as the end of a riding whip could give. Though charged by Miss Watson to let nobody in she returned in half a minute with a look of awkward dismay to hold the parlour door open for Lord Osborne and Tom Musgrave. The surprise of the young ladies may be imagined. No visitors would have been welcome at that moment, but such visitors as these – such a one as Lord Osborne at least, a nobleman and a stranger – really distressed them.

He looked a little embarrassed himself; and on being introduced by his voluble friend he muttered something about doing himself the honour of waiting upon Mr Watson. Though Emily could not but take the compliment of the visit to herself, she was very far from enjoying the call. She felt all the inconsistency of such an acquaintance with the very humble style in which they were obliged to live; and having in her aunt's household been used to the many elegancies of life, was fully sensible of all that must be open to the ridicule of richer people in her present home. Of the pain of such feelings, Elizabeth knew nothing. Her simple mind, or juster reason, saved her from such mortification. Though shrinking under a general sense of inferiority before her great neighbour, she felt no particular shame, and Emily could not but envy her.

Mr Watson, as the gentlemen had already heard from Nanny, was not well enough to be downstairs. With much concern they took their seats, Lord Osborne near Emily, and the obedient Mr Musgrave, in high spirits at his own importance, on the other side of the fireplace with Elizabeth. *He* was at no loss for words. But when Lord Osborne had hoped that Emily had not caught cold at the ball, he had nothing more to say for some time, and could only gratify his eyes by occasional glances at his fair companion. Emily was not inclined to give herself much trouble for his entertainment. After hard labour of mind, he produced the remark of its being a very fine day, and followed it up with the question:

"Have you been walking this morning?"

"No, my lord. We thought it too dirty."

"You should wear half-boots." After another pause: "Nothing sets off a neat ankle more than a half-boot. Nankeen galoshed with black looks very well. Do you not like half-boots?"

"Yes. But unless they are so stout as to injure their beauty they are not fit for country walking."

"Ladies should ride in dirty weather. Do you ride?"

"No, my lord," she answered, shortly. She had ridden regularly at Eversleigh; and at the moment he spoke her habit was hanging in a closet almost directly above his head. But she was somewhat impatient at the stupidity of a man who inquired whether she rode when it was common knowledge that there was but one old mare in the stables of the parsonage.

"I wonder every woman does not. A woman never looks better than on horse-back."

"But every woman may not have the inclination or the means."

"If they knew how much it became them, they would all have the inclination. And I fancy, Miss Watson, when they once had the inclination, the means would soon follow."

She repressed a second sharp reply and answered with more becoming civility:

"Your lordship thinks we always have our own way. *That* is a point on which ladies and gentlemen have long disagreed. But without pretending to decide it, I may say that there are some circumstances which even *women* cannot control. Female economy can do a great deal, my lord, but it cannot turn a small income into a large one."

Lord Osborne was silenced. Her manner had been neither sententious nor sarcastic, but there was something in its mild seriousness, as well as in the words themselves, which made him think. When he addressed her again it was with a degree of considerate propriety totally unlike the half-shy, half-assertive style of his former remarks.

It was the first time he had wished to please a woman; just as it was the first time he had had to consider what was due to a young lady in Emily's situation. As he was wanting neither in sense nor a good disposition his deliberations were not in vain.

"You have not been long in this country, I understand," he said, in the tone of a gentleman. "I hope you are pleased with it."

He was rewarded by a gracious answer, and a more liberal view of her face than she had yet bestowed.

"I myself have a great love of Surrey," he continued, thus encouraged. "I am seldom so happy as when riding in its lanes, or across its hill and heaths. There is a greater variety within a small compass in Surrey than I think you will find elsewhere. In a few minutes you can pass from a valley where all is cultivated, to hills that support but timber and sheep, or to moorlands which give sustenance only to birds and heather."

"You must not boast of hills to me, my lord. For I was brought up at Eversleigh in Shropshire; and to one accustomed to a view of Welsh mountains the Surrey hills seem somewhat puny."

"I will not compare them in size," he answered, with a smile, "but in everything else I think I have the advantage. For if the truth be told your Welsh mountains take up too much space. They usurp that part of landscape that should be set aside for meadows, cornfields and farmsteads. And in themselves they are somewhat rocky, better suited to goats than to sheep."

"Now you are speaking as a landowner, rather than as a lover of fine scenery."

"I am speaking as both," he said. "In Bedfordshire you have flat acres and great wealth. In Wales you have mountains and poverty. In Surrey you have variety and comfort. You have balance. You have woods and wilds enough for beauty and sport; orchards and snug fields enough for employment and prosperity."

"You have gone into the matter very thoroughly," said Emily. "In justice to Shropshire I must point out that it is only on the borders of Wales; otherwise I have no quarrel with your argument."

"Your uncle's estate there was of a considerable extent, I believe."

"It comprised a good number of farms," she answered.

"I did not ask solely out of curiosity," he assured her. "It is a subject that interests me greatly – the ownership and cultivation of land, I mean. I do not know that it is one of great interest to young ladies, but your indulgence in letting me speak on it is not without its compensation, for I am a poor talker on other subjects and would leave most of the work to you."

"There are certain topics on which no lady can venture, my lord. The niceties of sport and business and military matters are perhaps beyond us all. But leaving these out of the question I would rather converse with a gentleman on a subject that interests him, than listen to idle compliments, or feel that a special effort was being made to entertain me by a discourse on trivialities."

"That is a more reasonable view than some I know would take," he answered, and then relapsed into silence, brooding perhaps on other silences that had occurred in other conversations.

"I am told your lordship has recently purchased the estate at Stanton Lodge," said Emily. This was a large, handsome house, shuttered and empty, that she had seen at the end of the village.

"Some of the land only, not the house."

"Do you not think it a pity to separate a house from its land in that way?"

"I think it a very great pity; and if it should be the means of denying you pleasant neighbours, I should regret it even more. But the house has been untenanted these five years; and during that time the land has been left with a rascally idle agent, who has allowed it to sink to its present condition. I hate to see neglected land. I think it a crime that a man should own land – good farm-land – and not cultivate it properly. Such behaviour destroys the economy of the country. But estates should not be split up except as a last resort. Nothing is more sad than a great house that has sold its land to pay its owner's debts or make provision for younger sons. I have had to choose between two evils, and if you think I have chosen wrongly my justification must be that I waited five years for a purchaser of the whole estate to appear."

It was now Emily's turn to be silenced. He had not boasted of his duty, but the sincerity of his tone, more revealing than any boast, showed her how deeply he felt his responsibilities. Mr Howard might not have been able to give him an easy air, but he had certainly given him correct principles.

This was the end of their conversation. Lord Osborne's exertions seemed to have exhausted him. He was capable of nothing more, and sat for some minutes contemplating Emily while Tom Musgrave chatted with Elizabeth. In the end they were interrupted by Nanny, who, half-opening the door and putting in her head, said:

"Please ma'am, master wants to know why he hasn't had his dinner."

The gentlemen, who had hitherto disregarded every symptom, however positive, of the nearness of the meal, now jumped up with apologies, while Elizabeth called to Nanny to bring in the fowls.

"I am sorry it happens so," she added, turning good-humouredly to Mr Musgrave, "but you know what early hours we keep."

Tom had nothing to say for himself. He knew very well the hours they kept, and such honest simplicity, such shameless truth, rather bewildered him. Lord Osborne's parting compliments were all they should be, and he concluded by saying:

"My hounds will be hunting this country on Wednesday week. They throw off in Stanton Wood at nine o'clock. I mention this in the hope of your coming out to see what success we have. A walk is always more pleasant with some object in view – even such an idle one as that."

These last words were accompanied by the best smile he had been able to summon up during the visit. Whether it was in anticipation of the pleasure of their future company, or merely in relief at having concluded the call without upsetting a chair, which he had seemed in danger of doing on his way through the small and crowded room, was left in doubt.

Elizabeth looked at her sister in astonishment when their visitors had withdrawn.

"This must be you, Emily," she said. "Who would have thought of Lord Osborne's coming to Stanton? 'Tis good he did not come an hour earlier or he would have found me with the dried herbs. Indeed, it smells somewhat of fennel here still, though not more than is pleasant. He is certainly very handsome, but Tom Musgrave looks by far the smartest and more fashionable man of the two. I am glad he did not say anything to me; I would not have had to talk to such a great man for the world. Tom was very agreeable, was he not?

But did you hear him ask where Penelope and Margaret were when he first came in? It put me out of patience."

Emily said nothing. She had shown no outward embarrassment during the visit, but the colour of her cheeks heightened at Elizabeth's speech, and heightened still more when Miss Watson added:

"First Mr Howard is attentive to my father, and now Lord Osborne calls here! Well, you are certainly a beautiful girl, though you *do* look somewhat like me."

"Dearest Elizabeth, do not speak so. Any beauty I may have is not *in spite* of our resemblance."

"Believe me our resemblance has little to do with it. Margaret has the same features, but she is nothing to you. It is your bloom that makes you exceptional. Mine was not half so fine, and what with my disappointment and helping Nanny in the kitchen when my brothers were at home it did not last long. Still, if I can see you well married I shall feel I have done something."

"If I ever have any good fortune, I hope in some measure you will be able to share it," said Emily, earnestly. "But I must beg you not to jump to false conclusions. Nothing would distress me more than that you should attribute the recent call to anything but a desire to show civility to my father. Indeed as Lord Osborne owns the land hereabouts it is surprising he has not waited on him before."

"Now you are being *too* nice!" cried Miss Watson. "After years of hardly remembering to doff his hat as he rides by, Lord Osborne has suddenly taken it into his head to be intimate with my *father*."

"I am not suggesting intimacy, Elizabeth. I do not think this call is a prelude to *that*. The situations of the families are unhappily too different. I am saying that it is a civility that might perhaps have been paid before. It was you who told me Lord Osborne had recently bought the land at Stanton Lodge, which makes him almost a neighbour of ours. He might have considered that an opportunity for performing a duty previously neglected."

"Aye," said Miss Watson. "A nearer neighbour by a mile than he has been for the rest of his life." Then, seeing that her sister was becoming discomposed, she added: "But perhaps there is something in what you say. He is too high and we are too low. He cannot intend anything serious and it is best to take no notice. But Tom was here too, so everyone in the place will hear of it. You can count on *that*."

There Emily thought it best to leave the matter. Her own feelings were very mixed. To say that she was not flattered by Lord Osborne's visit would be to assert a very unlikely thing and to describe a very odd young lady. But the gratification was by no means unalloyed. His coming was a piece of attention which might please her vanity, but which did not suit her pride. She would rather have known that he wished the visit without presuming to make it, than have seen him at Stanton: that he had inquired about the extent of her uncle's estate, than have been questioned on the matter herself.

Among other unsatisfactory feelings it once occurred to her to wonder why Mr Howard had not taken the privilege of coming as well, why in fact he had not accompanied his lordship. After thinking it over she was willing to suppose that he had either known nothing about it, or had declined any share in a measure which, she soon began to believe, savoured as much of impoliteness as courtesy. Her father's remarks helped her to the latter conclusion. Mr Watson was far from being delighted when he heard what had passed, which he did on descending to take his tea with them that evening. Elizabeth's account seemed to wake more than usually gloomy memories, and he answered her somewhat peevishly.

"Pooh! Pooh! What occasion can there be for Lord Osborne's coming? If he was to come at all he should have come sixteen years ago, when I first moved into the district. But he did not choose to, and I have managed well enough without being noticed by the family."

"You would have been somewhat surprised at receiving him sixteen years ago," said Miss Watson, cheerfully. "For he would have been about nine years old at the time."

Emily again mentioned the purchase of the Stanton Lodge property.

"No, no. It is some fooling of that idle fellow, Tom Musgrave; or just ill-bred curiosity. I cannot return the visit. I would not if I could. It was not meant in earnest." And when Tom Musgrave was met with again he was commissioned with a message of excuse to Osborne Castle on the customary plea of Mr Watson's infirm state of health.

6

A week or ten days rolled quietly away after this visit before any event, beyond the customary bustle of the household, arose to interrupt the affectionate intercourse of the two sisters, whose mutual regard was increasing with the intimate knowledge of each other that such intercourse produced. Emily had not been slow to profit by her father's hint, and respect was soon added to regard – respect, not for Elizabeth's elegance, nor even, alas, for her management, but respect for character, for simple truthfulness and honest kindness.

The first circumstance to break in on their peace was the receipt of a letter from Croydon to announce the speedy return of Margaret, and a visit of two or three days from Mr and Mrs Robert Watson, who undertook to bring her home so that they themselves could see Emily. This intelligence filled the thoughts of the sisters at Stanton and busied the hours of one of them at least. Jane had been a woman of fortune and the preparations for her entertainment were considerable. Elizabeth, as was her habit, undertook the preparations with more good will than method, and Emily did what she could without actual interference to reduce the confusion. After an absence of fourteen years all her brothers and sisters were strangers to her; and she made ready to meet the party in some anxiety, and with a determination neither to be too nice herself nor expect too much from others. The event proved her anxiety justified and her determination not sufficiently deep.

Robert Watson was an attorney at Croydon in a good way of business. He was very well satisfied with himself both for his success and for having married the only daughter of the attorney to whom he had been clerk, with a fortune of six thousand pounds. Mrs Robert was not less pleased with *herself* for having had the six thousand pounds and for now being in possession of a very smart house in Croydon, where she gave genteel parties and wore fine clothes. In her person there was nothing remarkable, and her manners were pert and conceited. Margaret was not without beauty. She had a slight, pretty figure, and wanted rather countenance than good features; but the sharp and fretful expression of her face made her beauty little felt. On meeting her long absent sister, as on every occasion of show, her manner was all affection and her voice all gentleness; continual smiles and a very slow articulation being her constant resource when bent on pleasing.

"I am sure we shall be great friends," she observed, with much sentiment.

Emily scarcely knew how to answer such a proposition, and the manner in which it was spoken she could not attempt to equal. Mrs Robert Watson eyed her with much familiar curiosity and triumphant compassion. The loss of the aunt's fortune was uppermost in her mind at the moment of meeting; and she could not but feel how much better it was to be the daughter of a gentleman of property in Croydon than the niece of an old woman who threw herself away on an Irish captain. Robert was carelessly kind, as became a prosperous man and a brother. He was more intent on settling with the post-boy, inveighing against the exorbitant expense of posting, and pondering over a doubtful half-crown, than on welcoming a sister who was no longer likely to have any property for him to get the direction of.

"Your road through the village is infamous, Elizabeth," he said. "Worse than it ever was. By heaven, I would indict it if I lived near you. Who is surveyor now?"

There was a little niece at Croydon to be fondly inquired after by the kind-hearted Elizabeth, who regretted her not being of the party.

"You are very good," replied Mrs Robert, "and I assure you it went hard with Augusta to have us come away without her. I was forced to say we were only going to church, and promised to come back for her directly. But you know it would not do to bring her without her maid. I am as particular as ever in having her properly attended to."

"Sweet little darling," cried Margaret. "It quite broke my heart to leave her."

"Then why were you in such a hurry to run away from her?" asked Mrs Robert. "You are a sad shabby girl. I have been quarrelling with you all the way here. Such a visit as this I never heard of! You know how glad we are to have any of you with us. But I am sorry" – this with a witty smile – "we have not been able to make Croydon *assez charmant* this autumn."

"My dearest Jane, do not overpower me with your raillery. You know what inducements I had to bring me home."

"I only beg you will not set your neighbours against the place. Perhaps Emily may be tempted to go back with us and stay till Christmas if you do not dissuade her."

Emily was greatly obliged.

"I assure you we have very good society at Croydon," Jane continued. "I do not much attend the balls; *entre nous* they are rather too mixed; but our parties are very select and good. I had seven tables last week in my drawing-room. Are you fond of the country? How do you like Stanton?"

"Very much," replied Emily, who thought a comprehensive answer most to the purpose. She saw that her sister-in-law despised her immediately. Mrs Robert Watson was indeed wondering what sort of home Emily could have been used to in Shropshire, and setting it down as certain that the stories she had heard of the uncle's fortune were grossly exaggerated.

"How charming Emily is," whispered Margaret to Mrs Robert, in her most languishing tone.

Emily was quite distressed by such behaviour; and she did not like it better when she heard Margaret five minutes afterwards say to Elizabeth:

"Have you heard from Pen since she went to Chichester? I had a letter the other day. She seems to be doing little but ride all the time. She would be better employed in fixing Dr Harding, for there will be four of us now, instead of three, if she comes back Miss Penelope."

Deeply shocked as she was by the sentiment of this speech, Emily could not avoid noticing its tone. It was said in a sharp, quick manner, without any of the artificial sensibility she had heard before. Such, she feared, would be Margaret's ordinary voice, when the novelty of her own appearance was over.

The ladies were soon invited upstairs to prepare for dinner.

"I hope you will find things tolerably comfortable, Jane," said Elizabeth, as she opened the door of the spare bedchamber.

"My good creature," replied Jane, "use no ceremony with me, I entreat you. I hope I can put up with a smaller apartment than I am used to for two or three nights without making it a piece of work. I wish to be treated quite *en famille*. I do hope you have not been getting a great dinner for us. We had a good breakfast before we left, and some refreshment on the road, so are come prepared to eat your ordinary meals."

"I suppose," said Margaret, rather quickly to Emily, "you and I are to be together. Elizabeth always takes care to have a room to herself."

"No. Elizabeth has kindly given me half hers."

"Oh!" said Margaret, in a softened voice, but somewhat mortified to find that she was not ill used. "I am sorry I am not to have the pleasure of your company, especially as it makes me nervous to be much alone."

Emily was the first of the females in the parlour again. On entering it she found her brother alone.

"So Emily," he said, "here you are come back to your old home. A pretty piece of work your aunt Turner has made of it – O'Brien, I suppose I should call her now. By heaven, a woman should never be trusted with money! I always said she ought to have settled something on you as soon as her husband died."

"But that would have been trusting *me* with money," replied Emily. "And I am a woman too."

"It might have been secured to your future use without your having any power of it now. What a blow it must have been for you! Old Turner must have been worth fifty thousand pounds at least. I do not say you would have got it all, but you could have reckoned on half. I hope the old woman will smart for it."

"Do not speak disrespectfully of her. She was very good to me, and if she has made an imprudent choice she will suffer more for it herself than I possibly can."

"Everybody must think her an old fool. I thought Turner was reckoned a sensible man. How the devil came he to make such a will?"

"My uncle's sense is not at all impeached in my opinion by his attachment to my aunt. She had been an excellent wife to him. The most liberal and enlightened minds are always the most confiding. The event has been unfortunate, but my uncle's memory is, if possible, endeared to me by such proof of tender respect for my aunt."

"That is an odd way of talking. He might have provided decently for his widow without leaving everything he had to dispose of – or indeed any part of it – at her mercy."

"My aunt may have erred," said Emily, warmly. "Perhaps she *has* erred. But my uncle's conduct has been faultless. I was *her* niece and he left to her the power of providing for me."

"But unluckily she has passed on the pleasure of providing for you with the power. That is the long and short of the business. After keeping you at a distance from your family for such a length of time as must do away with all natural affection among us, and breeding you up, I suppose, in a superior style, you are returned upon our hands without a sixpence."

Emily, struggling with her tears under this unfair attack, said nothing.

"Has she written to you recently?" demanded her brother.

"No."

"You should write yourself. Circumstances may change; one does not know. A letter every month or so would not cost you much labour."

"You mistake me if you think such a correspondence would be a labour," cried Emily, with emotion. "But if my aunt does not write to me it is not fitting that I should write to her."

She was unable any longer to restrain her tears, which became obvious even to the slow eye of her brother.

"I did not mean to make you cry," said Robert, somewhat softened; and after a short silence, by way of changing the subject, he added: "I am just come from my father's room. He seems in very indifferent spirits. It will be a sad break-up when he dies. Pity you can none of you get married. You must come to Croydon like the rest and see what you can do there. I believe if Margaret had had a thousand or fifteen hundred pounds, there was a young man who might have had her."

Emily was glad when they were joined by the others. Mrs

Robert, exactly as smart as she had been at her own party, came in with apologies for her dress.

"I would not make you wait," she said, "so I put on the first thing I met with. I am afraid I am a sad figure. My dear Mr W., you have not put any fresh powder in your hair."

"No; I do not intend to. I think there is powder enough in my hair for my wife and sisters."

"Indeed you ought to make some alteration in your dress before dinner when you are visiting, though you do not at home."

"Nonsense."

"It is very odd you do not do what other gentlemen do. Mr Marshall and Mr Hemming change their dress every day of their lives before dinner. And what was the use of my bringing your last new coat if you are never to wear it?"

"Pray be satisfied with being fine yourself and leave your husband alone."

To put an end to this altercation, and soften the evident vexation of her sister-in-law, Emily, though in no spirits to make such nonsense easy, began to admire her gown. This produced immediate complacency.

"Do you like it?" said Jane. "I am very happy. It has been excessively admired, but sometimes I think the pattern too large. I shall wear one tomorrow which I think you will prefer to this. Yours is very neat, I must say. A little quiet for my taste, but it goes very well on you. Have you seen the one I gave Margaret?"

Dinner came, and except when Mrs Robert looked at her husband's head she continued to be gay and flippant, chiding Elizabeth for the profusion on the table, and absolutely protesting against the entry of the roast turkey.

"I beg and entreat that no turkey may be seen today. I am really frightened out of my wits at the number of dishes we have already. Let us have no turkey I beseech you."

"The turkey is roasted," replied Elizabeth, "and it may just as well come in as stay in the kitchen. Besides, if it is cut I am in hopes that my father may be tempted to eat a little, for it is rather a favourite dish."

"You may have it in, my dear, but I assure you I shall only be able to eat a *soupçon*. Really not more than a *morceau*."

Mrs Robert was fond of French words, though not always accurate in her employment of them. The occasional use of French, she considered, marked her out as a woman of education and gentility – as a woman, in fact, fully deserving of six thousand pounds.

In honour of their visitors they moved into the best parlour at the conclusion of the meal, and Mr Watson was prevailed on to join them there shortly after the arrival of the tea-tray. Robert, having investigated and passed judgement on Emily's affairs, started on his father's as soon as the latter was comfortably settled in his armchair.

"The meadows seem in poor condition, sir," he said.

"Yes," said Mr Watson, with a certain gloomy satisfaction. "They serve for the two cows and the mare; that is about all now. James tells me the ones by the stream get very marshy in the winter; but I have to keep my feet dry, and it is some time since I went that way."

"It is a pity you cannot be like your neighbours, sir, and get some benefit from the advance in corn. Every year it fetches a higher price."

"So they tell me," said Mr Watson. "So they tell me."

"A small outlay on improving the land would repay itself many times over," continued Robert, warming to his subject. "I have not looked at the stream yet, but I could do so tomorrow. It should not be a great matter to clear it out. An extra horse and another man or two should enable you to sow ten acres or more. Reckoning twenty bushels to the acre, and wheat at eight shillings a quarter, that would give you an additional hundred pounds a year."

He could not have looked more pleased if he had just made his father a present of the same amount. Mr Watson was less pleased than his son.

"I do not consider this an entirely fit subject for the drawing-room," he said, "nevertheless I must point out that you have quite neglected the debit side of your balance sheet."

"Let us say ten pounds for the horse," answered Robert, who needed but little encouragement to continue. "And twenty pounds to drain the land, mend the gates, and set the hedges to rights. That would be your capital cost. Another man would take twenty pounds a year and perhaps ten should be set aside for harvesting. You would still have a profit your first year."

"And whom are you suggesting as overseer?" asked Mr Watson, peevishly. "I am a little sickly for the task myself and James is kept busy as it is. Perhaps you think your sister Elizabeth could add the post of bailiff to her other occupations?"

Robert, disliking his father's tone, muttered something about James being able to manage.

"No; it will not do," said Mr Watson more politely. "Such schemes are good enough for a lawyer's office, but they do not suit the circumstances here. I am more likely to lose the little money I have on such a project than make myself rich."

"I hope we may be able to have a game of cards tonight," said Elizabeth to Mrs Robert, in the pause that followed.

"Not on my account, my dear, I beg. You know I am no card-player. I think a snug chat infinitely better. I always say cards are very well to break a formal circle, but one never wants them among friends."

"I was thinking of its being something to amuse my father," said Elizabeth, "if it was not disagreeable to you. We are too many for whist, but perhaps we could make a round game."

"By all means, my dear creature. I am quite at your service; *prêt d'accomplir* whenever you say the word. Only do not advise me to choose the game, that is all. Speculation is the only round game at Croydon now, but I can play anything. When there is only one or two of you at home you must be quite at a loss to amuse him. Why do you not get him to play cribbage? Margaret and I played cribbage most nights when we were not engaged."

The sound of a distant carriage was then heard. It was an unusual sound at that time of the day. Since Stanton Lodge had been untenanted the village contained no gentleman's family beyond the rector's; and few used the road except the Osbornes, who thereby avoided Wickstead and saved themselves a mile on the way to Dunford. It was from the direction of the castle that the carriage was coming. The wheels rapidly approached and stopped beyond doubt at the garden gate of the parsonage. Steps were distinguished along the paved footway that led beneath the window of the room to the front door. They were the steps of one man. After an interval of suspense the door opened and displayed Tom Musgrave in the wrap of a traveller. He had been in London and was now on his way home;

and he had come a mile out of his road merely to call for ten minutes at Stanton. He loved to take people by surprise with sudden visits at extraordinary seasons, and in the present instance he had the additional motive of being able to tell the Miss Watsons, whom he depended on finding quietly employed after tea, that he was going home to an eight o'clock dinner.

As it happened he did not give more surprise than he received. Instead of being shown into the usual sitting-room, the door of the best parlour was thrown open, and he beheld a circle of smartly-dressed people, whom he could not immediately recognize, arranged with all the honours of visiting round the fire. He stood a few seconds in silent amazement.

"Musgrave!" murmured Margaret, in a tender voice.

He recollected himself and came forward, delighted to find such a gathering of friends. He shook hands with Robert, bowed to Mr Watson, smiled to the ladies, and did everything required of him. But as to any particular attention towards Margaret, Emily, who closely observed him, perceived nothing that did not justify Elizabeth's opinion, though Margaret's modest smiles imported that she meant to take the visit to herself. He was persuaded without much difficulty to throw off his great-coat and drink tea with them. For whether he dined at eight or at nine, as he justly remarked himself, was a matter of very little consequence; and without seeming to seek it he did not turn away from the chair by Margaret, which she was assiduous in providing for him. She had thus secured him from her sisters; and after he had given Robert the last current of public news he was at liberty to hear her soft address as she spoke of her fears of his having had a most terrible, cold, dark, dangerous, dreadful journey.

"Indeed you *should* not have set out so late," she concluded.

"I could not be earlier," he replied. "I was detained chatting at the Bedford with a friend. All hours are alike to me. How long have you been in the country, Miss Margaret?"

"We only came this morning. My kind brother and sister brought me home this very morning. 'Tis singular, is it not?"

"You were gone a great while. A fortnight, I suppose?"

"*You* may call a *fortnight* a great while, Mr Musgrave," said Mrs Robert, sharply, "but *we* think a *month* very little. I assure you we bring her home at the end of a month much against our will."

"A month! Have you really been gone for a month? 'Tis amazing how time flies."

"You may imagine," said Margaret, in a sort of slow whisper, "what are my sensations in finding myself once more at Stanton. You know what a sad visitor I make. And I was so excessively impatient to see Emily; I *dreaded* the meeting and at the same time *longed* for it. Do you not comprehend that feeling?"

"Not at all," he cried aloud. "I could never dread meeting Miss Emily Watson, or any of her sisters."

It was lucky that he finished as he did.

"Were you speaking to me?" said Emily, who had caught her own name.

"Not absolutely," he answered, "but I was thinking of you; as many at a greater distance are probably doing at this moment. It is fine open weather, Miss Emily. Perfect for hunting."

"Emily is delightful, is she not?" whispered Margaret. "I have found her more than answer my warmest hopes. Did you ever see anything more perfectly beautiful? I think even you must be a convert to a dark complexion."

He hesitated. Margaret was not dark herself, and he did not particularly wish to compliment her; but Miss Osborne and Miss Carr were very fair, and his devotion to them carried the day.

"Your sister's complexion," he said at last, "is as fine as a dark complexion can be; but I still profess my preference for a white skin. You have seen Miss Osborne? She is my model for a truly feminine complexion and she is very fair indeed."

"I am getting a little warm here," complained Mr Watson, of whom nobody had taken any notice for some time. Robert had let Elizabeth settle her father into his chair without assistance, but now – a visitor being present – he got up himself and civilly moved it to a cooler place.

When the tea-things were removed Tom began to talk of his carriage. But the old card-table being set out in front of Mr Watson, with the fish and counters and a tolerably clean pack, the general voice was so urgent with him to join the party that he agreed to allow himself another quarter of an hour.

"What is your game?" he cried, as they stood round the table.

"Speculation, I believe," said Elizabeth. "My sister recommends it, and I fancy we all like it. I know *you* do, Tom."

"It is the only round game played at Croydon now," said Mrs Robert. "We never think of any other. I am glad it is a favourite with you."

"Oh *me*," said Tom. "Whatever you decide will be a favourite with *me*. I have had some pleasant hours at speculation in my time; but I have not played it for a long while now. *Vingt-et-un* is the game at Osborne Castle. I have played nothing but *vingt-et-un* of late."

"Why should we not play *vingt-et-un*?" cried Margaret. "I think it is a much better game than speculation."

Mrs Robert offered not another word in support of speculation. She was quite vanquished; the title of the new game made an irresistible appeal to her, and the fashions of Osborne Castle carried it over the fashions of Croydon.

"Do you see much of the rectory family at the castle, Mr Musgrave?" said Emily, as they were taking their seats.

"Oh yes! They are often there. Mrs Blake is a nice, good-humoured little woman; she and I are sworn friends. And Howard is a very gentleman-like sort of fellow."

"An educated man too, I consider," said Mr Watson.

"Indeed that is what I intended, sir," answered Tom carelessly, before continuing to Emily. "You are not forgotten I assure you, by *any* of the party. I fancy you must have a little cheek-glowing now and then. Were you not rather warm last Saturday about nine or ten o'clock in the evening? I will tell you how it was – I see you are dying to know. Says Howard to Lord Osborne –"

At this interesting moment he was called on by Margaret to regulate the game and determine some disputable point. His attention was so totally engaged in the business, and afterwards by the course of the game, as never to revert to what he had been saying before; and Emily, though suffering a good deal from curiosity, did not like to remind him.

Mr Musgrave proved a very useful addition to their table. He was excellently qualified to shine at a round game, and few situations made him appear to greater advantage. Though not perhaps a great claim to distinction, it was one he undoubtedly possessed, and should consequently be set down to his credit. He played with spirit, had a great deal to say; and without being a wit himself could sometimes make use of the wit of an absent friend. He had a way of retailing a commonplace, or saying a mere nothing, that had great effect at a card-table. The habits and jokes of Osborne Castle were now added to his ordinary means of entertainment. He repeated the smart sayings of one lady, the naïve remarks of another, and the blunt truths of the third. His admiration for the family bordered on veneration, but so attentive were his listeners that he even indulged them with a copy of Lord Osborne's overdrawing himself on both cards.

The clock struck nine while he was thus agreeably occupied; and when Nanny came in with her master's basin of gruel he had the pleasure of observing to Mr Watson that he would leave him at supper while he went home to dinner himself. The carriage was ordered to the door, and no entreaties for his staying longer could now avail; for he well knew that if he stayed he would have to sit down to supper in less than ten minutes, which to a man whose heart has been long fixed on calling his next meal dinner, was quite insupportable. On finding him determined to go, Margaret began to wink and nod at Elizabeth to ask him to dinner for the following day; and Elizabeth, not able to resist hints that her own hospitable temper more than half-seconded, gave the invitation.

"With the greatest pleasure," was the first reply. Then a moment afterwards: "That is if I can possibly get here in time. You must not think of me unless you see me."

And so he departed, delighted in the uncertainty in which he had left them.

7

Margaret, in the joy of her heart, under circumstances which she chose to consider as peculiarly propitious, would willingly have made a confidante of Emily when they were alone for a short time the next morning.

"The young man who was here last night, my dear Emily, and returns today," she said, "is more interesting to me than perhaps you may be aware." But Emily, pretending to understand nothing extraordinary in the words, made some very inapplicable reply, and ran away from a subject that was odious to her.

Margaret would not allow a doubt to be repeated of Mr Musgrave's coming to dinner, and the conversation at breakfast was confined to a discussion of what was to be eaten when they next sat down to a meal. Elizabeth's proposals were scouted as totally insufficient for a guest of such special importance, and finally Margaret went into the kitchen herself to harry and scold the maids and get in Nanny's way.

"Well," said Elizabeth, in some astonishment, "it is not often that Margaret does anything in the house. The suggestion is usually enough to bring on one of her headaches."

"It is not a habit she has picked up in Croydon," said Mrs Robert, quickly. "I have as many girls in the kitchen as I need."

"Leave her to herself," suggested Robert, with what Emily had to admit was admirable sense. "Then if the meal is not to the taste of her friend she will have only herself to blame."

"I planned to salt the pig this morning," said Miss Watson. "It is really my baking day too, but as you were both coming I did that yesterday. I would have done the pig as well, but it was two o'clock before I knew where I was."

"How much has he got?" asked Mrs Robert.

"Nine hundred a year," answered her husband, who knew the subjects most likely to be pursued by his wife.

"I doubt its going through. Margaret is a pretty girl, but he is entitled to look for some return for such an income. Five thousand at least."

The day was fine and Emily proposed a walk. Robert said he was going to make a survey of the stream; Mrs Robert did not think she had a dress suitable for walking the country lanes, and Elizabeth, after first wondering where there would be room enough in the kitchen for her to salt the pig, changed her mind and asked Mrs Robert if she would excuse her for an hour.

"Certainly, my dear Elizabeth. *Pas des excuses* to me, I pray. I have my work and I trust I can occupy myself for an hour. It is not very long after all, and if I find myself *ennuyée* I can always talk to Margaret."

A few minutes later the sisters left the parsonage together. They walked towards Dunford, thinking a great deal of the relations who had joined them since they had last walked together, but saying little. Indeed the little that could be safely expressed had already been said in the privacy of the bedroom they shared. There was no great diversion of opinion between them, only a difference in the intensity with which their opinions were held and in the emotions to which they gave rise. Elizabeth had too much good sense not to recognize hard-hearted prosperity, low-minded conceit, and wrong-headed folly when she saw them. But to her they were vexations to be disregarded when possible, and cheerfully borne when forced on her notice. To Emily they were faults of character that could never be ignored and should be publicly condemned.

"Though it is good for you, Elizabeth," she said, following her own thoughts, "that you *are* able to disregard them sometimes. Otherwise your life here would not have been worth living."

"Robert and Jane never stay more than a day or two. And Margaret is sunny enough when things go her own way. You must not be too nice."

"That is advice I must learn to follow," said Emily, with resolution. "Or at least I must so comport myself as to give the appearance of following it. I reached that conclusion last night. It is as necessary for my own peace of mind as for the comfort of those I live with. Now, pray, let us close the subject, and please tell me why you are taking me southward."

"Is not this the way you wanted to go?"

"*Wanted* to go, Elizabeth? I had no preference in either direction. I merely followed you."

Elizabeth regarded her with astonishment, and then sighed.

"Since *you* say so, my dear, I will believe you – though I doubt whether I would have believed anyone else. Did you not see the hounds this morning?"

"Lord Osborne's hounds?"

"Of course. As they passed this way over the fields from Stanton Woods shortly before breakfast, and as he invited you to come out to find him, and as you seemed particularly anxious for a walk to-day, I have put on my best pelisse to keep you company instead of salting the pig. Nor did I press Jane to come with us, you may remember."

"It is Wednesday!"

"Aye; 'tis Wednesday. My baking day."

"You are a good soul," said Emily, laughing, "but as I told you before, you mistake my interest in the gentleman. I did not see the hounds; I had forgotten the invitation; and my anxiety for a walk was more to escape what was *within* than to encounter what was *without*. Come, let us go back. You can salt your pig and I can take a turn or two round the church before I enter."

"It would be a pity to return now we are come so far."

"It would be an even greater pity to give the gentleman the opinion we were chasing him. If we are to walk, let us at least walk in the other direction."

Before they could settle the argument a very smart equipage, drawn by two perfectly-matched horses, and with two men in the Osborne livery on the box, appeared from the direction in which they had come, and forced them to step hurriedly to the side of the road. The carriage, which was Lady Osborne's best barouche, stopped abreast of them. The two ladies who were on the back seat, Mrs Blake and Lady Osborne, began talking almost before it had ceased to move. Lady Osborne's remark was brief and to the point.

"Have you seen them?" she shouted.

Meanwhile Mrs Blake, in a quieter voice, was greeting Emily, acknowledging Elizabeth's existence for the first time, and reminding Lady Osborne of Emily's great kindness to Charles at the ball two weeks before.

"Yes, yes," said Lady Osborne, impatiently. "I know all about that. She is a very well brought up girl, and so on. But the only point at the moment is whether she has seen the hounds."

"An hour to an hour and a half ago, your ladyship," answered Elizabeth, "going over the fields from Stanton Wood towards Millington."

"Good girl!" Lady Osborne swung open the door of the barouche. "Will you not come in?"

"Really, your ladyship –"

"Hurry up now, or they will get away from us."

With mixed emotions – awe for Lady Osborne's position, pleasure at Lady Osborne's commendation, and thankfulness that she had on her best pelisse – Miss Watson moved to obey, leaving Emily no choice but to follow. Their entry into the carriage was not made as expeditiously as Lady Osborne might have wished, for the opening of the door had exposed three dogs which now crowded to the entrance, and were only prevented from leaping into the road by Lady Osborne's threats and the exertions of the groom.

"Millington!" shouted Lady Osborne, as soon as they were settled on the front seat; and the carriage moved off at a smart trot.

It was a mile to Millington – a collection of farms and cottages between Stanton and Dunford – and Lady Osborne, prompted perhaps by Mrs Blake's politeness to Emily, had leisure enough for the courtesies required of her. She asked after Mr Watson; was told he was fairly well, and that Margaret and Robert and Jane, none of whom she had ever spoken to, were at the parsonage, before wondering aloud whether the fox had taken refuge in the spinneys of Millington Farm. Emily, after answering Mrs Blake's queries and inquiring after Master Charles, who was with the hounds, was fondling one of the dogs when she became aware that Lady Osborne was regarding her with approbation.

"I am glad to see you are not nervous of dogs, Miss Emily."

"Indeed your ladyship, it would be a poor person who was frightened of these setters."

"They are well trained. Though I did it myself I must say they are well trained. Cuff them please if they put their paws on your dress. I do not want them spoilt. I have no patience with people who let their dogs jump up on your chairs and mess your clothes. I would as soon think of putting my own dirty shoes on my furniture as let my dogs do such a thing."

Emily agreed that the proper place for an untrained dog was a kennel.

"I believe you are but recently come here," said Lady Osborne. "Unless I have been misinformed you were brought up by your aunt at Everton."

"Eversleigh, your ladyship."

"Indeed. And in what country is that?"

"Shropshire, your ladyship. It is only since my uncle's death and my aunt's second marriage that she has removed to Ireland."

Emily was startled by the laughter with which this reply was greeted. Mrs Blake too seemed shocked; and even the well-trained dogs turned their heads and looked at their mistress with surprise.

"Country, my girl. *Country*," explained Lady Osborne. "To what pack does the country belong?"

"To Sir John Freeman's."

"That is west of Shrewsbury, is it not?"

"Yes, your ladyship," replied Emily, to whom this seemed an odd way of fixing the locality of her old home.

"Did your uncle hunt?"

"Until the year before his death, when his health no longer permitted it."

"'Tis a sad time that for a hunting man," said her ladyship, in a truly sympathetic tone. "A very sad time."

Mrs Blake then expressed the hope that when Mr and Mrs Robert Watson had completed their visit she might be allowed the honour of waiting on Miss Watson. "For I suspect you are fully occupied with your family now," she observed, "and perhaps have no time for a new acquaintance."

Elizabeth said she was deeply obliged; but instead of suggesting a day, as Emily hoped, she agreed that she was indeed extremely busy, and was feeling somewhat guilty at that moment for having accepted Lady Osborne's invitation when she should perhaps have been salting the pig or attending to her guests. Mrs Blake was willing to pursue the question of her call further, and was beginning to ask whether Friday, the sixth of November, would be convenient, when Lady Osborne interrupted with an inquiry about the method used by Miss Watson when salting meat. Elizabeth described her method in detail.

"You do not add saltpetre?" said Lady Osborne.

"No, your ladyship."

"I always tell Twig to add saltpetre, especially with beef. It brings out the colour of the meat – a rich pink colour. It is not to everybody's taste, I admit, but I find it more palatable that way myself. The world is growing too refined for me. It cooks fresh meat till it has no taste, and it treats salt meat so that it turns a muddy grey. I confess I am old-fashioned. I like my meat red, just as I like my cheese high and my pastry heavy. There is more nourishment in that sort of food. And there was more colour in young folk's cheeks when I was a girl and we made our meals of such things, than there is today when we blow out our stomachs with soups and potatoes and that plant they call cabbage. Green stuff is suitable for cattle, whose intestines have been specially designed for it, but it does not agree with humans."

"I am a great believer in the beneficial effects of a certain amount of fruit in the diet of young children," said Mrs Blake. "But I must confess I am unable to credit the assertion that there is much nourishment in a cabbage."

They were now come to Millington, and the sisters were not required to carry on the conversation, for which circumstance Emily was grateful as the subject was not one she was used to discussing. They learnt that the hounds had passed by to the west more than an hour ago, but had recently returned through the hamlet at a walk and taken the lane to the east.

"To the spinneys!" cried Lady Osborne. "We will catch them up at the spinneys."

The carriage moved on again, but Lady Osborne was now too eager to allow much connected talk. Mrs Blake did not re-open the question of her call, and Emily was obliged to postpone her account of her father's pleasure in Mr Howard's sermon. She was very well pleased with Mrs Blake. She liked particularly the sensible, polite proposal she had made to visit them. Mrs Blake had obviously informed herself of their lack of a close carriage, and of the smallness of the rooms at their disposal for the reception of visitors. Without any open reference to these disadvantages she had suggested a course which took both of them into account. Emily's only regret was that Elizabeth had missed her chance of confirming the suitability of Friday, the sixth of November, for a call.

Her ladyship's forecast was correct. Within a very few minutes they heard the noise of the hounds and the encouraging shouts of the huntsmen. The carriage turned through an open gate into a firm meadow, and they came into view of the riders. Lady Osborne's excitement was now extreme; Mrs Blake had a mother's attention for the smallest figure among the field, and to both Emily and Elizabeth the scene was one of great interest. The hounds were engaged in a small wood not very far from them. Lord Osborne, on a fine horse, stood close to the wood, while men galloped to and fro to confer with him. Behind Lord Osborne waited the other riders, chatting together in small groups.

The arrival of the carriage was quickly remarked. Elizabeth, with what elsewhere would have been a blush of confusion, but which here passed unnoticed in the smiles of glowing pleasure that seemed universal, remembered in what she was sitting and with whom she had been discussing the salting of meat. She turned to Emily with a comical expression of dismay on her face, and said:

"Well, Emily, well! This is really most unexpected. I am really most surprised to be here. I believe that is Tom looking at us."

Mr Musgrave was not alone in regarding them. Colonel Beresford, a degree more elegant than anyone else on the field, and newly mounted on a fresh horse, exchanged greetings with Lady Osborne and examined her companions. His expression changed from one of disappointment, in failing to find Miss Osborne among them, to one of gallantry and admiration, in observing two not unattractive substitutes. Emily recognized Captain Hunter, with Captain Styles, who had danced with her and whose greeting she happily acknowledged, and Mr Norton. They were somewhat more mud-spattered than the Colonel, and one at least of them appeared to have had a misunderstanding with a brook. Even Lord Osborne took the opportunity of an unoccupied moment to raise his hat to his mother from the far side of the meadow.

"I believe Tom is coming this way," said Elizabeth.

But Charles Blake, crossing the meadow at a quick canter, was before him. He barely paused to greet them before starting his account of the morning.

"We have had such a run," he cried. "I kept up almost the whole way, but William would not let me jump the brook. I am sure I could have managed it. Captain Hunter went over beautifully, but Mr Norton went in with a great splash. They stop for nothing, those three. There was a great fence ten feet high, and Captain Hunter went straight through it. Captain Styles followed, and when the rest of us came up there was an easy gap."

"Remember that you are to follow William, and not Captain Hunter," said his mother.

"I have done all you said," he assured her. "We would have lost them after the brook if it had not been for the fox turning back. Indeed William was not sure it was the same fox, but he came back right to the brook and is got away altogether. Now we are looking for another. William says he will break out northward if we find him here, so you will have a fine view. We are going to take a line through that gap and along the track by the two haystacks. You will see us all. Lord Osborne will be with the huntsmen. Then will come Captain Hunter, Captain Styles and Mr Norton. They will go straight until one of them comes to grief. Colonel Beresford follows them, but a little more slowly. And Mr Cowdray from the farm beyond Wickstead always goes last, and is never in any hurry, and always gets there first, sometimes before Lord Osborne. He is the only one here who knows more than William, I think." He bade his mother and Lady Osborne a rather hurried farewell and turned to Emily. "Goodbye ma'am. I hope –" He stopped and searched his brain for something to say to the young lady who had danced with him. His next birthday, he remembered regretfully, as still a long way off. "I hope you may one day come riding with me and William."

Then he was gone; and Mrs Blake had the not unpleasing duty of acknowledging the compliments on his appearance, his manners and his seat on a horse, paid her by the other three occupants of the carriage. In this, as in other less difficult matters, she still showed herself a woman of ease.

"I am come to pay my respects to your ladyship and your companions," said Tom Musgrave. "'Pon my word, I must say that Charles shows a very good taste and a surprising swiftness in acting on it. He was with you before I had finished straightening my coat."

"You found in Stanton Wood?" said Lady Osborne.

"Within ten minutes, your ladyship. He headed dead south for two and a half miles, and I was beginning to think we would kill on the steps of the White Hart. But he doubled back and was lost in the brook."

"Was it the same fox?"

"Without a doubt. I would wager my horse on it. I assure you it was the same fox." In spite of his protestations Lady Osborne looked unconvinced. "I am glad you understood my hint last night, Miss Emily," he added.

"What hint, sir?"

"Why, I reminded you that it was fine weather for hunting, and here you are come out to watch us as you were invited. That shows a high degree of sensibility in a certain direction, I think."

For a moment Emily was too stupefied to reply. She realized with relief that Lady Osborne's own method of communication was too straightforward for her to read much into the circumlocutions of others, but she was more agitated than she cared to show about the possible effect of such words on a woman of Mrs Blake's understanding.

"You are entirely mistaken, sir," she said firmly, as soon as she had collected her thoughts. "I owe my presence here solely to Lady Osborne's invitation to mount in her carriage, proceeding from a chance encounter in the road. I did *not* follow the drift of your words last night; and I am still far from believing that you could intend any private meaning to a new acquaintance like myself during a public conversation with my family."

Mr Musgrave was unabashed. He was intimate with the Osbornes; nothing that could be said to him by one of Mr Watson's daughters could make him question the propriety of his behaviour.

"Well, you are here, which is the main thing," he replied. "And there is someone else coming to talk to you, I see. Miss Watson, I doubt very much whether I shall be able to get to Stanton in time for dinner today. I had best cry off now, rather than let you wait and be disappointed. I trust you will be so good as to convey my apologies to your brother."

Elizabeth barely had time to express her regret at the news, which she managed very civilly considering the trouble he had already caused in the house and the ill-humour his refusal would occasion as soon as it was known, before the other he had referred to was on them. This was Lord Osborne himself. He arrived with his cap in his hand, looking as awkward as he could look on a horse, which, as Emily had in justice to admit, was not nearly so awkward as he could look in a ball-room.

"A fine run you have given us, my lord."

"But did you change your fox or not?" demanded Lady Osborne.

"My men say so now," he admitted, directing his gaze anywhere except at the person he had come to see, "though I did not think so at the time and they did not correct me then either."

"Ha, Mr Musgrave! What do you say to that?"

But Mr Musgrave had nothing to say. He was so far from wishing to engage in any difference of opinion with Lord Osborne that he had already taken his leave.

"Rattle!" muttered Lady Osborne.

Lord Osborne regarded his horse, then the wood where his hounds were busy, and finally Mrs Blake.

"Charles had kept up well," he said.

Mrs Blake looked pleased. Lord Osborne cleared his throat and turned to his mother.

"I see," he said. "I see that you have brought some company with you, madam."

"Yes. It has been a pleasure to drive opposite two such healthy-looking girls."

Both Elizabeth and Emily dropped their eyes and busied themselves with the dogs in some confusion. Encouraged by this, and his mother's recommendation, Lord Osborne at last allowed his gaze to rest on Emily.

"I am glad you are come out," he said. "When you were not at the meet this morning I thought we had missed you for the day."

As Elizabeth said nothing, Emily forced herself to raise her head and confess, not only that she had forgotten about the meet, but that at nine o'clock the grass on the way to Stanton Wood would have been too wet for her shoes.

"We have gone into the question of half-boots before," said his lordship, with a slight smile.

"We have almost exhausted the subject, my lord."

Though he could think of nothing else to say Lord Osborne was unable to look away. There was perhaps some excuse for his scrutiny. The ride in the open carriage and Lady Osborne's blunt compliment had brought such a colour to her smooth cheeks that Emily could in truth be said to be glowing with health and beauty. Her eyes were still shining at the freshness of the scene in front of her; and a chance acquaintance might have supposed her mind to be formed on less serious lines than it was, so readily did her lips tend to form themselves into a complaisant smile.

"Well," he said again, "I am glad you are come out. I did not at first see who it was in the carriage."

"We too can congratulate ourselves on our good fortune and Lady Osborne's kindness," she answered, determined to make it clear to whom he owed her presence in the meadow. "The spectacle is delightful, is it not, madam?" she continued to Mrs Blake. "I can well understand Charles's excitement."

At this moment Lord Osborne's attention was called to his hounds, and he left them with the briefest apology. The other riders made way for him as he galloped by, skirting the wood in time to see the hounds come out on the north side in full cry after their quarry. Charles and William were already through their gap and hurrying along the cart-track.

"Forward!" shouted Lady Osborne. "Up to the top of the mound."

The carriage was driven on another fifty yards over the uneven ground, the occupants clutching the sides and the men on the box in some danger of being shaken off. From the top of the mound they could see the country to Stanton and beyond. It was a truly inspiring sight. The fox, indeed, who was responsible for it all, was somewhat difficult to make out; but they could easily distinguish the hounds, bunched together sometimes at a thick hedge, and then spreading out again over the open fields. Behind them came the hunt servants in their livery; then Lord Osborne on his tall horse taking the highest jumps with ease; and in an adjoining field the three young officers riding as though at a race. Away to the right, and still well to the fore after his good start, Charles passed between the two hay-stacks behind William. Dispersed in the rear was the rest of the field, except for a solitary rider who still stood on the mound with them.

"Which way is he going, Mr Cowdray?" shouted Lady Osborne.

"To the west, my lady. I'm thinking he'll cross the Stanton road, and perhaps the main road too."

They watched in silence for a few moments. Soon what had become almost a straight line of hounds and riders began to curve to the left.

"That's it!" cried Mr Cowdray. "He'll be making straight for the main road now." He lifted up his hat, clapped it down on his head, and with a final shout to Lady Osborne was gone.

They waited until the last rider was lost to sight behind the far hedges and the leafless trees.

"That was worth seeing," said Lady Osborne, sinking back in her seat. "There have been days when I have driven twenty miles through the rain and seen nothing. Let us make for Wickstead and try to pick them up again."

Their return journey was without incident. Elizabeth requested Lady Osborne to set them down by the gate of the parsonage, and both sisters thanked her ladyship for the kindness she had done them. Mrs Blake talked with continued civility; but to Emily's eye she seemed more thoughtful than she had been before they met the hunt, and nothing further was said about a call.

"Well!" said Elizabeth, when they had curtsied to the retreating carriage. "I did not know that your coming here would make such a change in my existence. Did you see Tom's face when he recognized me?"

"I cannot claim any responsibility for *this*," said Emily. "It was you who saw the hounds."

"In truth we may owe it to our complexions. It is good that some people like them brown. If I had been in any other company I would have laughed aloud at Tom; his mouth dropped open with surprise. Not that I found her difficult to talk to. Whoever would have supposed her interested in salting meat? And Mr James Tomlinson; he never took his eyes off us. James, whom I used to know as a boy, and who is grown so proud that he hardly remembers me. His mother will be out to call next week, you will see, and it will be the first time she is come to Stanton this year."

"Do you think Mrs Blake intends to call?"

"She did say something of it, to be sure, but Lady Osborne chipped in and I had no time to answer. I am glad I had on my best pelisse. I suppose we must now tell Margaret the news and see what she has done to the dinner. She will be cross as a cat, I can promise. You will want all your patience this evening."

They opened the gate and walked along the paved footway to the front door. Emily could not regret the morning. If she was to live at Stanton any attention that tended to raise her family in the eyes of the world called for her gratitude; she had too much sense to question that. But she would have been happier if the morning had turned out a little differently. As it was Mrs Blake had heard Mr Musgrave and had observed Lord Osborne. To be sure, she herself had treated the former's innuendoes with the scorn they merited, and had preserved a proper degree of modesty before the latter's admiration. There was nothing in her conduct that Mrs Blake could censure. But for reasons into which Emily did not enter as fully as perhaps she should, she wished the hounds could have found their fox in Millington Spinneys some ten minutes earlier than they did.

Her mind was by no means made more easy when Elizabeth paused outside the front door and addressed her thus:

"I will say nothing to the others, Emily. And I will say only this to you: you must prepare yourself. What difficulties there will be I do not know; but it is obvious that he admires you immensely, and you must not any longer pretend to be ignorant. That would only be foolishness."

Elizabeth then pressed her hand very warmly, and they went in together to face Margaret's ill-humour.

8

Margaret's ill-humour lasted for the remainder of the day, and reappeared when they met again the following morning. It had begun as an almost excusable vexation against Mr Musgrave for refusing to eat the dinner whose supervision had cost her several hours' work, and – if she was to be believed – a severe headache. As it progressed, however, the original cause was forgotten; everything that Elizabeth had done in the past few days became a source of peevishness. Margaret had just enough respect for Robert's and Jane's opinion to behave properly to *them*; but Emily, from whom she could expect nothing, found herself as guilty as Elizabeth within a remarkably short space of time. Elizabeth and Emily had received Mr Musgrave and Lord Osborne at Stanton while Margaret was in Croydon. Elizabeth and Emily shared a bedroom and possessed secrets from which Margaret was excluded. Elizabeth and Emily had known about the meet of the foxhounds, but had been too sly to tell Margaret. Elizabeth and Emily had gone for a walk without inviting Margaret to accompany them. Elizabeth and Emily had spoken to Mr Musgrave from Lady Osborne's carriage, and for reasons of their own had made him doubt the welcome he would have received at Stanton. Firm in her resolve to make the best of her situation, Emily bore her share of the complaints with outward calmness, however severely she was forced to condemn such behaviour in the privacy of her own mind.

Fortunately an event occurred soon after breakfast on Thursday of enough general interest to change the current of Margaret's reflections, and of such particular interest to Emily as to make her entirely oblivious of her surroundings for several hours. This was the arrival of the postman, who brought two letters. One was a brief note to Elizabeth to say that Penelope would be returning on Monday under the protection of some friends of Mrs Shaw's who were travelling to London. The second was addressed in her aunt's hand to Emily. As soon as she recognized the script she hurriedly excused herself and went upstairs to the solitude of her chamber. There, hardly pausing to sit down, she broke the seal and opened the letter.

Dublin,
24th October.

My dearest Emily,

I write in the greatest distress of spirits to inform you of a melancholy event of which I am sure you must still be in ignorance, for otherwise you would undoubtedly have communicated with me yourself, in spite of the little I have done recently to deserve such sympathy. Captain O'Brien, while attending to some private business which took him to the waterfront of this city, was set upon by a gang of dastardly ruffians, robbed, stabbed, and thrown into the waters of the Liffey. Though it is now more than a week since my happiness was thus destroyed I can hardly bring my hand to frame these words. His body was recovered the following morning and is now decently interred in the grounds of the Protestant Cathedral. I had often cautioned him on the dangers of late journeys to such parts, for since the July troubles these attacks have been only too frequent, but alas he was not the man to be infected by the faint-heartedness of a woman. Dearest Emily, do not neglect me in the hour of my misfortune as I neglected you in the time of my happiness. You are too generous not to forgive one who has been so sorely afflicted, and who has never ceased to love *you* however much she has loved *another*. The only shadow in the recent weeks has been the enforced separation from one I have always considered my daughter; and now that the cause for this separation has been so unkindly removed I look forward to a reunion with her more than anything in the world. At the moment I am beset by more business than one of my ignorance can attend to, and am at least happy in being able to call upon the services of Major O'Rorke, one of Captain O'Brien's friends, in my dealings with attorneys. Mr Childs is come from London and has been trying to impress on me that I have done a very foolish thing in marrying Captain O'Brien. He gives me advice to the exclusion of the sympathy I so much more urgently need. It is fortunate, he says, that Eversleigh is not yet sold and that he kept tight hold on the London properties. I am too distraught to understand it and leave Major O'Rorke to answer him. A competence is all I require, could I but settle in a cottage somewhere with my beloved niece. I trust you will write to me. Believe me, my dearest Emily, your sorrowing and most affectionate aunt,

Susan O'Brien.

After the first involuntary shock of horror was over Emily found much food for thought in this letter. Captain O'Brien had been almost a stranger to her, and an unfriendly stranger at that; nevertheless she needs must grieve at her aunt's unhappiness. Willingly did she forgive the silence that had endured since she had left Eversleigh, and willingly did she excuse the omission in such a letter of any inquiry about her present situation. That her aunt should think of her, that her aunt should desire her again by her side, was for the moment enough. She read these sentences again and tears of joy came into her eyes. Her immediate impulse was to run to the bureau and cover her pages with protestations of affection, and entreaties that her aunt would soon send for her.

Becoming calmer she began to wonder why indeed her aunt had not sent for her. There were difficulties to be sure; a journey of that nature would need a little arrangement. But Mr Childs had made it; why had he not engaged a respectable woman and taken Emily? And there were Mr Turner's cousins in Wimpole Street, the Seymours. They were people of proper gentility, and in such circumstances they would undoubtedly have spared a man and a woman to escort her. Then she wondered about Major O'Rorke. A thought which she endeavoured to dismiss came into her head – her aunt surely was not going to make a *second* blunder. Emily shuddered at the idea; it was impossible. A refined but too trusting woman could commit *one* mistake, but not *two*. But perhaps her reasoning was faulty; to her aunt it would not seem that her marriage to Captain O'Brien had been a mistake. Emily's perplexity increased. But about one thing she had no doubt at all: the proper person to do her aunt's business was her uncle's attorney, not Major O'Rorke.

She was still looking at the letter when Elizabeth entered the room.

"I am come to warn you that there is much curiosity downstairs over your letter," she said. "I do not know what you have been used to, but here there is little privacy about such things. You will be questioned by everybody and it would be as well to get your story pat before you descend. I must speak to Sarah about these candles – or perhaps it would be quicker to find new ones myself."

"If you can spare me a minute I will read you my letter. Captain O'Brien is dead."

"Heavens!" exclaimed Elizabeth, "I did not know he was sickly."

"It was an accident. An attack. A . . ." She hesitated at the word. "A brawl, perhaps."

Emily then read the letter aloud until she reached the first mention of Major O'Rorke.

"So now she wants you back!" said Elizabeth. "That is a strange way to behave to a niece. Still, you must go. It will be a great thing for you."

"Dearest Elizabeth, do not blame her! For fourteen years she has loved and provided for me. But there is no definite summons yet. You must not speak of it as though it was arranged."

"I will not speak of it at all until you give me leave; but I think you should inform my father."

Emily put the letter in a drawer and went to her father's room. As briefly as possible she informed him of Captain O'Brien's death and the likelihood of her aunt's requiring her presence in the course of time. It did not escape her father's notice that she could not quite explain either to herself or to him why her aunt had not already called for her.

"She may wish to know how she stands first," Mr Watson said.

"In what way, sir?"

"I mean with regard to money. Has she beggared herself?"

"Indeed sir, I trust not," said Emily, in some distress. "I think not from what she writes."

"You had best ask your brother," he said sadly. "The law is full of traps for unwary women. If she requires you I think you should go. I say nothing of your interest, but your first duty is undoubtedly still to her."

Emily thanked him and went downstairs. The possibility of *not* complying with her aunt's command had not entered her head, and she would have been faced with a problem beyond her solution had her aunt's and her father's instructions been at variance. In the parlour she told her story again to Robert and Jane and Margaret. Her summary was received with general astonishment.

"Well," said Mrs Robert, "that is an odd way of getting killed, to be sure. I am glad Mr W. lives in Croydon and not in Dublin. *Autres temps autres mœurs*, you know."

"So he is dead!" exclaimed Robert. "I wonder how much mischief he has done."

"And now I suppose you will go away and be rich again," said Margaret, rather more slowly than she had been speaking of late.

Mrs Robert sat up a little straighter on her chair at the thought that Emily might, after all, be worth six thousand pounds.

"She has not yet extended any definite invitation," said Emily, in answer to her sister.

"Some people are a little slow in offering their hospitality," explained Mrs Robert, with a happy smile. "I had almost forgotten I had invited you to return with us on Saturday. I hope you will now see your way to accept. Should your aunt suddenly call for you, you will more easily be able to make your arrangements from Croydon than from Stanton."

Emily thanked her. She admitted that she held herself at her aunt's disposal; but she explained that until a summons arrived she would prefer to remain in her father's house and take what might be her last opportunity for some time of becoming acquainted with her family.

"Where is the money?" demanded Robert. "Has Eversleigh been sold yet?"

"I do not think so."

"Then she will get it back. You must certainly write to her, Emily. It would be utter foolishness to let such a chance slip for a second time. Did she have anything in the funds?"

"I do not know. Such things were seldom discussed in my hearing."

"She will have lost one half, but the other will come back to her. You should get to Dublin as fast as you can."

"Even if I had the means, I could not go without her invitation. Such a course would be indecorous in the extreme."

"Fine sentiments will not make you rich, but quick action might. I could provide the means if necessary. It might even be worth my trouble to undertake the journey myself; I could say I had to escort you."

"Mr Childs is already in Dublin," said Emily.

"Childs? Oh yes, I remember. Turner had some London property, of course."

"My father suggested that you might be so good as to explain to me the ruling of the law in these matters."

"The law is clear enough," said Robert Watson, in a somewhat superior tone. "It would save us lawyers a number of unremunerative supplications from abandoned and penniless females if husbands and fathers would take enough pains to familiarize themselves with it." Then he went on to explain that at a woman's marriage all her personal property, including carriages, furniture and money in the funds, came into the possession of her husband, who also obtained a life interest in her real property – that was any land or estates that she might own. At the husband's death, his widow regained her title to her real property; and was also entitled to a third of the personal property of her husband if there were children of the union, or one-half of the personal property if there were no children. "Thus you will see," concluded Robert, "that if Eversleigh and the land in London have not yet been sold, your aunt will still be a rich woman, whatever she has lost in the way of money. The question of your going to Ireland is not a matter of decorum at all, but merely one of common sense."

"Thank you, Robert," she said. "You have made me more happy than I can describe."

"You will go to Ireland?"

"That I cannot do until I am invited. But you can rest assured that I shall write to my aunt today."

With this promise she left him; and as Robert chose to believe that it would not have occurred to her to write without his advice on the subject, he was tolerably content for the remainder of his stay.

Until she actually came to write it, her letter cost Emily a good deal of thought. There was so much of an unsatisfactory nature in the missive to which she had to reply that she felt she must exercise a certain restraint in her own composition. She must offer her sympathy and put herself unreservedly at her aunt's disposal, but she must not suggest she was awaiting an immediate summons.

Having thus prepared herself she sat down at the bureau, trimmed a pen and folded a sheet. Then the love she bore her foolish, trusting, indulgent aunt overcame her hesitations, and she covered her paper with the outpourings of a generous heart. Her aunt was, and always would be, she assured her, first in her affections. She grieved deeply at her loss and longed to offer the comfort of her daily companionship. Though she had found a true friend in her sister Elizabeth, she could not but look forward to the moment when she would leave Stanton behind her and return to her longed-for, familiar life. She would wait in daily expectation to hear again from her loved aunt.

It was not the letter she had intended to write, but she could not tear it up. Hastily she sealed it and dispatched it in safe hands to the post.

9

Robert and Jane left on Saturday; and on the following Monday Penelope arrived. With a quickly-beating heart Emily watched the scene from her bedroom. The carriage stopped, the postillion dismounted, Elizabeth ran up the path to the gate, and a girl of great beauty, with smiling lips and sparkling eyes, descended.

"You dear good soul!" she cried to Elizabeth, giving her an affectionate embrace, "how glad I am to see you. But where is my new sister? You are an amazingly mean correspondent. You have told me nothing about her except that she is safely arrived."

Elizabeth, with more sense of what was fitting at such a moment, invited the occupants of the chaise to descend for some refreshment. They refused; Penelope's boxes were handed out, and the chaise again set off.

"Why does not Emily come?" demanded Penelope. "I suspect you of having told her such tales about me as to make her nervous. How amazingly sorry I am to have missed Robert and Jane – or will you not believe me even if I say it? Indeed she would have been somewhat *de trop* herself just now. But I am on my best behaviour today for Emily's sake and will make no more jokes about Jane. I am glad my father was well when you wrote and hope he still is, or did I say that in my letter? I am also relieved beyond measure that the preserves turned out well, and my only anxiety during the last month, beyond a hope that Emily will like me, has been about the pickles. You never mentioned them and I have been in doubt whether they had all to be buried, like the cheese I put away and forgot when you spent a week with Miss Stokes."

She had now almost reached the front door and Emily could delay no longer. With a mixture of apprehension and expectancy she ran downstairs and seated herself in the parlour. Margaret was standing by the window.

"I see she has brought one more box with her than she took away," she said sharply; and then, turning to Emily, with a very slow articulation she added: "I trust, dearest Emily, you are not anticipating much of Penelope. If so, I fear disappointment is in store for you. She has not had your opportunities for education, and being without natural refinement herself she has not learnt to control her thoughts or modulate her voice. She says whatever comes into her head, whether it is true or whether it wounds, in a sharp and sometimes shrewish tone."

Before Emily had any opportunity of replying – had she indeed known *how* to reply to such a remark from such a person – the door opened and Elizabeth and Penelope entered. The merry voice, which was now fondly inquiring after the turkeys, and expressing its disgust that one had been sacrificed in honour of Robert and Jane, ceased abruptly.

"So this is Emily," it said.

Emily found her hands held, and her face and person subjected to a long scrutiny. Penelope was taller than she was; and she had to look up a few inches to meet the countenance of her sister. The complexion she saw was very fair, and laughing eyes were blue, and a lock of hair that had escaped the confinement of her bonnet was of a golden colour more often described in novels than encountered in life.

"Why, you are a beauty!" exclaimed Penelope. "I can say so honestly and admire you openly, for we shall never be in competition with each other. If I was Elizabeth or Margaret I might be more circumspect in my praise. Perhaps that is why I have heard nothing of all this."

"What is that you are accusing me of?" asked Margaret, with reddening cheeks.

"I am accusing you of nothing, my dear. I am admiring your modesty. No wonder you did not write and tell me how Emily looked. I should be in danger of thinking you were praising yourself, for she has your features though not your colour, which combines the attraction of the dark and the fair." This was said a little slyly; and Emily could not but smile at the satisfaction it gave Margaret. Penelope laughed, and continued to her new sister: "You have at least my smile, but I suspect you of having something else – something that is not so easily seen. I must warn you that I have nothing myself but what is on the surface – no character at all. You must ask Elizabeth and Margaret. They will tell you that I am quite empty-headed."

"I have given her a fair enough account of you," said Elizabeth, drily. "Your good points as well as your bad."

"When I know her better I shall require a summary of both," was the ready reply.

Penelope took off her bonnet and pelisse and dropped them carelessly on a chair. Her figure was more than good. She had a firm, ample bosom, fine shoulders and a graceful carriage. Emily did not believe Penelope's summary of her character, any more than she believed Margaret's or even Elizabeth's; but she saw that they might all contain a part of the truth.

"Well," said Penelope cheerfully, to Margaret. "I suppose you had no luck in Croydon as you have not yet demanded my congratulations. How is Mr Musgrave? Is he as unstable in his attentions as he used to be, or are you bringing him to the point at last?"

"Your mocking does not affect me," said Margaret, with disdain. "You would have had him if you could."

"I should have been delighted, my dear Margaret. To have married a man on such intimate terms with a nobleman, to have had all the backstairs gossip of Osborne Castle related to me daily, to have been assured that apart from Miss Osborne and possibly Miss Carr I was the most beautiful woman in the world, would have pleased me beyond measure."

"I should imagine Mr Musgrave to be somewhat more presentable than an elderly doctor," replied Margaret.

"And how did you come to hear of my rich admirer?"

"I learnt the story from Miss Stokes who had it from Mrs Shaw in a letter, so there is little point in your denying it. It is pity it is come to nothing, is it not?"

"It is sad indeed," agreed Penelope. "But the memory of his gout, his advanced age, and the inescapable suggestion of good port that clings to him even on breezy days in the open air, may in time allow me to recover something of my former spirits."

"You scoff because you had no success," said Margaret, sharply. "If you were to be Mrs Harding soon we would only have heard of his house and fortune."

"Since you have learnt part of the story, and are unlikely ever to meet the gentleman himself, I had better tell you the whole," said Penelope. "Indeed it would not otherwise be easy to account for my hurried return. But first I must remind Emily she is come to a household almost entirely consisting of unmarried women of marriageable age. We are getting somewhat anxious lest we be left on the shelf, my dear, which must excuse our preoccupation with a subject more refined young ladies never mention. Their thoughts perhaps may be concerned with the precarious position in this world of an undowered female, but never their lips. We, alas, are different. The problem is always before our eyes. Wherever we look it confronts us. We sleep with it, eat with it, walk with it, talk with it. In fact we have grown so familiar with the problem that, as you see, we have come to discuss it openly with one another. And now, my dear Margaret, having made my excuses, I will tell you the whole story of Dr Harding. He is comfortably situated, of about my father's age, and the uncle of Mr Shaw. Until last Monday he was as passionately in love with me as a complete absorption in his own affairs and a lively interest in the trade with Portugal would allow him to be. Mrs Shaw had set her heart on the match, chiefly to spite her husband, who had set his heart on the money. Mr Shaw, I should say, is very rich indeed, but grows more miserly with every fortune he inherits, and Dr Harding's would have been the sixth. I have had a hard time putting him off these last two months, and being too modest to understand Mrs Shaw's hints, which became eventually so outspoken that they could not rightly have been described as *hints* at all. However even I could not delay him indefinitely; and last Monday he made a declaration I could not pretend to ignore, although I was myself engaged at the same time in a very animated conversation about the excellent dinner we had just eaten. The subject was a favourite one with him, and had seen me safely through other delicate moments when all seemed lost. On Monday, alas, I did not start it in sufficient time, and I was forced to come out with an unequivocal refusal. Had he been ten years older or forty years younger I might have hesitated; but I fear he was either too young or too old for me. Mrs Shaw's chagrin was as great as her husband's gratitude, and I owe my place in the chaise today as much to his kind offices as to the fact that the courtesy did not actually put him out of pocket. If left to herself Mrs Shaw would have sent me home by stage."

"That is not quite the outcome I would have expected from the circumstances related by Miss Stokes," said Margaret.

"My dear sister, surely you do not credit me with the ability of inventing such a story? Or indeed of leaving Chichester of my own accord while the weather is so ideal for riding? You must refer to our good schoolmistress when she has heard again from Mrs Shaw. The word *refusal* has been so frequently repeated at Chichester lately I feel sure it will recur in her next letter – and you will hardly suggest that *I* addressed Dr Harding and that *his* refusal is referred to."

"Whether the story be true or not," said Elizabeth, "it is not fitting for you to speak of Mrs Shaw as you have done – no, nor Mr Shaw either."

Penelope regarded Emily for a moment with a rather impish smile before turning to her eldest sister.

"I think, my dear, you are come under a good influence since I saw you last," she said.

"I am not used to correct you, I know," said Elizabeth, somewhat self-consciously. "Perhaps I have neglected it too much of late. But if the story be not true you should not tell it; and if it be true then I cannot say that I consider Mrs Shaw a very suitable acquaintance."

"As to that, she is undoubtedly the most unsuitable acquaintance I have ever had. But she lives in the most amazingly diverting household I have ever been in; and apart from the past week, during which she suffered from headaches as frequently as Margaret when there is a broody hen to be fed, I have thoroughly enjoyed my visit, for I went riding almost every day."

"I suspect the poor mare will soon know you are back," said Margaret.

"Surely you do not ride the old mare!" cried Emily.

"Alas, I am permitted to no longer. Margaret is jealous because for me she trots to Dunford and for her she only ambles. But I have talked of my own adventures long enough. Pray tell me how you like our neighbourhood and what you think of Stanton and Dunford."

"Stanton and the neighbourhood I like well enough, but of Dunford I can say little for I have only been there once. However, as that was to a ball, which I greatly enjoyed, the little I can say is all praise."

"That is a proper way of putting it. The only justification for a town is to provide an assembly, and perhaps a milliner's. For, considered apart from these advantages, towns get in the way of the country, which I confess I prefer, to the most amazing extent. Elizabeth did at least remember to tell me that you had stood up with Mr Howard, which is more than I have managed to do, though I have smiled expressly in his direction more than once."

"Not only has she stood up with Mr Howard," said Margaret, "but Lord Osborne has called here, and Lady Osborne took Elizabeth and Emily in her barouche to see the foxhounds."

These events, which had previously been a source of displeasure to Margaret, now became a source of pride, merely by having occurred while Penelope was away and so being items of news she could communicate.

"Indeed!" cried Penelope. "I hope I shall be at the next ball myself and able to see her conquests with my own eyes. Or perhaps it would be wiser to stay at home, rather than risk watching my youngest sister steal my accustomed partners."

It was said with such good humour as to take all the offence out of the words; and Emily's heart warmed to the speaker.

"I do not think you need be in any great fear of *that*," she replied "But the matter may not be put to the test quite so soon. I have been wondering whether it would be fitting for me to go to a ball so soon after Captain O'Brien's death."

It was a point that had caused her a little concern during the past few days. She had never considered Captain O'Brien as an uncle – she had had but one *uncle* in her life – but he had married her aunt, and if only for the latter's sake some mark of respect might be due to him.

"Is Captain O'Brien dead?" exclaimed Penelope, and when the circumstances had been explained to her: "Well, my dear, I do not want to advise you to do anything contrary to your wishes, but he was neither a member of your family nor a member of the household in which you are living. That is the simple rule which was taught me and which is usually followed in these parts."

"Is it so sure that he was not a member of my family?" asked Emily.

Penelope hesitated.

"Since you put it to me like that, I am beginning to have doubts. He seems to be in a somewhat indeterminate position between a relative and not a relative."

"I will ask Mrs Edwards," said Elizabeth. "You are to appear with her, and if she does not object you may take it that no one else will see anything wrong."

Emily accepted the solution with gratitude. Of the people she had met since she arrived at Stanton Mrs Edwards was most like her aunt, and her decision on such a point could not be wrong.

Penelope's arrival made for an increasing bustle in the house; and though she enjoyed her new sister's company Emily was glad of an occasional evening's quiet conversation or silent reflection in her father's book-room. Further acquaintance taught her more about Penelope's character. There was no deceit in it; but a good deal of thoughtlessness. Margaret was often provoking. Her artificiality, her false sentiment, and her readiness to feel slighted, laid her open to teasing; but Emily sometimes wished Penelope would show a little more restraint with her wit. She resolved, when the opportunity offered, to speak to her on the subject.

The week that followed, however, gave her little opportunity for intimate conversation. Mrs Tomlinson came to see them, bringing her two daughters and several respectful messages from her husband and two sons. She even spoke of an engagement for dinner without actually committing herself to a specific day. Mrs Edwards and Mary, with a kindness that went beyond the empty expression of good intentions, called to invite three Miss Watsons to spend the night of November the tenth in Dunford and accompany them to the ball. Emily's position was put to her; and Mrs Edwards, after stating publicly that such scruples were a credit to her, and reflecting privately that Emily might soon be an even more suitable acquaintance for Mary than she had once supposed, said that in her opinion Emily should not pretend an emotion she could not feel.

"For Captain O'Brien's treatment of his wife's niece," she explained, "is not unknown in Dunford; and while your attending the ball will not be remarked, your wilful absence might in the circumstances be taken as affectation."

The matter having been thus admirably summarized, Emily, with Penelope and Margaret, accepted her invitation with much pleasure.

On the Thursday the four sisters drove to Dunford to pay their respects to Mrs Tomlinson and perform one or two other more pleasing and no less pressing duties. This time Mrs Tomlinson actually examined her engagement book in their presence, and had not the following week been rather too near, the next week rather too full, and the week after rather too far, she really might have fixed a day for them to dine in company with Mr James and Mr George. Against any slight disappointment they might have felt under this head could be set their good fortune in being escorted from the milliner's to the library by Captain Hunter, Captain Styles, Mr Norton and Mr Musgrave. It is an odd thing that two pretty ladies together are more than twice as charming as one pretty lady alone. The illusion – for illusion it must be – becomes more pronounced as we advance into higher numbers. Three pretty young ladies together are attractive to a degree; and there were few people (discounting Mr Edwards, to whom three was generally more lucky than four, magpies being in a class by themselves) who met the four Miss Watsons that morning and who did not go home to weary their hearers with an account of them. Mr James and Mr George Tomlinson, who passed them in the High Street, were not among the exceptions, and complained to their mother on learning that the four Miss Watsons had called at The Larches without being bespoke for their future entertainment.

"As they appear for some reason to be coming under the patronage of Lady Osborne it is only prudent to acknowledge the acquaintance," explained their mother. "Since they are all quite without fortune it is not incumbent on us to put ourselves out on their behalf."

Her well-dowered daughters nodded sagely. Mr James, a cautious young banker, said that an invitation to dinner was not an engagement to marry; and Mr George, a more adventurous young lawyer, said that he intended to put himself out far enough to dance with both Miss Penelope and Miss Emily at the approaching ball. Mrs Tomlinson, it is hardly necessary to explain, had not yet heard from Mrs Edwards of the fate that had overtaken Captain O'Brien.

On Friday the fire was lit in the best parlour, and the sisters assembled there early with their work. They passed a long morning, expectancy slowly giving way to disappointment and boredom. Mrs Blake did not come. Emily went to bed that night in a sad humour; and she needed all the comfort of Elizabeth's commonplace, cheerful philosophy before she could reconcile herself to the event and compose herself for sleep. The blow appeared less heavy the following morning; and it was chiefly to dissipate the last traces of its lingering aftermath that she asked Penelope to accompany her for a walk. Margaret who had just complained that the confinement of the previous day had given her a headache which would necessitate rest on a sofa for twenty-four hours, swiftly recovered and demanded to come with them. Since the morning two of her sisters had been invited into Lady Osborne's carriage, Margaret had made herself a member of all parties that set out on foot from the parsonage. This time her foresight was rewarded, for they had not gone far before they saw Lord Osborne and Mr Musgrave approaching on horseback.

"Musgrave," murmured Margaret to her companions, as soon as she recognized him. "If he were alone he would stop."

Her joy was great when Mr Musgrave realized that Lord Osborne had halted and dutifully drew rein himself.

"I am indeed fortunate," he cried. "The Miss Watsons brightened the streets of Dunford for me on Thursday, and today they brighten the lanes of Stanton."

Lord Osborne greeted them with more ceremony and asked if they had in truth been in Dunford on Thursday. For, he explained, he had been in the town that day himself and did not recollect having seen the three of them.

Penelope assured him cheerfully that they had been four on Thursday.

"Four?" he said in some surprise. He looked from one to the other as though trying to discover who was missing from the bevy in front of him.

"I see Miss Watson is not with you today," said Tom, readily. "I hope she is not indisposed."

"By no means," Margaret assured him, without feeling it necessary to add that Elizabeth was sorting out the apples that would not keep beyond Christmas.

"And the ball on Tuesday," said Tom. "I trust you are coming to the ball on Tuesday?"

Margaret told him they were; and there was then a brief silence. Tom gathered his reins together with the air of a man who must soon be off. Lord Osborne, however, had not yet done.

"I trust you will not take it amiss," he said, somewhat awkwardly. "I am, in fact, a poor dancer, Miss Emily. So poor that I am hesitant of asking any young lady to stand up with me. Nevertheless I should consider it as a very great honour if you would agree to a proposal of that nature."

Emily interpreted the strange words to contain an invitation to dance at some date in the future; and, concealing her surprise – for whatever she may have thought of Lord Osborne's feelings she had not expected *this* – she replied that she would be honoured.

"Shall we say the first two dances on Tuesday?" suggested Lord Osborne, with the more easy air of a man who had come safely over the stiffest hurdle.

"Had you not better wait, my lord?" said Emily, who was far from wishing a definite engagement. "You may not find it convenient to be at the assembly so early."

"If you will promise to stand up with me I shall be there."

There were but two courses open to her: either she must invent some story about her never engaging herself beforehand, or she must accept his invitation. As the former would have been as untrue as it was uncivil, she adopted the latter. Lord Osborne said he was extremely gratified, and looked at Mr Musgrave. Margaret too was looking at him; and with no bad grace Tom performed the duty at least half of those present seemed to expect of him by requiring the same two dances of Miss Emily's sister. His lordship then raised his hat, begged them, in a proper gentleman-like

fashion, to carry his respects to Miss Watson, and passed on, followed as usual by his obedient disciple.

Awkward he might still be; careless he was no longer, Emily was
thinking, when an unkind gust of wind brought back the somewhat
exasperated query:

"In heaven's name, Tom, how many sisters *has* she got?"

"I must run after them and tell him," cried Penelope.

"Hush, Penelope! He will hear you."

"Poof! He should know us by now. He was smacked more than
fifteen years ago for throwing plum stones at me from his mother's
barouche. Sam replied with half a brick which took a large strip of
varnish off the carriage, so Lady Osborne descended and smacked
him as well. I do not think she would have minded half so much if
he had just hit her son."

"I more than half-suspected that Musgrave would make an opportunity of asking me for the first two dances on Tuesday," said
Margaret.

Neither Emily nor Penelope made any reply.

"Musgrave's friendship with Lord Osborne is not without its
uses after all," Margaret continued. "It is unlikely that if he had
been alone Lord Osborne would have stopped. You are certainly
honoured, Emily; he seldom dances. I wonder whether he has heard
of the recent sad occurrence in Dublin?"

"I agree that Emily is honoured," said Penelope, discreetly. "But
as your sister, Margaret, I will tell you that either your eyes are
not as good as they were, or else that you are being wilfully blind."

"What do you mean by that, pray?"

"Lord Osborne stopped before Mr Musgrave. Lord Osborne
passed on before Mr Musgrave. It is according to precedent and all
that, I allow. But precedent does not demand that Mr Musgrave
should wait to invite you to dance until his lordship has invited
Emily. *Toady* is an unkind word. *Courtier* is perhaps more apt."

"You are jealous," replied Margaret, hotly. "You have been
jealous for the past two years because Musgrave prefers me to you.
As usual you seek to get your revenge with your tongue by calling
him names."

"I am not jealous of you, Margaret. I have had ample time to
consider Mr Musgrave's behaviour to myself, and to others, these

past two years. Jealousy is the last emotion my thoughts on the subject could give rise to."

"It is a pity," said Margaret to Emily, in a sneering tone, "that we did not encounter *three* young gentlemen just now. Then Penelope might have got herself engaged as well and we would have heard less of this courtier nonsense."

"Do not let us quarrel," suggested Emily. "We are come out to enjoy ourselves, and if we are to quarrel I at least shall return home and find some other occupation."

"You are right as always, my little moralist," cried Penelope, more gaily. "It would be foolish to quarrel on such a day. I shall agree that you are both very fortunate; I shall not attempt to deny it. I am quite outshone by my younger sisters, and I shall get what comfort I can from the fact that his lordship's horse and I admired each other immensely. Could he have spoken I feel sure that I too would have been engaged. Not even the knowledge of Mrs Edwards's certain disapproval on the grounds that we had had no proper introduction could have made me refuse him, for I have never seen such hind quarters."

"Of whom are you speaking *now*?" demanded Margaret, in shocked surprise.

"Lord Osborne's horse, my dear. Did you not see the look he gave me?"

10

Any lingering doubts Emily might have had about the propriety of her attending the ball were set at rest by a letter she received on the morning of the day itself. It was from her aunt, in answer to hers, but it was a very different letter from the one he had expected.

Dublin,
5th November.

My dearest Emily,

I was delighted to receive your letter, and I took the earliest opportunity of reading parts to Major O'Rorke, who agrees with me that he has seldom heard a more moving epistle. I am indeed touched by the sympathy you feel for me, and shall not soon forget how ready you were to forgive my neglect and to assure me of your love. My business here is almost concluded, and I see less of lawyers, English or Irish. I have been unable to understand what the fuss has been about; but it appears to have taken Mr Childs all this time to discover that I am still as rich as I ever was, which Major O'Rorke assured me of long since. Mr Childs could not have looked more solemn if I had been penniless. It is only recently that I have gained enough spirits to be able to face the prospect of a future without my dear partner, and so cannot yet speak of any definite plans. My friends here are much concerned that I should settle in Ireland as Captain O'Brien wished; but to me this is still a foreign country, though the kindness and sympathy of the inhabitants, who lack something of the reserve of the English, make me at times forget the fact. I shall write again to you soon, and hope meanwhile that my dear niece is well and happy.

Your most affectionate Aunt,
Susan O'Brien.

It was a letter Emily could not read without tears. She saw how her own careful upbringing, with its insistence on strict principles and correct behaviour, must have owed its inspiration entirely to her uncle. While that uncle was alive his example and influence had been enough to keep her aunt's conduct above any suspicion of reproach. After his death, his memory, and the association of the house in which he had lived, saved her from a blunder until Captain O'Brien began his addresses. Now, far removed from Eversleigh, among strange people and in a strange country, there was nothing but Mr Child's presence to defend her against her folly. All too soon would that presence be withdrawn; and Emily shuddered at the thought of the news that might then reach her. Indulgent, kind and generous, her dear aunt lacked the judgement that made such qualities noble, and without which they were little better than the vanities of a faulty understanding.

The immediate prospect of the ball and the preparations it entailed saved her from questions about her letter. Some time she must inform her father that Stanton would stay her home; some time she must bring herself to reply to her aunt. But for the moment it was good that she had something agreeable with which to occupy her mind. She dried her eyes and got her things together, determined to enjoy the evening to the limits of her power.

Her pleasure in being again a guest in Mrs Edwards's house was increased when she found she was to share a room with Penelope. They dressed, admired each other and arranged each other's ribbons, and were ready to descend.

"Are you not nervous?" asked Penelope.

"Nervous? No, I would not say that I was nervous. Excited perhaps, but not nervous. Are you?"

"Not I," said Penelope. "But then *I* have nothing to be nervous about."

"Nor I, I assure you," said Emily, earnestly.

"I have been very discreet," said Penelope, opening the door. "It has been difficult, but I consider I have managed it amazingly well. Let us go downstairs before you tempt me too far."

Mr Edwards filled in the interval between dinner and tea by telling the Miss Watsons' fortunes with a pack of cards. He had been in a somewhat gloomy humour during the morning, having entirely failed (to Mary's surprise) to encounter any auspicious omen since dawn. However the realization that he had *three* guests in the house cheered him considerably, and dinner was a lively meal. Mrs Edwards sighed when he fetched the cards; but the Miss Watsons treated their fortunes with such light-heartedness, while preserving the necessary outward respect for the fortune-teller, that even she felt able to notice what was going on, and observed that they were all to be congratulated on the likelihood of obtaining husbands before a twelvemonth was out.

They were at the ball at their usual early hour, and Mrs Edwards seated herself near the fire with Emily and Penelope on one side of her and Mary and Margaret on the other. In spite of her assurance to Penelope, Emily did now begin to feel something that might, without serious error, be described as nervousness. At any moment Lord Osborne might walk into the room – for she did not doubt· that he would keep his promise; she only feared lest its performance should be too marked. His dancing at all would be noticed. His dancing outside whatever party arrived from Osborne Castle would cause surprise. But his coming before the start of the ball – his claiming her in a manner that would leave no doubts in the on-lookers' minds about the dance having been promised in advance – these were things the mere thought of which made her heart tremble.

"Penelope," she inquired, in a voice barely above a whisper, "is it very unusual here to engage oneself beforehand?"

"It is less unusual than the mothers think, my dear. There must be many young ladies sitting round this room who will look more surprised than they feel when the honour of a dance is publicly requested."

"Dear Penelope, please do not distress me. You know there is nothing of that sort in my case. If I could have refused him without discourtesy I would. I fear a lot of people are going to remark it."

"There is little done in a Dunford assembly that is *not* remarked," said Penelope, and then seeing that Emily was really unhappy, she added: "Rest assured, my dear, I will see that you are not made over-conspicuous. Here he is. If necessary I shall remind him of the time he pelted me with plum-stones, and demand that he stands up with me twice to make amends."

Lord Osborne, with his accustomed attendant, was indeed approaching them. Emily was gratified in the extreme to find that instead of making straight for her, he came to Mrs Edwards, bowed, and stood chatting for a few moments. His manner had been at times so awkward that in her forecast of his behaviour she sometimes forgot to allow for the fact that he was a gentleman, and that his failures were the blunders of inexperience rather than want of breeding. In the past perhaps they could be said to have owed something to want of thought, but that would be no longer true. He had thought of little but Miss Emily Watson for the four weeks since he had first seen her.

Mrs Edwards had heard of his intentions through Mary, who had learnt the story from Margaret, but she had carefully refrained from comment in front of Emily. Her delight was as great as her surprise when he requested her to do him the honour of presenting him to her daughter, whom he knew well by sight, he explained, but whom he had not yet had the good fortune to meet. He then asked Mary for the second two dances before reminding Emily that she had promised him the first two. True to her word Penelope engaged him in lively conversation; but she was not called upon to propose herself as his partner, for he interrupted his account of how he came to purchase the horse she so admired to require the third two dances from her. Penelope acquiesced with a smile.

"I see you are not going short of partners tonight, my lord," she said.

He blushed slightly in a manner which did nothing to lessen the increasing good opinion Emily had felt for him since he entered the ball-room.

"No indeed," he replied. "Once I found that my first request was favourably received I was encouraged to make others." Then, with an expressive glance at Emily: "Had the first request been refused, I think it would have been some time before I could have gained sufficient confidence to try a second."

"I must give you a better opinion of yourself," said Penelope, gaily. "I shall let you into a secret. There are few young ladies in the room – very few indeed – who would refuse you the request of a dance."

"If I have chosen sisters," he said, after some thought and a little hesitation, "it might be that I hope they will discuss my imperfections as a dancer together, and give me the benefit of their combined advice when next I call at Stanton."

"I doubt whether you will have to wait so long, my lord. We are notoriously bad at keeping silent, and have the reputation of saying what we think with an abruptness that sometimes leaves much to be desired."

"As to that," replied his lordship, this time with no hesitation at all, "I have all my life been used to one who says what she thinks, and am not only accustomed to it, but frequently grateful for it."

Having made this excellent point, he bowed, walked across the room and commanded the orchestra to begin. Emily was conscious of the eyes of the assembly on her when she took her place at the head of the set. It was owing to his correct behaviour and Penelope's ready gossip – which together had made the whole party seem distinguished rather than one member of it – that the sensation was very much less unpleasant than she had feared. As soon as it was clear that Lord Osborne was to dance with Emily, Captain Styles and Mr George Tomlinson bowed in front of Penelope. She announced that it seemed to be a dead heat and selected Mr George.

"For," she explained, in a voice that reached not only Mrs Tomlinson but Emily in the centre of the room, "to send Mr George back to his sisters would be unkind. He is of no use to them at this juncture. And they are both charming girls and were good enough to call at Stanton a week ago."

Emily found Margaret by her side, the attentive Mr Musgrave having hurried to his usual place next to his lordship. Margaret was all smiles and sweetness.

"I trust, dearest Emily," she whispered, "you are as happy with *your* partner as I am with *mine*. What a night this is for us."

For some time Lord Osborne gave all his attention to the dancing. Later, encouraged by Emily's smile, his frown of concentration left him and he ventured a few remarks to which she replied very prettily.

"I trust that was not too awkward," he said, when the first half of his engagement was completed.

"Indeed, my lord, my sister was right. You are too modest."

"Your sister is very merry," he answered. "If I had not already enough to think about I should now be wondering how to answer her sallies."

Midway through the second dance the remainder of the party from Osborne Castle arrived. Miss Osborne and Miss Carr, with some officers who had dined with them, stopped soon after entering the room and stood talking together by the door. Lady Osborne, Mrs Blake and Mr Howard continued on to the entrance of the card-room. There Lady Osborne called a halt, and turned round to examine the dancers with a critical eye.

"I think my mother is about to offer us some advice," murmured Lord Osborne. "I trust you will not be embarrassed."

"Why no, my lord. We will put a brave face on it and answer her criticisms with the best performance of which we are capable."

Lady Osborne nodded once or twice in a brusque, satisfied manner, and remarked in a voice that was meant to carry no further than Mrs Blake that Miss Emily Watson looked by far the healthiest girl in the room.

"No man could have had a kinder mother, or one more solicitous of his well-being," explained her son. "But it may be that I owe my lack of ease in a ball-room, and other places where young ladies and gentlemen congregate, to the same source as I owe my lack of any offensively high opinion of myself. You must forgive my mentioning these things; but it is only in the last few weeks that I have seriously thought of them, and they are uppermost in my mind."

Here was intimacy indeed, thought Emily; almost too much intimacy for so short an acquaintance. She attempted to answer his words without echoing his manner.

"I am inclined to think that the spectators have judged your lordship to be managing very well in a ball-room."

"I have practised," he confessed, with a sudden youthful smile. "I have been practising since Saturday. You came some way to meet me the day I called at Stanton; you allowed me to talk of what interested me. I felt I owed you the duty of going at least this little way to meet you."

Here they were separated by the dance. She could not but be pleased by him, and her only unhappiness was in seeing Mr Howard follow Lady Osborne and Mrs Blake into the card-room.

The following dances were necessarily somewhat tame; and Mr Norton, who claimed her a moment after a somewhat vexed Penelope had been engaged by Mr Musgrave, must have found her a silent partner. She had much to think about. Here was a young man, a nobleman, rich and well-bred, of five-and-twenty, who admired her seriously enough to correct in himself the faults of which his admiration had, for the first time, made him conscious. That alone indicated a character above the average. It deserved more than her simple gratitude; it deserved her very earnest consideration.

Lord Osborne attached himself to their party for the evening; he (and consequently Mr Musgrave) showed Mrs Edwards quite plainly that he intended to take tea with her. Her good humour was such that Captain Hunter, Captain Styles and Mr Norton – for except when the dancing was in progress it was impossible to divide them – were emboldened to accompany her as well. A game was in progress at Lady Osborne's table when they passed through the card-room. Mrs Blake smiled at Emily; Mr Howard looked up, inclined his head slightly, and then returned to his play.

After tea she listened to Captain Hunter's account of the latest day's sport with Lord Osborne's foxhounds, and shortly before the final dance found herself seated again by Penelope. Lady Osborne's party had not yet departed and in spite of the lack of any opportunity for paying her respects to Mrs Blake, and the not very warm greeting she had received from Mr Howard, she still hoped the latter would dance with her.

"Apart from Mr Musgrave, whom I abhor, I have not done badly," said Penelope. "Notwithstanding the presence of a very pretty new sister."

"While there are candles enough in the room to see by, you will not want partners," answered Emily, sincerely enough. For she thought Penelope, whose fair beauty was quite different from her own, without serious rival among the company.

"I would prefer not to want a husband, my dear. My usual partners can be divided into two groups: the dashing but impecunious and the wealthy but circumspect. I have seen enough impecuniosity already in my life, and circumspection is too foreign to my nature to attract me, should one of its possessors ever be sufficiently distraught to put himself in a position he might later regret. Meanwhile it is nice to go to a ball. Whom do you hope to dance with now?"

While Emily was wondering whether to tell her, or how not to tell her, Lord Osborne demanded the honour himself. She had hoped he would not ask again; she was determined to refuse him, and she did. Not, as she explained with a smile, on account of any deficiency in himself as a dancer; she had enjoyed their two dances and the short conversation they had had; but their acquaintanceship was so short that she did not feel justified in occupying more of his time than was customary on such an occasion.

Lord Osborne was somewhat at a loss. He had been denied what he asked; but the denial had not been accompanied by any sign of displeasure.

"I trust I have not offended," he said.

"We are not so easily offended by compliments, my lord," Penelope assured him.

This merely increased his confusion. If the request had been a compliment, he inquired of himself, why the dickens had she not granted it?

"Is not that Mrs Blake just come in?" asked Emily, who had for some time been watching the door of the card-room. "I have a message for her from my sister."

"I will get her," said Lord Osborne abruptly, and turned on his heel.

This was not what she had intended; but she could not pursue him across the room. A little impatiently she waited the outcome of his application.

"Do not harry the poor man so," complained Penelope. "We are at the Dunford assembly rooms, my dear, not at the court in St James's. It is enough here, when you do not want to dance, to say that you are tired, or would prefer to sit, or something of that nature."

"I did not want to dance with *him*," she explained. "I have stood up with Lord Osborne once, and that must be enough for tonight. There was no need to bind myself not to dance with another if I chose."

"And who is that other, pray?"

Before she could answer, Mr Musgrave was bowing in front of her. Her care had been unavailing; all was now lost.

"Thank you," she said, "I do not intend to dance any more tonight."

Mr Musgrave regretted his misfortune in not having applied earlier, and moved a step to his right so that he was before Penelope. Penelope was far from pleased.

"I have already had the pleasure of standing up with you, Mr Musgrave," she said. "That, I am afraid, must suffice. I propose to sit with my sister."

Mr Musgrave, with a readiness that spoke more of the good opinion he had of himself than of his manners, pressed her to reconsider her decision. Penelope's eyes suddenly flashed in anger.

"Perhaps I should be honoured by your insistence after my refusal, sir," she said, "but I am wondering from whom you could have obtained permission to dispense with the usual courtesies. It could not be Lord Osborne, for he has taken my sister's denial as these things are usually taken by gentlemen. Is there, by any chance, somebody of higher rank than his lordship in the room tonight?"

Mr Musgrave reddened, bowed, and departed without a word. A moment later he passed in front of them with Margaret on his arm, as though to show that there was at least *one* Miss Watson who would dance with him as often as he cared to ask.

"Penelope, he will never forgive such a speech!" said Emily, in some alarm. His behaviour had been boorish, she knew, but their situation was not such that they could afford to make enemies.

"He?" said Penelope. "It will be out of his head tomorrow. At the next assembly he will come prancing up like a horse that has had too much corn just as he has done tonight."

Lord Osborne now returned to them with Mrs Blake. Emily made a place for her and said in some haste:

"I did not intend *you* to find *me*, madam."

"I was about to sit down myself for a moment and watch the dancing. I am indebted to Lord Osborne for bringing me here, where it is gayer. But you must not stay on my account. You will doubtless be dancing yourself in a moment."

"No, madam; I shall play but a spectator's part now until Mrs

Edwards takes us home. But I have a message for you. I am commissioned by my eldest sister to entreat you to do her the honour of waiting on her. You know, I think, how she is circumstanced, and your kindness in yourself proposing a visit when we last met allows her to suggest you name a convenient day."

This Mrs Blake readily did. She would be most happy to wait on Miss Watson on Thursday.

"It is no part of my commission," Emily added, "but I know that my father would greatly appreciate a call from Mr Howard if he could be prevailed upon to accompany you. As you are perhaps aware, Mr Howard introduced himself to my father at the recent visitation. My father was very much struck by Mr Howard's sermon. On his return home he stated that it was a long time since he had heard a discourse more to his liking."

"You are very kind," answered Mrs Blake. "My brother will be proud of praise from such a quarter. I will certainly press him to accompany me."

She was obviously well-satisfied at what had passed. If Penelope had read most into Emily's words and Lord Osborne least, Mrs Blake had read a comfortable intermediate amount – enough to convince her that Emily would not be displeased to see Mr Howard at Stanton. At this juncture, while the orchestra were preparing to strike up, the gentleman himself came in from the card-room, looked round at the company, and then walked across to them in answer to a cheerful summons from his sister. In a manner that to Emily at least showed his superiority to every other gentleman in the room he requested the honour of a dance. She could give him but one answer. He was unable to suppress a look of mortification, though it might have been less pronounced could he have read the conflict in her heart. In an effort to cheer him, Mrs Blake said:

"It is not for me to answer for a young lady, my dear brother, or I would perhaps have saved you the trouble of an application. Before you came up Miss Emily confessed that she felt herself unable to dance further with *anyone* tonight."

"We are in the same boat, Howard," said Lord Osborne, now apparently in the best of humours. "I too have been turned down."

Mr Howard replied with a few short phrases, and before Mrs

Blake could open the subject of the proposed visit, returned to the card-room.

Bitterly did Emily regret what had occurred. The assembly had no further pleasure for her, and she was as impatient as Mr Edwards, who had not had a very satisfactory evening, for Lord Osborne to leave them so that the party could return home.

"I trust you are not tired, my dear," said Penelope, when they were together in their bedroom. "I have restrained myself since Saturday, and now that we are alone with hours ahead of us I can do so no longer. I am ready to talk till the candles are burnt out."

"I was grateful for your restraint on Saturday," replied Emily.

"If Margaret had not been with us I would have plied you with questions. You are almost a stranger here. You cannot appreciate the amazing *oddity* of his asking you to dance, or of his behaviour tonight. It is without precedent. But that, it appears, is not all. I believe that there is another gentleman in the story."

Emily was not yet ready to discuss Mr Howard. She turned instead to a matter she had already determined to mention to Penelope, and which the evening's events had made appear of even greater urgency.

"Are you not sometimes afraid of making enemies with your tongue, Penelope?" she asked.

"It is not what one *says* that is important in this world, my dear, it is what one *does*."

"If one offends one's neighbours I do not think they will trouble to ask themselves whether they have been offended by words or deeds. Nor, should they take this trouble, do I think they will pardon the former more readily than the latter."

"Mr Musgrave's behaviour was unsupportable," said Penelope.

"I do not speak only of Mr Musgrave. Mrs Tomlinson cannot have been overpleased with the remark you made about her daughters."

"You are crediting other people with a sensibility equal to your own, my dear. Mrs Tomlinson was highly flattered at my telling the room her daughters were charming girls and had been civil enough to honour the penurious Watsons with a visit. What mother would not be?"

Emily shook her head.

"Come, my dear, if I say I am sorry will you forgive me?"

"Willingly," said Emily. "Though I do not know what _I_ have to forgive."

"I fear you have nothing, for I am not sorry at all. Nay, it is a shame to tease you. I promise I would have been sorry if I had in truth offended her. But I assure you I have not. The world has a better opinion of itself than you give it credit for – and a thicker skin. Now tell me what you think of Lord Osborne."

"I do not yet know him well, but I am inclined to think very much more favourably of him than I did at first. For some reason he has been at pains to correct the rather offensive carelessness he exhibited four weeks ago. For a man of his position to make such an effort to improve himself speaks highly for his character."

"And are you quite unable to guess the reason?" asked Penelope, with a smile.

Emily felt the colour come to her cheeks.

"I am not used to discussing such matters," she said. "Not only because I have had no sister with whom to discuss them, but also because hitherto there has been nothing in my life that could call for such discussion. However, I have Elizabeth's authority for saying he admires me, and I have certainly been distinguished. It would be foolish to pretend otherwise."

"Lord Osborne is very much in love with you, my dear."

"Penelope! You must not exaggerate! We do not yet know each other. I feel he admires me. I can admit as much to a sister. Admiration is certainly there. But you must not talk of love. He is still ignorant of my tastes and character and opinions. How could he love me?"

"As other men love. Having seen a pretty face and a sweet smile."

"If he thought those sufficient reasons he would deserve to be censured. I have given him no encouragement. Men do not fall in love without encouragement, and _that_ does not come until common tastes are discovered and mutual sympathy established. Our acquaintance has been too short for anything of that nature."

"I find your opinions fascinating to a degree," said Penelope. "Pray tell me what you think of Mr Howard?"

"It would help here if I brought in Mr Musgrave, who has ease without breeding. Lord Osborne has breeding without ease, Mr Howard has both. But there is more to it than that. He has sense and education as well; his understanding is superior to mine, which is what I require in a gentleman."

"In spite of the shortness of your acquaintance there would appear to be little you do not know about Mr Howard," said Penelope. "Had it not been for what you have just said I might be in danger of believing you in love yourself. Such a thing, of course, is quite out of the question."

"I *admire* him, Penelope. My father also admires him, so there can be no shame in my admitting as much."

"Now I understand, my dear. It is the same emotion as I feel for Lord Osborne's horse. However, I will not press the comparison too closely."

"I do not mind your teasing," said Emily, with a smile. "Indeed to me, who have lived so long without brothers and sisters, there is much comfort in being able to talk to one of my own age thus freely and pleasantly. But your teasing must not blind you to the fact that if I have given Lord Osborne no encouragement, Mr Howard has given me even less. I trust I shall never so completely forget the lessons I have been taught as to allow myself to fall in love until I am reasonably sure my affection is returned."

"These are very refined sentiments," answered Penelope. "My only fear is that if they are followed as circumspectly as you seem to expect by both a young lady *and* a young gentleman, the opportunity for a full and happy married life may have passed before the one gets to the point of proposing and the other to that of allowing herself to accept. Do you not think it would be for the benefit of society as a whole if the process could be speeded up somewhere?"

"Society as a whole does not strike me as in any danger of dying out in the foreseeable future. And for myself I am but nineteen, so I have time enough."

"I am thankful for the greater freedom you imply for Elizabeth, Margaret and *myself*, who are a little older."

"You speak as though you never had an admirer. Having watched the eagerness with which you were sought in the ball-room tonight, and indeed merely looking at you now, I cannot quite credit the suggestion."

"That is not fair, my dear. When I argue I must be allowed to take up a position entirely opposed to that of my opponent. If you like Mr Scott's ballads, I never read poetry; if you are somewhat critical of Mr Cowper, he is the inspiration of my life and I learnt a hundred of his lines by heart before breakfast. Otherwise there is no point in conversation and we must all sit around in dull agreement."

"I am grateful for the explanation," said Emily. "I now understand why some of the opinions you express are so strongly at variance with some of the others." Then she continued in a more serious tone: "If there is to be that frankness between us which I would like, Penelope, you must give me an account of a gentleman who, I believe, was once an admirer of yours – a Mr Purvis."

"Indeed I will; though it is a somewhat old story now," said Penelope, readily. "Purvis was a friend of Robert's for whom Elizabeth had very tender feelings. He was a humble fellow, with a total want of spirit. Very soon in our acquaintance he transferred his regard from Elizabeth to me. I was young at the time, and was so far from understanding what had occurred that it was not until Elizabeth reproached me that I had a suspicion of it. I confess I have never found it easy to imagine people in love with me – more especially one like Purvis to whom I was completely indifferent to myself. But within a month he met a meek little creature with two thousand pounds and that was the end of the matter. He was, as I have said, a friend of Robert's."

"You know that that is not what Elizabeth believes – even to this day?"

"Perhaps what Elizabeth believes is more in keeping with her vanity – that the change in his affections was one of *my* contriving. I told her once that it was not so; and when she did not choose to believe me I would not speak any more on the subject. But I should be sorry if my indulgence of my sister's vanity had caused me to forfeit your esteem. She is a good soul; but even she may be mistaken. And if I were given to stealing, I would steal gold; I would not pilfer farthings from a sister's drawer. I have many faults, my dear, but *meanness* is not one of them."

"If you are so well aware of your faults," said Emily, gently, "to mend them must not be difficult. It is the flaws in one's nature to which one is blind – that take one unaware and of which one is conscious only after they have occasioned some error, that are hard to correct."

"I must confess to a partiality for old friends," cried Penelope. "My faults have been with me so long that we have settled down together on affectionate terms. Indeed I would be a dull person without them."

To this Emily replied with only a smile. She was satisfied by the explanation, which accorded well with Penelope's character. She had already learnt that her sister was one of the least conceited of mortals and could hardly bother to tie a bow that had not some strict utilitarian purpose.

"If what you say is true – and I think it *is* true," said Emily, "Elizabeth was surely wrong in allowing her affections to become engaged before making sure they were returned."

"That is a sentiment which reflects great credit on your governess, my dear. But in life these things are less easy to arrange. Consider the case of Dr Harding. You censured me the other day for allowing him to come to a declaration when I had no intention of accepting him; yet now you tell me I should not have thought about him until I was certain he was at the point."

"That will not do, Penelope. You could hardly have chosen a more unfortunate example to support you. You have already confessed that at the beginning of your stay Mrs Shaw left you in no doubt of his intentions."

"No," agreed Penelope, laughing. "I cannot ask help from the doctor. My conduct there was disgraceful; and if he had been younger by thirty years or so and his suit worthy of serious consideration I should indeed be a heartless girl. But perhaps the reason I am not so critical of Elizabeth as you would have me is that I have made the same mistake myself. Some three years or more ago I thought myself very much in love with Tom Musgrave. I will not say I was sure of his affections, but I was certainly given encouragement, and I was foolish enough to believe he would in time return love for love. As soon as I realized he was trifling with me, as he has since trifled with others, I ceased to think of him. Nothing is now left but mortification at my feelings – not, thank heaven, at my conduct. You can imagine the uneasiness with which I have seen Margaret repeat my mistake – repeat it openly, without any sense of discretion or attempt at concealment. I have tried to warn her but she will not listen to me. She too will have to learn what I have learnt, and I am afraid we shall hear more from her than she and Elizabeth heard from me."

Penelope broke off her account for a moment. Emily looked at her in great sympathy. She had considered Mr Musgrave's behaviour objectional even before this revelation. She now judged it base beyond description.

"I say nothing of my taste in choosing Mr Musgrave," Penelope continued, more gaily. "Perhaps his manners were better then, but I am not a good judge in this case. He has been for some time past, and he is at present, the last man in the world from whom I would wish to receive any attentions whatsoever. That is all." She gave Emily a very friendly smile. "And now, my little moralist, you know me as well as I know you, though certainly no better. But I must confess that Lord Osborne and Mr Howard are not only more gentleman-like, but altogether more fascinating suitors than Mr Purvis and Mr Musgrave."

11

The weather was bad the next morning, and without consulting her guests Mrs Edwards dispatched a man before breakfast to inform Elizabeth that her sisters would be returning in the coach. Elizabeth replied that she hoped Mary would accompany them and be allowed to share their dinner, as she had a particularly fine piece of mutton she intended to roast; which request was readily granted. The coach was ordered at an early hour; and much interesting conversation was heard in Mrs Edwards's drawing-room after it had departed, concerning Lord Osborne's condescension in dancing with three of its occupants, and the possible effects of Captain O'Brien's death (of which Mrs Edwards now remembered to inform Mrs Tomlinson) on the fortunes of the four Miss Watsons and Mr Robert and Mr Samuel. As lively a conversation, though in some respects a more discreet one, took place in the coach itself and later in the parlour at Stanton. Sam was not mentioned, but Lord Osborne's name was frequently repeated; Captain Hunter, Captain Styles and Mr Norton were generally conceded to have been extremely agreeable; and Margaret more than once expressed the pleasure she had experienced in dancing *twice* with Mr Musgrave.

On Thursday Mrs Blake, and possibly Mr Howard, were to call. Mr Watson fortunately was well; and when informed by his youngest daughter that Mr Howard might be expected, said he would be very pleased to see him, and hoped they would enjoy a comfortable discussion in the quiet privacy of his book-room.

"Will you not come down, sir?' asked Emily.

"No, no. I am not in the habit of receiving people socially. Elizabeth will manage that. My illness is generally recognized and no secret to Mr Howard. He would not wait on me and expect to sit in a parlour."

This possibility had in no way entered Emily's calculations. Elizabeth, whom she informed of her father's decision, expressed no surprise.

"That is the best we could hope for, Emily. More often he does not wish to see people even upstairs."

As there was no appeal, Emily made the best of the matter.

"They must both be brought into the parlour," she said. "You will be talking to Mrs Blake. Perhaps I had better take Mr Howard upstairs."

"I expect you know best. My, we are getting high! To think of Mrs Blake calling. If I had not sat opposite her in the carriage I would be scared out of my wits. I wonder what made her suggest it?"

"It was not entirely her suggestion," confessed Emily. "You allowed me to say you would be ready to receive her should she repeat her offer to call. This visit is the result of our conversation."

The hour arrived and the visitors with it. Mrs Blake was cheerful, amiable and ready to converse. There was little for her to admire even in the best parlour at Stanton. She took her seat, looked round, and said that to her the presence of crowded bookshelves gave a room a friendly atmosphere. Mr Howard was as polite as he was expected to be; but the immediacy with which he desired to be taken to Mr Watson, on learning that he was upstairs, made Emily think that in his eyes the call was one he owed to his duty and the pleasure of a neighbouring clergyman, rather than to his inclination and the pleasure of that clergyman's daughters.

He had little to say for himself on the way upstairs; but when her hand was almost at the door of her father's room he did at last manage to speak.

"I am sorry I was kept so long at Lady Osborne's card-table on Tuesday," he explained. "I had looked forward to the pleasure of advancing our acquaintance a little."

She was already opening the door, and could do nothing but give him a smile and a grateful glance. He had acknowledged that the fault was his, and he must understand that her refusal had not been entirely a matter of unrestrained choice. She ran downstairs with a happy heart and passed a pleasant hour in the parlour. Elizabeth and Mrs Blake had much to talk about concerning their respective villages; Penelope made them laugh at her extravagant stories, and Margaret was on such laguorously good behaviour that Mrs Blake assumed she had not recovered from the fatigue of the ball, and kindly ceased troubling her with remarks that called for an answer.

Mr Howard then descended. So far from showing further signs of impatience he accepted a glass of wine and began a conversation about the contents of one of the books whose external appearance had pleased his sister. Emily knew the book well – it was Johnson's *Rasselas* – and listened eagerly to his opinion.

"When we consider that this book was written in less than a week," he said, "that what we read is uncorrected and would be considered by another writer as something in the nature of a draft, we can only marvel at the perfect symmetry of its design, and the classic proportion of its periods."

"Both are remarkable," she replied, "but I cannot concede that in either lies the chief charm of the book. It is a moral tale, and it is in the telling of the moral that the author excels."

"That is true. But I was speaking then of the extraordinary speed of composition, which would not influence the moral. A good man does not have to prepare each speech to exclude slander or evil thoughts; he speaks with natural goodness. An evil man produces evil words with equal ease. It is only when either has to dissemble that time and thought are required. Thus allowing for the failings to which the best human beings are at times subject, I would expect even an extempore anecdote from Dr Johnson to express a virtuous rather than a vicious sentiment."

Emily, though prepared to agree to the truth of these last assertions, suggested that the matter was different when the moral had to be worked into a tale. Mr Howard answered her, and the conversation was continued until Margaret interposed to say that reading usually gave her a headache. Mrs Blake then remembered it was time she returned to Wickstead on some business connected with her children, and called on her brother to take his leave.

"Lord!" exclaimed Margaret, when the visitors were gone, "if that is how you spent your mornings at Eversleigh, I would rather stay with Jane in Croydon and play cribbage."

12

Some days after this encounter Emily and Margaret were sitting together in the parlour with their work. Penelope and Elizabeth had gone to Dunford; Margaret had said she did not wish to go, and had pressed Emily with great urgency to stay at Stanton with her. As the day, though dry, was somewhat gusty, and as Margaret herself had been in such a good humour since the ball as to have become, if not a desirable companion, at least no longer an unpleasant one, Emily had consented. She now proposed a walk; if they chose one of the lanes, she suggested, they would be more sheltered from the wind than their sisters, whom she hoped were not getting too buffeted on their journey in the unprotected gig.

"I am quite prepared to take a walk, dearest Emily, but if we delay our start a little I suspect we may have an escort for it."

These words were accompanied by a look of peculiar meaning, which, with the words themselves, made Emily very uneasy.

"What have you arranged?" she demanded.

"*I* have arranged nothing; it is another who has done the arranging."

Emily remembered that some whispers had been exchanged between Margaret and Mr Musgrave when the latter had stopped his curricle at the parsonage-gate the previous day. She flushed in shocked disgust at what Margaret seemed to be proposing.

"If you hope to make use of me in connection with some – some *liaison* between you and Mr Musgrave, you will be disappointed," she said, with firmness. "You are my sister, and I sincerely trust you are intending no such thing."

Emily was pleased to see that such words brought a blush even to Margaret's cheek. She could, it appeared, be indiscreet; but there were at least limits to her indiscretion.

"Dearest Emily!" she cried. "You do not know how grievously you wrong me. Had I attempted to see Musgrave alone, I might have deserved a part of your censure, but I have not even done that. A hint was given me that Lord Osborne and Musgrave might call here this morning to invite us for a walk – that is all. We are four sisters. A little contrivance to ensure that a visitor can sometimes find less than four at home is surely permissible."

"I am relieved to find that the *matter* is not as serious as you gave me to believe," replied Emily. "But the *manner* was not well advised. Elizabeth is in a sense our guardian. She should not be kept in ignorance of what occurs here."

Margaret made no reply; and Emily could only hope that her rebuke had been taken to heart. She herself pondered a little on the difficulties of their position without either a mother or a loved aunt to guide them, make their arrangements and extend invitations on their behalf. Her own invitation to Mrs Blake, though entirely proper in every way, had been forced on her by the lack of such a person. It was not, perhaps, to one of Margaret's poor discernment, so very different from what Margaret had done for herself. She was about to address her sister in a kinder tone, and suggest that the best way to ensure that no harm resulted from Margaret's action would be for them to stay at home with their visitors, where they would be in some way protected by the presence of their father in the same house, if not in the same room, when a rap at the front door drove the thought from her head.

The gentlemen entered almost before she had time to compose herself. Their astonishment in finding only Miss Margaret and Miss Emily at home was expressed by the one in a glib phrase and by the other in a look of real surprise. Emily, who believed the falseness of the one as readily as she accepted the authenticity of the other, was grateful that Lord Osborne was himself in ignorance of the plan, and so could not reckon her as being a party to it. A walk was immediately proposed, and the proposal was as immediately agreed by Margaret, without any reference to her sister.

They started off in the direction of the castle. Though Lord Osborne commented on the badness of the surface of the road it was at least wide enough for them to walk abreast. This was not so of the lane into which they turned as soon as they were clear of the village. Lord Osborne was a speedy walker, and once the other couple had fallen into place behind he did not seem to mind how great the distance grew between them.

"We are in danger of losing my sister and Mr Musgrave, my lord," said Emily.

"There is no fork in the lane for three miles," he answered. "They have but to follow us and all will be well."

As the other two then came into sight round a bend some fifty yards to the rear, Emily contented herself with the knowledge that they were at least following them, and saved her energies for the two tasks of keeping up with her escort and addressing to him a few remarks about the recent ball. Lord Osborne replied rather abruptly and somewhat increased his pace.

"My lord," she cried, after a few minutes of further effort, "if our walk is not to degenerate into a race – if I am to have breath sufficient for the most spasmodic conversation – you will have to slacken speed a little."

He apologized, and did indeed for a short time walk a little more slowly. He seemed to be greatly preoccupied; and the only contribution from his side towards their conversation was a repetition of his complaint about the bad state of the road they had lately quitted. His eyes occasionally scanned the meadows between which they were rapidly passing with a fierceness that suggested these too in some way fell short of what was required.

"I am very fortunate," he said suddenly, "in having secured an opportunity for a private conversation with you today. It was an opportunity I was determined to make."

He spoke in such a hard abrupt tone, and cast another glance of such fierceness across the hedgerow, that Emily began to think he must have some complaint to make about her or her sisters. She wondered if they had perhaps disturbed his cattle or left open a gate on one of their walks.

"These are the meadows of Stanton Lodge, are they not?" she asked.

"Yes; and disgracefully full of thistles and other weeds," he replied.

"I am relieved to hear thistles named as a possible cause of your displeasure," she said, "for your eagerness to meet me, and the stern looks you have given the meadows, made me think that perhaps it was my sisters and I who had offended there. I confess we have taken several short cuts from the lane to the parsonage; and I trust your bailiff has not been complaining of open gates."

"Indeed he has not."

"Nor of furrows void of expected partridges?"

"No, Miss Emily. Not even of that," he replied, his features relaxing a little.

"I am glad to hear it, my lord. For as at this season of the year vixens are subject to more disturbance than two or three unmounted females can create, I can now face you as both a landowner and a sportsman with a clear conscience."

Lord Osborne smiled; his abrupt fierceness left him and he spoke in a tone that was still serious but no longer rough.

"You have a faculty for putting me at my ease, Miss Emily. I told you a little of my history the other evening; perhaps you now understand why I have not the ready manner of some others when addressing a young lady. I have been puzzling these last two minutes about the way in which I should speak to you, and now, because you have spoken with your usual friendliness, the problem does not exist any longer. I shall just speak as I feel."

"I am happy to have been the means of suggesting such advice to you," she replied, in some embarrassment, "for it is advice from which we can all profit, and to which your most intimate friends would subscribe. But I am at a loss to imagine a subject we could fittingly discuss at this early stage of our acquaintance and that at the same time requires such a serious introduction."

"The subject is marriage."

"That is *not* a suitable subject for us to discuss, my lord," she replied hastily. "I beg you to forget that you have mentioned it, as I myself most assuredly shall."

"No; you are too honest to shy away from it like that," he said. "If you are to refuse me, so be it; and with your permission I shall ask again. But you have made me brave; you have even made me fluent. I am going to speak, and you must answer."

"We do not yet know each other," she cried, in great

anxiety. "There is a seemliness about these matters that must be preserved."

She glanced round, but Margaret and Mr Musgrave were not in sight.

"I have not yet spoken," he said, still striding onwards with youthful impetuosity. "When I have, I trust you will tell me my faults – tell them even more explicitly than when I first called at the parsonage and you taught me there were ways in which a gentleman should *not* speak to a lady. For if you do not tell me my faults how am I to correct them, and so bring myself to such a condition that you are prepared to accept me as a husband? But perhaps I am walking too fast, for you seem a little flushed. We are now well ahead of the others and can afford to go more slowly. First as to this business of not knowing each other. It is at best but half true: I am quite certain that you know me better than anyone else does. With one sentence you can put me at my ease, which is not so simple a task that it can be performed by any stranger. I had flattered myself that I knew you, but of that you must judge yourself. The only proof I can offer is that I say nothing of any material advantages I am in the position of being able to grant the lady who becomes my wife, for I believe these would weigh less with one of your character than the plain statement that I honour, admire and love you to a degree that the poor words at my disposal can never adequately express. It is on my affection that I base my plea; though I should perhaps remind you that as my wife you would be able to dispense very substantial aid to *others* – to the villagers of these two parishes, to your family, and to anyone else who is fortunate enough to excite your sympathy. I know that to you the prospect of doing good to others would count more than any possible benefit to yourself. It would not alone recompense for some serious objection to the situation I am suggesting, but it might help to tip an otherwise even balance in my favour. That is my proposal, Miss Emily. Of my attachment I have already spoken; and I cannot believe that to one of your discernment it has come as any very great surprise. You have said you intend to refuse me, which has had the odd effect of helping me to a clear expression of what I wanted to say. I will claim no more than that it is clear. Its sincerity must make up for its deficiencies in other directions."

Emily had listened to his declaration with very mixed feelings. Unwillingness to listen at all had given way to sympathy and even to something not very unlike affection.

"My lord," she replied, "you have expressed yourself with a straightforwardness I am coming more and more to admire. You have done me a very great honour – so great an honour that I could not presume to take advantage of you by accepting it. I thank you most sincerely, but I must refuse. Let us wait here a moment, or better still turn back and meet my sister and Mr Musgrave."

"Surely you do not grudge me a few more minutes of your company?' he demanded.

"It is not that, my lord. It is only that I thought it would be easier for us both if we now concluded our walk as soon as possible."

She was agitated by what had occurred, and she had been moved to a surprising degree by the manner in which Lord Osborne had spoken. But she had always assumed that such painful interviews terminated with the young lady's refusal; and she had no very exact idea about the footing on which one should be continued. Her most unconventional suitor was walking on as though that was a matter not worth a thought.

"You must talk to me in plainer terms than you would use to another," he said. "There can be no question of taking advantage of me. I am far from offering that which I hope will not be accepted, so you must not expect any gratitude under *that* head. Talk to me as a friend for a moment. The faults you have shown me I have tried to correct. Tell me the others and I will do my best with them."

"You are putting too much on me," she cried. "You are treating me as though I was your superior. I assure you the world thinks very differently."

"Then I know you better than the rest of the world, which is what I have said."

"My lord, I will be quite frank, for otherwise I see we shall never come to an end. I had no alternative but to refuse your proposal for the reason that we do not know each other sufficiently well. I have been at Stanton hardly seven weeks. We have met barely half a dozen times. I have sat but half a morning in your mother's carriage. I have never spoken to your sister."

"But what on earth has my sister to do with *this*?" he demanded, in some exasperation. "She is to marry Colonel Beresford and will be out of the castle in a couple of months."

If it had not been for the seriousness of the occasion Emily would have smiled as she explained:

"In herself little, my lord. But the fact is a measure of the lack of acquaintance between our families."

"I see," said Lord Osborne. There was then a silence which lasted a full minute. "You are right. My family has neglected its duty in the past, and this morning's work has been part of the punishment."

"That was not what I intended!" she cried.

"But you are quite right. I see it very clearly, and shall do my best to make amends in the future. Where else have I failed?"

Emily found herself very near tears.

"It is not for me to give you advice, my lord," she pleaded. "You have a mother and a sister."

"Both of whom were amused at my efforts to fit myself for a ball-room," he said, "though I believe the inspiration of their laughter was different. One thought the trouble not worth taking: the other that no trouble *I* took would improve my clumsiness. It is you who have given me the encouragement I might have looked for elsewhere. Did I not hope you would one day agree to accept a closer relationship, I should be tempted to engage you for a sister."

"If in truth, my lord, I am to give you advice," she replied, in a voice that faltered, "I must advise you, as I am certain others would, to seek an alliance more in keeping with your situation."

"Fortunately I am in the position of being able to please myself. I have no younger brothers to be settled in the world, and my mother and my sister are well provided for. You are a gentleman's daughter and a gentleman's niece. I cannot believe you would fail to make a fit wife for a gentleman. It is but a day or two since I informed my mother of my intentions. She was surprised, I admit; but I do not think she was displeased."

"You have spoken to your mother!" she cried.

"Why yes. And I think you will find her ready enough to greet you when the time comes."

Emily was now seriously distressed. She was right – she knew she must be right – in refusing him. But she was wrong in believing he had not considered the step he intended to take with the proper seriousness. That he had already spoken to his mother caused her the greatest astonishment.

"I fear I am no longer able to take part in this conversation," she said. "If you will give me your arm to that gate and let me rest a little, I will try and recover myself."

"I have walked you too fast and burdened you with too much!" he cried. "Forgive me, please!"

With much solicitude he helped her to the gate, and waited until she was able to suggest that they retraced their steps. Again he offered her his arm, which she gratefully accepted. Her resistance was very much weakened; and had he now repeated his offer she might not have found the strength to refuse what was so sincerely demanded and what seemed in some ways so justly deserved. However, they soon encountered Margaret and Mr Musgrave, who were talking together in a very animated fashion, and they walked behind them until they reached the road. She did not feel the embarrassment she had expected in Lord Osborne's continued company. They seemed almost to converse in more intimate terms *after* she had refused him than *before*; and he made her free of any short cuts that took her fancy, and described the improvements he intended to the land of Stanton Lodge, in a very friendly and open manner.

At the gate of the parsonage they met Elizabeth and Penelope, who had just returned from Dunford.

"Miss Watson," he said, "I have been telling your sister that my family and I have been bad neighbours to you long enough. We pass here often; you must please make more use of us. I myself will be in the village once or twice a week this winter and will be happy to render you any service in my power."

Elizabeth was quite at a loss at this speech, but after a moment of hesitation managed to thank him in rather a surprised tone. The gentlemen then left and the four sisters went in together.

"What am I to suppose he meant by that?" demanded Elizabeth.

"Why, my dear, that he intends to help with the next big wash," said Penelope. "What else could he mean?"

"Perhaps Emily can tell us," suggested Margaret, in a very sly voice.

"I think it was only neighbourly courtesy. He accused himself

[123]

earlier this morning of having been a bad neighbour – though as the castle is two or three miles from here he has perhaps stretched the word somewhat far."

"Is that *all* the news you have to tell us as a result of your walk?" asked Margaret, in the same meaningful tone.

"What else do you expect?"

"Nothing, dearest Emily. Nothing at all. Only *I* have some very particular intelligence for you all. This morning Mr Musgrave did me the honour of asking me to become his wife, and I accepted. He is going to speak to my father tomorrow."

This was indeed very particular intelligence. Emily had not considered Mr Musgrave a desirable acquaintance for Margaret, and so should not strictly have considered him a desirable husband. As, however, a great part of her criticism of the gentleman was directed against his unstable, unconstant and flirtatious habits, and as Margaret herself was totally without taste, refinement, education or fortune, she could not but congratulate her sister with almost as much public pleasure as Elizabeth. Penelope too, with the same feelings as Emily, added her good wishes; and Margaret had the satisfaction of believing herself generally envied. Her sisters were as much inwardly astonished as they were outwardly pleased. It was not every day that a pretty figure, and a face with as much discontent as beauty, captured a handsome young man with nine hundred a year.

"Now be as frank as I have been," pleaded Margaret. "Musgrave gave me to understand that you *too* might have some news for us."

"I cannot go on pretending ignorance of what you expect, my dear Margaret," answered Emily. "But surely you cannot believe that in the *extremely* unlikely event of Lord Osborne's having any intention of addressing me he would take Mr Musgrave into his confidence first?"

"Not in so many words, dearest Emily. But one gentleman can often guess the intentions of another in these matters. Lord Osborne has openly expressed his admiration for you, and the opportunity was there. If it has not come yet you can expect it soon. Miss Osborne is to marry Colonel Beresford, though it is not meant to be talked about at present. Musgrave is determined to call Lord

Osborne brother somehow, so you can now count on his doing all in his power for you, I am sure."

This last speech was too much for Penelope's gravity and Emily's sense of decorum. The former turned to the window with shaking shoulders, and the latter went upstairs to reflect in solitude on the surprising events of the morning. Thoughts about Mr Musgrave soon gave way to thoughts about Lord Osborne. He had expressed himself well – extremely well. His attachment must be of the deepest, most serious kind. She must now respect him highly. But she must have been right – she must surely have been right in refusing a man whom she had seen for the first time five weeks ago. Then she remembered another man whom she had seen for the first time five weeks ago; one whom she had respected immediately, and whose conversation ranged further than the husbandry of land and the scything of thistles. The recollection convinced her that she really had been, in spite of her doubts, right in her refusal.

13

Mr Musgrave was to call at one the following day to speak to Mr Watson. Mr Watson considered Mr Musgrave an idle, empty-headed fellow, and was unable to join in the raptures Elizabeth gave way to when preparing him for the interview. But he was a poor man, he said sadly, and Margaret had never shown any qualities that recompensed for her lack of fortune or encouraged him to think a man of sense would have her. He could not therefore oppose the match. He had heard no real evil of Mr Musgrave, whose defects were probably common enough among young men of weak character, adequate income and no occupation. He was in hopes that the cares and duties of a family would do as much for Mr and Mrs Tom Musgrave as they had done for other couples, and that while distinction was not to be looked for, reasonable respectability would in time be theirs. It is to be regretted that Elizabeth, her head full of the glory of the alliance and the difficulties of preparing a meal worthy of it – for Tom would surely stay to dinner after such an application – did not listen to this just summary of the fate in store for the great majority of affianced lovers.

In due course the fire in the best parlour was lit; and Margaret, at her most elegant, established before it. By an arrangement agreeable to at least three of the sisters, Emily and Penelope passed the first part of the morning in the other room. After Mr Musgrave had seen Mr Watson he was to be allowed an hour or more in company with the young lady of his choice, with only Elizabeth, whose obligations towards the dinner would ensure her conveniently frequent absence, to overhear his secrets. Not till this happy interlude was past were Emily and Penelope to come forward with their congratulations.

That at least was Margaret's plan. The beginning of it was satisfactorily accomplished. Emily and Penelope heard a rap on the door at half-past twelve, betokening the punctual lover, and a few minutes later Elizabeth came in to say that Tom was with Margaret. In the kindness of her heart she dawdled with them a little before proceeding upstairs to see if Mr Watson would be able to receive Mr Musgrave somewhat earlier than had been arranged. It was at this point that the plan went wrong. The two sisters, alone again, were quietly discussing Mr Musgrave, and had just agreed that as he was shortly to become their brother they must forget their former criticisms and attempt to see only the good points of the gentleman, when they were startled by a loud scream from the other parlour. They jumped up and stared in astonishment at each other. At the same moment Mr Musgrave hurried to the foot of the stairs, calling:

"Miss Watson! Miss Watson! Miss Margaret has fainted!"

Emily and Penelope ran to the door, brushed past Mr Musgrave, and entered the best parlour in no little alarm. Margaret was lying on the sofa in the attitude made familiar even to Emily by numerous serious headaches. Her eyes were shut; one arm swung loosely towards the floor, the other was pressed to her bosom, and there seemed to be some congestion in her throat that interfered with her breathing.

"Water!" cried Emily.

"Yes, my dear," replied Penelope, with a calmness that surprised her sister, "a sprinkle of water will doubtless revive poor Margaret."

The words themselves seemed to have that desirable effect, for her eyes immediately fluttered and her lips moved.

"Musgrave," she murmured. "Where is my dear Musgrave?"

Emily, who for one moment had almost believed that Mr Musgrave's conduct must in some way have been responsible for her sister's collapse, was relieved to hear the affectionate inquiry.

"Mr Musgrave," she called, "my sister is recovered."

Mr Musgrave was standing in the doorway. With Emily encouraging him from before, and Elizabeth and Nanny, both of whom were trying to enter the room, pressing him from behind, he advanced towards Margaret. His ease of manner had departed; in a small room in the company of five females (a combination of circumstances that usually showed him to advantage) he was both agitated and self-conscious.

"I trust," he said, with some hesitation, "I trust you have fully regained your senses."

The ladies stood back and he took the place by Margaret's side that seemed to be expected of him. That particular lady sought for his hand with a very touching helplessness.

"Poor Musgrave," she murmured tenderly. "I am such a silly weak creature. But it is nothing; I am quite well now. I hope my faint did not alarm you."

"No," he muttered, perhaps still too disturbed to show his full happiness at her recovery. "I mean, of course, yes. It is not quite what one expects, you know."

"You had better lie down alone a little," suggested Elizabeth. "Nanny, there is the stuffing still to do."

"No, dearest Elizabeth," said Margaret, hastily. "Solitude would only depress my spirits; a little company might enliven them."

"But however did you come to faint? I have never known you do such a thing since you were twelve. To be sure, then you used to manage it half the Sundays through the summer."

"I had stood up suddenly. It was just when you went upstairs. Everything swayed and the room became quite dark. It stayed so for quite some minutes. Musgrave was talking, I think, but I could not hear what he said. I could not hear at all. I did not even know where I was. Then I felt myself falling and I think I screamed. The next thing I knew was dearest Emily leaning over me."

"How very unaccountable!"

"It was a most unpleasant sensation I assure you. I have no wish to go through it again. It was like a nightmare; indeed it almost *was* a nightmare, for I experienced a very horrible dream while I was unconscious."

"I did not know that people had *dreams* when they were *unconscious*," said Mr Musgrave.

"I can assure you *I* did," said Margaret, in a very gentle voice. "You yourself were present in my dream; but I would not tell you the story, for you appeared in a very bad light and not at all as the man of honour I know you to be."

[128]

"'Tis fortunate it was only a dream," said Penelope, looking with some curiosity from Margaret to Mr Musgrave.

"It is indeed. But I am recovered and have no right to hold Musgrave's hand in this manner before he has spoken to my father. Will you not speak to my father now, Musgrave?" she demanded tenderly.

The gentleman seemed very conscious that the eyes of the four sisters were on him. He flushed a little, looked for a moment towards the window, and at the bright, open autumn countryside beyond, and then muttered:

"Yes."

"I will show you the way," said Elizabeth, cheerfully, and led him out of the room.

Not till his footsteps were heard in the passage above was there any relaxation of attention in the room he had quitted. Margaret then got up from the sofa with a sudden movement that seemed to indicate a consciousness of complete recovery, and began to tidy herself before the mirror.

"This was Emily's fault," she said, in a sharp tone. "She has a very high opinion of herself, Pen – very high indeed. If she had not considered herself too fine for a certain gentleman who is above her by several degrees and many thousands of pounds I would not have had to go through this silly scene just now."

"I trust that no conduct of *mine*," said Emily, flushing, "indeed I am far from able to see or wishing to know how anything I have done could have caused your collapse."

"Then I will tell you," cried Margaret, turning round; but Penelope interrupted her.

"My dear Margaret, we know how deep your interest in our welfare is, but this is carrying it to excess. You must not let your sympathy for your less fortunate sisters mar the happiness of your betrothal. Be content with your public success; let us repine our failures in private. And should you require to faint again in the near future you would be well advised to study your breathing. It should be very quiet, barely perceptible, gentle as the fall of a petal. Not at all like that of a horse after a hard gallop."

Emily's error was forgotten. Margaret spun round to face Penelope with angry cheeks and trembling lips. Fortunately what might have been said was never revealed, for at that moment Nanny returned to tell them that Mr George Tomlinson's clerk had arrived with a key. Elizabeth's errand upstairs was completed and she followed hard on Nanny's heels. There must have been some mistake, she said. No one at the parsonage had asked for a key. Margaret explained that it was the key of Stanton Lodge, for which Mr George Tomlinson, the attorney, was in some way responsible, and that *she* had asked for it.

"Heavens! Are you to live at Stanton Lodge?" cried Elizabeth.

"It is not yet decided," replied Margaret. "But we are to look at it."

The lack of decision was soon apparent. Mr Musgrave's application was successful; and he came back to the room in a slightly better frame of mind than that in which he left it. For it is a remarkable fact that there are some gentlemen of such a peculiar nature that they can be highly gratified in being granted even what they have requested without very much enthusiasm. Mr Musgrave would have been insulted if Mr Watson had refused him his daughter's hand; Mr Watson, however, had not refused it; he had bestowed it with about the same amount of enthusiasm as it had been requested. And Mr Musgrave, this last fact having escaped his notice, was pleased to find he stood as high in the world's estimation as he did in his own.

When the congratulations were through Elizabeth spoke of Stanton Lodge.

"Stanton Lodge?" demanded Mr Musgrave. "What is this about Stanton Lodge?"

"You mentioned Stanton Lodge yesterday," said Margaret, hastily. "I have now got the key."

Mr Musgrave's gloomy frown reappeared. He looked again towards the window, through which the countryside had the same free, open appearance, and sighed with what seemed envy.

"Stanton Lodge we talked about, and Osborne Castle too," he said. "Have you got the key of that?"

"Do not be foolish, Musgrave," said Margaret, in a voice she had hitherto reserved for her sisters. "I have done as you suggested; that is all. If you do not wish to live at Stanton Lodge we need not; but yesterday you were saying it was very conveniently situated."

"It is near Osborne Castle – within two miles, I dare say. But beyond that it has little advantage."

"It is near my family," answered Margaret, sharply.

"To be sure it is," was the not overjoyed reply.

"For my part I should be well content to live in Dunford," said the young lady. "It was you who spoke of purchasing an estate in the country."

"Stanton Lodge is not an estate. Beyond the park it has hardly as much land as the parsonage."

"Then why did you talk of Stanton Lodge yesterday?"

"Let us at least go and see the house," said Elizabeth, to prevent a continuation of the quarrel. "It is many years since I have been inside, and a visit does not commit you to buy it."

Any relief from the immediate unpleasantness was welcome, and Emily and Penelope supported the suggestion with as much cordiality as they could summon. Their cordiality, however, stopped short of walking by the side of either Margaret or Mr Musgrave; and as the former had by now changed her original plan, evincing a determination at all costs *not* to be left alone with her future husband, Elizabeth was made to accompany the couple, while Penelope and Emily followed a little way behind.

"You are very silent, my love," said Penelope, when almost half the short distance had been accomplished.

"Penelope, I am thinking. I am thinking something I do not quite know how to put into words. Indeed it seems altogether too shameful to put into words."

"You may save yourself both the trouble and the shame, my dear, for I am thinking the same thought myself. Let us take it as said, and I will go on to add that Mr Musgrave appears to have the somewhat desperate look of a hunted man in his eyes. I have no experience in calculating these things, but I imagine the look will soon turn to one of resignation."

"In heaven's name, Penelope! We cannot permit this."

"One of the principals is determined that nothing shall prevent it; and the other, by his interview with my father, would seem to have burnt the last boat in which he might have escaped."

"I cannot tell you how disgraced I feel," said Emily, earnestly.

"I am far from feeling any disgrace myself," replied Penelope.

"In fact I am beginning to admire Margaret for the first time in my life. Perhaps I am influenced in her favour by the fact that the next month or two will probably see the end to our long and unsuccessful attempt to live together peaceably; but I do not think that is all. That my sister Margaret should be responsible for that *hunted* expression on Mr Musgrave's face speaks highly for her tenacity. I have always admired tenacity; it is the sign of the thoroughbred."

"You are joking again," said Emily, "but I know you now too well not to be aware that in your heart you, like me, consider marriage a serious undertaking."

"Yes, my little moralist, marriage is a serious undertaking. Birth, life and death are all serious undertakings; the trouble is that they are performed in the main by a great number of very frivolous people. You would not expect marriage to be considered as seriously by the savages of the Indies as it is by your sweet self. And you must put Margaret and Mr Musgrave and even your sister Penelope some way between yourself and those same ignorant savages."

"That is not true as far as you are concerned," said Emily. "You are not in a category with them."

"If I am not it is chiefly because I have decided, when I marry, to marry a man of honour. I confess I have come to have a rather prosaic view of marriage. If I can find in it a fair measure of stability I shall not ask for more; and stability, I feel, will be best ensured by choosing a man of honour. To me, Mr Musgrave has long seemed lacking in that quality, which I fear has never been conspicuous in my sister Margaret. Therefore I must conclude they are well-matched in at least one particular."

"Knowing what you now know you cannot approve of the match!"

"Let us look at the matter another way, my dear. Let us consider for a moment the possibility that some of us are intended to atone for the faults of our character in the circumstances of our present life – that poetic justice, in fact, far from being a fantasy of Mr Pope's, is a very real force. As I have told you before, I prefer Mr Pope to Dr Johnson, who seems to me too often sententious and dull, if not actually *ponderous*. I see from your expression I have gone too far, so I will hurriedly withdraw my criticism and merely say that at times he lacks a little of Mr Pope's ease and wit. Do not contradict me for the moment and I will promise to keep my opinion to myself in front of Mr Howard, so that you will never have *two* sisters to be ashamed of. You remember his words – Mr Pope's, I mean, not Mr Howard's:

> *Poetic justice, with her lifted scale,*
> *Where, in nice balance, truth with gold she weighs*
> *And solid pudding against empty praise.*

The potentialities of matrimony as a dispenser of poetic justice are almost unlimited. True, a miser can suddenly lose money; a bully can suddenly become a martyr to gout. Justice in each case is done and our sorely tried feelings are assuaged. But the satisfaction is a limited one: a single, though vicious, fault is punished by an isolated, though severe, penalty. Our admiration of fate, though deep, is not lasting. In marriages of a certain type, however, the grave alone puts an end to the tribulations of both parties. Pride must look at baseness, weakness at obstinacy, just as jealousy must look at indifference, duplicity at shallowness, until the day of that happy release."

"Even you, injured as you have been, cannot hope for such an outcome in the present case," said Emily.

"I do not hope it, my dear; nor, to tell the truth do I expect it, if by that you would take me to imply that both will indulge in daily regrets for this morning's work. I suspect that like other humans they will grow accustomed to their situation and pass lengthy periods without remembering it was due to their own choice and not forced on them by a malignant fate. They will be punished certainly; but not beyond endurance. Resignation will soon take the place of desperation; and if they could develop a few common failings they might even achieve an occasional bout of happiness."

Penelope stopped; and Emily said nothing for a few moments. She had been deeply shocked by what had occurred that morning; and even her fondness for her sister could not quite reconcile her to jesting in such a fashion on such a subject. At last she ventured a gentle rebuke.

"It pains me a little, Penelope, that you, for whom I have such admiration, should sometimes use your talents not to check faults, but almost to encourage them."

"We are made different, my love, and you must suffer it. You must read Mr Pope, as well. You would find that he is very far from condoning the extravagances of which he writes. I am by way of being a disciple of his, though a very humble one of course. I am still meditating on the lines I quoted just now. The exact significance of *solid pudding* has long puzzled me. Would you think it too far fetched to suggest that the author had Margaret and her very indifferent supervision of the kitchen in mind?"

"I will read more of Mr Pope," said Emily, "and will then endeavour to answer you."

They had for some time been walking in the grounds of Stanton Lodge, for the building itself, by the direct route, was but a short distance from the parsonage. The three they had been following, however, had chosen a detour through the shrubberies which now brought them out on the far side of the house and at a considerable way from it. This was the best impression of Stanton Lodge they were to be given that morning. The front before them, though not large, was of tasteful proportions, and the surface of the wide lawn it faced was pleasantly broken by clumps of carefully chosen trees.

"The prospect from the terrace must be charming," cried Emily. "Why have we not walked here before?"

"Indeed I do not know, my dear. We *used* not to walk here because of the agent responsible for the land, who once ordered us out in an amazingly rude manner. However, I believe the agent himself has since been ordered out by Lord Osborne no less summarily. We must see how we stand with Margaret and Mr Musgrave for the future."

But Mr Musgrave, whom they now joined, complained of the dwelling being too big and the estate too small; while a closer inspection of the house itself revealed faults which even Margaret, in her eagerness to impress her sisters, was unable to ignore.

"Quite out of the question," she said to Mr Musgrave. "I have seldom seen a house in such disgraceful condition."

"Not to be thought of," Mr Musgrave observed to Margaret, "even if Osborne would agree to sell back some of the land."

They returned home more directly than they had come, by way of the drive and the village street.

"I talked about Mr Pope on our outward journey," said Penelope, when they had once more dropped behind the others. "I will not start on him again. There is another subject I would like to discuss; but I am somewhat shy of opening it without your leave."

"What is that?"

"If you could indulge me with an explanation of the hints my sister let fall in the parlour about you and an unnamed gentleman I would be very grateful. As you may be sure that within the next day or two I shall hear a garbled account of the matter from Margaret herself, you can perhaps ignore the scruples that would otherwise prevent your speaking."

"Yesterday," said Emily, angry at herself for the blood she felt mounting to her cheeks, "Lord Osborne asked me to marry him."

"A refusal was I think hinted at," said Penelope delicately, after a short pause.

"I could not accept, and would not willingly listen to, the proposals of a gentleman I had met but half a dozen times."

"Say it again, my love. Lord Osborne has asked you to marry him and you have refused?"

"Yes."

Penelope gave vent to a long sigh.

"I say nothing of his castle, his fortune or his title; but I tell you frankly that I do not think I would have been able to refuse a young man with such very fine stables. If there is anything else you feel able to tell me I shall listen with considerable interest."

"In spite of myself I was impressed by his behaviour and his declaration. Less to my taste is the fact that Mr Musgrave seems to know of his request and my answer."

"He is more to be excused in confiding in a friend, than in his choice of that friend," said Penelope. "However, I am in no position to criticize him there. Well, you really do amaze me. I suppose his remark to Elizabeth was intended to mean that he does not consider his acquaintanceship with our family at an end."

"No, indeed; and it is there that I am least sure of the correctness of my conduct. He made his proposal, which I refused; and then, instead of leaving me or keeping silent, he continued to talk.

By the time we returned to the parsonage it was as though we had had an intimate and mutually satisfying conversation. I do not quite see *where* I was at fault, but I feel I must have been at fault *somewhere* for allowing such a thing to occur."

"I am no judge of conduct for one of your sensibility, my dear. However, should such a request be repeated, and should you have an opportunity for a further intimate conversation, you might take advantage of it to remind him that you have a sister who would be prepared to listen to him any time he cares to address her. I am sure you would manage the commission with great delicacy; and if you could include an account of my excessive fondness for horses I would have every reason to expect its successful conclusion."

This was the end of their discussion for the present, but it was far from being the last that Emily heard of a matter that seemed to have become unpleasantly public. Margaret tried to speak of it more than once; though as something further appeared to pass between Lord Osborne and Mr Musgrave in the course of the next day or two, which resulted in the latter being almost reconciled to his engagement, Margaret's manner underwent a change, and she even apologized for her early vehemence. Emily, however, had as little pleasure in being pressed to accept her suitor as she had in being blamed for refusing him. She was at this time grateful beyond words for Penelope's ready tongue. In front of visitors – Mrs Edwards and Mary, the inquisitive Miss Tomlinson, and even Lord Osborne himself, who called once with Mr Musgrave – she was never at a loss. Elizabeth was as discreet as she could be. She knew nothing of a proposal, would never dream of such an unlikely alliance, and saw Lord Osborne's call as inspired by friendliness to Mr Musgrave, who was of course to marry Margaret. Meanwhile Miss Stokes had given her a new receipt for ginger wine which required an excessive amount of sugar. Emily's affectionate respect for her eldest sister was as warm as her love for Penelope.

One conversation, however, could not be avoided. The visit to Mrs Blake, which had been delayed by bad weather, was finally undertaken. Mrs Blake received them with many expressions of kindness. Her brother, she said, was out, but if they would sit with her an hour he would certainly return. The visit was lengthened to well beyond this span; but though a horse was heard to enter the yard, which sound made Mrs Blake pleasantly expectant, it was shortly afterwards heard to leave again; and the Miss Watsons were forced to depart without having re-encountered Mr Howard. Emily was in low spirits when the party returned to Stanton, and these were not improved when Elizabeth told her that her father wished to speak to her. She went upstairs with an anxious heart.

Her father waited until she had made herself comfortable in the chair his evening companion usually sat in.

"Tell me, Emily," he said, "have you heard anything from your aunt since the letter announcing Captain O'Brien's death?"

"Yes, sir. I received a second letter two weeks ago, which I answered on Saturday. It was a matter I had intended to discuss with you when I had the opportunity."

"I am here by myself the greater part of the day," said Mr Watson, sadly.

"There was no urgency," replied Emily, with a slight feeling of guilt at having kept her father so long uninformed. "The letter told chiefly of the successful conclusion of my aunt's business in Dublin. No mention was made in it of my joining her; and as I have heard nothing since it would seem most sensible to dismiss the possibility of a summons and to accept the permanency of my stay at Stanton."

"That is the interpretation you attach to the letter?"

"Yes, sir."

"For your sake I must sympathize with you; for my own I am pleased enough at the way things have turned out."

Emily thanked him, and said with sincerity that she found herself increasingly happy in her new home.

"And now I come to another point which you may find less easy to discuss," continued her father. "Rumours have reached me that an offer has recently been made to you by a certain gentleman in a very high situation in the neighbourhood. As it appears probable that you will continue to live at the parsonage I think I must ask you whether these rumours have any foundation in fact."

Here Mr Watson paused, and in a very small voice Emily replied:

"They have some foundation, sir."

"I am surprised," said Mr Watson, raising his eyebrows. "I am very surprised. But in that case the reason for his visits becomes clearer. I have not met the gentleman myself, but I have made a few inquiries recently, and what I have heard is all to his credit. I am told he is an energetic and merciful landlord. He comes of an honourable family, and is not, I think, the sort of man to disgrace a name of which he must be proud."

Again Mr Watson paused. He had said nothing that required an answer and Emily waited in silence till he recommenced.

"It is certainly very astonishing, Emily. I had not thought of it before but I suppose you must be a very beautiful girl. I am not a worldly man; some would say I am not worldly enough. It is those who would doubtless affirm that it was your *duty* to accept such a very favourable alliance if you had the chance. I am too conscious of my own failings in similar matters to be as definite as that; but it is right that in your present position I should give you such advice as I am able. You know, I think, the circumstances of your family?"

"My sister Elizabeth has briefly described them, sir."

"We are entirely dependent on my living, which is not a large one. It is a fact you should remember. I will add two more. While it is not for me to pass on to others the commitments I am unable to fulfil myself – least of all to you who have only recently joined us – I must point out that as the wife of a man of wealth and influence you would be able to help your brothers and sisters without difficulty should they ever require it. And finally, if this young man of five-and-twenty, who has lived the normal, not over-studious life of one of his rank and position, has appreciated the finer points of your character, and shows himself sufficiently independent of the calculating materialism of the multitude to make you an offer of marriage, that offer deserves your very earnest, sincere and sympathetic consideration. That is all I have to say to you, my dear. I have neither the right nor the inclination to pry into your heart. I would like to sit alone for the rest of the evening. This talk has woken many regrets, and I have much to think about of a rather sad nature. Perhaps if fate had been kinder to me I would have performed my duty as a father a little more adequately."

Emily left him, but instead of going downstairs took refuge in her bedroom. The matter of Lord Osborne's proposal and her refusal now appeared in a different light; for it was this moment her perverse judgement selected to insist on the truth of a suspicion it had hitherto denied – the horse she had heard enter the yard at Wickstead was of course Mr Howard's horse. Mrs Blake's expectancy was sufficient proof. He had seen the gig and had decided to go away rather than meet the Miss Watsons. There could be no doubt about it. Through excessive over-refinement she had tried to prevent Lord Osborne addressing her. When he *had* addressed her she had refused him because of a foolish partiality for a man who had once danced with her, twice spoken to her, and now, realizing perhaps the thoughts she entertained, took the proper course of avoiding her. It was not before Lord Osborne she should have been so modest; it was before Mr Howard. Such was her immediate reaction to her father's discourse. Some minutes reflection, however, told her she was being too strict with herself. Her *thoughts* perhaps had been foolish; but to an outsider, ignorant of those thoughts, her *conduct* could not have appeared in quite such a bad light as she recalled it. Nevertheless she must be warned from this and her sisters' experience. With less excuse, she must not repeat Penelope's and Elizabeth's blunder. If Mr Howard desired her acquaintance he would doubtless seek it out; and until that occurred she would dismiss all thought of him from her mind.

14

Emily had told her father in all sincerity that she was happy in her new home; but the days that followed this interview revealed a somewhat formidable problem. She wished to atone for her treatment of Lord Osborne by a full return to her former friendliness – that was as far as she allowed her imagination to proceed; if any further reparation was required its initiative must not be hers – but her refusal of his offer was still recent, and a little interval must surely elapse before she would be able to behave in front of him with any naturalness. Moreover the December ball was approaching; and how would her conduct appear to onlookers if she accepted the invitation to stand up with the gentleman she would almost certainly receive?

Relief came from the quarter she least expected. With Margaret preparing for matrimony, and with a happy intimacy established between herself and her two other sisters – with nothing but pleasant prospects in front of her once the awkwardness of the next few weeks was past – Emily, on the last day of November, received the summons she had ceased to await from her aunt. The letter, which was part of a bulky package, had been written at Eversleigh.

Eversleigh,
25th November.

Dearest, dearest Emily,

I must entreat for what I do not deserve, and have forfeited the right to demand, that you will come to me at once. My eyes are opened at last. I have been a foolish woman, and would add that I have been grossly deceived as well, if the shame of my own folly did not prevent me. No; from you I will not attempt to hide it: I have been deceived, and have only my own imprudence to blame. What is much worse, dearest Emily, I have been unkind to one who has given me unexampled love and affection. I can see now how greatly I must have wounded you during the past few months. This is the bankers' order Mr Child has just given me; and I am requiring my cousins to send a man for you on *Wednesday, 2nd.* Of what has happened I will say nothing. I do not wish a young girl whom I have brought up, and who stands to me in the place of a daughter, to hear an account of my own *vain, frivolous* and *selfish* conduct. But I can see everything now, even the motives which prompted Captain O'Brien to address me. I hope for you by Friday evening and will certainly look for you on Saturday.

Dearest Emily, do not fail me. Mr Childs produced some letters in Dublin addressed to Major O'Rorke in Captain O'Brien's hand. Alas, that I was ever taught to read! But for the accident I would have been abandoned and penniless within six months. It is even now almost incredible. Beware, my dearest niece, beware of deceiving men. If we are ever to be parted again it will be at your wish, for I have learnt my lesson. Mr Childs says I am to tell you I am putting it out of my power to do you serious injury in the future. Be wiser than I have been. When it comes to you, preserve your fortune by discretion, and do not leave the matter to chance as I have done. I allowed myself to be blinded. I let myself be separated from those who cared for me. I have done as little to deserve your compliance as Mr Childs's exertions and poor Mr Jones's regard. Have I told you I returned to find him almost destitute and on the point of setting out for London on foot? Mr O'Neil, whom Captain O'Brien appointed to the living, refused to employ him, though I had stipulated that if Mr Jones was not himself appointed, as I wished, he must be allowed to continue in his old position. For how much misery have I been responsible!

Of Stanton and your own history you must tell me as soon as we meet. But you must not expect a similar openness from me, for the story is not a fit one for you to hear. I would say let it stand as an example, but I know you too well to believe you could ever be in need of such a terrible warning. It is I who must take it as such; and mercifully it has not come altogether too late. It has opened my eyes to many long standing weaknesses in my character. I must be *firmer* with myself and *more strict* with others too – though how could I be strict with you, my dear Emily, whose behaviour has been so much more correct than mine?

Come, I pray, to look after your foolish aunt, and to help her keep the stern resolutions she has made. If you have the opportunity please bring three yards of mauve ribbon, *not too bright*. I have mislaid some I bought in Dublin. We left in a great hurry and Mr Childs kindly escorted me here.

Mrs Seymour will undoubtedly send one of her own men to fetch you, so you will be in good hands. Take four horses where the post-master recommends it. Perhaps six yards of ribbon would be better. I long to see my dear, dear niece. My mind is confused and I fear this letter is not over-clear. It contains at the same time my shame for myself and my love for you; the knowledge that I do not deserve your obedience and the certainty that you would join me tomorrow in the most humble dwelling in the land if I were summoning you from there instead of from your old home. You will find me very changed. Half my furniture has gone, the house all at sixes and sevens and not half a dozen servants in the place. My poor, poor rose trees!

Your very contrite and

most affectionate aunt,

Susan O'Brien.

Very mixed were the emotions with which Emily perused her aunt's letter. Then she carefully destroyed it, together with the two other letters she had received at Stanton. Her aunt, who had been grievously at fault, was now aware of her errors. She was determined to make amends; she intended to provide in some manner for her niece's future; but to Emily all this was the less important than the many expressions of affection that occurred and re-occurred in the muddled letter. The dear, kind woman was herself again and required her niece's immediate attendance in the home they both knew and loved. Hastily brushing some involuntary tears from her cheeks Emily ran to her father's room and told him of the summons.

"I shall be sorry to see you go," said Mr Watson, when the matter had been explained to him, "but it is undoubtedly your duty.

From many points of view it must be a pleasant one, and in a worldly sense it is certainly advantageous. If I had not accepted your statement the other day I would be less disappointed."

"I hope, sir, that now I have made my sisters' acquaintance I may be allowed to visit them sometimes, and they me."

Mr Watson sighed. His spirits were low and he was not feeling at his best.

"Yes, I hope so," he answered, in an unhappy tone. "It is sad that we should grow fond of you and then have you thus abruptly taken from us. But that is the way of the world, I suppose, and I for one should be used to it. Sometimes when you read to me in the evenings I could imagine your dear mother was in the room."

To relieve his painful meditations Emily gave him the bankers' order she had received. After an examination of his cash box Mr Watson said she would have to send in to Dunford. He sadly wrote a letter to Mr Tomlinson on her behalf, which – the weather being inclement – he said she might send in by James. Emily then wrote a letter in her turn to Mrs Tomlinson, with whom the Miss Watsons were at last engaged to dine, and went downstairs to dispatch James and speak to her sisters. It was Monday; if she was to leave on Wednesday no time must be lost.

"I knew it would happen so," cried Elizabeth, "you were certainly born under a lucky star, Emily. You have brought us a big slice of it these two months; but you are a sweet girl and deserve anything that comes to you yourself."

"Dearest Emily," murmured Margaret. "This is sad news for me. Though I am to leave my father's house I had hoped to have *you* for a neighbour *whatever* happened. I pray that the intimacy which has given me so much pleasure in recent weeks is not to end with your sudden removal."

Less in answer to Margaret than as an honest expression of her feelings for her two other sisters, Emily replied that an invitation from Elizabeth would only require her aunt's permission before it was accepted.

"An invitation you shall have," said Elizabeth, readily. "You can visit us whenever you please and for as long as you please. You know how we live; it is nothing very fine; but you have fallen in with us very easily and will always be welcome."

Before Penelope could add the encouragement Emily longed to hear, Margaret spoke again.

"Visits between those forced to live apart are a great relief to hearts burdened with affection, dearest Emily," she murmured, in her most gentle, sighing voice. "You will understand of course that I do not wish to be separated by any considerable distance from Musgrave *before* our marriage. After that event I am sure both he and I would be happy to make the acquaintance of my aunt. Indeed, we would almost consider it our duty."

Penelope, who had been about to say something, now changed her mind and walked across to the window to look at the rain falling from the grey sky.

"You have boxes enough," said Elizabeth, "and it is no good trying to wash on such a day. What is not clean must go dirty unless tomorrow is fine. I will keep the rest of that nice bit of cold bacon we had for breakfast to make you some refreshment for the journey."

Emily thanked her; and then, as Penelope had still made no comment on her proposed departure, she shyly asked the sister she loved best to help her prepare her boxes. Penelope assented readily enough, and they walked upstairs together.

"I am no good at innuendoes, my dear," said Penelope, as soon as the bedroom door was closed behind them. "I will not sigh and say I doubt whether I shall be able to survive if I do not see my sister for the space of a month. Such is my confidence in my constitution that I truly think it probable I shall live in health for another fifty years. So I will leave the delicate circumlocutions to others and plainly state that if my aunt finds it convenient I shall have great pleasure in visiting her."

"I trust," said Emily, "my being of my aunt's household will not detract from the pleasure of your visit."

"There is a gentleness in my sister's nature that those of discernment must admire. There is an accomplishment in her mind that those of education must respect. And there is a niceness about her behaviour that those of spirit must tease. Were it not that she has warned me never to discover my partiality before being assured of its return I would confess I loved her dearly."

A blush of real happiness came to Emily's cheeks at these generous words.

"My warnings referred to attachments between the sexes, I think; not to those between sisters."

"You have already had one declaration from a sister this morning. I hesitate to burden you with another."

"One may be burdened with a false coin," said Emily, "but I have yet to learn that a golden guinea in one's purse can be a positive encumbrance."

"Then I will stop mocking and tell you straight out I love you. And if I am not high enough for Eversleigh you must bear to return here sometimes and be caressed and teased." Without further ado Penelope took her sister in her arms and embraced her most affectionately.

"I shall miss you sorely, dearest Penelope."

"And I shall miss you, my love. Let us confess as much to each other. Indeed we would be in a poor way if we were prevented from expressing what we *do* feel by the readiness with which Margaret expresses what she does *not*. I am considered a bad correspondent; but I think if you write to me, I will engage myself to answer."

"If you were coming with me on Wednesday my happiness would be great," said Emily.

"To be sure. It is a pity we have to be parted when we exercise such a good influence on each other. Were it not for the nice manners I have been taught in the past few weeks I would have told Margaret in the parlour that she had no reason to fear a separation from Mr Musgrave now that Miss Osborne was engaged and Miss Carr out of the district, which would have made her bad-tempered for the rest of the day. As for you, if you had not been somewhat coarsened by my company, you would have been preparing as expeditiously as possible to return to the refinement of Eversleigh instead of wasting your time clinging to me like this, with a mixture of tears and smiles on your sweet face."

"I must try and phrase it in a manner a little more in keeping with the truth, Penelope. You who have lived all your life with brothers and sisters will never fully understand the joy I have experienced in discovering someone I can love and trust and open my heart to without reserve. I must be happy because I am returning to my old home, but I must also be sad because I am leaving you behind."

"You are indeed a sweet person," said Penelope, giving her sister a final kiss. "And now there is one important matter we must discuss before you leave. Having accused me once of treachery with regard to that sad fellow Purvis, you must please run through a list of the young gentlemen in the neighbourhood on whom you feel you have a claim, so that I know the exact position with regard to each and do not offend you through ignorance."

"Indeed Penelope!" cried Emily, in haste. "I am far from – –"

"Pooh, my dear, you must not be shy with me. Let us go ahead without embarrassment. There are first the two Mr Tomlinsons. Mr James admittedly has not hitherto paid you much attention, but you may take it that as soon as he sees the order now on its way to him, and hears of your new situation, he would readily make amends for the past. Should he be at liberty between now and Wednesday morning you may even count on his calling; and if you ever return to Stanton, as I hope you will, he will assuredly see that you are given another opportunity to dine at the Larches. Come now, have you any claim on Mr James?"

"None at all," replied Emily. "Though by admitting as much I do not intend you to marry him yourself. You are far too good for the gentleman."

"You need be in no anxiety, my love. If you fail him he will return to Mary Edwards, who is the richest young lady of his near acquaintance."

"Alas, poor Sam!" cried Emily. "I have not given him a thought for days, and now I am to leave without seeing him."

"Alas, poor Sam indeed," agreed Penelope. "If it is fine tomorrow you must take your leave of Mrs Edwards in person and engage Mary as your correspondent. Should you be able to invite the daughter to Eversleigh that might incline the mother a little in our favour. As for the father, I can always run him down in the High Street to convince him of the propitiousness of an alliance with the family."

"I must certainly acknowledge Mrs Edwards's kindness to me in some way."

"I do not think *she* would see it in that light, my dear, but perhaps you meant something different. Let us return to our list. We next have Mr George Tomlinson. I have a weakness for his profession, which is that of the law; but the fact that at the last assembly he was prepared to dance publicly with an impecunious Miss Watson suggests that he will never rise as high in it as Robert or Purvis, both of whom I expect to end up as judges. What do you say of Mr George?"

"He is not for me."

"I am glad to hear it," replied Penelope. "Now we would ordinarily come to Mr Musgrave, but as he is at present engaged I will pass on in silence to Captain Hunter, Captain Styles and Mr Norton, whom habit forces me to consider together. It is here of course that I am most in danger. There is something about fair, pretty, scatter-brained creatures like myself and Miss Carr which exercises an almost irresistible fascination on junior officers. If I knew him better I would ask Colonel Beresford whether there was some peculiar military reason for the phenomenon. Be that as it may, the fact remains; and if you have designs on any of these dashing gentlemen, you must please let me know without false prudishness."

"I am without designs on any of them," answered Emily, merrily. "And could you attract Captain Hunter in my absence to the extent of making him neglect Mary Edwards, but without of course involving yourself in any permanent entanglement, you would earn my gratitude on behalf of my brother Sam."

"Before you met me you would never have made such an unladylike suggestion," said Penelope. "I will attribute it solely to your kindness in wishing to indulge me in what may be our last serious conversation, and herewith promise never to hold it against you. We now pass on to more dangerous ground. There is a handsome young nobleman living in a castle not very far distant from this spot called Lord Osborne. I do not suggest that he will transfer his regard from a sister to myself quite so readily as once did Mr Purvis. Nevertheless you are to go and I am to stay. So in spite of your blushes, my dear, I must ask your intentions towards the gentleman."

"Nay, Penelope, how can I reply to that!"

"Why, in as true a fashion as you can, my dear."

"Well then," said Emily, with scarlet cheeks, "*if* he had waited a few more weeks, and *if* he had continued to behave sensibly to me and courteously to my family – for that too I think important – I *might* have given him the answer he hoped for. But of course I cannot be sure."

"That is as clear an answer as I needed. There is but one more and my list is complete: a gentleman at Wickstead by the name of Howard. You see I do not limit you to Lord Osborne alone, for a lady must always be allowed a little latitude. There would be small amusement for the bystander if uncertainty about her final choice was not occasionally permitted to enter the story. What claim have you on the elegant Mr Howard?"

"None at all," answered Emily, firmly. "I hardly know the gentleman. I will confess to you that I once *almost* allowed myself to think foolishly about Mr Howard, who is an intelligent and in some ways an attractive man, but who has given me no encouragement whatsoever. We mentioned the gentleman the evening we shared a room in Dunford; and I mean it most seriously when I say I am glad you have made an opportunity, even as part of your jest, for me to correct any false impression I may then have given you. Penelope, after reflecting a good deal on the matter, I think it probable that Mr Howard returned to Wickstead while we were there, and on seeing the gig or being informed that we were within, retired again rather than meet us."

"The possibility had occurred to me," said Penelope, "and the only comment I can make is that if it be true I must rate Mr Howard's intelligence considerably lower than you do."

"If my conduct was slightly at fault, which it may perhaps have been, the correctness of his has taught me to amend it."

"Poof, my dear, what rubbish you talk! Your conduct could never be at fault. Mr Howard is a stupid dunce, and that is all there is to it. But I am happy to find there are no restraints on Elizabeth or myself save as regards Lord Osborne; for you may be assured that we humble folk do not aspire so high. He is yours as far as we are concerned."

"Dear Penelope, you are carrying your jest too far. I am not on those terms with the gentleman."

"I can jest no more, my sweet love. My mind is too full of your departure. It is seldom I give way to weeping, even in private, but I fear for once I am about to disgrace myself."

Emily saw with surprise that the smiling blue eyes were indeed full of tears before Penelope turned away in a belated effort to hide them. The sight almost brought her own to the surface again, when of a sudden the room was full of laughter. Penelope's movement had brought her to the window; she now stood beside it, well screened from below, looking down with an expression of the greatest delight on her face.

"He is come!" she cried, her tears forgotten. "It is more neatly fulfilled than Mr Edwards's most fortunate prophecy. He is come; and he is very, *very* wet."

"Who is come?"

"Whom did I promise you? Mr James Tomlinson, of course."

"He cannot have come on my account. It is not fifty minutes ago that I dispatched the notes."

"Not on *your* account, my dear. Do not flatter yourself. But on account of that order for so many guineas and the news that you are summoned back to Eversleigh to be your aunt's heiress. What is a hurried ride in the rain to one in search of a fortune? You must descend and thank him; that is the least you can do. Were I you, I should be *overwhelmed* by such *excessive* condescension, but I suppose you are too honest for such tricks."

"For shame on you!" cried Emily, part in fun and part in earnest.

"Alas it is true, my love. And I am such a complete artist I can play my part for my own satisfaction alone. But today I will be an audience for you, and you must divert me by being gratified in the *extreme* by Mr Tomlinson's *unexampled* courtesy. He will think you a very modest, sensible, well-behaved girl if you are."

"Oh Penelope," she cried, "who will be there in Eversleigh to talk nonsense to me?"

They went downstairs and were seated in the parlour by the time her sodden cavalier had attended to his horse and made himself fit for the company of ladies. He had been fortunate to encounter Miss Emily's messenger on the outskirts of Dunford, he explained, and had taken upon himself the honour of fulfilling her commission in person. He had no doubt that his mother would reply as soon as possible to Miss Emily's note, but meanwhile ventured to put Miss Emily's mind at rest by saying that his mother would not consider an engagement to dine should be allowed to interfere with a summons from Mrs O'Brien, for the former of course, could be repeated any time the neighbourhood was fortunate enough to be brightened by a second visit from Miss Emily. At this point he paused to take breath and hand over the guineas.

After a brief greeting to her sisters on entering the room Mr Tomlinson had addressed Emily to their complete exclusion. This was not because Mr Tomlinson, as Penelope had maliciously suggested, was consciously seeking a fortune. It was merely because to him, quite naturally and without any selfish motives whatsoever, those with money merited greater consideration than those without.

Mr Tomlinson, having got his breath again, went on to assure Emily that he would esteem it a favour if she would remember he was always at her service in any little matter; and that while he had no wish at all to bother a young lady with business he hoped Mrs O'Brien could be made aware of the fact that any transaction – – Here he sneezed suddenly; and Penelope, who had been listening to him with great attention, made a noise that began like a giggle and ended in a fit of coughing as she hurried from the room.

Emily wondered again what she would do at Eversleigh without Penelope to tease her, to talk nonsense to her, to love her, and to shock and divert her in such an undoubtedly unseemly manner.

15

Emily arrived in Wimpole Street on Wednesday morning in time to rest, go out in search of her aunt's ribbon, and change, before eating an elegant meal at the fashionable hour of six o'clock. The Seymours received her civilly. They had disapproved most strongly of Mrs Turner's second marriage, and though too well-bred to speak of the accident that had befallen Captain O'Brien with pleasure, they expressed their sympathy with his widow somewhat perfunctorily. Childless herself, Mrs Seymour had some nephews by the name of Turner who were, in her opinion, just as deserving of *Mr* Turner's money as *Mrs* Turner's niece. However, this was a grievance that had long since lost its sting; and in the past fourteen years Mrs Seymour had grown as fond of Emily as it was in her nature to be of one who was in no way essential to her comfort. That is to say, she was pleased to see Emily arrive, not sorry to see her go; frequently found herself admiring Emily's looks and behaviour when she was present, and seldom thought about her at all when she was absent.

After the meal Mr Seymour kindly examined the route, and gave it as his opinion that the journey from London to Eversleigh could not be accomplished by one in Emily's position in less than two and a half days. As Emily had never done it with her aunt in less than three she readily agreed. She was travelling from one loved person to another; and her emotions of both regret and anticipation were so strong that she was grateful for this interlude in which all behaviour was regulated by conventional courtesy – where any help she asked would be willingly accorded, but where no further demands would be made on her already divided heart.

By one o'clock on Saturday she was in Shrewsbury, and from there on the road was increasingly familiar. She leant eagerly forward in the chaise to get the first possible view of each successive landmark. Her excitement rose ever higher throughout this final hour of her journey; but when the carriage turned through the familiar lodge gates she let out a gasp of dismay. Could this wilderness be Eversleigh, which she had left barely four months ago? But it was indeed Eversleigh, where every tuft of grass, every clump of leaves, had once seemed individually known. A closer inspection showed that it was only the uncleared wrack of one autumn that littered the once tidy drives and paths and lawns; but the shock remained. Nor was it dispersed when she ran into a hall from which half the furniture had been removed and in which the rest stood where she least expected it. Then her aunt, so much greyer and more lined than she remembered her, appeared in the doorway, and a moment later she was in her arms.

"Oh aunt! Dearest aunt!" she sobbed, as the tears, which were not entirely tears of joy, rolled down her cheeks.

"I have been so foolish, Emily. Say you really forgive me."

"Oh aunt!" she said again, unable to give any other expression to her feelings than this single cry of anguished love.

"How glad, how *very* glad, I am to see you, my dearest Emily," said her aunt, and then herself gave way to tears.

It was some minutes before either of them were sufficiently recovered for conversation.

"Alas, how *changed* everything is," said Emily, at length.

"Do not say so, my dear," cried Mrs O'Brien. "I had hoped now you were arrived everything would be the same."

"It is so much bigger than I remember," said Emily, correcting herself hastily. "The parsonage is very small, and in comparison everything here appears enormous. Let us go into the drawing-room."

"Yes; they are waiting for us there."

"Who are waiting for us?" asked Emily, in alarm. "Dear aunt, I have been more than two days on the road, and am in no state to receive visitors."

"It is only Mr Childs and Mr Jones."

To her drawing-room at least, Mrs O'Brien had managed to restore something of its former elegance. The pianoforte and sofa, the tables and chairs, the carpets and curtains, were as Emily remembered them. Even her aunt's desk was in its familiar place. Two gentlemen rose up at her entry. They were both tall, thin and dressed in sombre clothes; but there the resemblance between them ended. Mr Jones was fair, and his vague blue eyes peered at the world with a kindly but somewhat anxious expression, as though hoping the onlooker would judge him as generously as he was prepared to judge the onlooker. His coat was patched and darned; it fitted neither his stooping shoulders, nor his long arms, for a stretch of naked wrist was always visible between his cuffs and his red, bony, restless hands. Emily saw none of his imperfections. He was her dear Mr Jones, with whom, and with whose second-best coat, she had been familiar since her earliest lessons.

Mr Childs's hair and eyes were black, and even his countenance was dark and gloomy. His coat came from the best tailor in the City of London, and if he had chosen to wear it as long as Mr Jones had worn his, it would still have fitted him to perfection. He bowed gravely to Emily; and Mr Jones, who had hurried forward with a great smile on his plain face and his long arms flapping loosely by his side, shuffled to a halt and performed an awkward bow himself. Emily acknowledged Mr Childs's greeting, and then impulsively ran to Mr Jones and kissed his worn cheek.

"Dear sir!" she cried. "I am so glad to see you!"

"Ah, Miss Emily! Thank you. I do not deserve . . . Dear Miss Emily!" Mr Jones pulled out a not very clean handkerchief, blew his nose, and wiped a stray tear from his eye.

Mr Childs had observed this latest manifestation of female vagary without surprise. He looked from the aunt to the niece and then shook his head gloomily.

"If I might have a word in private with Miss Emily I will not keep the carriage waiting ten minutes," he said.

"Surely tomorrow would be time enough," suggested Mrs O'Brien, in a supplicating tone.

"Madam," replied Mr Childs, in a voice void of all emotion save a sad patience, "I have now been absent from my desk on your affairs for some six weeks. Though always ready to help you to the best of my ability, six weeks appears to me an excessively long time."

He bowed again. Mr Jones extended his arm to Mrs O'Brien.

"Come, dear madam," he pleaded, and guided her gently from the room.

Mr Child opened his snuff box, snapped it shut, and addressed himself to Emily.

"I have not seen you since an unhappy event brought me here some two years ago. Since then much has happened. More by good fortune than good judgement the outcome is not as serious as it might have been, and instead of losing her entire fortune Mrs O'Brien is poorer than she was a few months ago by about three thousand, four hundred and sixty-seven pounds in rough calculation. You are a young girl, Miss Emily; but it has been my unfortunate experience that older people can act just as foolishly as young folk if they have a mind for it. I have therefore suggested to Mrs O'Brien, and she has agreed, that a certain proportion of her fortune should be made over to you, Mrs O'Brien retaining the right to the income as long as she is alive. It will not escape your notice that part of the temptation to which Mrs O'Brien has recently been exposed is thus being transferred to you. I was long a confidant of Mr Turner's and I feel it my duty to speak plainly on this point. You will possibly become the prey of fortune-hunters. They may not be as eager as they might otherwise have been in that you will not have the control of your money until Mrs O'Brien's death. Let us hope the event is long delayed, and that before it occurs you are securely married to a prudent and honourable gentleman in some respectable profession. That is all I have to say. I trust you will not take my discourse as intending any disrespect to Mrs O'Brien. Her intelligence compares very favourably with that of many for whom it is my lot to act. In conclusion I must add that chiefly through accident I have been able to save a respectable woman from a very melancholy fate. But unless you and Mrs O'Brien take warning from what has happened, distress, ruin and desolation are not avoided; they are merely postponed."

Here Mr Childs finished speaking. He looked mournfully for a moment at Emily, as though there was no real doubt in his mind that his most gloomy prophecies would in time be fulfilled; then he bowed and left the room.

It was not an occasion for gaiety, but with Mr Childs's departure an attempt was made by Mrs O'Brien, Emily and Mr Jones (who agreed to dine with them) to recapture a little of the innocent pleasure that had so often been theirs in the past. Emily gave an account of her journey, and after a short rest in her familiar room came downstairs with the mauve ribbon she had purchased for her aunt. It was exactly the shade Mrs O'Brien had had in mind, neither so dark as to be lost in the black, nor so light as to stand out in blatant contrast; and for some time all was brisk and lively. The candles were brought in early, Mr Jones built up a snug fire, and the curtains were drawn to hide the sodden leaves that lay unswept on the neglected lawns.

"I have one special piece of intelligence I must give you without further delay," said Emily, when Mrs O'Brien had finised praising the ribbon. "My sister Margaret is engaged to be married."

"Indeed!" cried her aunt. "How exceedingly interesting. But she is not the eldest, I think?"

"No; both Elizabeth and Penelope are older."

"That is not well arranged; but it sometimes happens when there is no mother. What is the gentleman's name?"

Emily told her. Her aunt seemed in special need of a little cheerful conversation, and for her sake Emily gave Mr Musgrave as good a character as her conscience allowed.

"Nine hundred a year!" said Mrs O'Brien. "That is more by three hundred and fifty than Lucy Waterman got, though to be sure we never considered her the most amiable of her family."

"We must not judge too hastily," said the charitable Mr Jones. "We must not judge too hastily. It is not my place to contradict you, dear madam, and I must agree that Miss Lucy did not perhaps have quite the easy manner of her brothers and sisters, for none of us is cast in the same mould. But I owe too much to the whole family, and particularly of course to her dear departed father, not to add that Miss Lucy felt keenly for the poor of the parish, and herself twice brought soup to my lodging when I was ill last winter."

"She was a high proud girl, with no reason at all for pride," said Mrs O'Brien. "Even you, Mr Jones, cannot deny that."

Thus pressed, Mr Jones could not avoid unwillingly admitting that at times, to those who did not know her well, Miss Lucy might perhaps have appeared, from shyness or possibly some other reason, not entirely innocent of giving the impression of being inclined to be, to put it bluntly, a trifle stiff. On her side, Mrs O'Brien admitted that Miss Lucy had behaved modestly enough during the farewell visit she had paid her, and then changed the subject.

"How did you find your poor father?" she asked.

"In truth, aunt, as far as his health was concerned I found him better than I expected. I had long pictured him in the same situation as Mr Waterman, who was confined to his bed half the year. That is not at all the case, for on no day that I was at Stanton did he fail to dress. It is want of spirits from which he chiefly suffers; and this I think is the cause of his seldom venturing beyond his book-room unless his duty requires it."

"Alas, he too has had much sorrow," said Mrs O'Brien. "He was greatly attached to my poor sister."

"It is indeed a sad thing to lose a loved one," agreed Mr Jones. "I think there are few afflictions to which we are exposed on earth that can cause deeper distress. It is not for me, who have never known the blessings of either wife or child, to minimize the pain of a sudden bereavement. But I suggest with all deference, dear madam, that upon reflection sorrow must give way to happier emotions. When we view the event in its true perspective, when we remember the joyful reunion to come, when we recall that the one we held so dear is no longer subject to aches of the flesh or sufferings of the spirit, we must surely find we have cause to rejoice, rather than lament."

"To be sure," agreed Mrs O'Brien, mournfully.

"What has happened now to Mrs Waterman?" asked Emily.

"She and her two youngest children have gone to her brother's, the other side of Shrewsbury," said her aunt.

Though no great intimacy had existed between Emily and Miss Lucy – who was nearest her in age of the late rector's family – the Miss Watermans and their brothers had been the only young people within walking distance whom Emily could visit in a social way. Mr and Mrs Turner had been acquainted with everyone of consequence in a wide neighbourhood; but, as Emily well knew, a call which required a drive in a carriage for its performance had something of ceremony about it which prevented its being too frequently repeated. She remembered the numerous unimportant comings and goings between Eversleigh and the parsonage and repressed a sigh.

"Has Mr O'Neil any family?" she asked.

"There is an unmarried daughter of some age between yours and mine, my dear," replied Mrs O'Brien. "As I have nothing against *her* I will not attempt to judge to which of us she is more closely allied. I visited them early this week and they returned the visit yesterday. In view of the way they have treated Mr Jones I have little inclination to pursue the acquaintance beyond what is essential for the well-being of the parish."

Mr Jones wrung his large hands together in a despairing effort to find something to praise in the conduct of the man who had deprived him of his small livelihood.

"We must consider both sides of the question, dear madam," he said anxiously. "We must fully consider the circumstances before we condemn him. As Miss Emily has just pointed out, Mr Waterman was confined to his bed the greater part of the winter months. He was unable to perform his duty here without my humble assistance. From what I have seen of Mr O'Neil I should judge him an extremely healthy and active man."

"The parish is scattered enough to require a curate, and the living is rich enough to afford one."

"Much good may be done by an energetic man fortunate enough to possess a horse," pleaded Mr Jones.

"And much harm may be done by a grasping man unfortunate enough to lack a conscience," replied Mrs O'Brien.

"He has a most melodious voice," cried Mr Jones, desperately. "I was as struck by his reading of the lesson on Sunday as I was gratified by the attention the congregation paid him. Nor was his sermon unedifying. He is qualified by both nature and education for the responsible position he holds. Before we sum his faults we must remember that none of us is perfect, dear madam."

"Ah, Mr Jones," said Mrs O'Brien, feeling for her handkerchief, "you need not remind me of my faults. For some days now I have been conscious of little else. I have shown myself a vain, foolish, frivolous creature, I well know."

"Nay, dear lady," cried Mr Jones, springing up in the anguish of his spirit. "I did not intend any criticism of *you*, whose bounty has perhaps prevented me begging my bread in the streets of London. It was to *myself* I referred. He had but to look at me to discern blemishes which would amply explain his not wishing for my assistance in the parish."

"You dispraise yourself too much, sir," said Emily. "I have known you walk five miles through wind and rain to cheer a sick child with a tale."

Quite overcome, Mr Jones retired into the darkest corner of the room to blow his nose.

"You are too good," he murmured. "You are too young, too kind, to see as the world sees. I assure you the world judges very differently."

"It was you who taught me, sir, that on some matters on which one has intimate knowledge oneself the world's opinion may be safely disregarded."

"It is my fault," said Mrs O'Brien, again in tears. "Had I remembered my responsibilities you would now occupy the position your labours deserve."

Fortunately dinner was then announced, and an end was drawn to a scene that was growing increasingly painful to all three. It was clear to Emily that more was changed at Eversleigh than the outward appearance of things. Labour and proper attention would soon restore tidiness to the estate and elegance to the rooms; occupation and company might in time revive her aunt's spirits. But in what manner could they re-establish the calm and decorous order of their lives that had grown up during the years Mr Turner had watched over them, that had survived his death, holding them still to their settled and habitual ways, and that had been shattered asunder by her aunt's second marriage? Mr Jones could not remain for ever dependent on Mrs O'Brien's charity; some proper station must in time be found for him, and he would leave the district. Once a week, and more often when there were parish matters to be discussed, Mrs O'Brien must be reminded of an enduring consequence of her folly. Emily herself must sometimes recall how she had been dismissed from her home. Things would not be as they had once been, in spite of her return. Would not both of them, thought Emily, be as restless and as unsettled in the future as they had been calm and contented in the past?

Their dinner passed quietly enough until Mr Jones realized he was wearing his old coat. The discovery distressed him so much –

not on account of vanity, for he had none, but because of the unintentional disrespect he had shown his hostess – that he quite lost his appetite for the latter part of the meal. On their return to the drawing-room, Mrs O'Brien requested a little music. Emily went to the pianoforte followed by Mr Jones. She was sadly out of practice; but she did not think her aunt would be over-critical of her performance, and she looked through the songs till she found a simple and familiar air. She had played the opening bars before Mr Jones interrupted her.

"A charming song, my dear Miss Emily," he said. "A most charming song. But not for my voice."

"I remember this as one of your favourite songs," replied Emily. "You have sung it a hundred times in this very room."

"I mean the words," said Mr Jones, blushing at the deceit he was forced to practise. "I fear I am no longer certain of the words."

"They are written down, sir."

"Please, Miss Emily," pleaded Mr Jones, "let me choose another."

While he searched the music Emily examined the song he had rejected. There were no notes in it beyond the range of Mr Jones's gentle baritone. The words surely were without objection, or it would never have come into her aunt's drawing-room. Then she understood: it was an Irish air, and she had once accompanied Captain O'Brien in it when he was but a new acquaintance at Eversleigh. Emily sighed ruefully. If such care had to be exercised over the choice of a song, life in her old home would be difficult indeed.

Emily played till she was weary, Mr Jones sang till he was hoarse, and Mrs O'Brien tried to pretend to herself that all was as it used to be. At last Mr Jones, who had a two-mile walk in front of him, took his leave. There were no horses at Eversleigh so Mrs O'Brien could not offer her carriage. But the offer would not have been accepted by Mr Jones. It had been made with regularity during the past twenty years, and during the past twenty years it had been refused with the same regularity. He appreciated the courtesy, it was more than he deserved, Mr and Mrs Turner were generous to a degree; but his over-shoes were strong, his health was good, and

he would not be the means of requiring a coachman and two horses
to perform a double journey merely for the sake of giving him a little
more comfort on a single one. On one occasion indeed, when the rain
was particularly heavy, Mr Turner, without consulting Mr Jones,
had ordered his carriage to the door and himself escorted Mr Jones
to it. Mr Jones was driven away leaning out of the window and protesting through the rain that though deeply sensible of the kindness,
it was in his humble opinion by no means essential, as he had no
doubt but that the inclemency was only a passing shower. It was unfortunately still raining the next morning when Mr Jones walked
the two miles up to the stables, and the two miles back, to inquire
after the safe return of the coachman and his horses. This gave him
a chill; and Mr Turner, who was a rational man, ordered Mr Jones
an umbrella from London instead of attempting to repeat his
kindness.

It was the same umbrella that Emily now fetched for him, with his
stout over-shoes, his worn hat and his shabby overcoat.

"Really, Miss Emily," said Mr Jones, somewhat embarrassed,
"such attention is not necessary."

She wondered whether, without impropriety, she might refer to
the misfortunes that had befallen him since they had last met.
Affection for her old master quickly conquered her scruples.

"I fear, dear sir," she said, "you have had a hard time of it these
past two months."

"Believe me, Miss Emily," he answered earnestly, "not for a lot
would I have forgone the experience. It has opened my eyes to the
true goodness and kindness of my fellow creatures. I am one who
has found it more blessed to receive than to give, if I may say so
without disrespect. In the humblest cottage in the parish I have been
pressed to sup, to sleep, to live if need be. It was not because I
wished to leave those I loved that I made my plan to proceed to
London; it was because I feared to become a burden on people who
have not always everything they need themselves."

"You have loved and served them," said Emily. "They would
love and serve you in return."

"I am very fortunate in my lot," replied Mr Jones. "There is
said to be much wickedness in the world, but I have not yet met
with it."

Before such simple faith she could only express her joy at having re-encountered her dear master.

She bid him good night and returned to her aunt with a full heart. Her first evening in her old home, she confessed to herself, had not been quite as happy as she had expected. Eversleigh, alas, had changed.

16

Many were the conversations that took place between Emily and her aunt during the ensuing two weeks. Some of these necessarily concerned Stanton; and great was Mrs O'Brien's surprise when she became aware of the true situation of her niece's family. Mrs O'Brien of course knew that her sister had made a poor match, and that Mr Watson had nothing beyond his living. But she had dwelt so long in luxury herself, and Mr Waterman's house had so little lacked comfort, that she had forgotten how scanty some livings could be.

"No pianoforte, no curate and no close carriage!" she cried. "And three daughters! It is no wonder that they are not yet married."

"If you are agreeable, aunt, it would be a great happiness to me to have my sisters visit here."

"Why yes, my dear," she answered kindly. "I must certainly do something for them when we are properly settled again."

Mrs O'Brien talked much of what she would do when they were properly settled again. More than once she referred to her past mistakes, but in general rather than particular terms, and more than once she assured Emily that she was a changed woman, that she would be stricter with herself in future, that she had determined to perform her duties and responsibilities with the same regularity as the late Mr Turner. Full of such resolves she would sit at her desk with lists in front of her for as long as twenty minutes. Having studied the lists and twice mended her pen, she would sigh, get up and walk restlessly to the window, through which she could see the top of the church tower beyond the leafless trees.

"If only there was some way of removing Mr O'Neil,' she would say; and her niece grew tired of explaining that there was none.

It was soon apparent to Emily, as indeed had been her suspicion since reading the muddled letter that had brought her home, that in spite of her protestations, her aunt's character was unchanged. Mrs O'Brien would never repeat the terrible mistake she had made; but that was the limit to what experience had taught her. Her heart was still good; and her understanding was still imperfect. Her spirits were now very low, but she was the woman she had long been: indulgent, sometimes foolish, full of worthy intentions and for the most part incapable of the application necessary to carry them to fulfilment. At Eversleigh all her meditations led her eventually to her own folly and its consequences. Had she been of a stronger character she would have realized this and triumphed over it. As it was, she was aware that even now her niece had returned, life did not resume its accustomed tranquil flow, while the reason for this still escaped her.

"I have been wondering, Emily," she said one day, "whether we might not perhaps be advised to spend the winter in Bath."

"Why aunt?"

"I have not been feeling well of late. I do not mean I have been feeling ill – but I have not been feeling cheerful. A change of air might do me good."

"Would you feel able to leave Eversleigh, madam?"

"Once we are properly settled again," replied Mrs O'Brien. "You are become a very beautiful girl these last two years, Emily, and I must not hide you here for ever. Or there is London; what do you say to London? Mrs Seymour could find us an apartment, and would be pleased to have charge of you for a few months. She made the promise many years ago."

"I would be an ungrateful niece," said Emily, with a smile, "if I agreed to a proposal that involved my leaving you by yourself each evening."

"Indeed, my dear, I should have company enough; and a novel interest of that kind is just what I require." Mrs O'Brien turned until the tower of the parish church came into her view. "My *duties* are here, I know," she confessed. "But my *interests* are here no longer. You are old enough to advise me, Emily. If you think we should pass the winter at Eversleigh you must tell me. You could invite one of your sisters to make up for the absence of the Watermans, and I would endeavour to fortify myself with the knowledge I was doing my duty. What do you say?"

"You are putting a great responsibility on me."

"Is it not better that we should share the responsibility?" replied her aunt. "I did not do so well by myself, and as it will one day be yours it is right that you should prepare yourself to meet it."

This was so true in itself, and so seriously expressed, that Emily felt it would be unworthy to put forward the pleas of youth and inexperience. If her aunt required her advice, no foolish modesty must prevent her giving the best advice in her power.

"Let me reflect on this for a few days, aunt," she said. "I would not like to speak on such a subject without consideration."

For a long time after this conversation Emily was silent. A project very dear to her heart, a project that had hitherto seemed impossible of fulfilment but which now appeared almost attainable, occupied her thoughts.

The following day brought her two letters. The first she read was from her brother Robert. He had apparently been fully informed about recent events, and his letter weighed the financial benefits she could expect as Lord Osborne's wife against those she could hope for as her aunt's heiress. But even this was not all, for the burden of Robert's advice was that she should secure herself in both positions.

Emily could not read such pages without blushing for the writer; and the knowledge that the writer was her brother caused her the deepest distress. She determined then that she would take no willing part in making Robert and Jane acquainted with her aunt; and that if such a meeting was inevitable she would fully inform her of Robert's character before it took place. But the letter could not be preserved for that purpose; it was too base to be kept; and Emily burnt it on the spot before opening the other, which was of a very different kind.

Stanton,
December 18th.

My dear love,

Before you left I engaged myself to reply to your letters and you must put it down to a stubborn determination to perform what I have promised that I am writing to you a mere two days after receiving your communication of the twelfth. If you are prepared to add a *small* amount of affection as an additional motive, you would not be *altogether* wrong; but as you may not yet be used to my peculiar style of composition (for it was, I think, a week or two before my conversation ceased to make you a trifle uneasy) I must explain that the *small* above is in truth large, and the *altogether* quite out of place. This is positively my last explanation and you must make the best you can of what follows. I am glad you had a safe journey, trust you are well, and am quite convinced you are behaving with perfect rectitude and reproving all excesses you encounter – if indeed you do encounter any in the elegant society in which you now find yourself. But there is little I can make sport of in your letter, and if, as I think probable, you were a little homesick for the quarrelling confusion of Stanton when you wrote, I hope that it is now passed, and that you are your sweet, happy self again. To be sure I will tell you *all* that has occurred. LADY OSBORNE HAS CALLED. (You will agree that this deserves capital letters.) We were fortunately warned by the obliging Mr Musgrave of the honour in store for us, so that Elizabeth and I had time to remove the flour from our elbows, (I was busy watching her make short-cake,) order the best parlour to be prepared, and arrange our dress, before she arrived in company with her son. With an openness I admired but was unable to emulate, Elizabeth informed her of her morning's occupation, and such was her ladyship's interest that I was on the point of asking Nanny to join us when I was engaged myself in an absorbing conversation about horses with Lord Osborne. Her ladyship would most certainly have joined in had not the stern look her son gave her kept her talking politely to Elizabeth. Her parting speech alone is worthy of a letter. She understood that Miss Margaret and Miss Penelope were in the habit of sleeping with Mrs Edwards on the night of an assembly, while Miss Watson stayed at Stanton with her father. If Mr Watson could be left for the space of three or four hours during the evening itself, Lady Osborne would be very pleased if Miss Watson would join her card-table for that period on the next return. She would undertake to fetch her and bring her back at the hours Miss Watson herself chose. It was *my* turn to stay at home, my sweet, but who were we to contradict the arrangements Lady Osborne was

[165]

so kind as to make for us? Elizabeth went upstairs somewhat breathlessly. On being told who was below my dear father *came down*, but more, I think, from curiosity to see the gentleman than from courtesy towards the lady. Nevertheless it was done: permission was given and the invitation accepted. He has seldom had more grateful (or more awed) daughters.

I have still more to say and have little space for the ball. Elizabeth, who in other circumstances would rather have been dancing, sat with Lady Osborne, Mrs Blake and Mr Howard. Lord Osborne stood up with Margaret, Mary Edwards and myself – in turn of course. I believe if Sam had been there he would have stood up with him, to show his feelings towards the family. Captain Hunter, Captain Styles and Mr Norton did their duty. Mr Edwards won and said it was a very gay ball.

Mr Musgrave is purchasing Millington Farm which we pass every time we go to Dunford. It is a bright, pleasant house, but Margaret is somewhat ashamed of the name and I expect it to become Musgrave Castle within the near future. As we lie midway between this and the other we see much coming and going of the two gentlemen. Mr Tom's has somewhat less land than Lord Osborne's, but a convenient amount for its size, neither too much nor too little. I am surprised that our future brother has shown so much sense, but suspect he has temporarily borrowed some from his friend, who has once or twice seemed a trifle distraught since you left. It may be this friend who is really responsible for the plans that are afoot for Millington. The meadows are to support neither Italian peach-trees, Guernsey cattle nor Havana tobacco: They are to grow corn and turnips and hay, and feed Shorthorns like the rest of the land hereabout. Perhaps it is because one knows them better that one expects one's family to be more foolish than one's neighbours, and so lays oneself open to so many pleasant surprises.

I have left the Tomlinsons' dinner-party to the end, because it is of least interest, though I am now conscious it occurred before all of what is set out above. You will never guess the names of the three gentlemen invited to meet us, so I will tell you without further delay; a Captain Hunter, a Captain Styles and a Mr Norton – all very gentleman-like young men belonging to the regiment stationed in the town. They made a good impression on me and I trust we meet them again. Mary Edwards was there as well, so perhaps but *two* of the gentlemen were invited for the *three* Miss Watsons, for I suppose young ladies without portions must not expect more than two-thirds of an officer in times of shortage. We would have been thirteen at table if all the family had been present, which Mary's father would never have forgiven when he came to hear about it, so Charlotte Tomlinson had to stay in her room with a cold. Anyone but Mrs Tomlinson would have invited Mr Musgrave and allowed poor Charlotte a proper meal; but even his engagement has not permitted her to forgive his trifling with her elder daughter last spring – if anything it has made it appear more culpable. Perhaps when we are mothers of marriageable daughters ourselves we shall understand. You are forgotten by no one; indeed the news of your departure excited considerably more interest than did the news of your arrival. I send you my love, and so would Elizabeth if she were not plucking fowls in the kitchen and so ignorant of her opportunity.

Your devoted and very affectionate sister,

Penelope Watson.

Forgive me, my dear, but I must add that the gentleman loves you and almost deserves you. If you could see your way to making him happy you would make me happy too, for there is an unpretentious honesty about him I more and more admire.

Emily's mind was made up before she reached the postscript to the letter. She ran to the drawing-room, where she found her aunt at her desk.

"Are you busy, dear aunt?" she said. "May I talk to you?"

"I have plenty to do, but no heart with which to do it. Pray talk to me as long as you like."

"It is on the subject we discussed yesterday."

Mrs O'Brien left her desk and came to the sofa.

"You think that we should spend the winter here?" she said, with an expression of resignation on her face.

"No aunt, I do not think that. It will come as a shock to you perhaps, but I think we should leave Eversleigh for good."

"For *good*!" cried Mrs O'Brien. "I should never consent to that."

"There was a time when you intended it," replied Emily, gently.

"That was when I had forgotten what I owed to Mr Turner. I am surprised that you, Emily, should encourage me to do so now."

"Dear aunt, my uncle desired your welfare beyond anything else in the world. If your continued residence here were not compatible with your welfare, he would not demand it. Neither of us can have doubts on that. There is much to do at Eversleigh, but it is not done because you have no heart for it. Action is forestalled by unhappy memories and mournful meditations."

"When we are properly settled," began Mrs O'Brien, and then stopped.

"Let us most earnestly ask ourselves whether we shall ever again be properly settled *here*. My uncle left us settled, and while we continued as though still under his direction all was well. I think it would be difficult indeed for you and me to bring things to the state he left them, and to us any other state will always seem short of what is desirable. That is the point I wish to make. You have spoken of a change of air and a new interest. The plan I would suggest provides both."

"What is your plan?"

"First I must admit that to *me* it has many and important advantages. I have tried to discount these when thinking of your welfare, and I acknowledge them now so that you may accord them the weight they deserve when you yourself consider the proposal. I suggest that you and I remove permanently to Stanton."

"To *Stanton*!"

"Yes, aunt. There is a house there but a few minutes' walk from the parsonage called Stanton Lodge. I went over it in company with Margaret and Mr Musgrave. It was too large for them, though it is smaller than Eversleigh; and there is not more land than is pleasant for the sake of privacy. The front of the house has a charming elevation and the prospect from that side is good. The house itself, however, is in bad repair and would need attention; that I think might appeal to you, for what we achieve there will always be in contrast to its present condition, whereas what we achieve here must always be set against the perfection we both remember. So much for the *house*. It is more difficult for me to set the attractions of the *neighbourhood* in the correct perspective. Here there is now no one we can visit in the course of a morning's walk. Mr Jones, of course, can visit us; but that is an indulgence which must quickly come to an end. Very soon, I fear, he will entreat you to help him to a situation, and it is not likely that you will find him one near-by. At Stanton there is my father, Elizabeth and Penelope. My father does not often visit, and not a great deal is to be expected from him in the way of companionship; Elizabeth is frank and kind; she is a ready talker, and will not displease you. Penelope I hope you will love as I love. I learnt today that Mr Musgrave has purchased a house a mile away. As I have told you, he is a man who appears to advantage at social gatherings, and he is generally considered agreeable. At Wickstead, there is Mrs Blake who will certainly visit us; and at Dunford there is Mrs Edwards. She is a very respectable woman, and her house has all the elegance you would expect to find in one situated as it is. An important neighbour would be Lady Osborne, whose son is a friend of Mr Musgrave's. I do not know that you would have a great deal in common with her, as her chief interest seems to be in dogs and horses; but I think she would pay you the courtesy you would look for. There are others, dear aunt; I cannot list them all. There would be a variety of company close at hand. My father is not rich; and for that and its consequences you must be prepared. You were so kind the other day as to say that you might perhaps do something for my sisters. If we go to Stanton Elizabeth and Penelope would repay you with much that you lack here – company, conversation, and cheerfulness. And if we go to Stanton I shall have all those I love close to me."

Emily stopped. She had said what was in her heart; her eyes were bright and her cheeks were flushed with the sincerity of her feelings. To her the plan gave almost everything she desired. If it were fulfilled she would possess at the same time all that was best in her two homes. She was only afraid that partiality had blinded her judgement, and that the benefits she saw accruing to her aunt would not exist in the view of another.

"Dearest Emily!" cried Mrs O'Brien. "Why did you not suggest this two years ago?"

"But I could not suggest it then. I did not know my family and we were still settled here."

"To be sure, but it would have saved me much misery. I will

write now to Mr Childs and your father. And to my cousins also, for if the house needs repair we will wait in London for it to be made ready. Eversleigh has become a reproach to me, Emily. That is the truth of the matter. Even your return has not made me happy here."

"Pray think it over, madam! I am glad you are not displeased, but it is not a matter to be decided swiftly."

"I thought it over while you were speaking. The scheme gives me the new interest I so urgently require. Later you can tell me its disadvantages and we can conspire together to overcome them. At the moment I can see nothing but what is of advantage to both of us."

"You will not forget Mr Jones?" Emily ventured to remind her. "We should not leave here until some arrangement has been made for him."

"I shall never again forget Mr Jones, my dear. I am going to ask your father if he would be prepared to have an assistant in his parish."

"Alas, aunt, my father is poor. The living is a meagre one, and however willing to comply with your wishes, he would lack the power. It is essential you do not mislead yourself on this point. There is but a humble parsonage with a number of small rooms. For servants there are only Nanny, two maids and James, who grooms the old mare, cuts the wood, milks the cows, and grows the vegetables. There is a small plot between the house and the road in which Elizabeth has planted flowers and herbs; there are some shabby stables at the back, and some neglected fields beyond. There is plenty of cheerfulness; but if you expect great elegance or refinement you will be disappointed and will perhaps blame me."

"Your father is my brother, Emily. He is my dear sister's husband. You have suggested the scheme; be content to leave its details to your foolish aunt. But why you did not suggest it two years ago I shall never be able to understand."

17

Mr Childs thoroughly approved of a move that would bring Mrs O'Brien within a quarter of a mile of her nearest male relative; and some four weeks after this conversation Emily and her aunt were established in a very comfortable apartment in Portman Square. There Mrs O'Brien attended to problems arising over furniture and servants; and there Mr James and Mr George Tomlinson addressed the many letters they found it necessary to write about the purchase and repair of Stanton Lodge. On strictly business matters they wrote to Mr Childs, but neither Mr James, nor even the more adventurous Mr George, was so neglectful of the future as to fail to keep Mrs O'Brien personally informed of all he was doing on her behalf.

Emily had every reason to be pleased with the results of her suggestion. The removal from Eversleigh had restored Mrs O'Brien's happiness; and the undertaking of her new enterprise had brought back her self-respect. For it is somewhat difficult for a rich and independent woman, treated with deference by members of both sexes, to retain a poor opinion of herself for very long. Not since they had left Eversleigh had Emily listened to a recital of her aunt's weaknesses, or heard anything of her determination to be more strict with herself in the future.

Penelope was engaged for a lengthy visit to London as soon as Mr and Mrs Tom Musgrave left for Tunbridge Wells; and greatly to Emily's surprise her father accompanied her. Mr Watson, however, stayed in Portman Square but three nights. He had himself suggested the journey, in order, he said, to pay his respects to the sister who had already done much for his family and who had promised to do more. His means were limited; by his exertions alone could he show his gratitude; and if those exertions proved somewhat less exhausting in the performance than he had anticipated no one was more surprised than Mr Watson.

He spent much of his stay closeted with Mrs O'Brien, and on his return home (under Mr Jones's care) took the first walk round his meadows in many years. Robert, he admitted to Elizabeth afterwards, had been right in one respect; the land was capable of improvement. A stout horse was acquired, the builders from Stanton Lodge repaired his barns and stables, and a young and energetic man was put under James. Later still, when Mrs O'Brien had made her final removal, her very comfortable coach found its way to the back-yard of the parsonage. His sister, Mr Watson explained, had said that her new chaise would be all that she and Emily would require in the way of a carriage in the future. While he did not intend to change to any great extent his accustomed habits, it would perhaps help to further the recent unexpected improvement in his health if he sometimes met his old friends. Perhaps on one day in the following week Elizabeth would arrange for a pair of horses from the White Hart so that he could visit Dunford in comfort.

It must not be supposed that Mr Watson grew suddenly worldly. For many years the simple pleasure he gained from his occasional excursions remained a source of surprise to him. Once or twice towards the end of his life he did indeed wonder whether his long mourning for his wife (that lasted in all some ten or twelve years), had not been at times a little selfish; then he would remember that his health had been so very poor until about the time of Mrs O'Brien's arrival in the neighbourhood that even if he had felt the inclination for company earlier he would not have been able to indulge it.

Nothing marred the joy of Emily and Penelope during their stay in London. Though Mrs Seymour found one rather a rattle, that one was not always unamusing, and the good looks of both could not be denied. They possessed another important quality in Mrs Seymour's eyes: they were of an exceptionally even temper. To whatever Mrs Seymour proposed, be it an invitation to a ball or merely an airing in her chariot, they would readily agree, subject only to Mrs O'Brien's permission. They were happy in each other's company; and Mrs Seymour, who studied the surface of life with such very close attention, judged them truly tasteful girls for seeming so happy in hers.

The two sisters were one day seated by themselves in Portman Square, waiting for Mrs O'Brien to return from a visit to a friend, when they heard a knock on the front door. It wanted but an hour to dinner and they did not expect a caller; but after a short pause footsteps approached, their door was opened and to their surprise Lord Osborne entered the room. For a moment he did indeed seem a little abashed at his daring. Reassured by their civil greeting, however, he made a passably good story of his being in London, wishing to pay his respects to his new neighbour, and then, on hearing she was not at home, being unable to resist the pleasure of informing Miss Penelope and Miss Emily Watson that their relations at both Millington and Stanton were yesterday well.

It was but the second time Emily had been in his company since the walk with Margaret and Mr Musgrave. The recollection caused her a moment's confusion; but she quickly recovered. The circumstances, she told herself, were very different. Then, she had been almost a stranger in a new home, and in some doubts about the duration of her stay in the district. Now, she and her aunt would shortly be established as his nearest neighbours of consequence, only excepting the inhabitants of Wickstead Rectory.

"Then you have heard the story of our proposed removal, my lord?" she said.

"I heard the news some weeks back, and it gave me great pleasure. I am glad Stanton Lodge is to be occupied again; and I no longer feel any scruples at having taken over the land, as I am told the arrangement suits Mrs O'Brien. Your sisters must be happy indeed."

"We are, my lord," Penelope answered, with a smile. "To begin with we were somewhat apprehensive at the thought that we were to be offered an example of elegant living almost on our own doorstep. Then we recollected the kindness of my sister Emily's heart, and are trusting to this that our rusticity will never be shown up by too obvious a contrast."

"For shame, Penelope!" cried Emily, blushing. "How could you say such a thing? His lordship might think you were serious."

[173]

"He has met me more than once before, my dear, and must surely by now be used to my extravagance."

"I am wondering whether it is that," replied Lord Osborne, "or whether it is I myself who am meant, rather than the family at the parsonage."

"Nay, my lord!" began Penelope hastily, and then stopped. "My lord," she continued, somewhat pink in the cheeks, "you are altogether too apt a pupil, if I may say so. I am more accustomed to teasing others than to being teased myself; and I am now so ashamed that I doubt whether I shall open my lips for the remainder of the afternoon."

"We are three very close neighbours," said Lord Osborne, with evident satisfaction. "There are consequently a number of maxims which lay down how we should behave to one another, but I cannot recollect any that advocate *silence*."

"Perhaps it is after all as well," replied Penelope. "For though it is an employment in which one can excel merely by keeping quiet, it is also that for which I have shown least inclination since I first went to school."

"There are more maxims that tell us of the *importance* of being on good terms with our neighbours, than there are those that tell us how to *achieve* or *preserve* those good terms," said Emily, with special emphasis. "We three are happy in having achieved harmony, but we are like to be neighbours for the greater part of our lives. Let us resolve not to hazard our harmony rashly, and hope that we shall be as happy in preserving it."

Penelope smiled; but the gentleman gave her a look which told her he had taken her warning with the seriousness she had intended.

"I trust it will not be through any careless action of *mine* that we fall out," he replied.

"You are come from the country, my lord," she continued, more gaily. "The first duty of a neighbour in such circumstances is to tell us the gossip which we have been so unfortunate as to miss."

"I would have done so on my arrival had it not concerned yourself. The chief topic of conversation in Wickstead, Stanton and Millington, and indeed throughout the greater part of Dunford, is the rehabilitation of Stanton Lodge and the approaching arrival of Mrs O'Brien and her niece."

"And throughout the remaining part of Dunford?"

"I fear that the only item I can offer besides a general satisfaction at the continued high price of corn, is one which concerns me. However, since you required gossip of your friends, Miss Emily, I must tell you what I can. For the past four weeks Mr Edwards has been prophesying my marriage."

This was not very welcome intelligence to Emily. Nor was it of a kind to which she could make any immediate reply. Penelope, however, readily agreed with Lord Osborne, who was smiling broadly.

"It is a matter about which I omitted to inform my sister," she said, with great amusement. "But if he is to be believed there is no hope for you."

"Why so?" asked Emily, in a small voice.

"According to what I understand of Mr Edwards's philosophy, accidents occur in threes," said Lord Osborne, "the second more serious than the first, and the third more serious than the second. Having attended Tom Musgrave on his marriage to Miss Margaret, and having given away my sister to Colonel Beresford, there is nothing for it but to be married myself very shortly."

"Indeed you must do what you can, my lord," cried Penelope, "for it would be unkind in the extreme to make Mr Edwards doubt the predictability of fate. At the moment, when the portents in which he believes inform him that the future is inauspicious, he can to some extent guard against it by wearing a green button-hole, or stubbing his toe on the doorstep, or exposing himself to the night air and developing a severe cold. But if his science is discredited he will be left as rudderless as ordinary mortals, with no more than his common sense, his conscience, and the conventions of society by which to regulate his conduct."

"If I thought you were talking seriously I should point out that with three such guides a man can come to little harm," said Emily.

"I can think of only one better, my dear," said Penelope, "but to spare your modesty I will not mention it. And before his lordship has time to disentangle that, I will swiftly inquire whether the business that brought him to London is successfully concluded, which gives him the opportunity of describing that business if he so desires, or briefly answering yes or no if he prefers."

"I will willingly describe it, Miss Penelope; and with your permission I will include a short account of a most interesting conversation that occurred in its course. I have been to Tattersalls, with the object of improving the line of my hunters. After that I went to Benson's Stables in search of a mare more in keeping with a lady of my mother's age. I trust you will not convict me of impertinence when I confess that I got into conversation with one of Mrs O'Brien's people at the second establishment. Without at all intending to pry into the man's business, I learnt that among other commissions he was buying some horses suitable for a young lady – for Mrs O'Brien's niece in fact. I expressed myself surprised, as I had once heard it stated that the young lady did not ride. He contradicted me flatly, and in no very civil terms. He implied that I was not only guilty of doubting his word, which was a comparatively minor matter; but that I was also questioning his horsemanship, which was a great deal more serious – for he himself had taught the young lady to ride, and had ridden with her since she was six years old."

Here he stopped; and Emily hung her head, aware that the falsehood of a statement to which her impatience had once provoked her had been discovered.

"And may one who is merely an outsider in all this inquire its moral?" asked Penelope, who had not been present when riding had previously been discussed between her companions.

"I had not intended my story to contain a moral," said Lord Osborne. "And indeed the only moral I can extract from it is that when one has been guilty of an error of taste one should forget the circumstances of one's blunder as soon as possible, which is perhaps not exactly what is meant by a moral. I was thinking of the future rather than of the past. If at any time any of the Miss Watsons find themselves mounted I shall be honoured if they will remember that my grounds are always open to them. Apart from myself they will often find another enthusiastic horseman there ready to make them welcome."

"And who is that, my lord?" asked Emily, conscious of little but the generosity of the remarks that preceded his invitation.

"Have you forgotten Charles Blake? He has recently constructed a steeple-chase course on which he spends much of his time. I would not advise you to follow him over his jumps, but if you can get him away from that particular corner, he will show you some pleasant rides through the plantations."

The two sisters had hardly thanked him when Mrs O'Brien entered the room, and the conversation became a little more formal. There was no doubt that Lord Osborne intended to make the best possible impression on the lady. He referred to his existing acquaintanceship with Mr Watson and his daughters, to which he was frank enough to attribute *part* of the pleasure of his call, but he was also at pains to point out that he had wished to meet the new mistress of Stanton Lodge as early as possible. He was proceeding directly to within two or three miles of the house, and was entirely at her service if there were any messages to be taken. Mrs O'Brien was concerned that he was in danger of missing his dinner. It was already dusk, nothing was to be gained by leaving before the moon was up; would he not do them the honour of dining with them? Lord Osborne regretted having to refuse the first invitation he had received from Mrs O'Brien, but the state of his dress left him no alternative. To which Mrs O'Brien replied that if that was indeed the sole reason for his hesitation he could set his mind at rest. The meal was to be a family one, as her nieces had been at a ball to a late hour the previous night. With his permission she would hasten it and they would sit down as they were. If, however, he would prefer to leave – for she admitted that she herself would not feel easy with a three- or four-hour journey in front of her – she would not attempt to keep him. At this point his lordship, doubtless thinking he had done all that was required of him in the way of politeness, said yes, in point of fact he would be very pleased to dine with them.

A ball had been mentioned, and it was not long before Lord Osborne informed Mrs O'Brien that two weeks from that day brought them to the second Tuesday in March and the last ball of the season in Dunford. As one who had been regular in his attendance for the length of the winter he trusted Mrs O'Brien would be settled in Stanton by the date mentioned so that her nieces could be present. The lady did not hold out much hope, and his lordship forgot himself so far as to give vent to a sigh. However, dinner was then announced and he ate such a meal as even his mother would have approved of, and which certainly convinced Mrs O'Brien that his health was in no immediate danger. She noticed also that while he *spoke* more to Penelope than to Emily, he *looked* more at Emily than at Penelope; from which she drew her silent and by no means unpleasing conclusions.

Lord Osborne could not sit with them long; very soon after dinner he departed, his head full of thoughts for the future, a few of which – such as his hope that Mrs O'Brien would shortly be acquainted with his mother – he was able to express aloud. Mrs O'Brien, as her custom was, then delivered judgement on her visitor. He was a handsome, well-mannered gentleman, and there was an openness about his countenance and character that was pleasing. Though the reports she had heard of Lady Osborne made her sound a little eccentric, she could not believe that the mother of such a son lacked any of the qualities she should possess.

A somewhat more intimate discussion of the gentleman took place in another room in Portman Square later that night – for though few ladies of Mrs O'Brien's age will credit it, neither Penelope nor Emily were in the least degree weary after their exertions at the ball of the previous evening. The details of the earlier conversation about riding had to be given, and Lord Osborne's generosity in drawing the moral as he did, rather than one concerning the inevitable discovery of falsehoods, had to be fully appreciated, before Emily ventured to suggest that one or two of her sister's remarks to his lordship had been a trifle free. To this Penelope would not listen.

"Pooh, my dear!" she said. "He adores my sister, and without doubt will one day be my brother. The sooner he grows used to me the better."

"Dearest Penelope, you must not make such assertions!"

"I make them only to you. I trust to your discretion not to repeat them in public."

"You may be sure of that," replied Emily, with an involuntary smile. "I will repeat them neither in public nor in private. But you are avoiding my complaint. I do not mind being teased – it is as well perhaps that I do not – but to be teased in front of Lord Osborne puts us on a footing of intimacy for which there is as yet no justification."

"It was with difficulty that I restrained myself from informing him that he and I had one most important thing in common," said Penelope.

"What is that?"

"Why, our love for you, you dear dull creature."

Emily sighed.

"I see you are determined to take no notice of me," she said.

"None whatsoever under that head. I am as I am made, my dear. I am no good at hiding what is open knowledge. But you will allow that I behaved very well in front of my aunt and permitted him to get through all the pretty speeches he had prepared without interruption."

"He is very much more easy, is he not?" said Emily.

"He has spent several hours in my company in the past three months, of which he seems to have profited," confessed Penelope.

"I feel I can respect him more now. He is no longer the overgrown boy he once was – nor even the more serious youth that he soon became. He is a proper *man*."

"This is very much more interesting than your moralizing on my loose tongue, my dear. Can you not admit to a sister that it was the memory of Lord Osborne that brought you back to Stanton?"

"Fortunately, Penelope," replied Emily, with a somewhat roguish smile, "I did not have to particularize to such a degree even to myself. My heart could recognize certain claims from Eversleigh, and others from the neighbourhood of Dunford. As things have fallen out I did not have to balance one claim against the other, or subdivide either into its different components."

"To one of your circumspection that must have been a most welcome accident," said Penelope. "But to a sister who is as vulgarly curious about your future as she is lovingly anxious for its happy outcome, it is poor comfort. You were once more open with me. Will you not tell me frankly the present state of your heart?"

"I will have no secrets from you, Penelope. Lord Osborne has my respect, but my *heart* is free."

"It is not engaged elsewhere?"

"My father, you, my aunt, Elizabeth and even Mr Jones own part of it; and there is a corner reserved for my brother Sam. But that section of most interest to the world – though why the world should take such interest in what is really a personal affair I have never been able to understand – is still free. Respect is a different emotion; it can be spread out between several gentlemen, and I have never hidden the fact that I respect Mr Howard, who is the one of whom I presume you are inquiring. But it would be an unpardonable weakness to have allowed my heart to become engaged in a direction from which I have had no encouragement."

"It is a weakness common to even the best brought-up young ladies," said Penelope.

"I am fortunate in having so far escaped it." Penelope seemed hardly convinced of her sincerity, and after a moment Emily continued: "Perhaps I owe you a further explanation, dear Penelope. You must remember that I am now in a very different situation from that which I was in three months ago. It might then have been said that it was my duty to hasten into marriage to relieve my father of the burden of my future upkeep. It might now well be argued, with equal truth, that it is my duty to postpone any thought of marriage until my aunt is comfortably settled in the new home I have encouraged her to make. This must be qualified a little however. One always has a duty to oneself; it must stop short of selfishness, but it nevertheless exists, particularly in the matter of marriage. Just as I would not marry three months ago solely on account of one duty, so I would not refuse to marry today solely on account of another."

"As you are accustomed, you have thought things out very thoroughly, my love; and the lucidity of your mind contrasts favourably with the muddled optimism of at least one of your sisters. I only trust you are not swept off your feet by some sudden attack for which you have not made allowance, and which is at variance with one of those duties whose enumeration made me somewhat dizzy just now."

"I too must trust I am never too severely tempted against what seems to be my duty," replied Emily. "But my remarks were meant to make it clear that there should now be no necessity for anything *sudden*. I am returning to Stanton as a resident. There will be time for what the future holds to develop in a leisurely and orderly fashion."

"It was made clear to poor Lord Osborne, and it is made clear to me," said Penelope. "I hope – as he is doubtless hoping at this moment – that *time* in this connection is measured in weeks and not in years."

"We shall see," said Emily, with a smile.

She was very content with the evening. Lord Osborne's attentions to her aunt had been all that she could have wished, and he himself was now a man she could respect. To end the day listening to Penelope's loving raillery was an indulgence of which she would not easily tire. Perhaps it would indeed come out as her sister so confidently expected. For the first time Emily allowed her imagination to wander a little into a future in which Osborne Castle played some considerable part.

But in spite of her assertions Penelope's own imagination, it appeared, was now proceeding in an entirely contrary direction.

"He is undoubtedly as *handsome* as Lord Osborne," she said as she snuffed out the candles. "But in that case you would never become your ladyship: which position, my sweet, your elegance would grace and your character undoubtedly deserves."

18

To the disappointment of Lord Osborne, Mr James and Mr
George Tomlinson, Captain Hunter, Captain Styles and Mr
Norton – for the *second* of these officers was beginning to find in
Miss Penelope Watson the true reason for an existence he had
hitherto believed dedicated to military glory alone, and the *first* and
third were becoming somewhat weary of his complaints at the length
of her stay in London – to the disappointment, then, of the afore-
said gentlemen, it was not till the middle of March that Mrs
O'Brien's furniture, housekeeper and new chaise arrived at Stanton
Lodge, and the house was declared ready for her occupation. Within
a week she followed in her coach, embraced her elder niece on her
doorstep, and set off with the younger on a tour of her new domain.
After bringing Penelope and her boxes to the front of the parsonage
the coach was taken round to the back and there left.

"My!" exclaimed Elizabeth, as she watched James and the new
man push it into the coach-house. "It is certainly very handsome. I
suppose it will need a great deal of polishing."

The following morning, in accordance with a promise carried by
Penelope, Emily visited her father and eldest sister. The short walk
took her past the cottage where Mr Jones now lodged; and this, she
thought, the first of many, many walks between Stanton Lodge and
the parsonage, brought home to her as no anticipation had done the
full convenience of her new situation. To have her dear aunt, her
old master, her father and her two loved sisters, within such a nar-
row compass was a pleasure too exquisite to put into words.

She brought an invitation from Mrs O'Brien for Mr Watson and
his daughters to drink a glass of wine with her later in the day. Mrs
O'Brien indeed would have engaged the Watsons and Mr Jones to
dinner immediately, but in spite of her father's visit to London

Emily had advised against so sudden a step. Let him but make the walk once or twice by daylight, let him once or twice meet at Stanton Lodge none but members of his own family, and Mrs O'Brien would perhaps be able to lead him on to accept her invitations as a matter of course. Mrs O'Brien had agreed; and after having greeted her father Emily delivered her message in the tone of one half-expecting a refusal. It was received with a readiness that surprised her. Yes; he had intended to wait on her aunt. His health had greatly improved in the past month, and it was right that while the improvement lasted he should be at the service of one to whom he owed so much. He would be with her in an hour.

Emily returned downstairs. Elizabeth she had not seen since she left the parsonage, and Elizabeth had not yet met Mrs O'Brien. Leaving Penelope to bring her father, she set out immediately with her eldest sister.

"It was Penelope's turn to talk last night and it is mine to talk this morning," Miss Watson began, when they were still in the hall, "though to be sure I have little intelligence to give you that you do not know already, but it is always refreshing to discuss pleasant news, is it not? I wonder what Miss Stokes will say when she sees me come in a coach to Dunford. You are a dear girl, Emily. You promised once that if you ever had good fortune you would share it with your family; and you have been as good as your word, where others in your position would have soon forgot us. I trust my aunt is not going to expect too much of me. What have I got to tell you now? Captain Styles stood out of two dances at the last ball. It is said he did so on Penelope's account, though she laughed heartily enough when I told her yesterday. He has only one thousand pounds beyond his pay, but I have heard there is a rich uncle in Norfolk. Margaret and Tom have been back three weeks. She has some fine new furniture at Millington and money to spend now, though she keeps good hold of it. I have been there three or four times and have not yet seen any waste about the place. It is boiled mutton for Tom all the week who was once so fond of oysters. I have heard her snap at him too about some gun he has bought; you would think it was *her* money he had used, not *his*. It is odd the way things turn out, is it not? To think of Margaret snapping at Tom Musgrave! However, he is married to her now and cannot undo what he has done. She is sick in the mornings sometimes, but of course she has not begun to grow big yet. And she wished me to say that Millington House is shown on some maps as Millington Farm, as it is a long time since it was occupied by a gentleman's family. I do not see that its name signifies myself. Look! That is the cottage where Mr Jones lives, did you know? If you have been acquainted for fifteen years there is little I can tell you about him, except that he walked three miles into Dunford and three miles back on an errand for poor Mrs Burton, who has taken to her bed and is not like to last long. You said once he was neither young nor handsome, but I do not agree he is either *old* or *ugly*, Emily."

"Indeed Elizabeth!" cried Emily, "I am sure I did not say he was. I could never have said such a thing about Mr Jones."

"Perhaps I wrong you, my dear, but that was the picture I had of him."

"I remember the occasion. You had teased me with having a young and handsome curate for a master. I replied that I did not think Mr Jones would call himself either young or handsome; but I would be as ungrateful as I would be unjust in seeking out terms of abuse for him. I would as soon think of doing the same for you."

"Then we are both agreed," said Elizabeth. "I understand you now; and as I never had occasion to repeat what you said, no harm has been done. I can judge his appearance myself, but I would be interested to hear his age."

"When I was five he was something over five-and-twenty. Now I am twenty he must be something over forty."

"It is a good age in a man," replied Elizabeth. "By then he has got over the indecisions of youth. If he makes up his mind, he will not easily be turned from his purpose by the wiles of a third party. It is a pity my aunt has no other living in her gift since Eversleigh was so unhappily thrown away. I suppose she has Stanton now instead, though *that* is not a living any of us would wish to see vacant. Lady Osborne called again when Penelope was in London. She gave me a large joint of Twig's salt beef which she said she had brought in exchange for a piece of my pork. I did not like her joint much; it had an unpleasant sharp taste. However, I was very polite about it when I saw her next, for I have a good idea who sent her, though the beef she must have thought of by herself. It is one way to pay a call. Mrs Edwards asked after Sam the last time I met her; that was since she knew about my aunt, of course. But I will never say anything against Mrs Edwards who has been so good to us for so many years. Miss Stokes says Mary is not so much against Sam as she pretended when she saw him at the wedding, and that if he were but to change coats with Captain Hunter she would have him as soon as her parents allowed. She thinks his position and his self too humble at the moment. His position he cannot help, but it is she who has made him humble by her behaviour. Captain Hunter is sure enough, even for a military man. But he expects to be with us for the month of May – Sam I mean – and may then have something to offer, for he talked much with Robert after the wedding about raising money to buy a partnership off Mr Curtis."

Miss Watson stopped gossiping as they entered the house, and permitted herself only one whisper to the effect that it was all much finer than the Edwardses' before Emily opened the door of a small parlour and presented her to Mrs O'Brien. Her father and Penelope would be following in an hour; meanwhile she had brought her eldest sister to make the acquaintance of her aunt.

Elizabeth, who had grown to accept life as she found it, and whose experience with the salt beef had strengthened her belief that great folk had their whims, was prepared for anything, and waited politely for Mrs O'Brien to reveal her particular eccentricity. Mrs O'Brien, however, asked only about the affairs of the parish, Mr and Mrs Musgrave, and the inhabitants of Wickstead and Dunford. To such questions Elizabeth replied with her usual readiness, and three-quarters of an hour was passed very pleasantly. Mrs O'Brien was then called away, and Emily and Elizabeth moved into the drawing-room to await the others.

"My aunt does not appear odd at all," said Elizabeth, when the door was safely shut. "This is a very fine room, is it not?"

"*Odd!*" said Emily. "What do you mean?"

"I meant that she talks very sensibly and shows a very ordinary interest in her neighbours."

"Dearest Elizabeth, do not let us misunderstand one another. What did you expect from my aunt?"

"I do not know what I *expected*, but after Lady Osborne I would have been surprised at nothing."

"Lady Osborne is the exception rather than the rule," said Emily. "You do not find either Mrs Edwards or Mrs Blake odd, do you?"

"It is *Mr* Edwards in that family; and Mrs Blake is certainly very refined. Perhaps it is a case of being either one or the other, for *you* are very refined yourself. And if this is the sort of house you are used to I do not wonder at it. The curtains for those windows must have cost what I spend on housekeeping in a quarter."

"Riches are by no means essential for refinement," said Emily, quietly. "True refinement exists in the mind and depends on less material things."

"Riches may not be essential, but I have no doubt they help," replied Miss Watson. "It is difficult to sit idle, and if one has no work to do I suppose one reads a book or learns the pianoforte."

"What do you intend to do today when your visit here is over?"

"I would have tidied the front garden and planted some seeds for the summer if James had not put the new man to it yesterday. Now I must find something else, for I am too old to become refined and have no wish to grow odd. Why do you ask?"

"Whatever you do I shall come and do it with you; for I fear that otherwise you will soon despise me for a lazy, useless female."

"No, my dear, you shall not. You are both happy and good, and I would not change you. But I will not be able to change myself either, so you must be prepared for my plain tongue and rough ways for as long as we are to live as neighbours."

"And am I to forget," cried Emily, with sudden tears in her eyes, "the kind welcome you gave me when I first came to Stanton?"

"Why, you were my sister. You were surely entitled to a welcome."

"Which you will always find in any house where *I* live," said Emily, warmly.

At this point Mrs O'Brien rejoined them with the news that Mr Watson and Penelope were walking up the drive. Emily rejoiced that she had brought Elizabeth with her earlier, and so allowed an opportunity for their talk. Her love for Penelope, she determined, must never make her forget what was due to her eldest sister.

The same afternoon brought Margaret and Mr Musgrave to Stanton Lodge. There was nothing to remark on in the behaviour of the former, which was all gentleness during the visit; but Emily could only wonder at the change to be discerned in the latter, who deferred to his wife in all things. She would willingly have believed that his was the happy obedience of a man deeply in love; but when she recollected the circumstances of the courtship, when she contrasted the easy address of the past with the somewhat harassed air of the present, she was obliged to discountenance that solution. But whatever the reason Mr Musgrave was a different man. The offensive gallantry was there no longer; and his manners had improved with its removal. He treated Mrs O'Brien, not with the patronizing politeness to which he had once subjected the entire family of Watsons, nor even with Margaret's subservient self-seeking, but with the proper respect due to one in her position.

"A very gentleman-like young man," said Mrs O'Brien, when they had gone. "I am by no means surprised that Lord Osborne should consider him worthy of intimacy."

The days that followed were busy ones for Mrs O'Brien and her niece. Their first visit to Dunford included a call on Mrs Edwards. The two ladies talked to each other in a very friendly fashion for more than an hour. Then Mrs O'Brien rose, the Edwardses were engaged to dine at Stanton on an early day, and Emily was recalled from her polite but somewhat guarded conversation with Mary on the window-seat. Mrs O'Brien said nothing until the carriage drew up at the library.

"She is to have ten thousand pounds on her marriage, I believe," she asked, before descending.

"So I have been told," replied Emily.

"It is a considerable sum, but possibly less would be demanded on the other side in view of Mr Edwards's peculiarities. I shall look forward to meeting Mr Samuel. However nothing can be done unless the young people are agreed."

"You are very good, aunt."

Mrs O'Brien shook her head. Mrs Edwards's misfortunes, on which she had fully informed herself, recalled events she remembered less and less often.

"I have been very fortunate," she said.

There were several ladies in the shop when they entered; but before Emily had time to decide whether any acquaintance was numbered among them, her attention was claimed in no uncertain manner by one of the opposite sex. It was Charles Blake.

"Good morning, ma'am," he said, in a voice loud enough to draw on them the immediate interest of all present. "I am glad you are come back to live among us, though the hunting is over for the season. I am to go to school in September."

"Good morning, sir," replied Emily, gravely. "I thought when the hunting was over you were to have lessons every morning in preparation for your school."

"I have had two hours today; and now I am come with mamma to change her books. There she is."

Mrs Blake was indeed regarding them. Any doubt Emily might have had about Mrs Blake's reception of her was set at rest by that lady coming forward with a ready smile and obvious pleasure. If the *brother* had reason to avoid her, the *sister* certainly had none.

"My dear Miss Emily," she said, "I am to welcome you back, I believe, and I do so most happily. I have no more forgotten you than Charles."

Mrs Blake and Charles were presented to Mrs O'Brien. Mrs Blake again said all that was required of her: she was but newly come into the country herself, but she was as pleased as the older residents with whom she had spoken that Stanton Lodge was once more occupied. She hoped to be allowed the pleasure of calling there shortly. Mrs O'Brien replied with equal courtesy. Mrs Blake then thought that tomorrow, being the twenty-sixth, her brother had some business at Stanton, and that if the day was convenient to Mrs O'Brien they might perhaps make the short drive together.

Even if circumstances had been different, Emily would not have repeated her previous proposal. But in the presence of her aunt, and without the excuse of a father to be visited, there could be no question of her suggesting that Mr Howard accompanied his sister. Mrs Blake indeed seemed willing to take back any message; but none was given. Mrs O'Brien would expect her tomorrow, Charles bowed most respectfully, and the interview was at an end.

Mr Howard did not come uninvited; and much of Mrs Blake's call the following day seemed unaccountably dull to Emily. Mrs Blake, who had the best-informed mind of any lady in Dunford and the surrounding villages, conversed with her usual ability; but it was not until her aunt required a description of Osborne Castle that Emily's interest was aroused.

"If you will not betray me to Lady Osborne, I shall say that the house is too old for convenience, and too new for grandeur, having been built some hundred and seventy years ago. That is not to say that it has no dignity. But for myself I would prefer a little more light, a great deal less carved oak, and a few rooms with modern furniture."

"The castle, then, is older than the title?"

"It was built under Charles I; and the family were ennobled by Charles II. There is a strong Stuart connection. I hope I have not made it sound too gloomy. I should be an ungrateful mother if I did not add that the grounds are both spacious and attractive, and that the plantations contain some very fine trees, for Charles has the run of both." Here Mrs Blake turned to Emily. "Since our meeting yesterday he has told me he hopes you will one day ride with him there."

"My sisters and I have only a general invitation," replied Emily, in some little confusion. "I did not think I should make use of it till Lady Osborne and my aunt had met."

"It is unlikely that the event will be long delayed. Had it not been that she was expecting the return of a horse from Colonel Beresford, Lady Osborne would have accompanied me this morning."

"It must be an extremely valuable animal," murmured Mrs O'Brien, who left the care of her horses to her coachman. "I trust it arrives without misadventure."

Mrs Blake went on to explain the particular friendship existing between Mrs O'Brien's niece and her own son Charles. While she had long forgiven Mrs Beresford – for the young lady who had not fulfilled her promise to Charles was now married to Colonel Beresford; and who knew what part that dance had played in the preliminaries culminating in this happy event – she would always consider Miss Emily one of the most unaffectedly good-natured people she had ever met for her action that evening. Though Emily was not insensible to the value of such a compliment from one of her own sex, she could not rid herself of the idea that there was something lacking in her pleasure over the visit. At last, her aunt still not having inquired after the Rector of Wickstead, and indeed seeming to have forgotten that Mrs Blake possessed a brother, Emily felt impelled – in the way of common politeness, she told herself – to ask news of Mr Howard.

Mr Howard was at that moment sitting with Mr Watson, who had promised to make him acquainted with Mr Jones. Then, after a moment of hesitation: would Mrs O'Brien and her niece dine at Wickstead on Wednesday week?

Mrs O'Brien would be very pleased to. She remembered now, of course, that Mrs Blake lived with her brother. It was remiss of her to have forgotten, but a new arrival must be forgiven a little uncertainty in the exact circumstances of her visitors.

Mrs Blake indeed lived with her brother. She had become a widow about the time Mr Howard had received the living from Lord Osborne. The rectory was large and the arrangement mutually convenient. But she had been thinking for some months past that she ought to provide herself with a house of her own, for it was in the nature of things that Mr Howard, who was some six years younger than she herself, would wish to marry now that he was settled. A widow with four children, however well provided for, would doubtless be considered something of an impediment by the average young lady of marriageable age as long as she shared his home.

Here Mrs Blake asked for her carriage, and Mrs O'Brien had barely time to agree with the good sense of what she had said, and to decide to herself that this good sense was of a very high order, before it was announced. Emily, full of sudden regrets that their visitor was to depart at this decidedly interesting point (for the possibility of Mr Howard marrying was, for some reason, no less engrossing than the architecture of Osborne Castle), accompanied her to the entrance. At the door of her carriage Mrs Blake turned back. Mrs O'Brien was engaged to dine with her on Wednesday week; did Miss Emily think Mrs O'Brien would prefer a small or a large party? For a moment Emily hesitated.

"My aunt has made a fair number of new acquaintances in the last week," she replied. "As she has not yet met Mr Howard perhaps she would enjoy the evening more if she were not required to meet anyone else with whom she was unfamiliar."

The remark was ill-expressed, but its sense undoubtedly pleased Mrs Blake. She gave Emily a very contented look, and said:

"It shall be as you suggest. My brother will ask Mr Jones, and we shall be only five."

At this moment Mr Howard himself came round the corner of the stables and advanced towards them. It is certain that Emily saw him before Mrs Blake; it is certain that within a very short time – within a few seconds of their mutual recognition, in fact – both Emily and Mr Howard were smiling; and it is certain that the gentleman's smile was not intended for his sister, who had her back towards him. The only point on which any doubt could exist was whether Emily or Mr Howard smiled first.

"Why madam," she cried, "here is Mr Howard!"

The gentleman was now greeting her, and she returned his greeting very happily. Mr Howard had been pleased to see her; consequently there was no reason to suppose that Mr Howard would ever *not* have been pleased to see her, and he was immediately absolved from the suspicion of avoiding her company at Wickstead.

He came from Mr Watson, he explained, and was pleasurably surprised at the improvement in health and spirits he had observed. Mr Watson had even spoken of visiting him at Wickstead when the weather grew warmer, which was an indulgence he had not hitherto felt justified in anticipating.

And had he met her old master, Mr Jones, Emily eagerly inquired.

Yes; Mr Watson had made them acquainted. Mr Howard had heard such stories of his unassuming zeal as made him look forward to the meeting, and he had not been disappointed in the impression he had received.

"I am glad to hear your good opinion, sir," replied Emily, "for I must warn you that my aunt O'Brien and I are prejudiced in this matter: an enemy of Mr Jones's cannot be a friend of ours. I will risk the charge of presumption and praise one to whom I have been in the position of pupil. I think Mr Jones without an equal in this world for benevolence and charity."

Mr Howard did not think she could be censured for her loyalty; and she could only be commended for her discernment, he added in a more serious tone, when he had had a moment in which to think over her words. Then he bowed, and it seemed that Mrs Blake could delay her entry into her carriage no longer.

"Ah madam! I am looking for my niece," said Mrs O'Brien's voice from the top of the steps. "We are about to decide which trees shall be lopped, which trees shall be cut, and which trees shall remain untouched."

Emily turned and saw her aunt, dressed for walking, descending the short flight. Mrs Blake presented her brother, who, with a swift look at his sister, immediately begged leave for them to accompany the ladies on their inspection.

"We shall be glad, sir, not only of your company, but of your advice."

"I do not know that we will dare offer *advice*," replied Mr Howard, "for at Wickstead we have been severely criticized for cutting down a walnut tree. Our neighbours saw its beauty and we felt its inconvenience, for it grew so close to the house as to dark the rooms."

"On the contrary, you must be well qualified to give advice," said Mrs O'Brien, "for your recent experience will allow you to sympathize with both sides, and judge between those who would fell and those who would spare."

"My recent experience enables me to promise you the criticisms of your neighbours, madam. Take but one dying tree away from a clump with which people are familiar, and they will complain that you have ruined the prospect for ever. That is a trait of human nature."

"I have found so myself," replied Mrs O'Brien. "But I have also found that after a year or two the same people will forget their first opinion and surprise you by praising what they earlier condemned. For that too is a trait of human nature. Are you not cold, Emily?"

Emily remembered that she had come out without a pelisse, and ran to fetch one. She rejoined the others to pass the shortest half-hour she had ever known. The value of her advice with regard to the trees was doubtful, as she found herself agreeing with Mr Howard in almost every particular. It became so marked that at one point she determined to *disagree*, which caused her to stumble into qualifications almost as involved as those of Mr Jones.

19

Mrs O'Brien's comment on Mr Howard was that he was a very much younger man than she had expected. She understood him to have been Lord Osborne's tutor; *companion* surely must have been meant, for he did not appear more than a few years older than his charge. She had not entirely expected a *young* rector at Wickstead, she added, with a slight frown.

"I trust you do not think him too young for his position, madam," said Emily. "I cannot claim to know Mr Howard intimately but I have never found any youthful foolishness in him; and my father rates him a most excellent clergyman."

"He is undoubtedly a man of sense," replied Mrs O'Brien. "His address and his manners are very good indeed; I could not pretend to the contrary. I suppose I am accustomed to think of a tutor as one of Mr Jones's age; and Mrs Blake, whom I met first, is not a young woman, though she did say that Mr Howard was her junior."

"She is six-and-thirty, I believe madam."

"Indeed!" said Mrs O'Brien. After a silence of some seconds she continued: "You have not yet ridden your new horse, Emily."

"No, aunt."

"I trust you did not lose your fondness for riding during the months you were without the facilities?"

"No, aunt. I thought it best to stay by you for the first few weeks here."

"You have been a great help to me, my dear, and it is right that those who call should know that this is now your home, although you were previously at the parsonage. However, I do not wish you to neglect your riding. You will always have a companion while Penelope is in the village. I would like to see you both go out next week. There are horses suitable for the two of you; I have just inquired."

"Yes, aunt."

"In view of Lord Osborne's invitation I do not think you need wait for his mother to call on me before entering his grounds. If there was any suggestion that she was *not* going to call, it would be a different matter. That is not the case, however; and from what I have heard of Lady Osborne she will not be displeased to see two well-mounted young ladies with whom she is already acquainted in the vicinity of the castle."

"Yes, aunt," replied Emily.

This conversation took place on Friday. On Monday, accompanied by her niece, Mrs O'Brien had occasion to drive beyond Wickstead. She had decided in her own mind that there was no immediate need to wait on Mrs Blake, and had almost dismissed Emily's suggestion that they should take advantage of the route on their return journey to do so, when her decision was rendered void by their meeting both the brother and sister at the gates of the rectory. To refuse to descend in such circumstances would have been ungracious, and Emily spent a happy hour talking and listening to Mr Howard.

Her happiness did not pass unnoticed. An hour before she was due to dress, Mrs O'Brien again mentioned Emily's untried horse. Her niece, who was by no means loath to ride herself, obediently asked permission to invite Penelope to ride with her. Permission was readily given, and the invitation as readily accepted. Tuesday morning saw the two sisters set out on horseback from Stanton Lodge.

"I hope, my dear, my aunt's final remark is as firmly fixed in your memory as in mine," said Penelope, as they turned northward on reaching the road.

"I do not recall any *particular* remark from my aunt this morning. She was pleased to see you, believed the weather would keep fine and thought we ought to have a groom behind us until we were familiar with the lanes and horses."

"Then it is a good thing I reminded you. My aunt hoped that now you had again begun, and had a sister for a companion, you would ride as regularly as you did at Eversleigh. This, I understand, was every fine morning when you had no more important engagement. I hasten to assure you that I have *no* engagements. Are we to enter the grounds of the castle?"

"My aunt saw no harm in it. What do you think yourself?"

"In truth, my love, you were invited. Unless my memory is at fault I was as well, in which case we might perhaps just peer through the gates and call for your friend Charles Blake."

"You were certainly invited, Penelope," said Emily. "Apart from anything else he could hardly have invited me *without* inviting you."

"I believe you are right. The pleasure of riding in his grounds, unlike those of standing up with him at a ball or refusing his hand in marriage, is one which he can safely offer any number of sisters simultaneously."

"Hush, Penelope!" cried Emily, glancing round.

"You may set your mind at ease. He is travelling at a most tactful distance – close enough to hear my screams should we encounter a gipsy, and far enough away for even *my* conversational tones to be inaudible. You have not seen the gentleman since we arrived?"

"No."

"Yet it is more than two weeks ago!"

"You must not exaggerate. It is two weeks precisely."

"You are bearing up very well, my love," said Penelope, with a side-long glance at her sister. "Did I not know it to be impossible in the circumstances I should say there was more colour in your cheeks than I am used to, and a suggestion of some special happy secret in your eyes."

"In self-defence I shall soon be forced to ask whether you have seen Captain Styles these same two weeks."

"It is rashly done for one of your refinement to compete with one of my immodesty in such a matter. First I shall say that Captain Styles, like a properly trained military man, undoubtedly has his sentries posted on the road between Stanton and Dunford. On the two occasions I have visited the latter place since my return he has appeared from behind a convenient corner with his two companions as soon as Elizabeth, Mary Edwards and I have begun to parade our new spring bonnets. And I must add that while Mr Norton is probably picking up a number of useful hints about the best way to

dry hazel nuts, and which feathers make the most economical stuffing for a comfortable pillow, my poor eldest sister is becoming un-
duly familiar with the lot of the very junior officers of the regiment.
It is a pity the two captains – so happily partnered themselves –
could not have picked a major to complete their trio. And now, my
dear, having demonstrated that it is quite beyond *your* power to
shame me, I shall return to the attack and say I wonder what it is in
the climate of Wickstead which causes all the young men of the
parish to admire Miss Emily Watson to such an amazing degree."

"All?" said Emily.

"I can think of three who profess their regard openly. There are
doubtless others who possess some unfortunate encumbrance in the
shape of a wife which forces them to keep their sentiments to themselves."

"Nay, Penelope!" cried Emily, a little consciously. "*One* such is
too many. Do not tax me with *three*."

"I will sum them, my love. There is first Lord Osborne. There
is second Charles Blake. And there is third Mr Howard."

"And these profess their regard openly?"

"I have said so," replied Penelope.

"Mr Howard is too – Mr Howard could never be – In short Mr
Howard is a man of the world and would not discover himself in the
public manner you would have me believe. You are teasing again."

"I notice that your denials relate only to the gentleman's *conduct*
and not to his *sentiments*, with which I must consequently assume
you are quite familiar."

Emily, her cheeks scarlet at her blunder, turned to Penelope.

"Pray tell me what Mr Howard said."

"Nay, my love, he is too much a man of the world to say anything."

"Tell me, Penelope."

"I shall expect some return for this. But in truth you are right.
He *said* little; his deeds spoke louder than his words. Mr Howard,
as you were told when we all met on Sunday and doubtless knew
even then, visited my father last Friday. Mr Howard's visits to my
father, I am informed, usually last an hour, after which he speaks to
such Miss Watsons as are prepared to receive him for five or ten
minutes, according to whether they are sitting in the ordinary or the

best parlour – for he is a tactful man – before returning home. On Friday, instead of coming on his horse, he came in his sister's carriage. I was sitting in the parlour – the *best* parlour, my love, for now we have my aunt's coach at the back I often sit in the best parlour to make it feel at home – and I heard Mrs Blake say as he descended that if he was resolved to be stubborn she would call for him in an hour's time. I found this so interesting that I sat and watched the clock for the length of his visit. Mr Jones too was overhead; but three-quarters of an hour had barely passed before Mr Howard hurried downstairs and informed Elizabeth that he was dependent on his sister for transport that day and must hurry off to Stanton Lodge. Thus my determination *not* to say how sorry we were to have missed him at Wickstead was not put to the test. This was perhaps as well; for my determination might have wavered at the last moment. A gentleman who intentionally avoids me must, in my opinion, be punished for his bad taste. I have found that a simple statement, and a frank, artless gaze can at times raise blushes of embarrassment even in those of the most blameless character."

"It is as well I do not believe your account of yourself," said Emily. "I trust you never repeat such things to those who do."

"Elizabeth, I fear, sometimes takes me at my word, but we remain good friends for days together now that Margaret has left us. Am I to take your observation as a sign that you would prefer not to discuss Mr Howard, whom we left hurrying to Stanton Lodge in case his sister went home without him?"

"I will say this for Mr Howard," replied Emily. "I think we have wronged him. I do not believe it was *his* horse we heard at Wickstead."

"And why, my dear, have you changed your previous opinion?"

"He greeted me on Friday with an openness – an obvious *pleasure*, I will say – that could not have been simulated. It is not possible to believe that a man would avoid me one day and so behave the next time he had a chance of meeting me."

"During the interval you have become an acknowledged heiress."

"For shame, Penelope! Can you suggest *that* of Mr Howard, who danced with me at the first assembly and who offered to dance with me at the second when it was well known I was penniless?"

"Nay, my dear, I do not seriously suggest it, but there is possibly *some* explanation of the incident at Wickstead." Penelope then paused a moment before continuing thus: "The most delightful trait in your character, my dear, if I may tell you the truth about yourself, is the entire suspension of your judgement and neglect of your principles where those you love are concerned. You are strict with the world and with yourself, and indulgent to the chosen few. This is a very revealing weakness. I benefit from it daily myself; so does my aunt, and so too does Mr Jones. Now apparently Mr Howard is to join us; and I despair for poor Lord Osborne, whom you have severely criticized from time to time. I have called it a *weakness*; but on second thoughts I retract the word. So generous a characteristic does not deserve the censure. Besides, it is an almost exclusively feminine peculiarity, which speaks well for it.

"There is much that needs answering in that, Penelope, but I will say first that I am glad you do not think it a failing to think well of those we love. However, your assumption that I feel the same emotion for you, my aunt, Mr Jones, and Mr Howard is quite, quite wrong."

For some time there was nothing to be heard except the thud of the horses' hooves and the jingle of their harness.

"I am waiting," said Penelope.

Emily felt her cheeks growing warm; and the knowledge that her sister had already seen a secret in her eyes did nothing to increase her ability to control her colour.

"Why then, dear Penelope," she said, "to you I shall confess that I have begun to think of Mr Howard. His behaviour on Friday, and again yesterday when we returned the call, was such that I need not be ashamed of admitting what is, after all, the truth. You cannot ask me to say more, and I would not have said so much if he had not shown me definite encouragement."

"I trust you will not *cease* to think of Lord Osborne before we have made some slight use of his hospitality – if, of course, it is permissible for a young lady to think of two gentlemen at the same time."

"She may perhaps *think* of two," replied Emily, with a smile, "but as soon as she has made up her mind she should put one out of her head. From what I have been given to believe, once the process has begun, it is usually soon completed."

"I am becoming anxious lest at the last moment I am denied the opportunity of trying out the paces of this very promising animal," said Penelope.

"Are those not the gates of the castle?"

"They are. If you can postpone your decision until we are safely inside I will promise to love either gentleman the instant you command me."

"In truth, Penelope," said Emily, softly. "I do not think it would be very difficult to love him."

As she was speaking a carriage drew out from between the twin lodges and stopped. It was followed immediately by a gentleman on horseback, who had apparently come up to speak to the occupant of the carriage.

"And that is Lady Osborne in her barouche," said Penelope. "Nobody else would set out in an open carriage in *March* – except of course the Miss Watsons, who cannot always help themselves. I wonder if that is the real secret of her partiality for us."

"We cannot enter uninvited while she is there," said Emily. "We had best ask her permission."

"A reference to Charles Blake would show the confusion of our motives, my dear. An assignation with the nephew of one gentleman in the grounds of the other would commit you to neither."

"Hush, Penelope!"

Her ladyship greeted them while they were still some distance away. She praised the condition of their horses, and as an afterthought remarked that they themselves looked very healthy too. Lord Osborne, for the rider was none other, expressed his pleasure at the encounter. His mother was about to make a call, he said, but he would be happy to show them the way to the plantations, and then bring them to the corner where they would usually find Charles when the boy was not occupied with his lessons.

"Yes," said Lady Osborne, with a somewhat reproachful look at her son. "I am about to make a call. And I am unable to refrain from observing that the pastime Miss Penelope and Miss Emily have chosen for themselves is more in keeping with the weather than the one you have chosen for me."

"Come, madam," said Lord Osborne, "you would not wish to show discourtesy to your new neighbour."

"It is no more discourteous to call on a wet day than on a fine one," replied his mother, tartly.

"I agree with you, madam," replied Lord Osborne, with commendable patience, "but we have already had a week of fine days. Should this weather continue for another month, and should you postpone your call till the end of that period, you would *then* appear discourteous."

"Should this weather continue throughout April it would be a very extraordinary thing indeed," said her ladyship. "There would be no harvest, the cattle would die, the country would starve, and there would doubtless be a revolution on the French model."

"We must trust, madam, that your prophecies are not fulfilled."

"It is not *I* who am prophesying them; it is *you*. I say it will rain tomorrow."

"Yes, madam. But if my memory serves me right you have said that for the past week."

"It is not seemly to argue thus publicly, Edward. I have said I will go, and I will go. I must beg your pardon, Miss Emily. I am looking forward to meeting Mrs O'Brien; but I should also have greatly enjoyed riding with you here. That is the long and short of the matter. I trust you will give me that pleasure another day. Mrs O'Brien, I suppose, is at home?"

"Yes, your ladyship."

Lady Osborne sighed.

"You will forgive me for asking; there would have been no point in undertaking the journey for nothing." Her ladyship then bid them good-bye and gave the command for the carriage to go forward.

"It is the weather," Lord Osborne explained unnecessarily. "It has been dry for the past week. My mother intends no discourtesy, but she has been waiting for a wet day."

His lordship led the way through the gates; inside the park he turned off the gravelled drive, and they were soon advancing abreast up a wide grass ride. The ground was undulating and well wooded; the castle nowhere visible from the road. Even the memory of Mr Howard's recent behaviour could not prevent Emily feeling a thrill of anticipation at the prospect that would any moment open before her. But their leisurely progress wearied Penelope.

"My lord," she said, "my horse is as eager to take advantage of this magnificent stretch of turf as I am myself. If I confess I am having difficulty in holding him in, and doubt my ability to do so much longer, I trust you will not believe me in any danger. I am seldom in danger on horseback."

Without more ado she urged her horse forward, and soon disappeared from view.

"She rides well," said Lord Osborne, who was more content with the situation in which he now found himself than his companion. The next rise in ground, however, brought them to a full view of the castle, and Emily quickly forgot her slight discomfort. The building was of red brick, and at first glance appeared disorderly in the extreme, with a broken sky line, and high fantastic chimneys. In place of the wide, equally-spaced windows, with which she had grown familiar at Eversleigh, and which were reproduced on a smaller scale at Stanton Lodge, there were innumerable irregular leaded panes; and in place of compact and separate blocks for house and stable, there was a suggestion of courts leading one out of the other, with no clear distinction where the castle ended and the outbuildings began. Of gloom there was none, but of quaintness a great deal.

"This is a view I have long wished to show you," said Lord Osborne, with simple pride.

"In truth, my lord, it is a noble group of buildings; and if I may say so without causing you displeasure it has a charming air of quaintness about it."

"*Charm* I know it has," said Lord Osborne. "But *quaintness* I am too much at home here to see. If you look more closely you may find that what appears irregular is but part of a more intricate pattern than you are used to. This is but your first view; I hope it will not be your last. As you said in London, we are like to be neighbours the greater part of our lives. I trust that you will be here often enough this coming summer to become – I will not say as familiar with it as I am, for that is impossible, but as familiar with it as one who does not live here *can* be."

She was pleased that he had fully understood, and as fully remembered, her words. Of a sudden she recalled how greatly he had improved himself, and how considerate he had been to her family since they had last been alone together.

"May I say, my lord, that it is not everyone who is granted such a generous neighbour as my sisters and I have found in you?"

Lord Osborne looked happy – almost too happy – and Emily quickly turned to meet Penelope, who was cantering towards them, flushed and excited.

20

Mrs O'Brien, with an entire disregard of the weather, arranged to return Lady Osborne's call the day before she was to dine at Wickstead; and Emily was at her aunt's side when the chaise drew up at the door of the castle.

The interior of the building was more in keeping with Mrs Blake's description than the exterior. There was a certain heavy ornateness about the wide hall they entered (to face the stuffed fox Charles Blake found so very life-like), the short corridor they traversed, and the large room they were shown into. *Distinction*, Emily realized, could exist without *elegance*. No one would wish to furnish a room in such a style today, and yet the room was impressive.

Three or four dogs, followed by Lady Osborne herself, rose up and greeted them as they came in. Lady Osborne, though eccentric, was well bred. Her red face and loud voice, her interest in dogs, horses, salt beef and other matters ladies customarily left to their grooms and housekeepers, could not hide her respectability. This attended her abroad, but in her own home showed most strongly. Like her drawing-room her ladyship lacked elegance; and like her drawing-room her ladyship possessed distinction.

As she was being welcomed Emily remembered that Lady Osborne had been told of her son's intentions some months earlier, and must presumably also know how his chivalrous offer had been received. The memory caused her some confusion. True, she had already met the mother since she had refused the son; but that meeting had taken place on a public road. Now she had entered her home – the house of which she herself might have been mistress – as an accepted visitor. She was glad to sit down in an inconspicuous corner and listen to the older ladies' talk.

Goodwill and courtesy can often take the place of common interests. Lady Osborne and Mrs O'Brien were dissimilar in character and taste; but goodwill, it seemed, had already been established between them. Lady Osborne complimented Mrs O'Brien on Emily's appearance, which was that of a healthy girl, accustomed to regular exercise. In return Emily's aunt complimented her ladyship on Lord Osborne's politeness, of which his call in Portman Square was so definite a sign. Lady Osborne had always considered Stanton Lodge a very fine residence; Mrs O'Brien believed there had been a book at Eversleigh containing plates of Osborne Castle. Her ladyship, going a long way to meet her guest, thought that Mrs Blake possessed quite a library of books. The number of volumes in the drawing-room of Wickstead Rectory had often caught her notice. Mrs O'Brien, after deep reflection, remembered having heard that the grounds of Stanton Lodge contained a spinney of some importance to Lord Osborne's hounds. Any requirements his lordship might have in the matter would be faithfully carried out.

Here the two ladies paused, well pleased with their progress, but both in need of a short rest.

"That is a very fine portrait, your ladyship," said Emily.

It was a portrait of Lord Osborne's great-grandmother, who had been a Miss Grey. The picture had been much admired, though Miss Grey had come from a Whig family and Lady Osborne herself was not over-fond of it. She had once or twice thought of removing the picture to another room, but it had always hung on that wall and it was a pity to change things. Did Miss Emily paint?

Emily modestly disclaimed any title to the accomplishment; but she was, she admitted, interested in viewing the work of others. Her ladyship then handed her a portfolio containing coloured prints of famous race-horses, and offered Mrs O'Brien a glass of madeira.

At this point the party was joined by Lord Osborne and Mr Musgrave, who had had some business together in the stables. In his present company the latter was a gayer associate than the married man who had called at Stanton Lodge. There was, however, slightly less of the impudence towards herself, as well as slightly less of the servility towards Lord Osborne, that Emily had found so displeasing when she first met the gentleman; and she again had no reason to feel ashamed of Margaret's husband.

Lady Osborne, still resting, appeared content to resign her duties to her son's friend, and these duties Mr Musgrave performed very creditably. After expressing his good fortune in meeting the callers, he gave a short history of the castle to Mrs O'Brien, requested her to admire the view from the windows and handed her some cake. Lord Osborne, meanwhile, brought Emily her glass of wine and gently removed the portfolio. This he put back on the table next to his mother, and then took up his station by her side as though to remind her of something she had forgotten.

Thus recalled, Lady Osborne engaged Mrs O'Brien and her niece to dine at the castle the following Monday. Lord Osborne looked pleased. His mother then turned to Mr Musgrave and hoped that if it was convenient he and Mrs Musgrave would join them. This too Lord Osborne approved of; but even this was not enough.

"Could we not include Mr Watson, Miss Watson and Miss Penelope, madam?" he said. "I do not think any of them have yet dined at the castle, for which we are much to blame, as they have lived near us for a number of years."

"Certainly," replied her ladyship civilly, and without more than a momentary look of surprise. "But is Mr Watson sufficiently well to dine out?"

"I have Tom's word for it that he dined at Millington last week."

"In that case I will write a note which perhaps Miss Emily will be good enough to deliver for me."

"It will not be necessary to trouble Miss Emily," said Lord Osborne. "I am passing that way tomorrow and will carry the note myself."

Emily was greatly moved by this unexpected courtesy. True, owing to the gentleman's exertions the families had become better acquainted since the beginning of the winter. But the difference in their circumstances was such that the proposed invitation must be considered a very high compliment indeed. She gave Lord Osborne a look most expressive of deep appreciation, which he answered with a slight smile as though to inquire: what else did you expect? Emily quickly dropped her eyes at this suggestion of a secret understanding between them. But indeed what else had she expected? This was how he had said he would behave. She knew his frankness; she knew his generosity; she knew he would always keep his word. Could life hold higher felicity than a union of true affection with a man so honourable? That he loved her she did not doubt; that she respected him, admired him, wished him well, she was as fully convinced. The thought came to her that if she had never met Mr Howard she would probably have now felt for Lord Osborne a regard equal to that which he felt for her; and she sighed at the realization that she might some day have to wound one who so little deserved her ill-will. She *might* have to wound him – she could go no further at the moment.

Emily was engaged in these not unpleasing reflections, and Lord Osborne was hoping she would soon raise her head so that he could see something other than the top of her bonnet, when Mr Musgrave was summoned from the room. Within a few minutes he returned. His gayness had disappeared; he was again the harassed man who had called at Stanton Lodge. He had received a message that Mrs Musgrave was not well, he explained. While he did not in any way wish to alarm the company by suggesting that she was seriously ill, he thought it best, now that his business with Osborne was completed, to return to Millington. Would her ladyship please excuse him? Lady Osborne assented, contenting herself with briefly recommending red wine and red meat. Lord Osborne was sympathetic, Mrs O'Brien disturbed, and Emily anxious. Margaret was her sister, and Margaret was in a situation that was not without occasional danger. All memories but these were forgotten. She did not know how Mr Musgrave had come to the castle; if it had been on horseback (with a look of entreaty at her aunt) could not the chaise take her to Millington to be of what help she could?

Mr Musgrave had come in his curricle which was now at the door. Miss Emily's offer was very kind; but he had no doubt that his presence would soon restore her sister to her customary health.

"Sir, if you are prepared to drive me I will accompany you. I may be of service; and should the report be exaggerated I can find my way home myself. It is but a short walk."

As for that she was welcome to come with him and reassure herself. He would undertake to return her to Stanton the moment she required.

Thus the matter was settled, and she left the castle with her brother-in-law.

"It is barely six months ago," he said, as he helped her in the curricle, "that you refused me the pleasure of driving you in this same curricle."

"The circumstances are now very different, sir."

"Yes," he replied, "the circumstances are now very different."

There was something in his tone that Emily disliked, and she did not pursue the conversation.

"Have you sent for a doctor, Mr Musgrave?"

"Ha! Doctor!" he said. "What is the need for a doctor?"

With that he cracked his whip and the horses set off at a very smart pace. Emily had never before been in such a carriage. Had the occasion been an ordinary one the entire lack of any protection, the fast pace of the horses, and the very insecure seat on which she was balanced would have caused her no little apprehension. As it was, her anxiety about her sister, and her astonishment at the seeming callousness of her brother-in-law, prevented any alarm on her own account.

Within a very short time they were at Millington, and Emily followed the gentleman, not upstairs as she had expected, but into the main parlour. Margaret was lying on a sofa, surrounded by the females of the household. Her eyes were shut and her hartshorn was held most pathetically some little distance from her nose.

"Well, here I am," said Mr Musgrave, in a voice that was both weary and resentful.

"Dear Musgrave," murmured Margaret gently, not opening her eyes, "I shall be all right now *you* are returned."

Perhaps taking this hint, or perhaps well-trained in these emergencies, her maid, cook, housekeeper and other servants returned to the work from which they had had an hour's respite. Even Emily felt there was something familiar about the scene; and she remained by the door with the uncomfortable feeling that she had unwittingly intruded where her presence was not required.

"Where have you been?" asked Margaret, a little less gently.

"I had some business with Osborne."

"You did not tell me you were leaving Millington."

"I told you yesterday I had some business with Osborne, and you made such a noise that I put it off till this morning."

"You have no right to leave me in my condition without warning," said Margaret, sharply. "How should I know where to find you if I had had an accident?"

"You have found me easily enough as it is. I had not been at the castle an hour before I was called away."

"Why did you not take me with you?"

"You have a household to look after, madam. A woman's place in the mornings is in her house; not at her husband's side preventing him doing his business."

At this point Margaret so far forgot her ailment as to sit up and scold her husband in the most vigorous manner.

"That is a very easy thing to say, Mr Musgrave, and I am sure your business with Lord Osborne must have been of great importance, concerning as it doubtless did some dog or horse. Other gentlemen are pleased to take their wives with them on a morning call and I cannot see – – But Emily!" she exclaimed in the most gentle voice. "Why did you not say you were here?" She stood up, walked across the room on very steady feet, and embraced her sister. "This is a most happy meeting. I was so bored I did not know what to do. Let us have some sandwiches and cold meat."

Mr Musgrave observed the greeting with a somewhat sour expression.

"This is a remarkably quick recovery, madam," he said rashly.

"I am not at all recovered," said Margaret, coming back to the sofa and looking for her hartshorn. "I was welcoming my sister, that is all. It is the duty of one of us to do so; and your neglect of it threw the burden on me, ill as I am." Here she lay down on the sofa again and closed her eyes.

Emily now wished most heartily that she had taken Mr Musgrave's advice and stayed away from Millington. If the early argument had been painful to listen to, the present one, concerning herself, was unbearable. She tried to interrupt with the request that she be taken home to inform her aunt that Margaret's condition was not as serious as had been thought; but neither of the principals would listen to her. When Margaret learnt from her husband that Mrs O'Brien and Emily had been calling at the castle, and that Emily had come, not on a social visit, but to help a sister understood to have been suddenly taken ill, her anger at having been left at Millington increased. The original complaints were gone through again in greater detail; and not till Mr Musgrave had admitted that he had been wrong to have business with Lord Osborne, wrong to do that business at Wickstead, wrong not to have welcomed Emily, and very wrong to have believed his wife recovered when she was only trying to make amends for his discourtesy, did Margaret allow herself to sit up a second time and repeat her invitation to Emily.

No inducement she could offer would make Emily stay in the house after what had occurred. She would not be happy till she had reassured her aunt, she said; it was but a mile to Stanton Lodge; and as Margaret did not wish to be left alone she could walk the distance.

"What will my aunt think?" cried Margaret. "Musgrave will drive you, of course. I wonder you did not suggest it yourself, Musgrave."

Neither Emily nor Mr Musgrave made any reply to this; and they did not break their silence until Emily was again in the curricle, and the curricle itself on the road.

"Will you please drive more slowly this time," said Emily. "I am no longer in any anxiety and I am not accustomed to this sort of carriage."

"I beg your pardon," said the gentleman, and immediately reined back his horses until they were going as steadily as she could have wished. Mr Musgrave was somewhat red in the face, and kept his eyes firmly fixed on the road ahead. "You have seen my humiliation," he said suddenly, after a few moments. "My God, if I ever offended you or any other of your sex, I am being punished for it."

"I am her sister, and you are her husband," replied Emily. "However distressing the scene we have just witnessed, I do not think we should comment on it."

"You are her sister," said Mr Musgrave, "but you are also a woman of judgement and sense. You need not tell me your opinion of such behaviour."

His ready compliance with her request for a slower pace, and his tribute to her sense where six months ago there would have been an empty compliment to her beauty, raised her brother-in-law in Emily's regard. He had indeed been punished for his past flirtations; even Penelope would grant that. Emily felt she owed him what comfort she could offer.

"Much may be due to her present condition," she said. "We must hope that this is but a temporary phase."

"I wish I could so deceive myself," said her companion bitterly, "but I know her too well. I will say nothing of what happened earlier, but I had not been three days married before something of the sort occurred. I met an old friend at Tunbridge Wells, and we started talking and forgot the time. Ha! What a life for a man! I tell you" – they were now passing Stanton Parsonage – "I tell you neither good old Miss Watson, nor Miss Penelope, though she has a tongue, would have treated me like this. As for you, Miss Emily – –"

"Hush, sir," said Emily. "This is most improper talk."

"Yes; it was most improper behaviour as well," said the harassed Mr Musgrave. "Happy is the man who learns in time. Why I did not enlist in the Militia I do not know."

The few minutes that remained of their drive were spent in silence. At the door of Stanton Lodge Mr Musgrave handed her out, bowed, and in a very humble tone wished her good morning. Severely though she condemned his past conduct, Emily could not but pity his present situation.

21

Emily did not see her sisters that day; and soon after she had had breakfast the following morning she walked to the parsonage to warn them of their visitor, to discuss the possibility of a ride, and to tell Penelope what had occurred at Millington.

"It is not *today* I expected to see you, my love, but *tomorrow*," cried that young lady, when Emily entered the parlour.

"Pray why tomorrow?"

"To hear an account of the dinner at Wickstead, of course, you dull creature. But perhaps you have merely come to ask me to ride?"

Here Elizabeth bustled into the room, her arms full of soiled sheets.

"Nanny told me you were come, my dear. Forgive the linen; I am getting ready for the spring wash. Has Penelope told you our news?"

"No; she has told me nothing."

"'Tis Sam," said Elizabeth. "He is to have his month's holiday and is arriving today week. It is great news, is it not? But the aggravating thing is we are to dine on Monday with the Edwardses. My father is to go too. If only it had been a few days later I would have sent Mrs Edwards a note about Sam."

"You are to dine on *Monday* with the Edwardses?"

"Yes. Two days before Sam arrives. It is very annoying. It is good weather for my wash, however, and my daffodils are very fine. Are you not riding this morning?"

"That we have still to decide. I have brought you intelligence of another invitation for Monday."

"*Another!*" cried Penelope. "Can Mrs Tomlinson have heard of something further to our advantage? It is but two weeks since we dined with her."

"It is not Mrs Tomlinson, Penelope. It is Lady Osborne. Lord Osborne is to call on my father this morning to invite Mr Watson and his daughters to dine at the castle on Monday."

"My!" said Elizabeth, dropping the sheets. "To dine at the castle! My!"

"It is very close," murmured Penelope. "Indeed I am not sure that this does not put him ahead, for we have no invitation to Wickstead tonight. How much importance, my love, is to be attached to an invitation to the lady's family in the peculiar language you would have me believe current between refined young persons contemplating matrimony?"

Emily blushed faintly even as she smiled; but she made no attempt to answer her sister's sally in front of Elizabeth.

"My, it is very unfortunate," continued Miss Watson. "Mr Edwards so dislikes being put off. An engagement once postponed brings sorrow; twice postponed illness; and thrice postponed death, I think it is."

"But you must not put him off," said Emily.

"It would only be on your account, my dear, for to be sure I would feel more at home with Mrs Edwards than in the castle."

"On my account it is not necessary, but you should remind my father he is already engaged for Monday."

"Aye; and Penelope must not ride till Lord Osborne has been. And I must tell Nanny she will have to prepare the wash without me. I am beginning to be busy with nothing to show for it like all the rest of you. I had best get this linen out of the way to prepare for his lordship."

"And I will rearrange Penelope's ribbons, if she will permit me," said Emily.

The two sisters went upstairs together and Emily retied her sister's bows. Afterwards Penelope examined herself for some time in the glass.

"No, my dear. It will not do," she said at last. "You wish to make me demure; and I am not demure. I fear I am somewhat pert."

She was about to set the ribbons to rights when the sound of voices in the garden below drew her to the window. She beckoned to Emily, who crossed the room to see Mr Jones and Elizabeth engaged in a very cheerful conversation across the daffodils.

Yes; the bulbs were very fine, were they not, Elizabeth was saying. They had been given her by Miss Stokes many years before. That was to say Miss Stokes had given her a dozen or so, and this was the result. Mrs Burton was surprisingly better; but of course the winter had been mild and the spring early. He himself looked well too. It was a remarkable warm day, was it not? Almost like summer. Would he come in for half an hour? Both Penelope and Emily were within and would be pleased to see him.

Miss Watson was too kind. It was somewhat early for a call, and though it was difficult for him to refuse so generous an invitation he did not feel that he ought actually to take advantage of it when he was, in point of fact, on his way to Nettlebank, however severely tempted to enter for, say, just a quarter of an hour, unless he could be assured that he would not thereby be keeping her from her household duties. He was particularly fond of daffodils himself. Those at Eversleigh had been very fine; and while it was not for him to judge between Mrs O'Brien's display and Miss Watson's, the other had admittedly been on a somewhat larger scale, though for his part even *one* daffodil of that precise size and colour that Miss Watson alone seemed able to grow might be said to be without serious rival when considered as an object of beauty. It was but four miles to Nettlebank; if Miss Watson was really so charitable as to offer him hospitality for ten minutes before he set out so that he could pay his respects to dear Miss Emily, and of course Miss Penelope, he did not wish to give her the impression of being unwilling to accept her kindness – more particularly as perhaps later in the day his coat and boots might be so dusty as to impel him to refuse a possible second invitation, so perhaps if he might just for five minutes . . .

With this Mr Jones allowed himself to enter the door that Elizabeth had been holding open for some little time. Penelope sighed.

"Mr Jones is becoming very poetic; but Elizabeth remains as prosaic as ever. Could I but bring him to a declaration I should be forgiven for the treachery I did not commit in regard to Purvis."

"Penelope!" cried Emily, in a shocked tone, "you must not think of such a thing!"

"Why not, pray?"

"Because I am sure Mr Jones does not think of it himself."

"He is certainly a humble man," replied Penelope. "It will be no easy task. My good sister seems partial to those of humble disposition; though in other respects I will not compare the two gentlemen."

"I am glad you appreciate Mr Jones's worth," said, Emily, earnestly, "but I see you do not know him. I must warn you that he is some forty years old; and further that he is not a man who would think of himself in the role you have suggested. He has a great affection for *all* human creatures, but the idea of particularizing, of forming an affection for *one* individual to the exclusion of others, is foreign to his nature. However, even if this were not so, there is his situation. He is penniless except for the post he fills. I am not asking for sympathy on his behalf, for his needs are few, but even if his income were doubled it would hardly support a wife."

"Let us consider your points one by one, my love. First his age. Mr Jones is forty and you are twenty; there is, I admit, a great difference between those two ages – a whole lifetime, in fact, from your point of view. But I am nearly four-and-twenty, and the difference between Mr Jones and myself is reduced by some odd law of mathematics to about eight years. Elizabeth is nine-and-twenty; and the difference between Mr Jones and Elizabeth is, by this same law, almost negligible. Secondly, there is Mr Jones's humility about the role he is destined to play in this world. This I have already admitted will be my chief obstacle; but I am full of confidence. Thirdly, there is Mr Jones's situation. This is where my aunt is to help me, though she does not know it yet. Fourthly, there is Mr Jones's general affection for mankind. To this I can only reply that Mr Jones and my sister Elizabeth are in love with each other."

"If you have nothing beyond your own assertion to support you I need not take you very seriously. For you have accused *me* of some very remarkable sentiments before now without any sure foundation."

"It was after the second ball of the season, was it not?" said Penelope, with a bland smile. "I suggested that Lord Osborne was in love with you, and that you were almost in love with Mr Howard. I must apologize that events have proved me so very wrong."

Emily blushed. "Even so," she said, uncertainly, "I cannot believe you are right with regard to Mr Jones."

"Then I suggest, my dear, that by some tactful method of your own, whose contrivance I may safely leave to one of your delicacy, you discover my aunt's opinion on the subject."

"I will indeed," replied Emily.

"It is a project very dear to my heart," said Penelope, more softly than she was wont. "In addition to a natural feminine inclination for *anything* that savours of match-making I confess to a particular wish to see Elizabeth married. I have many memories of her struggling to perform the duties of a mother to those not much younger than herself, who were, let us say, not uniformly grateful for her efforts. To see her settled in the same house, a mother in her own right and busy at last in the highest purpose our sex is fit for, would give me a very real satisfaction. Do not misunderstand me, my love. I would hasten no one's departure but my own. Indeed I would be tempted to accept the proposal Miss Stokes is daily expecting me to receive from Captain Styles if I could be assured that by so doing I would make room here for Mr Jones."

"I see I have not misjudged the true kindness of your nature," said Emily, much moved by the serious part of this speech.

"Indeed you have not. I have beguiled you all this time with my gossip so that my second-best pair of lovers would not be disturbed."

"We must go down," said Emily, recollecting herself. "I had meant to tell you about Margaret and Mr Musgrave. That must wait another occasion for I intend to be gone before Lord Osborne arrives."

"What have you to tell me about them I do not already know?"

"A long story; I cannot tell it now. However, it ended in his almost confessing in so many words that he wished he had chosen you or Elizabeth."

"To be preferred above Margaret?" cried Penelope. "My dear, I am exceedingly flattered. I am only surprised he said nothing about you."

"He began to, but I cut him short. I felt I had already heard too much."

"I would have been too inquisitive to know who else was on the list," said Penelope, opening the door. "After Elizabeth, you and myself, doubtless come Miss Tomlinson, Miss Osborne certainly,

Miss Carr probably, and poor Jane Layton. Then there would come Miss Buckley, Alice Hammond, and others of whom I know nothing. I do not say we would all have had him; the uncertainty must be a great part of his punishment."

When they entered the parlour Mr Jones was on his feet in the middle of the room, apparently occupied in straightening his coat.

"Ah, the young ladies," he said, looking slightly embarrassed. "Dear Miss Emily; Miss Penelope. Miss Watson was so very kind – though I had not noticed the omission myself and I did say that perhaps it was neither the time nor the place for such a very personal service – however she suggested, and had made considerable progress in overcoming my objections to her proposal – –"

"Pray put me out of my suspense, sir," said Penelope, "and tell me what my sister Elizabeth has suggested before my imagination quite runs away with me."

"I was on the point of doing so, Miss Penelope. It concerns my coat. I do not know if you have noticed – I see no reason to suppose – –"

"He has lost a button from his coat," said Elizabeth. "I have asked him to remove the garment so that I can sew on another."

"That is precisely it," said Mr Jones, dropping his eyes bashfully.

"Now that we know the worst there need be no more hesitation," said Penelope. "Kindly surrender the garment as you are commanded."

"Perhaps some other time," began Mr Jones, going an even deeper shade of red.

"You must not expect to be so well chaperoned every day, sir," said Penelope, now smiling broadly. "There are three of us here this morning."

Mr Jones looked unhappily round the room; there were three young ladies in front of him, and there was not even a pianoforte behind which he could hide.

"There is surely another parlour," he said. "Could I not remove my coat in there, leave it outside this door with a knock warning you of its presence, and then perhaps trust you to repeat the process when the reparation is completed?"

"Come, dear sir, you are being very foolish," said Emily, midway between tears and laughter. "My sister wishes to render you a small service. I require you to submit."

With that she took hold of his coat at the shoulders, and Mr Jones apologetically slid out of it.

"Have you the button, sir?"

"He has lost it," said Elizabeth, looking in her work-basket.

"I have certainly *mislaid* it," said Mr Jones, "though whether in the literal sense of the word, I have actually *lost* it or not, I do not yet know."

"But you cannot at the moment produce it?"

"No," he admitted. "I cannot produce it. Miss Watson was so good as to proffer me the loan of one of hers."

Here he cast a look of such tender gratitude at Elizabeth that Emily began to think there might, after all, be some truth in Penelope's contention.

"I can offer you a choice between two," said Elizabeth. "Neither is an exact match I fear; one is somewhat too large, and the other somewhat too small."

"Either will do, Miss Watson. I shall be more than satisfied with either. Which ever will be least missed."

"You may take your choice, sir. The larger is a spare one of mine that has not been required, and the smaller has been discarded by my father."

At this information on their origin, Mr Jones drew near and examined the buttons. The large one was bright blue and a great deal too fine for his sombre coat, on which the small one would not have been noticed. But the large one had belonged to Miss Watson. After a long scrutiny he picked it up with his thick, red, clumsy fingers.

"That is a very elegant button, Miss Watson," he said, in a gentle voice. "It is a remarkably handsome button, if I may say so. I do not know how long it is since I have seen such a very fine button. Unless I am mistake even Mrs O'Brien has not one to match it. My only fear is on account of its being somewhat too handsome for my second-best coat."

"Then, sir, you must choose this," said Elizabeth, putting forward the other.

"Since you have been so generous as to offer me a choice I will

[217]

choose the larger. I do not think I am greatly given to a habit of personal adornment, and in this one instance perhaps the small vanity will be forgiven. I assure you I will long treasure the button in memory of your goodness in performing so kind a service for me this day."

Nothing more was said. Elizabeth bent over her work and Mr Jones watched her with a very tender expression. Within a short time the task had been completed, and Mr Jones, again fully clothed, displayed the button on his chest. Mr Jones and Emily then took their leave, he to continue on his way to Nettlebank, she to return to Stanton Lodge.

Emily did not now doubt that Mr Jones loved her sister, and that Elizabeth fully returned his affection. Whether Mr Jones was himself aware that his sentiments for Miss Watson were very different from his kindly feelings for the rest of his fellow creatures, she could not be sure; but she clung sufficiently to the opinion she had put forward to Penelope to believe him innocent of any plans terminating in matrimony. That he, Mr Jones, with all his obvious imperfections, could be loved as a husband is loved by a wife, would never enter his head. His humility was too great for such conceit; and even if it were not there was still the matter of his situation. Elizabeth was penniless; but his own circumstances were such that he could no more afford to think of a penniless wife than he could hope to aspire to a rich one.

Emily sighed. Like Penelope she would be happy to see her old master and her eldest sister settled in modest comfort. Then her thoughts turned to her personal affairs and the state of indecision of her own heart.

She sighed again. In spite of her indecision it was a very happy sigh.

Emily's indecision lasted but a few more hours. Some twenty minutes after she, Mrs O'Brien and Mr Jones (in his carefully preserved best coat on which there was a full complement of buttons that matched) entered the drawing-room at Wickstead that evening, it was resolved. She then allowed herself to acknowledge that she was as much in love with Mr Howard as it was proper for her to be until she had received his formal proposals. How far her present emotion fell short of that which was to succeed his declaration must be left to the reader to determine; but it is an admitted fact that there is a sympathy between certain members of the body in consequence of which no correctly brought-up young lady is able to bestow her whole heart until her hand has also been requested. It must not be supposed that Mr Howard behaved in any very remarkable fashion during these twenty minutes. His conversation was sensible rather than brilliant; his manners pleasing rather than extravagant. But his welcome had been warm; and there was a happiness about his eye and his smile whenever these alighted on Mrs O'Brien's niece that left Emily in no doubt of either his feelings or ultimate intentions. Such assurance was enough. She readily conceded that she was in love with the gentleman, that the sentiment had been present in a mild form even at the October assembly, and that in spite of her refusal to think of him during her absence at Eversleigh and in Portman Square the sentiment had grown progressively stronger since that early date.

Outwardly nothing was changed. To Mrs Blake she again admired the pleasant but irregularly shaped drawing-room, with its window cut away to the ground, and heard for a second time that this was the new rector's innovation. In the dining-room books and music, riding and Osborne Castle, were discussed; and – as she was now growing accustomed – Emily found herself agreeing with Mr Howard on all matters where taste allowed two opinions. The conversation might have become somewhat insipid had not the two elder ladies occasionally put forward a contrary view. This, however, they did with admirable tact; and further variety was added by Mr Jones, who in several speeches tried to reconcile the different judgements.

Charles and his brother and sisters came into the drawing-room during the very short period in which the gentlemen sat over their wine; and Mrs Blake began to talk of schools to her guests. Mrs O'Brien had no experience of boys; she agreed that in their case there might be much to be said for a school; but a girl was, in her opinion, best educated at home. Mrs Blake agreed. She would go so far as to say that where a good tutor could be provided, and where there was a father to advise and control, even a boy should stay at home. Her situation unfortunately was not that of others. Her brother had helped her through a difficult period, but she could not expect that he would always be free to devote his whole attention to *her* family. It was thus that she had come to her decision to send Charles to school.

"The decision does you credit, madam," observed Mrs O'Brien, "though in some respects it is a pity Charles must be taken from his tutor. Those who know Lord Osborne and your son cannot form other than a very high opinion of Mr Howard's abilities."

That gentleman and Mr Jones then came into the room, and Mrs Blake, after asking permission of her guest, repeated the praise to her brother with real pleasure. He took it in not quite the sense she had intended.

"You are right, madam," he said to Mrs O'Brien. "Osborne is as true a man as I ever wish to see. I am proud to have been accepted as his friend."

With this judgement they were all agreed; and Mr Jones was spared the difficulty of having to vindicate the character of a gentleman he did not know.

Mrs O'Brien said little on the way home. When Mr Jones had bid them good night, and they were sipping their warm wine and water before going to bed, she inquired whether Emily had found the evening an enjoyable one.

"Yes, aunt."

"Mr Howard is a sensible man, is he not?"

"Yes, aunt."

In the pause that followed Emily remembered all she owed her aunt. She remembered too that Mr Howard's behaviour during the evening had been such as to make the time peculiarly appropriate for the disclosure of a small part of her secret. In a voice she tried hard to keep from becoming over-tender she added: "I would go further than that, madam. I confess I find Mr Howard a man of very superior understanding."

Mrs O'Brien sighed. The admission had been slight in words, but it had confirmed all that she herself was thinking.

"I fully meant my praise, both of Mr Howard and his pupils," she said. "My remark was not intended as an idle compliment to Mrs Blake. Mr. Howard is in possession of a fair living; and as the sister has four thousand pounds apart from what her husband left her, we must presume the brother to have at least an equal sum. In short, an alliance there would be respectable from every point of view. Nevertheless one in the position of a mother may be excused from hoping . . ." Here Mrs O'Brien broke off. "Your happiness will be my happiness, Emily, wherever you find it; but you must not be too hasty. You do not see Mr Howard very often, do you?"

"No, aunt. He is, one must suppose, busy with his duties."

"I trust so. Yet I do not think you were particularly intimate with Mrs Blake when you were at the parsonage."

"We did not meet very often, but Mrs Blake was always most friendly when we *did* meet."

"You must remember that should they desire any *special* acquaintance they can easily seek you out," said Mrs O'Brien. "I shall be happy to receive Mrs Blake whenever she cares to wait on me; and of course they must be invited to dine with us in due course. We are getting somewhat full of engagements. On Monday we go to the castle; on Wednesday to the Tomlinsons; and on Thursday I mean to ask the Edwardses again, as Mr Samuel will be here. Did I tell you that Dr Richards gave me a very fine account of your brother the other day? I have been speaking to your father about him."

"Dearest aunt," said Emily, "you are very good. I trust – I trust most sincerely that I have not disappointed you."

"No, Emily. And you yourself, I am sure, are too sensible to take my small warning amiss. There is another point on which you can give me some information. Has your sister Elizabeth any admirers of whom I might be in ignorance?"

"I do not think so. There was a gentleman by the name of Purvis to whom she was once attracted, but some years ago, I understand, he married another."

"She is not young," said Mrs O'Brien. "She has struck me as one who would not ask for a great deal. She is a very *practical* lady, is she not?"

"Yes, aunt. And a very kind one."

"To be sure, my dear. It is a delicate matter, but the knowledge that she would not necessarily be called on to move out of her home in the event of some unfortunate accident might predispose her to accept what to others would seem a very modest situation."

"Yes, aunt."

"You think I am right, my dear?"

"I am almost sure of it."

Mrs O'Brien sipped her wine very contentedly.

"Your father is not a worldly man, Emily. It is a sad thing when daughters are left without a mother. Penelope is a girl any mother would be proud of. Is not one of those three officers attached to her?"

"I believe so. But Penelope discusses the matter with so little embarrassment that I cannot believe *her* heart is affected."

"It might be that she was not yet sure of the gentleman," suggested Mrs O'Brien.

"Truly, aunt, I am not able to make up my mind. We do not hide much from each other and she has not been silent on the subject. But she has jested about it as she jests about everything, which has been the most effective way of concealing her wishes. However, I think that if she had come to some *conclusion* as opposed merely to some *hope*, she would have told me."

"I have nothing to say to her jesting to you, Emily, but I trust she does not jest to the gentleman. Nothing is more likely to cool a man's ardour than wit."

"Were a gentleman to become fully acquainted with Penelope's character I do not think he would find much to complain of, madam."

"I will not criticize your favourite sister, my dear. We must hope that Captain Styles appreciates her as you do; and I do not think Penelope would have reason to regret any confidence you felt able to repeat to me. This has been a most interesting conversation, and has left me much to think about."

Within a week it was generally known throughout Dunford and the neighbouring villages that Mr Jones was to be the next rector of Stanton, and that whatever Mrs O'Brien was to do at some later date for her other nephew and nieces, Sam was to have four thousand pounds immediately to buy a partnership off Mr Curtis, and Elizabeth the same sum on her marriage. In Croydon, where the news was received in an aggrieved letter from Millington, it caused little satisfaction. It was very like a woman, Robert told his wife, to think that a man who had established himself by his own exertions had less expenses than one who was just beginning in the world. He himself, after three months' consideration, had been on the point of agreeing to lend Sam some money at six per cent, which was a very low rate considering the lack of security, when his aunt had made his brother a present of twice the sum. It was, to say the least of it, hardly business-like. And surely something was due to Tom Musgrave, who had taken Margaret without a penny.

Mr Robert Watson then wrote a long letter to Tom explaining the difference in value between four thousand pounds now, and four thousand pounds in ten, fifteen and twenty years' time. He trusted a favourable opportunity would arise in which Tom could bring the matter to his aunt's notice. As some hard things have had to be said about Mr Musgrave's character in the foregoing pages, it should be recorded that the gentleman spent two hours trying to unravel the calculations, and then put the letter away in a drawer and forgot about it.

22

Two days after the visit to Wickstead, Mrs Blake, as though aware of Mrs O'Brien's warning, called at Stanton Lodge on her way to Dunford. She usually followed the other road, she explained, which was a great deal kinder to the springs of her carriage; but now that she had become acquainted with Mrs O'Brien she hoped sometimes to vary her route. Emily's aunt received her very politely. If there was any regret in her heart, her own breeding and the obvious happiness of her niece prevented her showing it. Mrs Blake, assured of her welcome, wondered if Miss Emily would care to accompany her to the town. She intended nothing more serious than a visit to the library; but the weather was good and she would undertake to find time for any small commissions of her guests. Mrs O'Brien was appealed to. She suppressed a sigh and gave Emily a note for Mrs Edwards. Then, kind, generous and indulgent as ever, she engaged Mrs Blake and Mr Howard to dine with her two weeks from that day. To make it quite clear that Mrs Blake's visit had her fullest encouragement she came out herself to hand her niece into the carriage of the lady Emily hoped soon to call sister.

The next two hours were happy ones for Emily. Their conversation, she afterwards admitted, was confined to minor matters. Mr Howard, of whom Mrs O'Brien had not forgotten to inquire, was barely mentioned; but even the familiar subject of the bad state of the road, which was brought forward again to excuse Mrs Blake's previous neglect of the route through Stanton, took on a special interest when discussed in such circumstances and with such a companion.

"It certainly does put things in a different perspective," said Mrs O'Brien that evening. "We are of course to dine at the castle on

Monday, and there can be no question of our wishing to be on any but the very best terms with such an important neighbour as Lady Osborne. Nevertheless, Emily, a young lady cannot be too discreet. It would perhaps be as well if you rode in the other direction occasionally."

Emily did as she was bid; and on Monday evening, when the Musgraves, the Osbornes, Mrs O'Brien and Emily (but not Mrs Blake or Mr Howard) met at the castle, Margaret asked her sister where she and Penelope had been going when they passed through Millington that morning. Aware that Lord Osborne was listening, Emily answered that she thought it time she became a little acquainted with the country round her, and consequently Penelope and she had ridden almost to the foot of the downs beyond Millington spinneys.

Lord Osborne looked somewhat grieved, but said nothing. It was for the best, Emily assured herself. If they were to be no more than friends she owed him the earliest warning of the fact that she could give. She had so high an opinion of the gentleman she did not doubt they would remain friends.

Sam arrived on Wednesday night; and on Thursday morning, a trifle earlier and a trifle more quickly than she had made the journey before, Emily walked from Stanton Lodge to the parsonage. A tall, handsome young man, who would have looked very like Penelope if it had not been for the strongly masculine cast of his features, introduced himself as her brother and gave her a warm greeting.

"This is very pleasant, is it not?" said Elizabeth, when they were all seated in the parlour. "We have had much luck these last few months. Margaret is married, Sam is on the way to being settled, and I have arranged things so that I have nothing to do this morning but sit here and talk to you. To be sure my aunt is responsible for most of it, for if we were not to dine with her tonight I should be thinking of the dinner myself. Emily has been a good sister to us, Sam; for without her my aunt would still be in Shropshire."

Sam was very ready to agree with Elizabeth. He was in the difficult position of owing much to those he did not even know. Could he not call on Mrs O'Brien there and then without waiting for the evening?

Emily told him that her aunt was still busy with her morning duties, but hoped to see him and his sisters in about an hour's time. Meanwhile would he not tell her something of his circumstances at Guildford?

Sam, whose candid manner had already made a favourable impression on his new sister, willingly complied with her request. Both Mr and Mrs Curtis were respectable people, and Mr Curtis had by far the best practice in the town. There were two daughters, the elder of whom was married to an officer in the navy. Mrs Curtis, it appeared, had once held the belief that the younger might take the surname Watson with some advantage to both Miss Alice and Mr Samuel, neither of whom saw the matter in quite the same light as the good lady herself. A period of some difficulty had followed, during which Sam had felt it best to behave with absolute correctness to Mrs Curtis, and at the same time hold himself available day and night to Mr Curtis so that his employer would never, even for so short a space as one evening, wonder whether he might somewhere find an assistant more suited to his taste. Sam was sustained in his resolve by the good understanding existing between him and Miss Alice, and the suspicion that his pretty friend had more than a little admiration for a certain clergyman in the neighbourhood, whose living was not commensurable with his merits. The perseverance and proper conduct of the three young people brought their reward. About the middle of the winter Mrs Curtis had begun to speculate on the possibility of Miss Alice being provided for in some other way than the one she had first planned. Soon afterwards Mr Curtis started to drop hints of a possible partnership. He was no longer young and would be happy to hand over part of his duties and part of his income once Miss Alice was married. Now, thanks to Mrs O'Brien, the matter was as good as settled. The clergyman's calls were openly looked for by the daughter; the father was expecting an increase of leisure during the summer; and Sam's relations with the mother had returned to their former cordiality.

"My!" exclaimed Elizabeth. "This is news to me. It is time someone told Mary Edwards what you have refused for her sake."

Sam blushed, and for some minutes appeared less confident than he had been during the recital of his story.

"The refusal left me in a subordinate and even precarious position," he said.

"But that is past," cried Penelope, "and you will soon be as rich as my faithful Dr Harding, though not as fat, I hope. There is something in the medical profession that makes for constancy, is there not?"

Emily approved of Sam's modesty as much as of his candour. She had already found sisters she could love; now she had found a brother. There was much happiness, she realized again, in being one of such a family. To have around you those of your own age who wished you well in all your undertakings must add pleasure to success and remove the sting from failure.

Penelope, Sam and Elizabeth had begun another discussion, and she herself was contentedly listening to them, when there was a knock on the front door.

"It will be Mr Jones," said Elizabeth, promptly. "He promised to come this morning to meet Sam."

With no change of colour, but with a cheerful air of expectancy, she waited for Nanny to show in the gentleman who had taken Mr Purvis's place in her heart. Her brother and sisters were as surprised as she was when Mr Norton entered in his place. Penelope was the first to recover. Was Mr Norton *alone*, she inquired.

Mr Norton, however, was too worried to notice the remark, much less to reply to it. After the briefest possible greeting to Elizabeth he walked quickly up to Sam and said:

"Mr Samuel Watson?"

"Yes, sir."

"I was told at Millington I might find you here. There has been an accident."

"Good God!" cried Elizabeth. "Is Margaret ill?"

Even Emily was disturbed. There was something in Mr Norton's manner which told her the accident he was reporting was a more serious affair than one of Margaret's periodic prostrations on a sofa.

"No, Miss Watson. Pray do not be alarmed. None of your family is affected, but there has been an accident in Millington Spinneys. One of our party went to Dunford for medical attention but has not yet returned. Fearing the consequences of a long delay I went to Millington to ask help of Mr and Mrs Musgrave. By them I was told that Mr Samuel Watson was probably here, and I have come to entreat his aid."

"I am at your service," said Sam. "But please tell me what has occurred that I may prepare myself a little."

"There is a leg broken," said Mr Norton. "I will tell you more on the way."

"Then I shall need splints and bandages Elizabeth, what can you give me for splints and bandages?"

Before Elizabeth had time to reply Mr Norton spoke again.

"Will you not bring your instruments?" he asked.

"For a broken leg?"

Mr Norton bit his lip.

"Sir, I had meant to be discreet, but I had best be blunt. A man's life is at stake. There has been a meeting; and an officer lies in Millington Spinneys with a ball in his neck in imminent danger of bleeding to death."

All their alarm returned to the ladies; but there was now added another emotion, and it was with a look of shocked horror that they gazed on Mr Norton.

"You cannot have been so foolish as to have fought a duel!" cried Elizabeth.

"Not I, Miss Watson. I was but my cousin's second."

"Then it is Captain Hunter!"

"Hunter fired the accursed shot. He swears he meant to aim wide, but a hare got up at his feet the moment he fired, and poor Styles is not like to last long unless your brother can help us."

"I have not much here," said Sam, "but what I have I shall bring. Elizabeth, get me some linen."

Sam, who was by far the calmest and most collected of those present, ran out of the room and up the stairs. Elizabeth followed. Her alarm, and even her horror, had been brief.

"Foolish creatures!" she exclaimed impatiently, as she passed Mr Norton. "It is time you grew a little sense."

Mr Norton did indeed look somewhat foolish. He was barely older than Emily, and the events of the morning had been almost too much for him. His faith in the necessity of a strict sense of military honour had been strong when he set out from Dunford at an early hour. His anxiety over his cousin, who fired the shot, his friend, who received it, and his own self who witnessed the action, had greatly lessened that faith. Elizabeth's impatient feminine superiority now caused him to wonder whether a strict sense of military honour, which could threaten such unfortunate results, was in truth worth possessing.

Emily saw little of this at the moment. When Captain Styles's name was mentioned she had gone to Penelope and now stood by her sister's side.

"It is Captain Styles who has been wounded?" she said.

"Yes, Miss Emily. Our only hope lies in your brother. If we can pass the matter off as an accident things will not be too bad. I trust you will not betray us. If Colonel Beresford hears of what has been done there will be an inquiry, and the consequences may be serious. It is too late to think of now, but the whole quarrel was over nothing at all – a game of cards where the stakes were a few shillings."

"No one in this house will betray you, sir," said Penelope. Emily was relieved to find she spoke in a firm voice and with no trace of special distress. "Who is with Captain Styles now?"

"Mr Hammond. Captain Hunter went off immediately to Dunford for Dr Richards, but is not returned. Poor Styles! If anything happens to him it will be the end of all of us."

Sam and Elizabeth than came downstairs.

"You had best lend me your horse," said Sam. "It will save time. I know the spinneys and will undertake to be there over the fields in a very few minutes. If you will escort Miss Watson to my sister's house at Millington she will be at hand should she be needed."

The unhappy Mr Norton, glad to have some of the burden taken off his shoulders, readily agreed. Emily immediately offered her aunt's chaise; but Elizabeth refused, saying she would be at Millington before the horses were harnessed or even the old mare had been put in the parsonage gig. With a final appeal to them all from Mr Norton to speak of the matter as an accident, the three departed.

"Sam will do everything that can be done," Emily hastened to assure her sister. "I will wait here with you till we have some news."

"I thank you, my dear, but you must not be needlessly anxious on my behalf. I am as shocked as you by what has occurred, but Captain Styles is not a man I could be on more than friendly terms with."

"Is this true, Penelope? Or is it merely to spare me uneasiness?"

"It is true, my love. Willing though I was to respond to your pleasantries, I fear they were very wide of the mark. And talking of pleasantries, I chose a wretched moment to ask Mr Norton whether he was *alone*."

"He had something else to think of, and did not notice you," said Emily.

"Aye. Did you ever hear of such wicked folly? That three good friends could fall out over a game of cards! They must have been in liquor."

"I am relieved at least you do not have to suffer for it. I need be anxious now only for Captain Styles."

"Before you rekindle your anxiety tell me whether my dear Sam came up to the description I had given of him," said Penelope.

"Prior to the interruption," replied Emily, with a smile, "I had decided that Sam's character was composed half of yours and half of mine; and I asked myself what could be better than such a mixture. After the interruption, however, he exhibited qualities of decision and action which were peculiarly his own. And so I was answered."

"Thank you, my dear. Now you may be as anxious about Captain Styles as you please. In spite of their stupidity I cannot help feeling anxious myself."

The two sisters walked together to Stanton Lodge to tell Mrs O'Brien that Sam had been called away, and then returned to the parsonage. They had many hours to wait; and their day was not a happy one. That the officers who had danced with them at the winter assemblies, who had so often conducted them through the streets of Dunford, and who had supplied them with so much cheerful conversation throughout the recent months, had now laid themselves open to censure and perhaps even to public disgrace, was not a pleasant thought. At last Sam and Elizabeth returned, and having first assured them that Captain Styles was no longer in any great danger, they recounted the story of the day. It was good he had been sent for, and that Mr Norton had had the courage to admit the true position, said Sam. The ball was at the base of Captain Styles's neck, and while it remained embedded there was little hope for him. Sam had extracted it on the spot with such instruments as he had. When Captain Styles had recovered a little, he had been moved to Millington, where he still was, under the care of a sensible woman

Sam had found in the house. After some hours Captain Hunter had returned with Dr Richards, whom he had been following over the countryside, and the doctor had been good enough to approve of what had been done.

"He went further than that!" cried Elizabeth. "He said you had probably saved the gentleman's life."

Sam admitted that this was the doctor's opinion.

"'Tis a pity we are all bound to secrecy," continued Miss Watson. "It is to be a riding accident and Captain Styles is to have fallen on a stake. It would be better if some people in Dunford learnt what Captain Hunter has done this day."

"You are a loyal soul," said Penelope, "but before you take away Captain Hunter's entire reputation, pray remember that we have been seen more than once in his company of late."

"Captain Hunter indeed fired the shot," said Sam. "But we must believe its aim was accidental. And speaking as a surgeon I would find it difficult to judge between the good sense of a man who shoots and that of another man who stands up to be shot at."

Miss Watson found nothing she could disagree with in this sentiment, and merely added:

"I still say it is a pity they do not all know."

"Rest content, my dear," cried Penelope. "Dunford is a small place, and however much we talk of gentlemen falling on stakes, it is only a matter of time before someone else talks of them shooting each other in the neck."

However even in Dunford such rumours took a little time to travel. When the Edwardses arrived at Stanton Lodge – Mary and her mother somewhat blown about the face, as the new moon rose an hour or so before sunset and Mr Edwards had consequently lowered the windows of the coach soon after starting in an effort to catch a glimpse of it – Mary had heard nothing of a duel, and little of an accident. She greeted Sam civilly, but without warmth, and inquired whether it was true that he had attended Captain Styles at Millington. Sam replied that it was; and there for the moment Mary left the matter.

It was a party of a dozen people. Mrs O'Brien had invited the Watsons, the Musgraves and Mr Jones as well as the Edwardses; and nothing that could raise the importance of the occasion had been neglected. There was a certain sympathy between Mrs Edwards and Mrs O'Brien. The two ladies were able to read each other's thoughts and comprehend each other's motives even more readily than is usually the case with those interested in the possibly inter-dependent future of a young lady and a young gentleman. Mrs Edwards had well understood the point of Mrs O'Brien's invitation, and had come prepared for a display of elegance that caused both her husband and her daughter a little surprise. For some days it had been known that Sam was now in a position to seek his happiness. The present party was to show that the young lady who was to make him happy would enter a family of adequate respectability. The Watsons of Stanton Parsonage, now that Mrs O'Brien had come among them, must not be undervalued by their old friends.

Mary, seated next to Sam at dinner, and separated from her mother and father, Mrs O'Brien and Mr Watson, by the Musgraves and Mr Jones, returned to the subject of Captain Styles.

"He is not badly hurt, I hope," she began.

"It is something more than a scratch," replied Sam. "I think Captain Styles is more comfortable lying in bed at Millington than he would be sitting at this table."

"But physicians are usually inclined to exaggerate the importance of an illness," said Mary. "I do not mean it personally to you, of course, but that is the natural tendency of the profession, is it not?"

"So it is sometimes believed," said Sam.

"Dr Richards did not consider his injuries by any means negligible," said Elizabeth.

"But he too is a physician, my dear," said Penelope, "so we can hardly use him as an argument against Mary's proposition."

"However, he is well acquainted with the officers," said that young lady, "and after having attended them through a season of fox-hunting must be familiar with their careless attitude towards minor injuries. If *he* regards the accident as a severe one, Captain Styles has my sympathy."

There was nothing particular in the words, but the tone was not a pleasant one. Sam however accepted Mary's remark with outward good humour, and for a short time all was peace. Then Mary began again. Had Captain Styles been alone at the time of the accident?

"No," replied Elizabeth. "His *friends* were with him."

"I would have been surprised if that had not been the case. They are inseparable, are they not?"

"They are indeed. *We* were surprised that they had asked Mr Hammond to join them this morning."

"Mr Hammond! That is most unusual. Perhaps they had raced on the downs or something of that nature. Has anyone heard how the accident occurred?"

"I understand that the horse was fortunately unhurt," said Penelope.

"The military are at times, and not least when on horseback, an imprudent company," said Mary. "But I confess I admire them. They have more dash than others in riding and jumping. You have but to compare the state in which Captain Hunter, Captain Styles and Mr Norton return from hunting with that of Mr James and Mr George Tomlinson. But of course an officer is accustomed to see things in a more adventurous spirit than a civilian gentleman; what is a burden to the latter is a small affair to the former. A ride at night is nothing to a military man. I have heard that Captain Styles left London at six o'clock one evening last winter, and was attending our assembly by nine."

This speech distressed Emily and Sam, angered Elizabeth, and delighted Penelope. Before the others could reply she said:

"I fear you have the advantage of me, my dear Mary. I confess I find myself unable to admire a man solely on account of the facility with which he gets his neck injured. It is after all something that occurs almost inevitably to the more violent type of criminal."

Mary flushed; but she found an unexpected supporter from further up the table.

"I agree with you, Miss Edwards," said Mr Musgrave. "There is much to be said for a soldier's life."

"The military are indeed a brave lot," said Mr Jones, who had followed the conversation more closely than Mr Musgrave, "but I would not have them praised at the expense of those in other walks of life. With great respect to Miss Edwards there is only one profession which is entitled to higher praise for the ready services its members render their fellow creatures than that which Mr Samuel Watson follows. I refer to the profession of which I am a humble, unworthy and fortunately entirely unrepresentative sample myself.

If we are to make a list of the men to whom humanity owes most, then physicians must surely come very near the top. I trust I have in no way offended you. Those who know me well will not, I think, accuse me of a habit of making dogmatic assertions; but this is a subject on which I have thought much; and the conclusions I have come to in the past have been reinforced in recent weeks by the generous manner in which Dr Richards has spared no pains to help an elderly villager of this parish on my applying to him on her behalf. However, nothing I have said must in any way be taken to imply that I have anything but a high opinion for the special virtues of the soldier. I am too fearful myself to belittle courage in others."

Mary could not continue her argument in face of this. She acknowledged that Dr Richards was a benevolent man; and then allowed Emily to change the conversation. The point had been made however; and Sam's sisters were left in no doubt that, in spite of the elegance by which they were surrounded, Mary had reason to believe their brother a dull fellow, lacking the liveliness and ardour likely to appeal to a discriminating young lady.

The knowledge was the more difficult to bear in view of the day's events. At such a moment even Emily could have asked Mary whether she thought that perhaps some limit should be put to the high spirits of an officer, and on which side of the limit she would have placed the pastime of shooting one's best friend in the neck. Elizabeth was only prevented from divulging the secret by Sam's watchful care; and she recompensed herself for the suppression by telling the story of Miss Alice Curtis to Mrs Edwards in the drawing-room while her brother was drinking his wine. When the gentlemen joined them, Mary and Emily played; and Mr Jones, still uncertain whether or not he had offended the former by his outspokenness, lifted up his humble baritone in praise of military valour.

The party broke up early. The elders reckoned it very enjoyable; and Mr Edwards was so busy with his praise on the return journey that he entirely forgot his pursuit of the new moon. To some of the others it had been less satisfactory. The Miss Watsons' usual good humour had been ruffled; Sam had begun to think a month either too long or too short a time to stay at Stanton; and Mary was in that state of annoyance with both the outside world and herself that sometimes follows the ill-manners of a young lady.

"Yes," said Mrs O'Brien, "I think it all went very well, and the meal was not one I need be ashamed of. Emily dear, I do not wish to hurry Mr Jones, but the hints I have dropped in the past few days have had no effect whatsoever. The songs he chose tonight, for instance, were hardly those that would have appealed to Elizabeth."

23

The next morning was wet enough to put any thought of a ride out of Emily's head. At twelve o'clock, however, the weather changed with a suddenness to be expected of April, and white clouds in a blue sky replaced the earlier greyness. Mrs O'Brien took advantage of the break to go to Dunford; Emily, who hoped to see as much of Sam as she could during his visit, asked to be excused from accompanying her.

She was seated alone in the small parlour, wondering if the ground had dried sufficiently for the short excursion to the parsonage, when Mary Edwards was shown into the room. As Emily rose to greet her she saw that her visitor was in some agitation.

"Are you alone?" asked Miss Edwards.

"I am indeed. And I will ask you the same question. Are you come by yourself?"

"Yes. My mission is not a pleasant one; but I would not have you think it was forced on me. It is one I have chosen myself – I will at least claim that credit. Dear Miss Watson – dear Emily, if I may so address you – I have made my journey to apologize for my conduct last night, and to beg a service of you. Some short time ago I heard that so far from Captain Styles having been hurt in an accident yesterday, he was wounded by one of his fellow officers. It is true, is it not?"

"Yes," replied Emily. "It is certainly true."

"And you and your family knew it when I spoke last night?"

"We did; but we had been asked to keep the secret in the hope of hiding the matter from Colonel Beresford."

"How foolish and empty my talk must have sounded!" cried Mary. "I am deeply ashamed."

"You have made amends, Mary. And if the service you require

of me is to pass on your apology to my brother and sisters, it is one I will readily perform."

"I am not so contemptible as that. Where I have offended I will make restitution myself. But I cannot boast of my bravery, for what I had intended to ask was for you to come with me. There are certain circumstances which make my unaccompanied intrusion into the parsonage just at this moment exceedingly difficult."

This caused Emily some uneasiness. The only circumstances she could think of that would make Mary's contrite arrival at her father's house other than welcome was the existence of a definite engagement between the young lady and Captain Hunter or Mr James Tomlinson.

"Unless you have some particular intelligence to impart beyond what you have told me, I am quite sure that my sisters will be glad to see you. But I will certainly come with you."

"Dear Emily, I will not pretend to misunderstand you," said Mary, with a slight blush. "I do not think you will ever hear the particular intelligence to which you have referred. 'Tis a pity you and I were not more frank with each other earlier, but my position has not been an easy one. If you can spare me a few minutes I will enlarge on it; and I trust that you will not judge me too harshly." Emily assured her that nothing was further from her intention. Mary then paced restlessly up and down the room for a moment before continuing thus: "I have been acquainted with your brothers and sisters for as long as I can remember, and have an affection for all of them. But for many months before your arrival I could not meet one of your sisters without some hint being given me of Mr Samuel's intentions. I will not say that they were always unwelcome; but how was I to treat such hints, who had never heard, and indeed have *still* never heard, any hint of his intentions from himself? I am not pretending to excessive refinement. There are few of us who have never been flattered by a whisper from a sister of a brother's preference. But in my particular circumstances it became more and more difficult for me to converse with your family with my old freedom. Some time after your arrival your sisters ceased to embarrass me, and we have got on a little easier; but there are unhappily others to whom the talk seems to have spread. To my misfortune I live in a town; and I can hardly do an errand in the streets without encountering Miss Stokes, or someone of that nature, to ask me when a certain gentleman is coming over from Guildford."

"Dearest Mary!" cried Emily. "This is intolerable! You are now making me ashamed."

"*You* have no cause for shame, certainly. But I am nearly done. During all this time I have had no one in whom I could confide. Until very recently you yourself lived without brothers or sisters; I am still in that position. You were made aware of my parents' attitude to your brother almost the day we met; so on that score I need say nothing, except that mercifully it is now somewhat changed. If I have appeared to show too great an interest in another gentleman it has been partly to silence gossip I very much dislike, and partly, I must admit, out of – I do not quite know what. But I do not think I would have been constrained to act as I did if your brother had ridden over from Guildford once or twice in the past year, or made some other small sign himself that I was not entirely . . ." Here Mary broke off. She had been very frank, but there was a limit to what she could say at the present juncture to Sam's sister.

Emily was both surprised and moved. She had prepared herself for a confession concerning Captain Hunter, and had heard instead that Mary loved Sam. She herself had lately learnt the joy of a confidence shared; and that part of Mary's story that touched on her isolation excited all her sympathy.

"Dear Mary," she said, "let us be friends from this moment. You will not allow me to apologize on your behalf, but you must accept my apologies on behalf of my family."

"I told my story to excuse myself, rather than accuse others. I like your brothers and sisters, and I have been quite as much at fault myself. If you will but help me through the first few awkward minutes I have no doubt we will soon return to our old intimacy."

This Emily promised again, and for a short while the young ladies talked of their pleasure in making each other's real acquaintance after having been on formal terms for so long.

"Is it true that Sam – I mean Mr Samuel – really saved Captain Styles's life?" Mary then asked.

"Dr Richards has said so, but you know the tendency of physicians to exaggerate."

Mary smiled, though she still looked somewhat ashamed of herself.

"I see you are Penelope's sister," she said. "Did he really re-move the ball in the spinney where Captain Styles fell? I have only heard the story from my father, who learnt it in the White Hart this morning."

Emily now indulged her guest with a full account of the previous day's happenings as far as she knew them herself, and in one par-ticular – Sam's cross-country ride to the scene of the fight – as she imagined it might have occurred. Mary listened with gratifying attention.

"There is something of gallantry in that, is there not?" she said. "To gallop straight to the help of a wounded officer. One needs must admire conduct of that nature." The young lady paused, looked pensively out of the window, and sighed deeply. "Only I do not understand how a man who has the decision and spirit necessary for such an action should on other occasions hesitate so lamentably. Mrs Curtis must be a very shabby, scheming woman, do you not think?"

It seemed to Emily that it was for Sam rather than for her to answer this speech. Instead of making the attempt she asked if Colonel Beresford's views on duels were known.

"He is of course a military man himself," said Mary. "He has been heard to say that there *are* situations in which no gentleman would wish to avoid fighting. But I am told that ordinarily he would take a very strict view of a quarrel over some hasty words. How-ever, in the particular circumstances . . ." Mary stopped and shook her head. "I must not fall into the mistake for which I have just blamed others," she said.

It took Emily a few moments to think out the connection from Colonel Beresford, through his wife, who had been Miss Osborne, through the lady's brother, herself, her sister Penelope, until it finally reached Captain Styles. She laughed.

"I fear there are some weaker links in your chain than you ima-gine," she said.

"Dearest Emily, forgive the impertinence," said her visitor; and then added shyly: "Do you not yourself, just at this time – these last few months, for instance – find things very perplexing, and sometimes act in the opposite way to that in which your feelings prompt you for reasons which are, to say the least of it, not really adequate? It is not well expressed, I fear. I am not accustomed to speak of such things."

Such an ingenuous confidence, betraying the full extent of Mary's love for her brother and the difficulties she had had to face unaided for so long, again woke Emily's compassion.

"I will admit to you, Mary, that during the past winter I had suspicions I have since found quite unfounded, but which made me very unhappy for a short time."

"It is odd, is it not?" said Mary, with a deep sigh. "Of course I still do not know. . . . Or perhaps I should say I am not quite sure. . . ." Here she stood up. "They dine early at the parsonage; perhaps we should go. I trust your sisters will forgive me."

"I trust you have forgiven them."

"*I* have nothing to forgive," Mary hastened to assure her, so well pleased was she with her short conversation and her new friend. "I have been embarrassed sometimes, I must confess; but loyalty is a quality I value very highly. If I was so fortunate as to have a brother I hope I would be loyal to him. Looked at in that light the matter appears very different, does it not? Their loyalty to one another was what first attracted me to the three officers, though yesterday's events have greatly lessened my admiration. However, I must not pretend I have anything but friendly feelings for them, or have objected to being in some small degree distinguished. That is allowable from the military. It is not quite the same with Mr Tomlinson. One cannot accept attentions from a near neighbour like that without implying something serious in return. I was careful not to take any latitude there. He is grown into too cautious and calculating a gentleman for me. Let us go in the carriage, as it is still somewhat damp underfoot."

As Emily prepared herself for the drive and the walk home she had determined to make, she could not but wonder at the very young and unformed mind now revealed beneath Mary's formal, almost prim exterior. Then the memory of her companion's situation returned to silence criticism. That Sam would soon mould such a mind to correct principles she doubted no more than that its present weakness was due to the deception forced on it by the silliness of Mary's father, and the lack of sympathy with its simple wishes shown by Mary's mother.

Mrs Edwards's coach was at the door, and Mary and Emily were about to enter it, when a barouche, so smart and shining that it could have had but one owner, was seen approaching.

"Surely that is Lady Osborne," said Mary.

"I think so."

"Why then if Mrs O'Brien is not at home – Emily, you have quite restored my confidence. If Lady Osborne decides to descend I shall – I am sure I shall – be able to face your dear sisters without difficulty."

"Let us see," replied Emily. "It is unlikely that she will descend when she knows I am alone."

Here, however, she misread her ladyship. On being informed that Mrs O'Brien was in Dunford, Lady Osborne got out of the barouche, admonished her dogs for trying to follow her, walked twice round Mrs Edwards's coach, made a slight adjustment to the harness, and then dismissed Mary with an apology for the liberty she had taken.

"My respects to your mother, Miss Edwards; and I trust you will forgive me, but I like to see things properly done." As the coach drove off, her ladyship continued to Emily: "He is an idle, slovenly fellow. Mrs Edwards does not use her carriage enough. She should have the horses harnessed every day instead of letting the fellow grow fat in the kitchen while a boy exercises them. However, that was not what I came about. I have not yet looked at the grounds here since Mrs O'Brien had the timber seen to. As it has now dried up nicely perhaps you would be so good as to conduct me round to the front."

Somewhat surprised, Emily replied that she would be very pleased to; and with Lady Osborne at her side she set off to the nearest walk.

"You have not ridden towards Wickstead this past week?" said Lady Osborne, suddenly.

"No, your ladyship."

"I trust you have not given up your riding."

"By no means."

"I am glad of it. Nothing keeps a girl so healthy as constant exercise on horseback."

Emily said nothing. She could no more believe that Lady Osborne had made the visit to talk about her riding than to criticize Mrs

Edwards's coachman. The event proved her right; for as soon as they were some distance from the house Lady Osborne admitted as much.

"I am glad Mrs O'Brien is not at home," she said. "There is a certain matter I wish to discuss with you personally. It is what I believe you would call a delicate matter, and it was for that reason I suggested a walk in the open air where there is less chance of our being overheard."

Emily began studying the path at her feet. There was but one delicate matter that could be discussed between Lady Osborne and herself; but what did her ladyship mean to say, and how was she to be answered, when nothing had yet been expressed in words by the one who must speak out before anything could be decided?

"I am told you are a very refined young lady," continued Lady Osborne, "so I will not embarrass you by asking whether my son has made you an offer. I shall say instead that I know he has, and that I know too you have refused him." They had now come round to the front of Stanton Lodge, and Lady Osborne stopped to examine this view of the building. "Though modern, it is as respectable a house for its size as I have seen," she said. "It would make a very convenient secondary residence for the castle, though I do not hold myself with this habit of banishing one's mother from her accustomed home. If two ladies cannot agree, then they must disagree, and that is the end of it. I am glad it is now occupied." Lady Osborne turned her back on the house and walked on. "However, do not misunderstand me. Neither you nor I are seeking a fortune, Miss Emily. Our conduct has proved it – yours by refusing my son, and mine by not objecting to his choice when it was first brought to my notice. If you will forgive me saying so, you were not then what the world considers an eligible match. But I have never cared much for the world's opinion. I thought you an honest, healthy girl when I first saw you, and I think so now, in spite of all I have heard of your refinement."

Embarrassment was obviously an emotion Lady Osborne did not understand and for which she would make no allowances. Emily realized that nothing would be gained by permitting herself to become embarrassed, and she resolved to speak out.

"Your ladyship is very good. I have been more than grateful for your kindness both to me and to my family recently. But I feel I should ask – in fact I *do* ask – your ladyship's intention in opening this subject with me."

"I have no great intention, Miss Emily. You must not think I have come as a deputy on behalf of my son. He does not know I am here, and would, I am sure, have something to say of my interference if he heard of it. But I thought you and I might have a frank talk by ourselves for a change, instead of exchanging small politenesses in other people's company. There are several things I would like to say to you. One is that my son is greatly improved this past winter. He is more of a man than he was, and does not hesitate to tell me what I am to do at times. That is as it should be, and I am proud of him; though I must confess that when he first started practising to dance I felt very uneasy. There is another point on which you should be informed: he has been exceptionally healthy ever since he was a boy. He had the measles when he was six, but that is an infection even healthy people sometimes succumb to. Good health is in the family. His father was killed in a hunting accident, as you may have heard; it was in a strange country, and he jumped fifty feet into a quarry, which was the end of him, though there are worse ways to die than on horseback. He was a considerably more healthy man than your father, though I am relieved to hear that Mr Watson is better of late. I mean no criticism of you, of course. Miss Watson and you are the healthiest girls I have seen in the district. Miss Penelope seems very vigorous as well, in spite of her fair colour. Poor Tom Musgrave has drawn unlucky; I suppose he was misled by the rest of you." Lady Osborne turned round and obtained a second view of Stanton Lodge, now somewhat hidden by trees. "I have been happy to find that Mrs O'Brien too is a healthy woman," she added. This, however, was said in a more pensive tone and did not seem part of her main discourse. "Tell me, Miss Emily, do you like my son?"

Emily, who had recovered a little of her composure during this long speech, blushed again as she said:

"I consider him a very honest, honourable gentleman."

"But that does not answer my question," replied Lady Osborne.

"Then I will say yes, your ladyship," she replied, quite scarlet in the face. "I like your son very much. I would rejoice most heartily to hear he was affianced to some lady of merit and rank equal to his own."

"We are of the wrong party to match easily in rank," said her ladyship. "I am not altogether unacquainted with some of the Whig families in the distinct, but I am not on such terms with them as would encourage my son to seek an alliance among their daughters. Nor would I wish to be. I am proud of my family as it is, Miss Emily. We do not have to look for perpetual aggrandisement. We are not place-hunters. We have our position and we will maintain it as long as we are able. There are those who go to court, and there are those who go into trade; and there are others who are content to do their duty in the station in which they have been placed by providence. That is all that need be said. Edward must marry, of course, for without that the name could not survive. The girl he chooses will become one of his family. If she is a healthy girl, capable of performing her duty and keeping my son to his, she will be welcomed very sincerely."

All the oddity of her companion could not prevent Emily's being moved. Open gratitude and strong denials struggled for expression at the same time; and for a few moments she was in danger of confusing Lady Osborne by the simultaneous disclosure of both. Then she collected herself. She could not refuse proposals that had not been put to her, and she must say nothing that could be taken as encouragement of a suit she did not intend to accept. Her purpose must be made clear before they parted. Wondering how this was to be achieved, she could for the moment only bow in answer to her ladyship's very generous speech.

"You like dancing, I believe," said Lady Osborne, abruptly.

"Yes, your ladyship."

"Good. I propose to give a ball. Today is Friday. I shall give a ball next Wednesday. Wednesday is as good a day for a ball as any other, is it not?"

"Certainly, your ladyship."

"My daughter did well enough for herself without putting me to this trouble last winter," said Lady Osborne. "She and Colonel Beresford were content with the public assemblies in Dunford. However, as I have said, you are very refined."

"I do not know Mrs Beresford," said Emily, hastily, "but I have seen her, and I am quite sure she lacks nothing that taste and education can give a lady."

"I have a cousin in London who goes in for that sort of thing," explained Lady Osborne. "My daughter spent two years with her; she had balls enough then I suspect. Elegance and refinement are all very well in their way, Miss Emily, but they will not help you manage a great house, you know. An honest housekeeper is important; but in the end it is you who are responsible to your husband for the money you spend. Wednesday next, then, is convenient to you?"

"Yes, your ladyship. But are you not overestimating the importance of my presence? I shall merely be a guest there, like the others, though a very grateful one."

"I hope you do not intend to *refuse* my invitation," said Lady Osborne. "I shall send a man out later today with the cards, one of which, I need hardly say, will be addressed to Mrs O'Brien."

"I would find it difficult to refuse *any* invitation from your ladyship," said Emily. "But if an acceptance of this particular engagement is to presuppose the acceptance of some future request that need not be specified, then I would most certainly have to take the risk of offending you by a refusal."

Lady Osborne appeared genuinely puzzled by this remark.

"Is the acceptance of an invitation to a ball in itself nowadays considered as signifying a willingness to marry the gentleman of the house?" she asked. "I confess I am out of touch with these things."

Embarrassment had already been left behind; Emily realized that she must now pass beyond the ordinary restraints of modesty and reserve.

"By no means. But in view of our previous conversation – In short, your ladyship, as your near neighbour, and one very sensible of your kindness, I shall always be honoured to accept your invitations, provided my acceptance entails no obligation beyond what is customary in the way of gratitude, respect and civil conduct."

"I cannot compete with all that," said Lady Osborne, bluntly. "I will only say I shall be pleased to see you and your family, to whom I also mean to send cards, on Wednesday next. I am glad it is settled. And now I think I had better find my carriage before my dogs get too impatient."

They then turned their steps towards the carriage, Emily not entirely satisfied that she had made her point with the lucidity she had intended. It would have been clear enough to one of Mrs Blake's understanding; but was it clear to Lady Osborne? Emily sighed. She could not help liking her eccentric companion; and she hated the thought of wounding the son of whom that companion was so justly proud. However, she had done her best; she had spoken plainly. But there was a limit beyond which she could not go. She could not tell her ladyship that she would be unable to accept her son because she meant to accept Mr Howard as soon as he addressed her.

"I hear the officers have been duelling," said Lady Osborne. "I trust it is not about one of your family. It is bad for a girl's reputation if men start shooting each other over her, though she may not be to blame herself."

"Your ladyship!" cried Emily, in alarm, "I hope there has been no report of that nature. I was told myself that the duel was over a quarrel that occurred in the course of a game of cards."

"I believe that is right. It was your *brother* that was mentioned; not your *sister*. I had mixed it up, but I remember now. Colonel Beresford is said to be grateful to your brother. He seems to have taken a very serious view of what is really a very unimportant affair. If officers are not to let off their pistols sometimes there seems little point in their having them. Your brother is in practice in Guildford, I understand?"

"He is about to purchase a partnership there."

"I am not partial to physicians myself. In minor matters a proper diet is better than a doctor; and in major matters they do not seem to have much skill. No doctor has yet learnt to cure a broken neck. However, they have their place, like others in the world. No duel should be fought without a surgeon in attendance. There is my carriage. I have enjoyed our walk, Miss Emily, and I hope you feel a little better acquainted with me. You are a very civil, pretty girl, you know, though I am not credited with much judgement in that direction by my family. My respects to Mrs O'Brien."

When Lady Osborne had gone Emily went into the house and sat down. Her mind was very disturbed, and she hoped to compose it a little before encountering her family. But as she went through the interview to herself, instead of becoming quieter, she became more agitated, and her cheeks refused to return to their normal colour. That such remarks had been addressed to *her*, and that *she* had replied as she had, seemed in retrospect very surprising. Had she really told Lady Osborne that she would be unable to attend the ball if her presence there was to imply the acceptance of some unspecified future offer? The most brazen woman's cheeks would have flushed at such a recollection; it was certainly not the way Miss Emily Watson ordinarily spoke. Lady Osborne must have a very forceful character to make her so forget herself. And how was she ever to face her ladyship again?

After some minutes of these and similar thoughts Emily decided that anything was better than sitting still and recalling memories that made her ashamed. Indeed she could no longer sit still. Action of some sort had become a necessity. Without more ado she got up and hurried towards the parsonage.

She caught a glimpse of a carriage – not Lady Osborne's barouche, for that would have sent her home again – in the yard of her father's house as she passed; and she was the more surprised to find Elizabeth and Penelope alone in the parlour when she entered.

"Is not Mary here?" she said. "And where is Sam?"

"They are gone to look at something in the church," replied Penelope. "Or perhaps it was at the outside of the church – I have really forgotten. Elizabeth was unable to go because of the dinner, and I was to join them as soon as I had put on my pelisse."

"I am so happy for Sam," said Elizabeth. "Mary said she had come from you, so I suppose you know about it. She has heard of the duel and wished to beg our pardon for her silly talk last night. It must be half an hour ago that Sam said something about the church and they went on ahead of Penelope, who did not follow. My dinner is spoilt, but I do not mind. Perhaps I had better see if my father is prepared to wait, or would like something now."

With this Miss Watson rose, and having again told Emily that she was very happy, which indeed she looked, went out of the room

"And so there is now an understanding between Mary and Sam," said Emily.

"There was an *understanding* when they left the house, my dear. If they stay away much longer we must assume a betrothal or a serious quarrel. Doubtless their faces will tell us which has taken place."

"She has spoken to me very openly. She is very young and not very sensible. However, I have no reason at all to believe her anything but well-intentioned. She will at least be in good hands in Guildford."

"Which of us is sensible compared to you?" asked Penelope. "I must put in a good word for Mary. If one's father exhibits the silliness of an old woman, one may surely be excused the errors of a young girl oneself."

"You are touching me on a sensitive spot, Penelope. I have had a very remarkable conversation since seeing Mary, and I am by no means sure that I acquitted myself in it as sensibly as I should."

"With Lady Osborne, I suppose, whose visit prevented you accompanying Mary here?"

"Yes," said Emily, and proceeded to give her sister a very full account of the interview.

"Well, my love, a ball at the castle will be very enjoyable," said Penelope, when her sister had finished.

"*You* may enjoy it, but I do not think *I* shall. You must please be serious for a moment, for I want your advice. I know I have accepted it, but I am not sure whether I ought to attend. My aunt will wish it, but she will not require it if I am not well, for instance."

"I feel that to fall back on such a stale method of avoiding one's obligations would be more discourteous in the present case than usual," said Penelope. "Besides, you might one day have reason to regret you caused Lady Osborne to alter her high opinion of your health. However, I will be serious. You must remember that Mr Howard is rector of Wickstead. If he had a London parish the matter would be simple; you could go and stay with Mrs Seymour until he came to the point. But if you avoid Lord Osborne beyond what you have already done in the way of not riding in his park – if you refuse this invitation, for instance – you may find you have also avoided Mr Howard, which I take it is not your wish."

"He is to dine with us today week."

"Then I am sure you will have a pleasant evening," said Penelope, and a moment later added in a different tone: "In truth, my love, I very sincerely hope you will. You have not met him recently?"

"I met him on Wednesday."

"Indeed! You have been very secretive about the meeting."

Emily smiled and reddened slightly.

"I had not intended to keep it hidden; and being with my aunt in Dunford when it occurred I could hardly hope to. But we have had other things to talk of since Sam arrived."

"I wish you no unkindness, my dear, but I would not have you meet him again before next Wednesday."

"It is not likely, I fear, for I felt compelled to tell Mrs Blake in his hearing that I expected to be making Sam's acquaintance at this time. But pray why should I be limited to one meeting a week?"

"I was thinking that it would be a pity if Lady Osborne were to cancel the invitations we have not yet received. And my hope is not entirely selfish. You cannot continue under false colours. It is better to show the whole neighbourhood at one time that their surmises about you are incorrect, and that your carriages, however respectable, will never bear a coronet. The ball should be given and you should go to it. Once there you should so behave that your intentions become clear to everyone."

Emily thought this over in silence for some moments.

"It will be a disagreeable ball," she said.

"Could any ball attended by Mr Howard be disagreeable?" asked her sister.

"I mean that it will have disagreeable *aspects*."

"We will face them together, my dear. That is you and Sam settled, I am glad to say. Now I have only Elizabeth and myself to think of."

"My aunt has been complaining that Mr Jones will not understand her hints."

"There are hints and hints," said Penelope, "Mrs O'Brien's, I fear, are somewhat genteel. However, I am myself prepared to talk to Mr Jones any time it can be conveniently arranged."

"He is a good man," said Emily. "But Mr Howard . . ."

"Mr Howard is a passably handsome clergyman, with a fair income and a respectable character. He is entirely unworthy of a rich, generous-hearted, tender-spirited, and very beautiful girl.

However, as he loves you and you love him, I see no point in interfering."

"Ah, Penelope," said Emily, softly, "if I could but know that you would be half as happy!"

"I am not without hopes of doing something for myself one day. It has just occurred to me that Captain Hunter's wounded heart will shortly need as careful attention as Captain Styles's wounded body."

24

Penelope's wish was granted. Emily did not meet either Mrs Blake or Mr Howard again before the ball. However, one encounter of some importance to the inhabitants of Stanton did occur during this period. The two sisters were returning on foot from Millington one morning, whither they had accompanied Sam, when they were overtaken by Mr Jones.

"Dear Miss Emily! And Miss Penelope, is it not?" he called, as he came up to them. "This is a very fortunate encounter. I am in no fit state to offer myself as an escort to two such elegant young ladies, having made a circular tour which has taken me some four hours. Nevertheless, if you will forgive my muddy boots I would esteem it a great honour to be allowed to continue my journey at your side."

"You are always welcome to walk with us, sir," said Emily.

"And at this particular moment," added Penelope, "you are the more welcome in that our latest argument has just reached the gratifying conclusion of mutual agreement. The road, we have decided, is disgraceful; and it is time something was done about it."

"I cannot claim that the surface is, in the strict meaning of the words, either *firm* or *flat*," said Mr Jones, anxiously. "And though it is, of course, used by others of greater importance than myself, who could easily make do with a track across the fields, we must remember that those responsible for its upkeep have other preoccupations, not the least of which is the constant repair and maintenance required by the main road running through Wickstead, which, taking an impartial view of things, might be said with truth to bear a heavier traffic."

"I fear you have misunderstood me," said Penelope. "Our argument about the road is *finished*. We gave due weight to the points you have advanced, and in spite of them we reached the *termination* recently disclosed to you. I might add that we allow ourselves to discuss the state of the road but once in every four-and-twenty hours. Our daily indulgence has this morning been stretched to its limit, and we cannot reopen the topic till tomorrow. I must therefore request you to advance some entirely *fresh* subject for discussion."

"Indeed!" said Mr Jones, who had listened to this speech with a very puzzled expression. "Indeed!"

For some moments the party proceeded in silence.

"Well, sir, have you nothing to suggest?"

"It is not that, Miss Penelope. I assure you it is not that. There are as many subjects for discussion as there are objects in the world around us. But I was thinking."

"Of what, sir?"

"The road," confessed Mr Jones, with a blush. "I fear I was wondering why you limited yourself in this arbitrary fashion to but one conversation on it in each four-and-twenty hours. It would not, I confess, have occurred to me to lay down such a very definite ruling for myself about what could not be considered in any way a moral problem."

"You are apt to take my sister's statements with a greater seriousness than they deserve," said Emily, smiling. "Pray trouble yourself with this particular one no longer. What news have you to tell us as a result of your walk this morning?"

"I have had the painful task in two or three humble households of correcting gossip," said Mr Jones. "It comes about, of course, because the accident befell an officer. Certain folk appear more credulous over the behaviour of an officer than over that of one whose name they have been long familiar with, and who has lived among them all his life. If the accident had occurred to Lord Osborne, for instance, I cannot imagine that he would have been accused of having taken part in a duel."

"And has this been rumoured of Captain Styles?" asked Penelope.

"Did I not say so? I believe I forgot; but it was the point I meant to make, of course. People are too apt to credit any story of rash or foolhardy behaviour on the part of a young officer. However, in fairness I must make it clear that as soon as I pronounced a willingness to believe evil reports to be in itself no less reprehensible than the conduct alleged in those reports, the speakers were in all cases reduced to silence."

Emily and Penelope, like the humble inhabitants of the cottages, were reduced to silence by Mr Jones's dictum. After some moments of reflection his former pupil said in a low voice:

"Dear sir, you have a strong propensity for believing the best of others. I trust you will never have cause to regret this most admirable trait."

As was his habit in moments of embarrassment, Mr Jones fumbled for his handkerchief and blew his nose.

"You are too good," he said. "I do not deserve – In short it was not my design to draw attention to myself. Let us talk of something else. Have I told you that Lady Osborne has distinguished me to the most remarkable degree by including my name among those to whom she has addressed invitations for the coming ball? I realize, of course, that it is but my position as a willing if unworthy servant of Mrs O'Brien's and Mr Watson's that has caused her to take such a step. Nevertheless the condescension is very great. I could not be considered an ornament in even the lowliest ball-room; but I will endeavour, by such small means as lie in my power, not to disgrace my kind protectors."

"You will, I trust, dine with us on the evening in question and give us the pleasure of your company in the carriage," said Emily, who knew Mrs O'Brien's responsibility in such matters.

"My dear Miss Emily, what am I to say!" cried Mr Jones, in alarm. "I have already accepted Miss Watson's kind invitation to proceed with her party. The offer was made, and I yielded to it without expecting I would thereby affront Mrs O'Brien."

"You are already engaged, sir, and there can be no question of an affront."

"And my father is to have the honour of your company instead of Mrs O'Brien," said Penelope. "My sister, my brother and I have reason to congratulate ourselves."

Mr Jones blew his nose a second time.

"I am distressed to observe," added Penelope, "that my sister's skill with a needle and thread is not what I had believed. The blue button she sewed on your coat the other day appears to have come off already, and to have been replaced by one more in keeping with the sober hue of the others."

"Indeed you wrong Miss Watson," cried Mr Jones, blushing deeply. "It is through no fault of hers that the button is not visible. For reasons of my own, I myself removed the blue button and substituted this more ordinary one in lieu."

"It is not every man that is so proficient in what is usually considered a female accomplishment," said Penelope. "I do not wonder that you have a different opinion from the rest of your sex on the usefulness of mine, and show slightly less inclination than is customary to exchange the freedom of a bachelor for the cares and responsibilities of a married man. Have you a cold, Mr Jones?"

"A cold, Miss Penelope?"

"Yes. Surely that is the third time you have blown your nose since joining us?"

"I do not think I have a cold," said Mr Jones. "No, I am sure I have not. But your remark for a moment confused me. While I do not wish to give the impression that I consider the comparatively simple task of sewing on a button in any way beneath me, the inference you deduce from this faculty of mine – that because of it I would willingly dispense with the ministrations of a wife – is, I must assure you, not altogether correct. The matter is rather the other way about. It is not my few domestic accomplishments that are responsible for my unattached state; it is my unattached state that is responsible for these few accomplishments."

"I am relieved to hear you have no criticism to make of marriage itself. From the lack of example you had set I imagined you had some prejudice against it."

"Indeed, Miss Penelope, it is far otherwise," said Mr Jones, with emotion. "I yield to no one in the high opinion I hold of marriage. But I fear you do not fully appreciate my position. I am, dear Miss Penelope, a man rich in friends, rich in health and happiness, rich in the untold blessings of a merciful providence. Nevertheless I am what the world calls a poor man, a very poor man. Apart from many personal shortcomings, which are such that I could expect no young lady to look on me with favour, my impecunious state means I would be unable, quite unable, however deep and sincere my feelings, to address her."

"In one particular you grievously wrong yourself, sir," cried Emily.

"Dear Miss Emily; dear, dear Miss Emily," replied Mr Jones, heedlessly blowing his nose, "you see me still with the loving and uncritical eyes of a child. I cannot believe that others are so blind to my failings."

"I am myself more interested in the other objection Mr Jones has advanced," said Penelope. "I know there are philosophers who hold that only those in possession of riches should be permitted the pleasures of a wife and children, and that these should be denied the needy from fear they become burdens rather than pleasures. It has been claimed by some that this policy would result in a lessening of the unhappiness in the world; but to me there has always seemed something suspect in their reasoning. I confess I am surprised to find Mr Jones among them."

"Dear Miss Penelope!" cried Mr Jones. "I am at a loss for words . . ."

"This discussion is becoming rather too personal," said Emily, much moved by the distress of her old master. "Should we not discontinue it?"

"Surely Mr Jones will not object to giving us his opinions?" said Penelope.

"More than that," cried the unhappy gentleman. "I *must* give you my opinions. I cannot bear the thought that you should so grossly misrepresent me to yourself. It wounds me deeply to feel that such false ideas are current about me in Stanton Parsonage. I conceive of marriage founded on mutual love as the highest condition attainable by humans, and would deny its blessings to no one, rich or poor. That is my honest general opinion, and in the strictly general sense there are no exceptions to it at all. I trust – I most earnestly trust that you now fully understand me."

"I understand you except as regards one small detail," Penelope continued relentlessly. "You deny no man, rich or poor, the right to marry; but you deny yourself the right because of your poverty. I am, I confess, not greatly accustomed to logical disputes; but there seems to my untrained mind a contradiction there."

"You are confusing a general opinion with a particular instance," said Mr Jones, wildly waving his handkerchief. "I have explained my circumstances. I can do no more."

"Perhaps it is because I am a female that I am at heart more interested in particular instances than general opinions," said Penelope. "Let us, however, strike a balance. You must be a little less general; I will be a little less particular; and we will both assume mutual love to exist in my imaginary cases. If a rich young lady is addressed by a rich young gentleman, you think she would be justified in accepting him?"

"Most assuredly."

"And if the lady is not rich, but the gentleman is; she is not to be censured for agreeing to his proposals?"

"Why no, Miss Penelope."

"And if the riches belong to the other party before the marriage; should mutual love exist, the lady is entitled to accept the gentleman?"

"If the motives of both are honourable there can of course be no no objection."

"And if both the lady and gentleman are poor, though sincerely in love, the lady is still allowed to take her happiness if it is offered to her?"

"There must be bread to eat!" cried Mr Jones. "I must tell you, Miss Penelope, that at one period in my life I was forcibly reminded of the great importance to the human frame of a sufficiency of nourishment."

"I myself have not been accustomed to riches, sir. My family is not one that has been brought up in luxury, though it has not known starvation. Assuming there to be bread enough to eat, but none to waste, you would allow the lady to make sure of the one chance of happiness life offers by accepting her poor suitor?"

"I would not presume to assert she was *wrong*," replied Mr Jones.

"I myself would assert she had made a very honourable decision," said Penelope. "I can conceive of no more honourable existence for one of my sex than that of sharing the world's burdens with a loved partner. But I can easily see that if the gentleman had a low opinion of the lady's worth, if in fact he thought she would prefer an existence of idle gentility to one of useful toil, he would hesitate to address her. Did you say something, Mr Jones?"

"I was about to say – In brief, I thought perhaps you had attributed a somewhat unnecessarily low motive to the gentleman's silence."

"It would be that or pride," said Penelope. "Either he doubts the lady's worth, or he is too proud himself to think of a situation in which his wife works at his side instead of gracing an empty drawing-room for the length of the day. Between such motives I find little to choose. However, I am glad to find you in entire agreement with my estimation of a lady's duty in this matter. Be she rich or poor, and be her suitor the one or the other, she has but to consult her heart before refusing or accepting him. Indeed, Mr Jones, I think you have judged better than you know, for it is in truth by the heart alone that the better part of our sex decides."

Stanton church had been in view for some time; and nothing more was said until they turned the last corner that hid Stanton Parsonage. Then Penelope spoke again.

"Here is my home, and here I must bid you goodbye," she said. "It is as pleasant to return home as it is to set out, is it not? I trust I may long have such a home to return to. It will be a sad day for Elizabeth and myself when we have to leave it. The knowledge that the time must inevitably come when we are cast adrift does not make the prospect any easier to bear. We can only hope that the day itself is far distant."

"Indeed," cried Mr Jones, with unfeigned sincerity, "I most earnestly hope so."

"Goodbye, sir," said Penelope. "I have greatly enjoyed your company and our discussion. Goodbye, dearest Emily."

The other two continued on their way, Mr Jones very thoughtful, and Emily with some feeling of shame. Surely Penelope had said too much. A hint to one of Mr Jones's humility was permissible; but to put the poor gentleman so consistently in the wrong, to attribute to him such a series of uncharitable opinions and shabby motives, was hardly just. She felt that she owed him an apology.

"Is not this your lodging, sir?" she asked.

Mr Jones looked up, used his handkerchief once more, this time to mop his brow, and finally put it away.

"Why yes, Miss Emily. I had not realized where I was. But if you will permit me I will walk on to your door."

They had almost reached the limit he put to his journey, when he said:

"Miss Penelope has a very lively mind, has she not?"

"Yes, sir."

Mr Jones looked at her with no little anxiety.

"You have yourself told me from time to time that she is not always serious."

Here, it seemed, was Emily's chance: she had but to agree that Penelope was not always serious and apologize on her behalf. Mr Jones would readily forgive, and all would be as it had previously been. That, without a doubt, was the way she would have acted if she had never left Eversleigh. But she was no longer able to judge so simply. Mr Jones trusted her. A word from his former pupil would still every doubt that Penelope had raised. But was that the reassurance he required? She remembered Elizabeth's sewing on the button; she remembered Mr Jones's secretiveness about its disappearance; she remembered Mr Howard and the longing in her own heart. This final recollection decided her.

"Dear sir," she said, "my sister sometimes exaggerates in her talk. But her admiration for your character is as genuine as her interest in your welfare. I am sure, *quite* sure, that she would never intentionally mislead you."

It had been done. She left him and ran quickly within.

"You are very flushed, my dear," said Mrs O'Brien, whom she encountered in the hall. "I trust you have not been walking too fast."

25

In common with many others, Emily was conveyed to Osborne Castle at the appointed hour on Wednesday. She would perhaps be required to go through some unpleasant moments in the course of the evening, but the thought could not diminish her great happiness, her joyous, trembling expectancy. One consideration dominated all others; the time was fast approaching for Mr Howard to declare himself. That the moment would come soon Emily did not doubt; and no surprise on either Lady Osborne's part or her son's must be allowed to check her determined course of behaviour at the ball. No consideration of *their* feelings must prevent her making *hers* clear beyond the possibility of future misunderstanding.

A good number of people were in the drawing-room when Mrs O'Brien and her niece entered. One glance sufficed to tell Emily that this good number did not include Mr Howard, and almost before she made her first curtsy she was engaged for the two opening dances by Lord Osborne. It had occurred to her, as these things are apt to occur to a young lady before a ball, that if Mr Howard had happened to jostle her in the passage, or had chanced to be standing by the door as she entered the drawing-room, she might have been able to tell his lordship she was already engaged. She smiled now at the memory of her idle musing. Mr Howard was a gentleman of some thirty years of age. That his affection was deep and would be lasting were facts vouched for by his character; but this same character would also see that his affection was not displayed by behaviour more suited to one as young as Mr Norton. Emily sighed happily. She had chosen worth, integrity, education and manners. She had refused position, riches and nobility. She had never wanted violence, infatuation or impetuosity. She did not now regret her choice, even though Mr Howard had not been standing by the door.

"You are looking very beautiful, my love," said Penelope, while Mr Watson was trying to explain his presence, which was still causing him some slight surprise, to Mrs O'Brien. "I am almost grateful Captain Hunter is not here to see you, for then my schemes would undoubtedly have come to nothing. But I have been wondering whom I am to dance with now my favourite three officers are not come. Mary at least has Sam, as you will notice if you look behind me; but as nothing has yet been said to Mr Edwards they can hardly be allowed more than two dances together."

"Was Captain Hunter not invited?" asked Emily.

"He was certainly invited, for Lady Osborne is not deterred by a few pistol shots. It is Colonel Beresford, to whom I have just been presented, who is responsible for his absence, and Mr Norton's and Mr Hammond's too. I nearly asked the Colonel if he was prepared to do duty for the gentleman, two of whom would certainly have stood up with me. There is Mr George Tomlinson, however, and perhaps even Mr James, now it is known what my aunt is doing for Elizabeth. In that connection I have something to tell you, but it cannot be said here. Indeed I am saying far too much as usual."

"You are saying it somewhat loud," said Emily, in a low voice.

"I am surrounded by my family, my dear, and they are so used to me they do not listen any more. I see that the gentleman who has the shortest distance of all to go has not yet arrived. However, he was not only invited, but accepted, I have learnt, so you must not distress yourself. Perhaps it is only Charles who has lost his gloves at the last moment. Are you engaged at all?"

"In the first two dances."

"With Lord Osborne?"

"I could not refuse."

"It would have been difficult, as he owns the house; it would have been ungenerous too, as the ball is doubtless only given to allow him an hour or so in your company. It makes him appear somewhat reckless, does it not? He could have hired the parlour at Stanton for a fraction of the cost."

"Hush Penelope."

"I mean no harm, my love. I had intended to be there myself to chaperone you."

There was still no sign of Mrs Blake, Charles or Mr Howard

when the party began to move into the ball-room. This was a high apartment, with a very fine gallery; and though Mrs Blake might perhaps have complained of the amount of carved oak both in this gallery and in the vaulted ceiling, she would have found few to agree with her that evening. Lady Osborne seldom gave a ball; but the general opinion of the company was that her skill – or perhaps her housekeeper's – had lost nothing through disuse.

The music began. Lord Osborne came forward to claim his partner, and with an ease that contrasted most favourably with his behaviour at the first winter assembly in Dunford, conducted her to the place of honour. The distinction did not pass unnoticed. There were few ladies present who did not feel their existing suspicions about Lady Osborne's reasons for giving a ball fully confirmed. Something of this general contentment – for nothing is more satisfactory than having one's judgement proved correct – reached Emily, and she decided to give Lord Osborne the warning she owed him without further delay. He was too open, and she liked him too well, for her to leave him any longer with expectations she could not gratify.

"I do not see Mrs Blake," she said at her first opportunity. "Nor Charles, nor Mr Howard. I hope no one is ill at the Rectory."

"I trust not. I saw Howard this morning and he assured me he was coming, which I took to mean the whole party. That is your brother with Miss Edwards, is it not? I shall look to you to introduce me in the course of the evening."

"He will be honoured, my lord. Mr Howard and his sister are to dine with us the day after tomorrow. I trust the meeting will not have to be postponed."

"I do not think it likely," replied Lord Osborne, with a smile. "You know my mother well enough by now to be sure that she would not have chosen a sickly tutor for me. Yours is a remarkably handsome family, Miss Emily. I see it has two distinct strains. There is your brother, Miss Penelope, and perhaps Mrs Musgrave on one side, and you and Miss Watson on the other."

There was no special compliment to his partner in this, but he was gazing at her with such manifest admiration as he spoke, that, though she would willingly have listened to his commendation of her sisters, she thought it best to return to her own conversation.

"There are more headings than one under which her ladyship's choice could be approved," she said. "Mr Howard, surely, has qualities besides his health to recommend him. In education he stands very high. In so far as I can presume to judge his character, it is superior to that of others. And though I have not myself yet had the opportunity of hearing him preach, my father has praised both the substance and the method of his sermons in very complimentary terms."

"I am inclined to reckon both you and Mr Watson very good judges," said Lord Osborne. "In fact, I will tell you this, Miss Emily, I admire Howard more than any man living, and I am particularly glad you share my good opinion. As for hearing him preach, it is possible that you may have an opportunity for that in the future."

Emily now regretted that she had added her father's praise to her own, but she was not dissatisfied with the short conversation. She had made her point; it would not be long, she hoped, before Lord Osborne recalled it, and asked himself what it implied.

For the rest of the two dances Emily said little. She praised the room, and the very handsome arrangements that had been made, but in as restrained terms as were compatible with politeness. Nothing must be allowed to suggest that her interest in the ball or the castle was different from any other quest's.

Shortly before the end of the second dance Mr Howard came into the room without his sister or Charles. That he lacked companions, and that he seemed far from at ease himself, made Emily think that she had been right in her apprehension of something having occurred at the Rectory. For a moment her heart beat at a more urgent pace. Mr Howard, indeed, was safe; he was now talking to Lady Osborne; but she had feelings of more than ordinary affection for Mrs Blake and her family.

"There *is* Mr Howard, my lord," she said. "But I see no sign of Mrs Blake or her son."

"Why yes; there is Howard," replied Lord Osborne. "I was sure he would not fail us."

"He appears somewhat upset. I trust there has been no accident or anything of that nature."

"He is late, and has to make his apologies which is not always an easy matter. I assure you, Miss Emily, that if anything untoward had happened at Wickstead, we would already have heard of it. Our first intimation would have been a message for assistance, not Howard's lonely presence at a ball. However, that is the end of our dance. You are not yet acquainted with Colonel Beresford, I think. If you will allow me to present you, I will have a word with Howard, and send him along himself to reassure you. It is no misfortune to meet him at a ball, for he is a better dancer than I am, as you may be aware."

It was an honest, generous speech, revealing the entire man in its openness and lack of jealousy.

"You are very good, my lord," she murmured. In spite of all her resolution her voice was a little tender. He was always good, and in this case he was certainly right. If anything was seriously amiss at the Rectory Mr Howard would not have come up to attend the ball. She could not be unhappy merely because he had come alone.

Lord Osborne presented her to his brother-in-law, reminded her of her promise with regard to Sam, and then withdrew. Colonel Beresford was an elegant officer of very good family. The Watsons, of whom he had not been greatly aware during the early part of his stay in the district, had recently come rather more to his notice. He was grateful to one for preserving the good name of his regiment; and his brother-in-law was said to be distinguishing another. He believed them to be worthy folk – could there be a more worthy action, for instance, than preserving the good name of a fine regiment – but he had been surprised to find their appearance so uniformly good. Indeed to Colonel Beresford, who was by way of being an experienced judge in these matters, the appearance of at least two of the young ladies – the one with whom he had just danced and the one to whom he was now talking – was something more than good.

"I, too, must request the honour of an introduction to Mr Samuel Watson," he said. "I understand that he attended one of the officers of my regiment recently with beneficial results."

"He was fortunate to be at hand when his services were needed, sir."

"The regiment must also consider itself fortunate," said the Colonel. "As is often the case in such circumstances there has been some gossip over what, after all, was only a riding accident. Had it had fatal results the gossip would have been more widespread."

"Undoubtedly," said Emily.

She had hoped to learn what was in store for her unfortunate acquaintances; but if the duel was, in spite of everything, still to be regarded as an accident, the less she said on the subject the better. Perhaps Colonel Beresford sensed her curiosity. He glanced at one of his officers for a moment and said:

"We are not a full complement this evening by any means. Three of my officers are under orders to proceed abroad, and could not be spared from their preparations."

"Indeed, sir! To a distant station?"

"To a somewhat remote outpost in the West Indies," replied Colonel Beresford, with obvious satisfaction.

Penelope, who had left her sister and her partner to speak to Mrs Edwards, now returned and took the chair at Emily's side. Preparations were being made for the next two dances, and the Colonel asked Miss Emily Watson to stand up with him. Emily looked towards the door where Lord Osborne and Mr Howard were still in conversation together. She was unhappy to have to refuse the Colonel, she said, but though she had not yet given a definite promise, enough had been said about the second two dances for her to be under the obligation of keeping them open. Colonel Beresford replied that in that case he would apply again in the next interval, and after giving the ladies a final bow, went in search of his wife.

"And what," asked Penelope, "has been said about the next two dances that allows you to refuse one gentleman without having promised another?"

"Very little has actually been said," confessed Emily, with a slight blush. "But Mr Howard is come and Lord Osborne intends to send him this way."

"I noticed the gentleman's entry, my dear, but I am surprised to learn he needs other encouragement than what his own eyes give him before taking so obvious a step. And furthermore, though I hesitate to suggest that either of your admirers would stoop to sharp practice, it would seem to a disinterested observer that Lord Osborne was retaining him by the door, rather than sending him this way."

"I think he will come before the music starts," said Emily, gently.

"It is possible, my love. It is indeed possible. I believe you once before tried to keep a dance for Mr Howard, though without success. I wish you better fortune this evening. Do you realize that this is the first ball I have ever attended in the district at which my presence is not due to Mrs Edwards's charity? The same could be said for the four of us. Some acknowledgement is surely due to the lady. It would look very pretty if we advanced down the room in line, wheeled, curtsied in front of her, and solemnly intoned our gratitude, would it not?"

"You are as right in intention as you are wrong in method. I think she would welcome our thanks now that we are all so independent. You should have remembered the fact when you were talking to her just now."

"I did, my love," replied Penelope, with a look of complacency. "And she said that I was a very civil young lady. Notice, please, that I did not openly brag of my politeness, but cunningly induced you to draw it out of me. It was cleverly done, was it not?"

"It was. And in return I shall tell you that Captain Hunter is under orders to proceed to a remote station in the West Indies, and looks like being too busy with his packing to say goodbye to *any* of his acquaintances."

"My poor heart!" said Penelope. "Its affections must return to Captain Styles immediately. To be recovering from wounds in Surrey – even in Margaret's house – is a better fate for a man than exile to a tropical island. He knew what he was about when he exposed his neck, after all. I believe my brazen talk to poor Mr Jones is bearing fruit. When Elizabeth and I were helping each other dress she let fall a casual remark about our not really requiring a spare bed-chamber any more, with you and Margaret close at hand, and the probability of Sam staying with the Edwardses in the future. My dear, here is your gentleman, but he does not look very happy. I trust there is nothing wrong."

Mr Howard was approaching them, but without any expectant smile; and their friendly greeting seemed to embarrass, rather than please him.

"I have not yet seen Mrs Blake this evening," said Emily. "I trust she is not unwell."

"It is kind of you to inquire," he replied. "Osborne informed me you were anxious. My sister has a slight headache, which made her decide not to come tonight, but she is not ill."

In answer to a further question he told them that Charles was in his normal health, but that his mother had decided he could not attend the dance without her protection.

Emily was alarmed, not by his words, but by his manner. He stood in front of them, very ill at ease, looking sometimes at the floor, sometimes at the musicians, and occasionally – for a few short seconds – at the two young ladies. This was not the Mr Howard she had known since she returned to Stanton; it was not even the Mr Howard she had known in the early months of the winter. Could it be that Mrs Blake was more ill than he pretended; or could it perhaps be that the public nature of the encounter, which was taking place under the watchful eyes of a great number of chaperones, was embarrassing him? But this latter suggestion she discounted. Mr Howard was a grown man; he was a gentleman of very adequate address. His preference had been made plain in front of Mrs O'Brien and Mrs Blake. He must be as well aware as she herself that their liking for each other would soon have to be disclosed to others, and that nothing was to be gained by pretending a less close acquaintance than existed. Nevertheless *something* had disturbed him. Was it her remark to Mrs Blake that for the few days after Sam's arrival she would be occupied in making her brother's acquaintance? But surely that was natural enough; even a lover could not take exception to so innocent a wish. Whatever the cause of his displeasure she determined that no effort would be spared on her side to restore him to humour.

"I am sorry to hear of Mrs Blake's headache, both on her account and Charles's," she said, with a friendly smile. "Indeed, if I had but known of it in time, I would have asked if Charles could have accompanied me, I would have undertaken his guardianship with pleasure."

"You are very good," he replied.

"And I must remind you, sir, that you are engaged to dine with us on Friday. It will be a real blow if Mrs Blake is not recovered and our meeting has to be postponed."

The music had started. Mr Howard said that his sister would, of course, write a letter if unable to fulfil her promise, and then stepped in front of Penelope and requested the honour of a dance.

The young ladies were both so surprised that the gentleman had to repeat his request, which he did in no very polished way. Penelope, for once at a loss for words, stood up with a flushed face, while Emily bit her lip. Then ignoring Mr Howard's arm, Penelope preceded him to the set, which was rapidly filling up; and Emily was left in unenviable isolation.

It had been done intentionally, of that she as sure. If he had been pleased to see her, if he had hesitated, if he had seemed shy like a lover instead of embarrassed like a – she had no word to describe one ashamed of his gratuitous rudeness – if there had been anything to suggest that he would have preferred to dance with her, she would have gladly forgiven his dancing with Penelope. But there was no excuse; his act had been deliberately designed. He seemed even to wish that its intentional nature should not be misunderstood; and for the moment anger predominated over the painful feelings in Emily's heart. Base, mean, and despicable were the words she used to herself to describe him. Never, never again, in any circumstances, would she treat Mr Howard with anything but the utmost coldness. Nothing would make her vary her attitude; she would not pursue her acquaintanceship with Mrs Blake, and she would see no more of Charles. Mr Howard was treacherous. He was unprincipled and dishonourable; and she could only congratulate herself that he had, for some reason, exposed his true character before it was too late.

An inquiring glance in her direction from Colonel Beresford, standing near the head of the set, woke her to the awkwardness of her position, and she blushed. The young ladies round her had been claimed by their partners; she must find her aunt without delay. She got up, and with all the unconcern she could summon, began her journey. Then she heard a step behind her and felt her arm taken. It was Sam.

"This is very fortunate," said her brother. "I had just gone to see that my father was comfortably settled in the card-room; and in truth" – lowering his voice slightly – "as I am not supposed to dance with my sisters there was but one person here I wished to stand up with. Let us walk up and down a little and improve our acquaintance by discussing our neighbours."

She gave Sam a very grateful glance. It was his fate it seemed, to be at hand when wanted; just as it was his habit to take decisive action while others would still be parleying.

"You are very thoughtful," said Sam, after almost a minute of silence.

"Yes, Sam. I have something to think about. I am grateful for your arm, and I must tell you that there are at least two gentlemen here who wish you to be presented to them. But do not let us talk for the moment."

The awkwardness of being alone was over and she could turn her whole attention to Mr Howard's behaviour. Her anger was still very strong, but it was not enough to call him shabby, base, and treacherous. She must recall their acquaintance and see – not if there was an *excuse* for him, for there could be no excuse for wounding a heart that had innocently responded to open attentions – but if there was any discoverable reason for his conduct. She had been attracted to him while staying at the parsonage. Whether he had or had not ridden into the Rectory yard while she was calling there with her sisters she could not now be sure; but the point had lost its significance, for there had been no doubt of his welcome when she returned to Stanton. He had admired her, and had made his admiration clear. They had met as acknowledged friends, and from that meeting their intimacy had progressed very rapidly. His sister had twice said in front of Mrs O'Brien that there was no obstacle to his marriage. The same sister had driven her into Dunford; and they had spent some pleasant hours together during which the unspoken knowledge of their probable future relationship had been a bond and not a restraint between them. And now he had thus brutally shown her that he desired her affection no longer. There *could* be no reason for such behaviour. Emily reddened, and the tears came into her eyes. But she would not give way to them; she would not ask to be taken home; she would stay as long as her aunt wished to stay. She would dance with Colonel Beresford for the next two dances, and with Lord Osborne as often as he required it. Mr Howard must not be allowed to know what he had done.

Sam found her a chair when the dances were over and she forced herself to reply to his cheerful talk. Mr Edwards was playing whist; and Mary, seated near her mother who knew her secret, was a livelier, more lovely, more glowing girl than the prim young lady Emily had been introduced to six months previously. Fortunate Mary, thought her observer; she had given her heart to an honest man and would never have occasion to complain of treachery.

"She is in good looks tonight, is she not?" said Sam, proudly.

"She has good reason. I am sure you will never give her cause to be otherwise. Nothing has yet been said to Mr Edwards?"

"No. Mary thinks it best that I should wait for a specially favourable opportunity. It has not been easy for her in Dunford, you know. I shall be glad to take her to Guildford. Here are Penelope and Mr Howard. I think – it is a little early to dance again, but I think – yes, if you will please excuse me."

Penelope had come back to her, Mr Howard following somewhat awkwardly a few feet behind. Sam bowed, and though it was too early for him to dance again with Mary, left to talk to her mother, or perhaps merely to stand in front of his lady and receive her smiles. Mr Howard muttered his thanks and Penelope sat down without replying. There was a long and embarrassing silence. Mr Howard was standing two yards from them. He did not talk himself, and his presence prevented the sisters from talking.

"Our dance is over," said Penelope at last, very coldly. "You have returned me to my sister. You doubtless have other duties in the room tonight. Pray do not neglect them on my account."

"I do not think I am required elsewhere at the moment," replied Mr Howard, with an effort to appear at his ease. "And perhaps the most serious duty I am neglecting is that of conversing with you. I trust you will help me make amends, for you have the reputation of being a witty speaker, and the pastime needs the willing participation of at least two people. It is a very brilliant company tonight, is it not?"

"If I have the reputation of being a witty speaker, and if my performance has disappointed you, I must apologize," said Penelope, her eyes flashing. "My only excuse is that I have been thinking a great deal about an incident which occurred recently in the neighbourhood, and which raised in my female mind a multitude of speculations concerning masculine *honour*. It is not for one in my position to question the motives and actions of officers or indeed of other gentlemen, but I am unable to avoid observing that I myself prefer a less complicated pattern of behaviour, in which friends remain friends, brutality is avoided, promises are kept, and expectations fulfilled."

Mr Howard's face became very red.

"I am not excusing," he began, "I would not excuse, nor should others, behaviour that must be condemned. I would not excuse it in *either* sex."

He then bowed and left them.

"He is not *excusing*, he is *accusing*!" cried Penelope. "How *dare* he?"

"Hush!" said Emily. "We will be remarked if you are not careful."

"It is *unpardonable*! I cannot tell you what I feel. How *dare* he — to my sister of all people in the world?"

"He has heard something," said Emily. "I would rather it was that than — I do not know what — than he should wound me for the pleasure of wounding, I suppose."

"Shall I take you home? Shall I be ill and ask you to take me home? I will do what you think best."

"I think it best that we should pretend nothing has happened — not to each other, not to him, and not to my aunt — but to the rest of the world. If Sam had not arrived when he did, I might not have managed it. Now I feel strong enough."

"I do not mind what he has heard. That he should dare to believe ill of you proves his utter lack of worth. I cannot say the knowledge makes it easier to bear *now*, for it does not. But in time it does make it easier to bear, that I can promise you. To know him utterly base and contemptible means you will recover as completely as I have done; but one is apt to distrust one's judgement afterwards and to think twice before one listens to other men. My dear love, I would have saved you from the experience if I could."

"You will stay close to me this evening?"

"I will stay close to you always," replied Penelope, tenderly.

"We do not have to look far for comfort. Both Elizabeth and Sam are happy."

"And are you to have no happiness, who made theirs possible? But I will not distress you; we will talk of it only when you open the subject yourself. Supper is to follow the next pair of dances. I shall not dance without you and we had better be prepared to find my aunt."

"You must dance if you are asked, Penelope. I meant only that you would come back to me afterwards if I was alone."

"We shall see, my dear."

They were not however to sit either alone or with Mrs O'Brien for very long that evening. Emily had been deeply hurt, and she knew that many painful weeks were ahead of her. But Penelope's company, Penelope's knowledge of her situation and sympathy with her suffering, made what had happened bearable and prevented public disgrace. A few minutes later, when Lord Osborne joined them, she was able to answer his high spirits with a smile. How little one could judge from first impressions! Mr Howard's ease had hidden a mean, uncharitable disposition; Lord Osborne's awkwardness had disguised as honest and as generous a nature as she could ever hope to meet.

"Has Howard left you already?" he said. "The shabby fellow. I hope he reassured you, Miss Emily. Our neighbour has only a headache and there is nothing seriously amiss, though you would not guess it by Howard's gloomy face. Miss Penelope, may I please have the honour of the next two dances? Before you accept, or before you refuse perhaps I should say, I must warn you that supper is to follow them, for we once agreed to turn our back on subterfuge in our dealings with each other and speak out honestly."

"To be really outspoken is a pleasure I am too seldom allowed to indulge in in company," said Penelope. "However, since you have given me such a lead, I will confess that I am highly flattered by your offer. Even my determination not to be separated from my sister for any lengthy period this evening is somewhat shattered by it."

"Nay, Penelope," cried Emily. "This is carrying your determination too far."

"I have not refused him yet, my dear. Indeed, he is my host and he knows I am not able to refuse him. I have merely given him an *opportunity*, of which I am sure he is going to take full advantage."

Lord Osborne was still in the highest spirits; but a slight diffidence appeared in his smile at this. It was a touch of true modesty that did nothing to lessen the high esteem of his two companions.

"I am indeed being put to the test if my poor speeches are to be judged against those you invent for me in your imagination," he said. "I do not know if you will consider it worthy of the opportunity you have made for me, but I can only say that I understand Colonel Beresford hopes to dance with Miss Emily while I dance with you, and that I think it unlikely you will be separated by any great distance from your sister at the supper table."

"Had you not reminded me you had turned your back on subterfuge I might have believed that in the small matter of some prior arrangement of places at the table you had come to some secret agreement with Colonel Beresford," said Penelope.

Lord Osborne blushed.

"There can be no subterfuge when a matter is thus openly discussed beforehand," he replied. "Perhaps I should forewarn you of something else. My mother is going to ask you to ride in this direction on the next fine day. She has a new mare of which she is very proud."

"It is two weeks since we were in the park," said Emily. "If it is convenient to my aunt we will certainly accept her ladyship's invitation."

For the few moments between this remark and Colonel Beresford's arrival nothing was said. They waited for the music, not in the awkward silence that had endured while Mr Howard was with them, but in the easy intimacy of friends. Emily would willingly have prolonged such a period of comparative peace until the end of the ball, but this could not be. Colonel Beresford claimed her, and she had to respond to his elegant gallantries for the length of two dances and during the interval for supper. Afterwards came other partners, each of whom had to be answered and talked to, so that she was heartily glad when Lord Osborne asked her a second time, and she could stand up with one who respected her wish for silence, who was content merely to look, who did not require to be entertained.

When the ball at last came to an end and she followed her aunt into the darkness of the carriage, her relief was indescribable. It was no longer necessary to smile; she let her features relax, and immediately felt the tears flow down her cheeks. Her aunt silently pressed her hand, and within a few minutes she was able to find her handkerchief and regain control of herself. The strain was over. Whatever the next few weeks contained, she would never have to suffer as she had suffered that evening.

"I fear you did not altogether enjoy the ball," said Mrs O'Brien.

"No, aunt."

"I would have taken you home if you had asked, but it was better that you should stay – much better. I was proud of you, my dear. Many of us can behave well in prosperity, but it takes courage and character to stand up to adversity. You have had your reward; nothing was noticed. And I must tell you that everywhere Miss Penelope and Miss Emily Watson were spoken of as the most beautiful girls present. That must be some consolation."

"Yes, aunt," she replied. But she found more consolation in the assurance that nothing had been noticed than the statement that she had been universally admired.

"Lady Osborne said something to me of having acquired yet another horse. She hoped you would see it, or ride it, or feed it – I do not know what."

"Penelope and I have agreed to go towards the castle tomorrow if it is fine."

"That is very sensible of you, my dear." Mrs O'Brien was silent till the carriage turned into the drive of their home. She alone among the onlookers had missed nothing of what had occurred – for discounting Penelope, knowledge of the intimacy between Emily and Mr Howard was still confined to the two households at Wickstead and Stanton. Mrs O'Brien was not displeased to find that the gentleman's ardour had cooled, but she was both surprised and angry that anyone should slight her niece. She said nothing of this, however, nor of her determination to cancel the engagement for Friday evening. "Perhaps the day will come," she continued, "when you will wonder at tonight's disappointment. But I will never press you to leave me, my dear. You can be assured of that. You are still a young girl and we can manage very happily by ourselves for several years yet. If you like to go straight to your room I will bring you some warm wine myself."

26

When Emily awoke the next morning it was fine; and for the first time in her life the look of a bright sky was distasteful to her. If it had been raining heavily she need not have ridden, visitors could not have called, and she would have had a four-and-twenty hours' respite in which to accustom herself to her changed circumstances. For it was not easy to realize without reflection how greatly her circumstances *were* changed. The man she had hoped to marry – the man she had confidently looked forward to marrying – was not for her. He whom she had thought of differently from others, she must no longer think of at all. Fortunately there had been no public engagement, and so there would be no scandal; but in her own heart she had considered herself engaged, and she had expected the event to be announced soon to the world. Now, in spite of her unhappiness, she must grow used to considering herself un-attached, the possible object of attentions from other gentlemen. A broken engagement, however disagreeable itself, would at least have preserved her from any immediate anxiety on that score. Emily sighed. Though she would never be pressed, she was not ignorant of her aunt's hopes. How easily she could have fallen in with them if she had never met Mr Howard!

After a few tears Emily sighed again, and determined not to give way to weakness. She had been disappointed; but she was not abandoned, ill-treated, scolded or unloved. No one could be kinder than her aunt; she had only to ask and plans would immediately be made for them to stay in London or Bath. The knowledge that escape was possible would perhaps mean escape would not be necessary. She had Elizabeth and Mr Jones, Sam and Mary Edwards, to think about and talk to. And she had Penelope, who knew her whole story, ready at all times to comfort and protect her.

"I will not tease you today," said her sister, when they were riding together. "I will say instead that I have thought much of you since we parted last night, which perhaps you have been good enough to guess; and I will do my poor best to cheer you. But first please tell me how you are."

"I am unhappy," replied Emily, "I will not try to hide it. But others have been unhappy before me, and have recovered; and I have determined to do the same. I intend to be busy, and you are going to see much of me at the parsonage in the next week or two. I am sure Elizabeth will find me an occupation, if it is only darning Sam's shirts. Pray let us talk about anything except last night."

"I have a lot to tell you about this morning, my love. In spite of the late hour at which we went to bed we have already had two visitors. They were both very welcome ones, so you can guess their identity without any more of my hints. We had hardly finished our breakfast when a sour-looking coachman brought his horses to stop at our modest gate. My! (Elizabeth, I need hardly explain, is the speaker.) My! What on earth has brought Mrs Edwards out so early? But it was not Mrs Edwards at all. A very pink and happy Mary descended from the carriage and came in to sit with us. The coach went into the yard, but came out straight away, facing the direction of Dunford, and waited with obvious impatience. My! said my eldest sister again, are you going back so soon? For you see we like to observe the proprieties at the parsonage, and not until we have exchanged the latest gossip do we remember those errands in the kitchen or upstairs that Sam and Mary find so very convenient. We do not dart out and leave them alone as soon as she arrives – even Elizabeth, who is much kinder-hearted than I am, does not. But this morning, proprieties went to the wind; the matter was too urgent altogether. A blushing Mary informed the three of us – not outright of course, but with certain ladylike circumlocutions – that it would be as well if Sam went in with her immediately, as Mr Edwards had fortunately fallen downstairs on his way to breakfast, and was at that moment seated on a sofa with his leg up, waiting an unexpected request that would bring exceptional good fortune."

"So it is all settled!" cried Emily. "I am so glad."

"Yes, my dear. And it is a mercy we do not have to push my father down the stairs when we need his assent to anything particular, for ours are somewhat steeper than Mrs Edwards's. However, you interrupted my story. As a result of Mary's account of the accident that had befallen her father, Sam accepted her kind offer of a seat in the carriage on its return journey. The offer had been addressed to all of us, of course, and Elizabeth, with that regard for the proprieties I mentioned just now, said she would accompany them, as her monthly visit to the provision merchant was about due. They were on the point of setting out when Mr Jones arrived, several shades more pink, and several degrees more embarrassed, than Mary, and asked if he might see my father. So Elizabeth stayed behind, and Sam and Mary set off alone. Pray do not tell of us. We have behaved not too badly at Stanton Parsonage for a good number of years; but things are now coming to a head and we dare not miss our opportunities. Mr Jones went upstairs, and Elizabeth and I sat down. It was not that Elizabeth had nothing to do; it was only that she wanted to prepare me for something she imagined would be a considerable surprise: which she did in her ordinary sensible and unaffected way. Marriage, of course, was not immediately thought of; but if in the course of time, when Sam was settled, there was no speedy prospect of my settling myself, she hoped I would take a sympathetic view of some arrangement which involved the spare bed-chamber being in permanent use. I replied that should I be fortunate enough to secure Mr Jones for my brother, and it became a choice between his being kept upstairs in the spare bed-chamber, like a relative one does not wish one's acquaintances to meet, or my setting up permanently with one of my brothers or sisters, I would unhesitatingly choose the latter. However, as I pointed out, there seemed a third alternative which she had not considered. This was that the gentleman should join our household as an acknowledged and accepted member on equal terms with the rest of us. I did *not* add that I expected it would be a mere year or two before he would cease to feel called upon to apologize for entering a room, or taking a chair, or accepting a plate of food, for that would have been unkind; but I fear there are a great many long and involved apologies in front of me. While I would, by no means, my dear Miss Penelope, actually go so far as to pretend I wished to remain *outside* the room when you are so thoughtful as to invite me to come *inside*, I have not, in the strict sense of the word, at this precise moment, made up my mind whether it would be less inconvenient of me to disturb you in the parlour, or to seat myself on these very comfortable stairs, where I might possibly be in the way of those wishing, in the ordinary course of their duties, to *ascend*, or – looking at the matter the other way – *descend* them. Forgive me, my love, I mean no criticism of your worthy teacher. He is a good man, and I am a disrespectful girl by nature, and habit too, I fear. Well, I made my little speech to Elizabeth, and it was very kindly received. She kissed me and said I was a dear creature, which of course I knew before; but that it was my home as well as hers and my father's and she did not want to make it less comfortable for me. I asked her if she was happy, and she hoped I would one day be as happy myself. She thought it unlikely, however. Mr Jones was not rich; but who else would have agreed to an arrangement whereby she could still look after my father, and carry on with her ordinary tasks in her familiar home? And though Mr Jones was not rich, he was good, generous, worthy, respectable, clever, honest, grateful, hard-working, kind, intelligent, pleasant, etcetera, etcetera. I have forgotten the list, and may have misquoted her; if *young* and *handsome* were actually omitted in words, this was on account of modesty alone, for they were sufficiently vouched for by her manner. Since we were now gossiping as intimately as sisters do on these occasions, I allowed myself to ask whether Mr Jones had expressed himself well. Elizabeth, with an honesty of which I would have been incapable, admitted that he had not really expressed himself at all – at least not on the subject at issue. The pair of them seem to have confined their discussion to their respective places of residence. *He* hoped she would not feel under any necessity of leaving the parsonage, either in the lifetime of my dear father, or in that of his humble and altogether unworthy successor designate. *She* thought the proper home of a beneficed clergyman was in his parsonage, and could see no real reason why in certain circumstances the removal should not be anticipated. It is as well my father has been forewarned, or he might think Mr Jones's call this morning was for the sole object of sub-renting a part of his house."

"Elizabeth owes much to you, Penelope."

"Poof, my dear, I have expedited matters a little and saved my aunt the indelicacy of being outspoken, that is all. It is not to be supposed that Mr Jones could have held out long against a bevy of determined females. We have not much further to go. Let us trot a little on the edge of this vile road."

Without waiting for her companion's assent Penelope increased the pace of her horse, and Emily had perforce to follow. Once inside the castle grounds Penelope urged her horse forward again so that they arrived flushed, breathless and smiling at the point where Lady Osborne was waiting while her son conducted Charles over his jumps.

"That was a fine sight," cried Lady Osborne, with obvious pleasure. "The two prettiest girls at my ball cantering towards me not ten hours after I had bid them good night. I wonder how many young ladies are spending the morning on a sofa clutching their hartshorn!" Her ladyship laughed at the picture, and slapped her thigh with such force that her new horse, not yet used to her ways, pranced nervously. "Whoa, my beauty!" she cried. "This is my new mare. What do you think of her?"

"She is a fine creature," said Penelope. "Indeed she is so fine she is driving other thoughts from my head, and I do not know which to praise first, your ladyship's ball or your ladyship's horse."

"You may praise both," replied Lady Osborne. "And I will forgive a little surprise on the former subject, for I am becoming used to my neighbours' astonishment that I can still give a good ball. From their tone last night you would have thought it was something altogether different from other pastimes – or perhaps it was I who was altogether different from other women – I do not know which was uppermost in their minds."

Emily realized that she had not thought of Mr Howard since the beginning of her ride. For that she must be grateful to Penelope's lively talk; and for the fact that she had come on Lady Osborne with her usual colour in her cheeks, and was so spared questions that would have distressed her, she must be grateful to Penelope's forethought in setting such a sharp pace for the last part of their journey. She quickly complimented her ladyship on her arrangements, added a message from Mrs O'Brien, and retold two or three laudatory remarks she had overheard. Then, her duty done, she stopped, hoping that she would never have to speak of the evening again. Before Penelope had finished her speech, Lord Osborne and Charles joined them; and for some moments they had to attend to two separate conversations. Lord Osborne was bidding them good morning at the same time as Charles was complaining of his bad luck in missing the ball, and demanding to know if they had watched his progress over the course of jumps.

"We were all watching you," said Lady Osborne, untruthfully. "But you were following someone. Now show us you can manage them on your own."

"That I will, your ladyship," replied Charles, wheeling his horse away from them.

"Well, was I not right?" said Lady Osborne, looking at her son.

"Indeed, madam, you were," he replied, with a very tender glance at Emily.

"Edward thought you would be numbered among the young ladies with hartshorn on their mothers' sofas this morning," explained her ladyship. "We have been arguing furiously since breakfast."

"I said nothing about sofas, nor hartshorn either. It is an article of which I know very little. But since you have given me away thus unceremoniously I will admit to our companions that I did say they had danced almost as much as was possible yesterday evening, and that I would not have been surprised if they had slept late this morning."

"As you have had the grace to admit you were in the wrong, I will not press the point," replied his mother. "Besides if we carry on our arguments in public our companions may believe there is something acrimonious about them. For the life of me I cannot understand why people are shy of arguments. There is nothing I enjoy so much as a good argument where both sides are determined they are right, and refuse to budge from their opinions. It is only with my family I can indulge myself these days; everyone else is become so nice. And even Colonel Beresford spent some minutes yesterday trying to convince me we both thought alike though we expressed ourselves differently. I do not wish to think alike. I wish to have my own opinions."

"That is a most interesting point of view, your ladyship," said Penelope, happily. "I have greatly admired the mare you are riding today. Pray, what is your ladyship's opinion of the animal?"

"Ha!" cried Lady Osborne, with zest. "You are thinking to catch me, Miss Penelope, but you will not, for I have had a good argument about her already this morning. Edward says she is too nervous for me, but I do not agree. She has spirit, that is all, and I like spirit. When Edward chooses a horse for me it is always something very placid and quiet. When I choose one for myself it is something altogether brisker. One of you shall ride her some day and tell me what you think."

Lord Osborne did not look very happy about this suggestion though he said nothing. Emily thought no less of him for his care of his mother, but decided that it was not an argument in which either she or her sister could properly take part.

"I fear Charles has promised more than he can perform," she said. "His horse has refused the third jump thrice."

They watched Charles, now somewhat red in the face, put his horse at the jump for the fourth time, only for the animal to turn away at the last moment and almost unseat its rider.

"Do not let it master you," shouted Lady Osborne. "You must go on now until you succeed."

The boy, who was not wanting in courage, tried again to make his horse jump, and again failed.

"I will go over with him," cried Penelope. "It is a shame to stand here and watch. We have made him too conscious."

"What! You will go over the jumps?" said Lord Osborne.

"It will not be the first time, my lord. Though I must admit I have not yet had an audience apart from my sister."

"They have been made higher since you were last here," said Lord Osborne. "They are a fair height now even for Charles."

"And does that mean she is not to jump them?" asked his mother. "She is a fine rider, Edward, and can certainly manage anything that Charles Blake can manage."

"Miss Penelope is indeed a fine rider," replied Lord Osborne, "but she cannot jump better than her horse."

Penelope, however, had not stayed to listen. She trotted to the first of the jumps, calling on Charles to join her.

"I am not going to lead you," she said. "We will go over together. And after we have done it, we will go over by ourselves just to show them we can. Come, sir."

The two riders put their horses into a canter, and took the first jump side by side; then they cleared the second; and then the third, which had given Charles so much trouble a few minutes before.

"And what do you say to *that*," demanded Lady Osborne, with a very satisfied expression, as though she herself had been in some way responsible for the feat.

"It is well done," replied her son, good-humouredly. "You know, Miss Emily, I believe my mother thinks I wished it otherwise."

"Rubbish, sir," replied Lady Osborne. "No son of mine could wish to see a horse fail. It is not pleasant even to jest about such things."

Emily smiled; and then, realizing that Lord Osborne's eyes were on her, she blushed a little. The sympathy between Lady Osborne and her son was not quite the same as that between her aunt and herself; but she knew it was founded on similar trust and affection. For a moment she could not avoid thinking that, with all its outward strangeness, the castle family would not be a difficult one for a newcomer to fit into, provided always that newcomer could contribute an equal trust and affection herself.

The two riders had cleared the fourth and fifth jumps in the same easy style, and were now approaching the last. This was no higher than the others, but somewhat broader, comprising a ditch as well as a fence. The horses took off side by side but seemed to swerve in mid-air and collide together. Both of them stumbled on landing. Charles's horse recovered and continued on its way, with its rider lying precariously over its neck; but Penelope's horse fell, and Penelope herself was thrown heavily on to the ground.

"My God!" cried Lord Osborne. "She is down."

The horse struggled to its feet, walked a few steps, and stopped. Penelope tried to rise, and then lay back on the grass.

"Penelope!" cried her terrified sister.

"She is hurt! Quick, Edward!" shouted Lady Osborne.

Her ladyship galloped to Penelope's side, accompanied by her son and a number of dogs. For a moment Emily was too horrified to move; then she set her horse after them as quickly as she could. Lord Osborne was on the ground, and Lady Osborne was in the act of dismounting, when she arrived on the scene. Penelope, though very white, was at least conscious; and Emily's worst fears were dispelled.

"This is your doing, madam," cried Lord Osborne angrily, as he knelt down. "I would not have let her do it if you had not been by."

"Indeed, my lord, you wrong your mother," said Penelope. "It was my own wish to jump, and it was my own carelessness that was responsible for my fall. But I do not think –" She stopped, and with Lord Osborne's help attempted to stand up. She succeeded in getting to her feet, but the position was too painful to maintain and she immediately sank on the gentleman's shoulder.

"Let her lie down, my lord," cried Emily, and helped him gently lower her sister to the ground.

"My bones are still whole, I trust," said Penelope, biting her lip. "But I am badly shaken."

"Where are you hurt?" asked Emily anxiously.

"It is my back, my love. I can move, but it is very painful. I fell on a stone, I think."

"Do not fret, my dear. Nor you, Miss Emily," said Lady Osborne. "She has stood up so there is no great harm done. I have had some experience of these things. I confess I would have been anxious if she had not stood up, for she took a nasty fall. She is undoubtedly in pain, but you need not fear anything else."

There was such assurance in this speech that all her hearers were in some degree comforted.

"I am sorry, madam, I spoke as I did," said Lord Osborne. "I was greatly distressed; and I would never have forgiven myself if Miss Penelope had been seriously hurt."

"Do not waste time with apologies," said Lady Osborne. "Get us a hurdle. It will be better than if you carried her. She does not weigh much and we can manage it by ourselves."

"And a doctor, please, your ladyship," said Emily.

"Certainly, my dear. Send a man for Dr Richards – or would you prefer your brother? He is nearer, of course."

"He is in Dunford this morning, I fear. Let us have Dr Richards immediately. And pray let nothing be said to alarm my family until we have learnt his opinion."

"Did you hear, Edward? And you, Charles, collect these horses. We do not want all the men running out to look for us."

Lord Osborne went back along the course of jumps to find a hurdle; and Charles set about catching the horses. Lady Osborne, kneeling at Penelope's side, gave her a very friendly smile.

"You will soon be well, my dear. Do not take any account of your sister's tears."

"They are partly tears of relief," said Emily. "That my sister is still whole and can speak to me is more than I dared to hope when I saw her fall."

"I have seen many falls and it was certainly a nasty one, for she was thrown over on her back. But there can be no important injury now we have seen her stand up. One cannot stand up, even for five seconds, with a broken leg or a broken back."

"Your ladyship does not like to be bothered with apologies," said Penelope, "but I must ask you to bear just one. I shall apologize once for the trouble I am causing you, and then leave myself in your hands."

"That will do very nicely, my dear. It would be a poor creature who could not help another after a riding accident. We will put you to bed here; and Miss Emily shall stay by you until you are well. Edward was quite right, of course. I should not have let you be so rash."

"Your ladyship," said Penelope.

"Yes, my dear?"

"Had we not better invent a different excuse than a mere riding accident? We do not want the neighbourhood to believe that you and I have been indulging in a duel."

Lady Osborne laughed.

"You are a brave girl," she said. "You will soon be well!"

Lord Osborne returned with a hurdle; and as gently as possible they put Penelope on it and carried her to the castle. The staircase was fortunately wide enough for the hurdle, and they were able to take Penelope into the room that had been allotted her. She winced a moment when she was put on the bed, and Lord Osborne apologized for his clumsiness. The pain of her journey had been considerable. Her face was now very white, and it was with no trace of her usual smile that she said:

"I am the best person to judge, my lord, and I do not think you are clumsy. Believe me, I am very grateful for what you have done."

"I will not burden you with a speech," he replied. "You have but to ask for anything you require. I will leave you to your sister, but I will stay within call until Dr Richards has told us what is amiss."

He looked at her very compassionately for a moment, bowed, and left the room.

Emily spent an anxious hour and a half waiting for the doctor. Her sister indeed reassured her, not only with words, but with a better colour and a more cheerful expression as soon as she was allowed to lie still. Emily's anxiety in consequence had not the frightening urgency of the moments immediately following the accident. Nevertheless until she could hear the truth from the doctor, and inform her family in precise terms of what had occurred, she could not be easy. Towards the end of her wait she heard the sound of a carriage; and though aware that Dr Richards usually travelled on horseback she ran hopefully to the window. It was not the doctor; it was Mrs Blake. Emily drew back quickly. If she was to stay at the castle for any length of time a meeting would be inevitable, but she trusted she would be spared one until she could prepare herself a little; her present state of uncertainty over Penelope left her no time for thought about the Wickstead family. After a very short time Emily saw the carriage drive away, and Lady Osborne came upstairs to tell them of Mrs Blake's call. The lady had heard of the part Charles had played in the accident. She had driven up immediately to ask after Miss Penelope, and offer her services – which was very civil of her, in her ladyship's opinion, as she had not been well enough to attend the ball the previous evening. Lady Osborne explained the position, and had promised to send a message to the rectory after the doctor's visit. She did not think Miss Emily wished to be bothered with an inquiry at such a time.

Emily begged to be excused from seeing *any* visitors except those of her own family until Penelope had recovered. Her sister was already improved; Lady Osborne could see for herself; but movement was still as painful as ever, and Emily would require all her energy to nurse her, which duty, with her ladyship's permission, she had determined to undertake herself. Lady Osborne poured them both a glass of wine, and struck a bargain with her guest. Miss Emily was to do the nursing and could have the adjoining room to sleep in;

she need meet no visitors; but in return she was to come downstairs for meals and eat under Lady Osborne's eye. Nothing was so fatiguing as nursing, and, as she herself had said, the task would require all her energy. Emily readily agreed.

Dr Richards was then brought in. Twenty minutes later Emily ran downstairs to write her messages. Lord Osborne was pacing restlessly up and down the hall in front of the stuffed fox.

"What has he said?" he demanded.

"Oh my lord! My lord!" cried Emily, happily. She could pronounce nothing else. The tears of joy and relief in her eyes ran over her cheeks.

"You need say no more, Miss Emily. Your expression is enough to tell me all is well. I cannot begin to explain how relieved I am. I have been standing here these two hours in bitter remorse. I should have stopped her. I should never have permitted it. She is so gay and adventurous; I would never have forgiven myself if she had permanently injured her back. It is too ghastly to think of. I will have the jumps removed today."

"No, my lord," she said. "No. Poor Charles!"

"Then you will give me your solemn promise *now* that neither you nor your sister will ever go over them again."

"Willingly. For myself and for her."

"At least I will have that half-buried stone dug up. I cannot tell you what I have pictured. She is so quick, so easy, so smiling – it would have been cruel. But tell me – what is the doctor's exact opinion?"

"She is badly bruised, my lord; but Lady Osborne was right. There is no injury to the spine. She will have a painful day and a disturbed night. She will sit up tomorrow and feel very stiff. She may get up on Saturday and lie on a sofa. She may walk a little on Sunday. And on Monday I may take her home."

"You have made me very happy," said Lord Osborne. "Dear Miss Emily, you have made me very happy."

27

Penelope's recovery was as rapid as Dr Richards had predicted, but the time-table attendant on it was a little advanced. On Friday afternoon Lady Osborne remembered that her daughter's sitting-room, not used since her marriage, was on the first floor of the castle. The room was dusted, a fire was lighted in the grate, and Penelope was informed that it was hers as soon as she cared to take possession of it. Emily would have preferred her to carry out the doctor's instructions to the letter; but Lady Osborne and Penelope, with the argument that these instructions had been based on the assumption that a flight of stairs stood between the patient and a sitting-room, forced her to give way. Penelope got up; and with her sister's help was brought to a sofa in the little chamber. There Penelope ate her dinner while Emily was served with more than she could eat in the dining-room. There they all drank tea, played cards, argued in turn with Lady Osborne, and passed a pleasant evening.

On Saturday Penelope was in the room earlier. She could now walk without pain, though she was still stiff enough to make movement awkward. The sofa in Stanton parsonage had, during the course of many years, been occupied by Margaret; Penelope however lay on hers with an elegance that one not familiar with the family would have judged the result of long practice. Emily and – for the greater part of the morning – Lord Osborne, sat by her, and waited on her. After some hours Lady Osborne came into the room and looked at the scene, not with any active displeasure, but with a certain bewilderment. Miss Penelope had had a riding accident. There were definite occasions in a lady's life – of which riding accidents and child-birth were the chief – when that lady was entitled to lie on a sofa. Similarly, where a gentleman was concerned, either a riding accident or an attack of gout might prevent him following the active pastimes his choice would naturally lead him to. Lady Osborne was not without sympathy for Miss Penelope; all that she could do in the way of providing beef-steak, port wine, a sofa and a good fire, to speed her recovery, she had done. Company of course was frequently required to keep up the naturally depressed spirits of one confined to a single chamber. But that two healthy people should share this confinement with apparent pleasure during a period of broad daylight on a fine spring morning was something her lady-ship could not understand.

"Have you been out today, Miss Emily?" she asked.

"No, your ladyship."

"You are feeling quite well, I hope?"

"I am feeling very well. Your ladyship looks after her guests too carefully for them to become ill under her roof."

"Nevertheless it is not healthy to sit in the whole time. I have noticed it with dogs. I think you should go out for an hour. I am sure Miss Penelope will spare you for such a period, and I will my-self undertake to see that she lacks nothing meanwhile. She knows we shall all be with her this evening, and she will not expect us to stay in her room the whole day. If you have no business yourself, Edward, you might show Miss Emily the walks."

"I have twice urged them to go riding, your ladyship," said Penelope, "but they would have none of it."

"I will do as your ladyship suggests and go for a walk," said Emily, hastily. "If I am seen riding it will be hard to convince my aunt that my presence here is due to a wish to help my sister."

Lord Osborne asked if he could accompany her. A few minutes later they left the castle by a side door and began ascending the gentle slope behind it. Emily had spent a busy, agreeable morning. Each sign of Penelope's recovery had cheered her. The accident itself, and the strong emotions that had accompanied it, had driven her own unfortunate circumstances into the background of her thoughts. The memory of Mr Howard's treachery was still with her, but it was as though time had already cured – not her afflic-tion, but the immediate pain of it in her heart. In the past eight-and-forty hours she had been taught in the most effective manner pos-sible to count the blessings she still possessed. They were far from negligible. She had lost nothing in reputation; she still had her family and friends; she still had Penelope, whom, for some moments of terrible anguish, she thought she had lost.

"You are very silent, Miss Emily," said her companion, in a quiet tone.

She started.

"I was so deep in thought I had almost forgotten you were with me," she replied. "I fear that sounds very impolite, but it is not meant so. You and Lady Osborne have taken us into your home so generously, so spontaneously, that I am in some danger of forgetting I am here as a temporary guest with but one case hurriedly packed after my written instructions."

"You do not mind being brusquely sent on a walk when my mother thinks it good for you?"

"No, my lord, I do not mind. I would go for a walk in a thunderstorm to please one who is so good to my sister. But we have been so much in each other's company the last few days I had forgotten I owed you my attention."

"But I too was thinking," said Lord Osborne. "If it is not impertinent, pray tell me what so occupied you?"

"I was counting my blessings, my lord, of which the chief, as you may well guess, is that my sister is so much better than she might have been."

"Yes. For that we must all be grateful."

Lord Osborne did not seem very inclined for conversation himself, and for some minutes they walked on in silence. Then, in the same quiet, serious tone, he said:

"Miss Emily, some months back, after a very short acquaintance with you, I made a certain proposal. I see now that being the person you are, you could have given me only one answer. Since then, after a period in which we were parted, and which gave me leisure to think more seriously than I had been used, we have seen each other regularly, and have, if I may say so, become friends. I hope you will not accuse me of being too hasty if I now ask whether your answer to my proposal – which I consider myself still bound by – is likely to change in the course of time. Though you wished, I think, to wait before deciding, and though I agreed to wait, there are circumstances in our present situation which impel me to importune you without further delay. I need only mention one. You are now acquainted with my mother's character. I was very pleased when she first said she intended to give a ball; it made an opportunity for me to talk to you and dance with you. But she gave the ball with certain assumptions in her mind; and unless you share those assumptions your position is going to grow increasingly difficult. So too is mine. You know how greatly I admire you; but I did feel, towards the end of Wednesday evening, that you were not as happy as you were at the beginning. Whether this was due to a realization of other people's expectations or not, I do not know; but it must be my chief excuse for speaking to you now. However, I have learnt my lesson, and only you and I are aware of this conversation. You are a guest here, and you have recently been subjected to a severe shock. Do not hurry with your answer. There is a seat on top of the mound. You can stay there and I can come back in ten minutes; or you can wait till you are fetched away – whatever you please. However you answer, my attitude to you will not change; and I trust we may always remain friends."

Emily's first reaction to this speech was one of gratitude. An impassioned proposal was more than she could have borne at such a time. She could only have refused it in curt terms. But Lord Osborne had set out the exact difficulties of her position with a sympathy that surprised her. He had left it open to her to answer how and when she would. She could refuse; she could accept; she could tell him she would accept at some later date. But whatever her decision one condition must be fulfilled; her answer must be absolutely definite. What she pledged she must perform. If her answer was *no*, it must be *no* for ever. If it was *yes*, it must be *yes* without regret. And if it was a promise of yes in the future, the promise must be kept whatever happened in the interval. Such a man deserved no less.

As they climbed towards the little mound, she considered her answer. Mr Howard was not for her. Her affection for her companion differed from the love she had once felt for Mr Howard, but it was a very true, a very deep affection. There would surely be much happiness for her in the union he proposed. She hesitated. If she had never met Mr Howard she knew there would have been no need for hesitation.

They reached the top of the mound and stood for a moment by the seat on which he had suggested she should wait. Beyond them, a little way to the west, was the village of Wickstead, with its church, rectory, cottages, and the house Mrs Blake had talked of purchasing. She could see them all clearly and her mind was made up. She was not very old; perhaps another chance of happiness would come later. With the memories that were in her heart she could not honourably promise any affirmative to the gentleman at her side.

"Do not go, my lord," she said. "I will give you my answer now. I am deeply grateful for the honour you have done me, but what you propose cannot be. As I think I once unwittingly gave you the impression that I was critical of your behaviour to my family, I must now say without reserve or ambiguity that no one could have been more attentive, more courteous, more truly generous, to my father and brothers and sisters than you have been during these recent months. I trust my answer today has not made you regret your conduct. I myself will be proud to remain your friend if you will permit it. This will be the last time we talk together with such intimacy. You must therefore permit me to say that I honour and respect you as I honour and respect no other man."

"If we are to remain friends, I hope we shall often talk together," said Lord Osborne, very tenderly.

"I hope so too, my lord. But this must be the last time we talk on this subject. In view of what you have said I can ask you, when my sister and I have left here, to tell Lady Osborne what has occurred, and to explain that my answer is irrevocable. It will always be an honour for me to know her, but I would be grateful if she could be left in no doubt at all of my inability to accept your proposal."

"That I will do without fail."

Emily felt herself very near tears. She had said what she meant, and she had said it clearly. But there was one more thing she wished to say.

"It is not for me to give you advice, my lord, but you have been kind enough to call me your friend. Forgive me if I say you owe it to your mother, to your family, to your name and to yourself, to marry. I would most sincerely ask you to forget me and marry someone more worthy of you. And now I would be grateful if you would let me rest here for a little alone."

"I will let you rest," he replied. "Part of what you have suggested I may one day do. But the other part, your wish that I should forget you, is likely to remain long unfulfilled."

He bowed and was gone. Emily sat down on the bench and wept – not because she had refused him, but because she had had no alternative. She did not regret what she had done; but she bitterly regretted the circumstances that had forced her to do it.

After some time she saw a figure making its way towards her. She was about to withdraw down the path when she recognized Charles Blake. The path, she realized, must be a short cut between Wickstead and the castle. She had not seen Charles since the accident; she dried her eyes and prepared to tell him of her sister's recovery.

"Good morning, ma'am," he said.

"Good morning, Charles. Are you not riding today?"

"No. I am not allowed to ride until Miss Penelope is better," he told her, in a gloomy voice. "When I shall be allowed to jump again I do not know."

"But my sister *is* better. You must tell your mother."

"Is she up – Miss Penelope, I mean?" he asked, brightening a little.

"Yes. She is sitting on a sofa."

"But not out walking yet?"

"No; she is not out walking yet."

Charles sighed.

"I am to wait until she is out walking," he explained.

"That is very hard on you," said Emily.

"I know."

There was a short silence.

"What have you been doing this morning?" she asked.

"I have had a lot of lessons and groomed my horse. Now I am going up to see the other horses. There is not much else to do."

"I see."

The boy stood for a moment kicking his heels. He looked first at Wickstead, and sighed; then at the castle, and sighed again. He was undoubtedly very bored, and Emily pitied him for his enforced inactivity.

"Surely Miss Penelope would not be offended if I rode," he said. "She will not get better quicker if I do not."

"Perhaps not, Charles. But if your mother has said you should not ride, then you must not question her decision. Tell her that on Monday we intend to go home."

"Very well."

"I have seen the badger now," said Emily. "Do you remember telling me of the stuffed badger? It is half-way up the stairs, is it not?"

"Yes. But I like the fox best. It is the biggest fox I have ever seen. . . . Which do you like best?"

"I have not really considered yet. I will look at them when I go back and decide."

"When you marry Lord Osborne you must put them together in the hall," said Charles. "People do not often see the badger when they visit as it is."

The young lady was very surprised.

"When I *what*?" she demanded.

"When you marry Lord Osborne."

"And who said I was going to marry Lord Osborne?"

"Mr Musgrave told my uncle on Wednesday afternoon that it was the reason for Lady Osborne's ball. It was probably to be announced at supper, he said. I suppose now you must wait till Miss Penelope is out walking."

For almost a minute Emily sat in silence with a whirling mind and racing heart. He should not have believed such a story, of course; but when the source was her own brother-in-law – her sister Margaret's husband – how could he not believe it? Charles became somewhat anxious at her prolonged silence.

"Should I not have mentioned it?" he said. "I am sorry, ma'am. It was the badger I was thinking of."

"You are not the one at fault, Charles. Others are older than you and should know better. But as I hope you will grow up an honourable man I must tell you now that one does not speak of such things unless one is quite sure one is speaking the truth. Much harm may be done, and much unhappiness caused, by careless words on such a subject. I hope you will remember that all your life. I repeat that it is not your fault; and you have done me a service by telling me what has been said about my intentions by others. In return I will tell you that I am *not* going to marry Lord Osborne, either now or at any time in the future. For the moment that can be a secret between us. That is all I have to say. Good-bye, Charles."

"I am very sorry," repeated the boy, who had not quite been able to separate the praise and blame in this speech. "Good-bye, ma'am." He looked for a moment at Emily, and then turned and ran on towards the castle stables.

He should not have believed it, and in any case he should not have behaved as he did. But if he *had* believed it, her conduct towards him during the past month must appear in the most unfavourable light, heartless at least, almost vicious. If he *had* believed it, it was no wonder his behaviour was awkward and his expression miserable. He must have felt as she had felt. And then anger at Tom Musgrave so took hold of her that she felt herself flushing to the forehead. He must repair the injury he had done. She had another brother. Sam would see to it that he withdrew his wicked words; and perhaps in time, in three months or so when the misunderstanding had been cleared up, and the pain it had caused had been forgotten, she and Mr Howard might come together again. A great joy flooded into her heart. The beauty of the spring landscape, to which she had hitherto been blind, stood open to her eyes. The castle was charming; the park was very fair; Wickstead was the most beautiful of English villages. For some minutes she gazed at them in turn; then she was seized with a longing to share her happiness. She must tell Penelope. Now, immediately, she must tell Penelope.

Emily got up and turned towards the castle. With a step so light it seemed hardly to touch the ground, she hurried back to her sister. In a corridor of the castle, before she reached the hall, she met Lord Osborne.

"Excuse me, my lord," she said hastily. "I am going to my sister."

"Pray give me five minutes first. I have something to tell you."

"Will it not wait?"

"No, Miss Emily. I must tell you now."

His manner was urgent and there was something grave in his tone. She looked up in alarm. Her eyes were accustomed to the bright day outside, and in the dark corridor she could not see his face with any distinctness.

"Surely there is nothing wrong," she cried.

"I trust you will not think so."

The gentleman opened the door of what seemed to be his library, and she obediently entered the room. He followed.

"I have some important news for you," he said. "It is not alarming, but I think you will find it surprising. I hope very much it will please you. Your sister has just this moment agreed to become my wife."

"My lord," she cried. "You and Penelope! I am certainly surprised. But I am very, *very* pleased. But I am astonished, I confess. Oh my lord, I am so glad."

Overcome with her surprise and her pleasure, she sat down. Lord Osborne began speaking, but it was some little time before she could pay him enough attention to follow his words.

"When I began to feel for her as I do, I cannot tell you," he was saying. "She was your sister; I thought that one day she would be mine; of course she was dear to me. But when I saw her almost lifeless on the ground, when I paced the hall with terror in my heart waiting for news, I knew I loved her more than one loves a sister. For the moment it was enough to know that she was well; I imagined I was completely happy. But yesterday I allowed myself to consider possibilities which, I assure you, I would have put out of my head if a definite engagement had existed between you and me. Though no such engagement existed, I still felt bound. Nor would I have wished to go to your sister while there was still any doubt at all in my mind about your feelings. It has not been easy for me these last two days; I hope you will not think I have behaved ill. I hope you will understand the many motives which have influenced me and which I am so clumsy at putting into words."

"You have not behaved ill, my lord. But I am wondering whether you have not behaved too well. While I am still confused let me say what I shall not be able to say in an hour's time. Suppose I had accepted your offer this morning?"

"My opinion of you has not changed, Miss Emily," he said simply. "I have always thought the man who marries you will be very fortunate. I think so now."

For a moment Emily was silent. There was a prospect of almost unlimited felicity before her. She would not now need Sam's services; the news could not be kept secret for long. Mr Musgrave would be contradicted in a more precise manner than would be achieved by the mere retraction of his wicked words. Surely it would not now require the three months she had allowed before there was complete understanding between her and the man she loved best. Half that time, a mere six weeks perhaps, would see her personal happiness secured. And for the immediate present there was the promised union between the man and the woman who stood only below Mr Howard in her affection.

"I have been made very happy by your news, my lord," she said. "I have long been at a loss to place the affection I feel for you, but now the matter is cleared up. I can confess I love you as a sister should."

"It is a relationship of which I shall always be proud," he replied. "And it is a relationship I must rely on to secure me your forgiveness on one small point. Your sister would not listen to me until I had given her a short account of the interview that had just taken place between you and me. Something was due to her. Something was due to all of us. I took the liberty of telling her that you had decided, since your arrival in the castle, that a union between us was for ever impossible."

Emily smiled.

"There have been few secrets between Penelope and me, my lord. I do not think she could have been very surprised at your news."

"I did not notice whether she was surprised," confessed the gentleman. "I was more occupied – in short, you will understand. But she has asked for you. I hope you will tell her yourself that all is well."

"Indeed I will." Emily got up with the intention of hurrying to her sister's room; but at the door she paused. "My lord," she said, "forgive me for asking, but when is the news of your engagement to be announced?"

Lord Osborne looked suddenly as youthful as Mr Norton.

"Your sister and I, Miss Emily," he said, "are perhaps more impulsive and more impetuous than in your heart you might wish us. I do not doubt that in the future we shall often ask your advice; but on this occasion we are going to act without any discretion at all. Our only excuse is that I am as sure of my mother's approval as she is of her father's. I am now going to spend five minutes with my mother. Her constitution is strong, and she will doubtless be upstairs very shortly. I am then going to ride to Stanton and return as rapidly as politeness permits. As soon as that is done, say within half an hour, I hope to begin receiving the congratulations of my friends." Still smiling very youthfully at her, he opened the door. "I trust you are not shocked?" he said.

"The only conclusion I can draw, my lord, is that you and Penelope suit each other very well. No; I am not going upstairs just yet. I have an errand outside that will occupy me for a few minutes."

28

Her errand done, Emily came back along the corridor, passed the stuffed fox in the hall and the stuffed badger on the stairs and ran into Penelope's room.

"You laggard!" cried Penelope. "I told him to send you straight away, and I have been waiting here ten minutes at least."

Emily ran to the couch and embraced her sister.

"My darling Penelope," she said. "I cannot tell you how happy I am."

"And now you will never believe I told you the truth about Purvis," said Penelope. "As soon as I accepted him – not Purvis this time of course – I knew I was done for. Elizabeth will not speak to me; Sam will kill him in a duel; and my aunt will not give me a shilling. I shall be pointed at in Dunford as a terrible example of the black treachery that can exist in a sister."

"Do not jest, Penelope. I have some news for you."

"But my news will keep the whole neighbourhood talking for years. The reason I agreed he should tell *everybody* is that I dare not tell *anybody* myself. What do you suppose is now happening at Stanton? My! I thought it was Emily you were going to marry! But seriously, my love, what are we going to do? It is you who will have to support me now; and even if you are by my side I shall blush for shame every time I am congratulated."

"Dearest Penelope, you have not listened to me. I tell you I have some news myself."

"You mean you have accepted Mr Tomlinson? I did not know he had called."

"Penelope, be serious, *please*."

"My love, I am listening. What have you to say?"

"I have been talking to Charles Blake. It was not some slander about my behaviour that Mr Howard gave credence to. It was the definite assurance from Mr Musgrave that an engagement between Lord Osborne and myself was to be announced during the ball on Wednesday evening."

For some seconds Penelope was silent.

"He had no right to believe it," she cried suddenly. "It was not possible. He is not worthy of you. He should have – –"

"It was a story from my own brother."

"I do not care whom it was from. I still think –" Penelope stopped and sighed. "But I suppose you wish me to forgive him?"

"*I* have already forgiven him."

Penelope sighed again.

"Very well, my dear. I will forgive him. Mr Howard, that is, not Mr Musgrave. You must be almost as happy as I am."

"I am very happy."

"Come, my love. Let me kiss you again." Penelope embraced her very tenderly, and then continued in a quieter tone: "If the engagements could be announced together the world might be satisfied. Apart from that I can see no way out of our fix. *You* opened the ball with Lord Osborne on Wednesday; and *I* was the only Miss Watson Mr Howard danced with."

"I can hardly expect – In short, Penelope, after what has occurred it will be at least four weeks or so before there is no constraint between us."

"Four weeks is a long time, my love. Could you not make it a little shorter?"

"We do not meet very often," said Emily. "There was a very close intimacy between us. Now it has been destroyed; it is not to be supposed it can be built up again at the first good-morning."

"If it is only a matter of opportunities I will willingly arrange some. If I undertook to double the number of meetings could you not see your way to halving that four weeks? Two weeks is about as long as I can bear to be considered a scheming woman, and I assure you I shall be thought one until your engagement is announced."

"I do not know. I do not at all know what the future will bring. Let us talk of your happiness."

"With pleasure, my love. And I shall begin by saying I cannot thank you enough for refusing to marry my future husband and thus allowing me to fix him in the moment of his blackest despair."

"Unfortunately for your jest he has told me the whole story."

"Then he has done a lot of explaining today, for he has told me the whole story too. I hope the two stories tally. He says that since the day he saw you, he has considered me his sister. He admits that I have grown an increasingly dear sister, and that recently he has had reason to believe that his brotherly affection for me was hardly to be matched in even the most united families. Nevertheless it was not until he felt me lifeless in his arms, and pictured a long and painful existence in front of me on a cripple's bed, that he realized I was destined for another role – should he, of course, be able to extricate himself from an unfortunate previous entanglement with the daughter of some impecunious local clergyman."

"You can never regret having discovered that the man you are going to marry has a sense of honour above all other men," said Emily.

"That is a point you must not press too closely, my dear. A sense of honour which obliges him to address my sister when he finds himself in love with me is a masculine attribute with which I can hardly be expected to sympathize. However, with all his quixoticness I love him, and I suppose that is the end of the matter."

"I have been very blind, have I not? Pray, how long have you loved him?"

"I do not know, my dear. In a sense I have loved him for fifteen years, since the day he pelted me with plum-stones in fact, for that was the first time I was distinguished by a gentleman outside my own family. And in another sense I have loved him since the day I knew he loved you. And in a somewhat different sense I have loved him since the moment he stood at the foot of my bed and apologized for his clumsiness, when he had just handled me with a tenderness of which I did not believe a man was capable. But as I am speaking to you, who are such a nice judge of a young lady's conduct, perhaps I should say that I never thought of him for myself until he promised me his whole heart. That would be the correct behaviour, would it not?"

"I fear these things are easier to teach in a lesson than to practise in real life," said Emily.

"If my memory is not at fault I once suggested as much myself," said Penelope. "But perhaps we had better not inquire too closely into the exact moment at which I began to love his lordship. Let it be sufficient that I am pledged to love, honour and obey him and never jump a horse for the rest of my life. It is amazingly well arranged that we are to be settled so near each other, is it not? You and Mr Howard shall dine with us every Sunday. I shall speak about it to the dear lady who is to be my mother as soon as she condescends to come upstairs."

"Dear Penelope, do not assume too much. Give me a little time to readjust my feelings."

"I am giving you two weeks; did I not tell you just now? And you are not to worry. You are going to have the gentleman though Lord Osborne has to promise him a bishopric in return. I doubt whether he has the influence to implement his promise with the present ministers, whom I must now begin to dislike much more than I did before, but Mr Howard need not know until you are safely married."

"It is not on those terms that I would have him," said Emily, gently. "Only if his heart wills it."

"His heart shall will it, my love. You got me a husband, and the least I can do is to get you one in return. Will you do an errand for me?"

"Most certainly."

"Then pray walk over to the rectory and ask Mrs Blake if she has a reel of light blue thread to lend me. Elizabeth packed my sprigged muslin, you know, and it has a small rent in the back which I must mend before I come down to dinner tonight. Mrs Blake will doubtless ask how I do; and you can say I am doing very well indeed, and have just got engaged to Lord Osborne."

"Nay, Penelope, I could not do such a thing."

"But someone must break the news to her, for it is not to be kept secret. And to Mr Howard too, of course. What is more natural than that you, my sister, should perform the task? Mr Howard is a gentleman, and so could hardly say that Lord Osborne was making a rather mean alliance, which he might be tempted to do in other circumstances. Come now; it is but a small service I require of you."

"It is one I shall refuse."

"Be careful, my love. You should know by now that I am quite ruthless in achieving my ends. If you will not do *my* message you might find yourself doing one for Lady Osborne."

Emily began to feel seriously alarmed. Her sister, with the best cause in the world, was at that moment as assured and confident as she was smiling and beautiful.

"Penelope, there are certain reasons – there is at least one definite reason, why I cannot go to the rectory or do anything else that could put me under the suspicion of attempting to meet Mr Howard today."

"If you wish to be excused you must tell me the reason."

"Very well," replied Emily, blushing. "I will tell you. It is very probable that by now Mr Howard knows of your engagement."

"Indeed! And how did he come to hear of it?"

Emily was now quite scarlet.

"After what Charles Blake had told me, and having learnt from Lord Osborne that there was to be no secret about the matter, I felt justified in telling Charles it was *you* who was going to marry Lord Osborne – not *I*."

"You know, my love," said Penelope, after a little thought, "you are really very much more sensible than I once supposed. Perhaps we have had a good influence on each other. Perhaps you are a little less over-nice, and I am a little more nice, than when we first met. But you have certainly done your part. The next move must be up to the gentleman. After that it will be your turn again."

Then the door opened and Lady Osborne brought the gentleman himself into the room. He gave Emily a look in which humble apology, happiness and love were so intermingled that, even in her embarrassment, she began to think that perhaps the two weeks Penelope had allowed them might be reduced to one.

"Mr Howard called to ask how you were," said her ladyship, in a very brusque tone. "To save him a double journey I told him what I had just learnt myself, and brought him up here to congratulate you. But I must say you are a pair of very sly girls."

Mr Howard was still looking at Emily, who had dropped her eyes, and did not give the congratulations that had been promised. A little pink in the cheeks, but smiling broadly, Penelope faced the lady who was soon to be her mother.

"This is a very inauspicious start, your ladyship," she said. "To be called sly in public like this."

"I say what I think, Miss Penelope," replied Lady Osborne. "You know that."

"Indeed I do, your ladyship. Were it not for the respect I have for you, I would be tempted to suggest that in this instance you have thought wrong."

"I repeat that you are a very sly girl, Miss Penelope. And I do not think you have any respect for me at all."

"I will confess that I have a greater affection," said Penelope. "Lord Osborne's mother has been uniformly kind to me since I have known her. I trust that at this moment she is not going to withhold the few words of welcome without which I can accept no one's congratulations. For my part, if a promise is needed, I promise to perform my duty to both her and her son with all the strength, love and tenderness of which I am capable."

"If it comes to that you are welcome enough to marry Edward," said Lady Osborne. "You have made a quick recovery and must be a healthy girl. You are certainly a brave one. It is not every young lady who can jest when she cannot stand. But it does not alter the fact that you are very sly. When you are in my position you will know what I mean."

"If providence ever puts me in your position, your ladyship, I trust I shall be able to look about me with the same lack of regret and pride of achievement."

Lady Osborne allowed herself a rather grim smile.

"I see I am going to be greatly flattered in the future," she said. "That too is a sign of slyness, you know."

"Your ladyship must learn to distinguish flattery from truth. There are at least two subjects on which I shall ask your advice with no other motive than that of profiting by it. One of these concerns horses. The other I need not go into at the moment, but it is a matter in which you were wise enough to engage Mr Howard's help."

"It is as well you intend to ask my advice when it comes to bringing up your sons," said Lady Osborne, bluntly, "for you will certainly get it. And what do *you* think of this news, Miss Emily?"

"I was privileged to have a private conversation with your lady-ship some days back," replied Emily. "If you can recall what I said to you then, you will realize that I was somewhat more prepared for this morning's work than you were."

"Aye. I do not doubt that you dropped a lot of hints. But I am no good at understanding hints. I like people to be open with me."

"Your ladyship is surely requiring too much," said Penelope. "You were informed as soon as an engagement was agreed upon. You could hardly expect either my sister or myself to inform you in advance of an event which, as I am sure you will be the first to agree, did not rest *entirely* with us."

"You must not twist my words, Miss Penelope. There has been a lot going on behind my back; that is what I meant. However, I will say no more." Lady Osborne looked at the two sisters in turn. Miss Emily had a good many thousand pounds; Miss Penelope had nothing. Though she had not sought it, she regretted the loss of the fortune. Younger sons could have been provided for out of it, and daughters could have been dowered. But she had once been prepared to accept Miss Emily empty-handed; and having expressed her displeasure at having been tricked, she accepted Miss Penelope. "What is done, cannot be undone," she continued. "You are a handsome girl and a good horse-woman, and you have a lively tongue. I expect I shall be proud of you. Come Mr Howard; you are very slow at congratulating Miss Penelope. She is to be part of my family, you know, so I trust you do not disapprove of her."

Mr Howard assured her ladyship that her son could not have made a better choice. He then came forward and congratulated Penelope with great sincerity. He had been glad – he could not tell her how glad he had been to hear the news. He had always admired Lord Osborne. There was no more worthy gentleman in the country. Then his eyes strayed again to where Emily was sitting, and he lost the thread of his discourse. His sister, he said, hoped very much she would be allowed to entertain the two Miss Watsons before they left the castle.

"Miss Penelope, there can be no question of your coming down today," said Lady Osborne, suddenly. "We have been going rather faster than the doctor intended, and it may not be good for you. The muscles in the back are very important to a woman. It does not do to overstrain them. I have told Edward to explain to your family that I shall keep you here till Friday at least."

"I do not at all object to being your guest," said Penelope, "but it is only an hour ago that your ladyship was encouraging me to come downstairs for dinner."

"That matter is now quite different, my dear. I will arrange that you are provided with an adequate meal upstairs. And I do not doubt that Edward will often be with you to the neglect of his other affairs. I see now what has kept him within these last two days."

"In this, as I hope in other things, I shall be happy to obey your ladyship," said Penelope, and then turned to Mr Howard. "You see, sir, that I am to be kept a prisoner in this room," she continued. "I wonder whether you or Mrs Blake would take pity on me sufficiently to find some means of sending me a book. I am sure there are a number of books in the castle, but just at the moment I would like a novel or something of that nature, and I do not think her ladyship is a great reader of novels."

Lady Osborne sniffed.

"You are quite right," she said. "I am *not* a great reader of novels. Nor will you be, when you have this house to look after. By all means ask your sister to lend her a novel, Mr Howard. It will be the last she will read here for many a day."

"I could of course send someone up with a volume," said the gentleman, "but if Miss Emily would care to accompany me to the rectory for the sake of the walk she would be able to choose one likely to appeal to her sister."

"That is a very good suggestion," replied Penelope, "though I had not thought of it myself."

Emily could think of no good reason to advance against the journey. Lord Osborne would soon be back from Stanton; he, his mother and Penelope would have much to talk over that did not directly concern her. In addition, for the past fortnight until the evening of the ball, she had longed to be alone with Mr Howard. But now that the opportunity had come, and even though she knew that Mr Howard was as responsible as Penelope for making it, she felt a great reluctance to leave the protection of her sister.

"I have, sir, but this moment returned from a walk," she said in a small voice.

"But you could not have gone very far," said Lady Osborne. "There is no point in us all sitting in and Edward certainly will. Perhaps you would be so good as to tell Mrs Blake that though your sister is in a sense recovered, I do not wish her to be put to any strain until she is quite well. You are both to be here till Friday at least; Mrs Blake's invitations are always welcome, but I intend to make sure that Miss Penelope's back is as strong as it ever was before I let her out of my sight. You will doubtless be able to make the point politely, which is, of course, what I would wish."

After this there could be no more hesitations. With the knowledge that what she had once thought would take three months might now be accomplished in as many days, Emily rose and accompanied Mr Howard from the room.

They left by the front door of the castle. Together they made their way round the building and began to ascend the path they had both separately hurried down that morning.

"They are well matched," said Mr Howard.

"Lord Osborne and my sister?"

"They too. But I was thinking of the two ladies we have just left."

"Why yes," said Emily.

Lady Osborne and her sister were perhaps better matched than Lady Osborne and she herself would have been. Though she liked directness, there was at times a directness about her ladyship that was almost overwhelming. But Penelope could equal her; Lady Osborne would never make a remark that Penelope could not cap if she wished. Then Emily ceased thinking of her sister and listened to Mr Howard.

"I came to the castle today," he said, "less to ask your pardon than to see if there was any chance of my ever being allowed to ask it. What I said on Wednesday night was quite unforgivable. It must have caused you distress at the time. I know it has caused me the deepest distress since."

"What you said, sir?"

"Yes. I will not repeat the words; I am too ashamed of them. But to suggest, even indirectly – though I do not think it was very indirect – that your behaviour should be condemned, was so grossly unfair, so vilely untrue, that I do not know what apology I can make to reinstate myself. Miss Emily, you have heard, I think, how I was misled. You are generous and good by nature. I ask very humbly: can you find it in your heart to forgive me?"

"I forgave you, sir, as soon as I heard what you had been told and by whom," said Emily, quietly. "But it was not your words that hurt me most; it was your manner and your actions."

"And those too?" asked the gentleman. "Can you forgive those?"

"Yes, sir," she replied, hardly knowing what she said, but happily aware that all was now well between her and the man she loved. "I fear I shall always find it difficult to refuse what you ask."

"Dear Miss Emily, you are kinder to me than others in your position would be. You are gentleness itself. I owe you many explanations, but I fear I cannot proceed in a logical sequence. When I have not been misled, when I have listened to one who has at all times been your friend, I have not disguised the very real affection I have for you. My feelings are such that when I believed you were destined for another – in spite of the very high opinion I have of that other, and the knowledge that he is in many ways my superior, more generous, more trusting, more open perhaps, certainly greater in the eyes of the world – my mind was in a state of turmoil. It is not yet fully recovered, or I would speak to you in a more orderly fashion. All I can think of now is that I love you to the extent of my power, that I am quite unworthy of you, and that you will honour me beyond my deserts if you will agree to my proposal. Miss Emily, I am offering you my hand and my name and my heart. Will you consent to become my wife?"

"It is a position, sir, I should be very proud to accept," she replied. "I can think –" Her joy was so great that her voice faltered for a moment. "I can think of no other position in the world which would promise me greater felicity."

"You have made me very happy," said Mr Howard. "There is a bench on top of the little mound. Let us sit on it a moment and look at Wickstead. It is a fair enough spot by itself; with you to share it, no man could ask more."

For the second time that morning Emily sat on the white seat and looked at her future home. What she had pictured an hour ago as requiring three months, had already come about. The step that was to inspire all her future life, even as it was to justify all her past, had now been taken. The odd reluctance to be alone with Mr Howard had quite disappeared. She knew that she could never have too much of his company. They talked of their happiness, of Mrs Blake, Penelope and Lord Osborne, and again of themselves.

"Sir, there is a point that has long been puzzling me," said Emily, at last, "and as I shall require you from this time forth to hide nothing, and always speak the truth to me – as I most assuredly shall do to you – I now require an honest answer. Will you promise me one?"

"I will. What is your question?"

"When I was staying at Stanton Parsonage before Christmas, I called at Wickstead in company with my sisters."

"I know what you are going to ask. I did indeed come into the yard while you were there."

"That was but half of my question. I want to know why you did not come into the drawing-room."

"I will tell you, Miss Emily," he replied. "I knew by then that Lord Osborne had asked you to marry him. And I knew too that he intended to ask you again."

"Then I am in a very unfortunate position," said Emily. "Lord Osborne has not only asked Penelope to marry him, but she has accepted. As your wife am I to be denied the pleasure of seeing my sister on that account? Or will you perhaps allow *me* to see her while *you* wait in the yard?"

"But there is another fact you have not taken into account. Already at that time I loved you. I have never loved Miss Penelope to that degree."

"Ah sir, you loved me and so you avoided me?"

"No; I avoided you because I thought no one of discrimination could prefer me to him. All my hesitation must be put down to that."

"You are too humble, sir," replied Emily, very tenderly. "That is all I can say now."

"Others see us better than we see ourselves," continued the gentleman. "Affection has perhaps prejudiced my sister. It was she who encouraged me on your return to Stanton. It was she who said that I was not to pay too much heed to the speculations of the world, or indeed to the wishes of one or two ladies."

"She has been a good friend to me."

"She has been a good friend to us both," said Mr Howard. "May I not tell her the news?"

"You may tell her; but no one else must be told till I have spoken to my aunt. Perhaps I should go back now. I do not know how long we have sat here."

"Have you forgotten the book?"

"The book, sir? What book?"

"The book you are to bring to your sister."

Emily blushed.

"Why yes," she said. "I *had* forgotten the book. I have had something else to think of, you know. I must fetch it without further delay."

"No harm will be done if we sit here a few more moments," said Mr Howard. "There is a quality of gentleness about you, and a sweetness in your smile, that I have not yet had time to describe. Now I am no longer in any uncertainty, I will, with your permission, tell you a little of the feelings that have moved me, and the thoughts I have been thinking, since my sister introduced us at the Dunford assembly some months ago."

Emily said nothing; but the very tender and loving look she gave him seemed to the gentleman sufficient consent. It was not till another hour had passed – the happiest hour so far in Emily's life – that he reminded her again of the book.

29

Little remains to be told. For four-and-twenty hours – and in some households for even longer – Lady Osborne's opinion was shared by her neighbours, and Penelope was considered a very sly girl. But as the news of the second engagement slowly spread more than one lady remembered having had her suspicions that something of that nature would very probably occur. No lady, however, had been so definite as Mr Edwards, who recalled having promised Miss Penelope, Miss Margaret and Miss Emily Watson husbands before the twelvemonth was out when he told their fortunes in November.

If Mrs O'Brien was surprised at the news, she did not show it to any marked degree; if she was disappointed, she soon forgot the fact. She had in the early days quickly established goodwill between Lady Osborne and herself; but it was not to be supposed there could be any great intimacy between characters so dissimilar. Her friendship with Mrs Blake, however, became very deep as the years passed. If Surrey was her favourite county, she became fond of explaining, it was not because of any particular beauty in its scenery, or any specific virtue in its soil; it was solely on account of the convenient closeness of its habitations. In Shropshire she had been accustomed to driving five or ten miles to pay a call. In Surrey she had a multitude of friends and relatives within a radius of three. And when her niece left her there were few days on which she did not walk to the parsonage, or on which one of the three adult inhabitants of the parsonage did not visit her at Stanton Lodge.

Of the three sisters Penelope married first. As Lady Osborne very truly said, the castle was there; it was large enough to accommodate one more; she did not object to another carriage – indeed it was the custom, was it not – but there could be no question of buying a lot of new furniture merely because Lord Osborne, like his father, grandfather, great-grandfather, and others of the line, had chosen himself a wife. Soon afterwards, in the presence of but a dozen people, Elizabeth was married to Mr Jones in her father's church; and some months later, Emily was a bride herself.

A decision on which of the four weddings that joined a Miss Watson to the gentleman of her choice brought the greatest felicity will be left to the reader. As a guide it may be said that while Margaret found rather less than she had expected in marriage, and Penelope rather more, Emily found the perfect union of two equally-matched hearts that her education and upbringing had always taught her to regard as the due reward of good principles and correct behaviour. It surprised her only that those who had painted the picture to her when young had used such cool and restrained language to describe a state to which no superlatives could do justice. As for Elizabeth, the event so far exceeded what she had dared to dream of that she was unable to avoid the public expression of her happiness at frequent intervals as long as she lived. It was on these occasions that a faint – a very faint – hint of pride could be observed on the usually humble, self-effacing countenance of Mr Jones. Those who are perfect themselves will doubtless condemn him for these frequent lapses into a worldly sin as severely as he deserves. To the author the fact that he long preserved a rather large bright blue button in his unpretentious stud-box goes some way to redeeming the only serious blemish in his character that has yet been brought to notice.

The road through Stanton village was soon mended, to the great detriment of the conversation of the district. The surprised surveyor received by one and the same post incensed letters from Mr Howard, Mrs Blake, Lord Osborne, Lady Osborne, Mrs O'Brien, Mr Watson and Mr Musgrave, threatening to report the matter to a higher authority if action was not taken immediately, followed a day later by a most courteous letter from Mr Jones, pointing out the great inconvenience suffered by the poorer villagers, in almost all weathers, on account of the not entirely undefective state of the surface of the highway. Being somewhat nervous about his position, the surveyor set all the men under his charge on the task, and made a very creditable job of it. Mr Jones then wrote expressing his gratitude.

It was the younger Lady Osborne who conceived the idea of presenting Mr Jones with a horse for his personal use. The gift, of course, had to be seriously belittled before Mr Jones could bring himself to accept it; and never was Penelope's patience so tried as when asserting that a horse out of her own stable was useless either as leader or wheeler, was too oddly coloured to match for a curricle, was too light for farm work, was not sufficiently spirited for Lord Osborne, was too awkward in pace for herself – in short was quite useless either to her or anyone else. She was so weary when it was at last done that it was with resignation rather than surprise that she would later meet Mr Jones on an errand of mercy in the country lanes, still afoot, leading his horse from verge to verge where the going was softest.

It was, he would assure her, an excellent horse, really a very noble creature. He could never be sufficiently grateful to her ladyship for giving it to him. And while he would not go so far as to say in so many words that Lady Osborne had been in any sense *wrong* in her description of the horse, he must in fairness point out that it had most handsomely responded to all his calls on it. In answer to her ladyship's exasperated query about why he did not *ride* the animal, he would reply that he often did, particularly in the evenings when his wife might be getting anxious about his prolonged absence, and on days when he could not otherwise get through his work. That, however, was but part of his happiness in her ladyship's gift. Blessed at home by the loving companionship of his wife and infant daughter, he was comforted in his weekday labours by the friendship of one of God's creatures, which followed willingly where he led in the mornings, which walked beside him in the twilight of the evenings, and which waited patiently for him with never a complaint or moan.

Lady Osborne would then hurriedly pass on in her carriage before she was tempted to say anything that would hurt Mr Jones's feelings. She would frown, sigh, shake her head, then smile and shrug her shoulders. To her husband she would say she did not know whether he was more foolish than good, and that she might as well have given him a dog. And to Emily she would say that she was having a large umbrella made in London, so that Mr Jones could keep his own and his horse's head dry during the rain, instead of only the latter as at present.

Nothing has yet been said of Sam, whose marriage to Mary Edwards took place in Dunford at an early date. Mr Edwards, having seen four magpies a few days after he had learnt from his wife that his daughter was in a certain condition, refused to go into the country throughout the whole of six months, and in due course was rewarded by being told he was the grandfather of an eight-pound boy. He cast up a most surprising horoscope for the child, in which a throne figured largely, but fortunately did not live long enough himself to wonder where he had miscalculated.

The letter Mrs Robert Watson wrote to Emily on her engagement contained many elegant French phrases. It was not, however, so remarkable as the one, almost entirely composed in that language, which Penelope received. Both letters were acknowledged, but thereafter intercourse between the two sisters and their brother's wife was slight. Robert himself continued to prosper, though not, for some reason, to the extent that might have been imagined from his early success. He remained through life a prudent, industrious attorney, with a small mind much occupied by very small matters. His affairs seldom allowed him to leave Croydon, where Mrs Robert's parties were considered very select by those on her list. On the few occasions he revisited the neighbourhood in which he had grown up, Robert stayed at Millington, where he and Jane felt most at home. A suggestion that this was because only Tom and Margaret among his brothers and sisters would not notice the squabbles that so frequently took place between him and Jane, has recently come to my ears. While there may be some truth in this reasoning it should also be remembered that the Howards, the Osbornes, and Mrs O'Brien were very much richer than the Robert Watsons; and that though the Joneses were very much poorer, they were so little ashamed of their poverty that conversation with them soon became very dull to those whose chief interest was material prosperity.

As for Tom Musgrave, I fear that some moral is inescapable. He had gained his chief ambition. He was as closely connected with Lord Osborne as he could become once Mrs Beresford had made her choice. But though to the end of his life his friend was always pleased to see him on the hunting field, or to ride round his fields and advise him on his husbandry, their intimacy seemed to have decreased rather than increased since marriage had come to them. Tom, a little wiser, a little kinder, and a great deal less gay than he had once been, a better if a more unhappy man, realized what others had realized before him, that the means used to attain one's ambition are as important as its attainment. Of his false words to Mr Howard, it need only be said that they were uttered in a mood of gloomy vanity after a particularly aggravating interview with Margaret when his self-respect was almost exhausted. When he realized his falseness he paid a special visit to Emily to apologize for them. He had thought it would be so, he told her. He was very sorry if he had caused her pain.

The road, as has been explained, was soon mended; and Mrs Howard's visits to Dunford, to get a new book from the library or purchase a length of spotted muslin from the milliner's, could be made without damage to the springs of her chariot by the road with which she was most familiar. Prompted by feelings different but equally to her credit, she stopped often on her journeys at Osborne Castle, Stanton Lodge, Stanton parsonage and Millington House (still shown on many maps as Millington Farm). Love took her to the castle, to be teased, to gossip and confide in her dearest sister. Affection and gratitude took her to Stanton Lodge, to sit with her aunt for many a spare half-hour. Regard and respect took her to the parsonage, to share for a few minutes Elizabeth's busy domesticity, and hear again of the goodness of Mr Jones. Charity alone took her to Millington, to listen to Margaret's complaints, and perhaps smooth over some quarrel. It was on these visits, it was generally said, made without preparation and undertaken in addition to her ordinary engagements, that Mrs Howard's gentle manner and ready smile appeared most to advantage. Those who knew her better, however, thought differently. It was in the nurseries of Wickstead Rectory and Osborne Castle, in their opinion, that Mrs Howard was happiest. Mr Howard, who must be presumed to have known her best of all, never gave his opinion; which suggests that there were occasions when she was even happier, and leads me to suppose that Mrs Howard loved her husband even more than she loved her children.

Advertisement by the Author

There are two sorts of Janeites. To the first Jane Austen is above criticism of any kind and even her fragments are sacrosanct. Neither this note, nor the preceding story, is meant for them.

But there is, I hope, a second category of admirers. I mean those whose delight in her books is equalled by their regret that her books are so few. For these, and for those who aren't Janeites at all, I have written this note and what I am the first to admit is a poor substitute for the book we might have had.

The fragment of *The Watsons* was given its title and first published by J. E. Austen Leigh in 1871 in the second edition of his *Memoir*. From the watermarks of the MS he deduced its date of composition as between 1803 and 1805. This places it after *Northanger Abbey*, *Sense and Sensibility* and *Pride and Prejudice* but before *Mansfield Park*, *Emma* and *Persuasion*. He answers the question of why it was left uncompleted by suggesting that Jane Austen had placed her heroine in too humble a social position, and put away the book when she realized her mistake. R. W. Chapman (*Jane Austen: Facts and Problems*) suggests that *The Watsons* may be a sketch for *Emma*. Anyone who has attempted to study Jane Austen's language, style and method of work must owe a great deal to Dr Chapman's painstaking scholarship. I gratefully acknowledge my debt; but, with respect, the fragment is a false start rather than a sketch. I find it easy to believe that Mr Austen's death in 1805 interrupted the work, and that when his daughter started writing again six years later she had lost interest in *The Watsons*.

To my knowledge two completions of the fragment have been published: *The Watsons* by Edith and Francis Brown (Elkin Matthews and Marrot, Ltd, 1928) and *The Watsons* by L. Oulton (Hutchinson, 1922). The story of the former is said by Mrs Brown, a great grand-niece of Jane Austen, to follow her intended story as handed down by family tradition.

Both books are extremely difficult to obtain, and both end by providing Emma (my Emily) with Mr Howard as a husband after she has had attentions paid to her by Lord Osborne. There are further similarities. Mr Watson twice dies; his daughters twice remove to Croydon, and Lady Osborne twice has designs on Mr Howard. I can have no quarrel with the end, for it seems to me implicit in the beginning. But in other ways I find both books less satisfactory. One is a slight lack of Jane Austen's wit. Another is what I would call the *tempo* of the writing. The original fragment is a *leisurely* opening; it is the start of a long book, not of a short one. Yet it comprises about a half of Mr Oulton's book and almost half of the Browns' book. I find this a pity. It means that the characters so deliberately introduced are rather hurriedly dispatched. It also means that in the second half incidents are crowded one after the other in a very un-Austenlike manner. The rapid journeys in one book make one almost dizzy.

It is easy to criticize. I must start on the harder task of justifying myself. In my version the original fragment is less than a quarter of the book (the transition takes place in the third paragraph of Chapter 7). And here I must make a confession that gives ample opportunity for those I have criticized to retaliate. Unlike them I have altered the original fragment. I offer three excuses for this: the reader's convenience; Miss Austen's presumed intentions; and my own requirements for a book in which both characters and incidents were to be fresh, and not pale imitations of characters and incidents that occurred in existing Jane Austen books. It is the last of these that is important, but we had better consider them in turn.

The first need not detain us. An example is the Watsons' family vehicle. In the fragment it is called a "chair". It was open and needed only one horse. But the use of the word in this sense was at no time common, and I have called the vehicle a gig. Mr Collins, you may remember, had a gig. A few other alterations are due to this compromise between period atmosphere and the modern usage of words.

With regard to my second excuse, we can only guess at Jane Austen's intentions by studying what she did in fact do to the MS. I have not seen it; but in her book *Jane Austen And Her Art*, Miss Mary Lascelles tells us that there are many corrections in Elizabeth's conversation bringing out the character of the speaker, and lightening and brightening the fragment. It seems to me certain that if Jane Austen had completed the book, the opening would be more vivid and more witty than the version she left us.

This brings me to my third point. As it stands the fragment is a trifle pedestrian. It is full of promise of a good story and it has a sufficiency of characters; but which of them do we immediately love? Elizabeth Watson, of course, but who else? And who is to develop into the dimensions of a Mr Collins, a Lady Catherine de Bourgh, a Miss Bates or a Mr Woodhouse? Superficially the ingredients – the characters if you will – are perfect. We have an ailing father, four unmarried daughters, and one married and one unmarried son. We have a bachelor peer in the neighbourhood, with a flirtatious bachelor friend, a mother and an unmarried sister. We have a highly eligible clergyman with a widowed sister near by. In the town of D. we have an almost unlimited quantity of officers from a colonel downwards, a young girl with rich parents and two eligible young men, the sons of a banker. In the distance there is a rich elderly doctor, a young man who jilted the eldest of the four sisters, and finally a wealthy aunt who has just made a misfortunate second marriage to an Irishman.

What is missing? Nothing, I suggest, except a lack of salt. Almost everyone we need is present; but if they are developed as they are introduced to us in the original fragment many of them are going to become either too dull, too unpleasant or too like an existing Austen character.

Let us look briefly – very briefly – at the more important as Jane Austen left them. Mr Watson is sickly and peevish. He threatens to become a rather unlikeable Mr Woodhouse – a fault in two ways from my point of view. I have consequently made him more sad than ill, and allowed him to cheer up when his material position improves.

Elizabeth Watson is perfect as she is. I have tried not to change her and to provide her with the husband she deserves.

Penelope Watson seems to be a mixture of the two unpleasant Misses Steele – even to the extent of chasing a doctor. I wanted a foil to my rather correct heroine, and Penelope as she now stands is my creation.

Margaret Watson has a distinct if repellent character, and I have left her as I found her.

Emma Watson needed her name changed so I called her Emily. To me at one stage she threatened to turn into another Fanny Price, my least favourite Austen heroine. Others have seen her resemblance to Emma Woodhouse. I have tried to give her enough spirit to keep her distinct from Fanny, while also keeping her as gentle and as well-behaved as when I first met her. I hope I have done her justice.

Robert and Jane Watson are adequate characters as they stand, but not pleasant enough to make favourites of. In any case, as others have pointed out, Mrs Robert resembles Mrs Elton. There are thus two reasons to keep her in a minor role and to prevent the removal to Croydon.

Sam Watson hardly appears in the original. I can find no clue whether he was to marry Mary Edwards or not; but I thought it fair to give Emily one brother she need not be ashamed of.

Mr and Mrs Edwards and Lady Osborne possess good manners, and ample breeding but little else. To avoid dullness I have taken liberties with two of them. I also had to be careful that neither lady resembled Lady Russell or Lady Bertram, and that Lady Osborne's attitude to Emily was different from Lady Catherine de Bourgh's to Elizabeth Bennet. As she now stands the blame or credit for Lady Osborne is mine.

Lord Osborne has "an air of coldness, of carelessness, even of awkwardness". The awkwardness and lack of offensive pride save him from becoming too like Darcy. I have let him develop as I think he was intended, giving him perhaps a little more charm than he had.

Mr Howard is, I am sure, destined for the role of hero. I feel a little guilty about him as I am certain I haven't done him justice. But he threatened to develop either into an Edmund Bertram in one direction, or an Edward Ferrars in the other. Perhaps I took the easiest course; but worthiness is difficult to depict at length without dullness.

Tom Musgrave is an admirable character as presented. I trust I have given him the wife he deserves.

Mrs O'Brien, rich and childless, is too useful to the Watsons and the story to be left in Ireland. I have brought her back to fulfil the function she might have been intended for.

Mr Jones, like Penelope and Lady Osborne, is my creation. Unlike them he, almost alone, does not appear in the fragment. But who else was there to fulfil the role he is eventually pushed into, gently by Emily and ruthlessly by Penelope?

These then are my explanations and excuses; and I must add one more. The first MS of my version came to over 160,000 words. This is longer than most English publishers favour these days. Even when I had cut an entire chapter about Mr Jones in London, the MS was still overlong. So I then pruned the original fragment and the completion impartially – though not, I admit, with the same easy conscience. What remains is offered to the second category of Jane Austen's admirers mentioned at the beginning of this note, and others, with all of Mr Jones's humility. I am sure I have made a number of slips. I apologize for them, and for letting a pair of understudies, as it were, usurp the place reserved for the principals. But even Jane Austen herself once allowed an orchard to bloom in midsummer; and even the *Encyclopaedia Britannica* (14th ed.) slips when it says there aren't any duels in Jane Austen's books – as any reader of *Sense and Sensibility* will discover. As a last effort to draw attention away from my failings, can anyone tell me how Mr Bennet's estate was entailed on a Mr Collins without, of course, introducing a change of surname which should surely have been mentioned if it had occurred?

J.C.